# PLAY ME FALSE

### E.R. WHYTE

Copyright © 2022 by E.R. WHYTE

All rights reserved.

No portion of this book may be reproduced in any form without written permission from the publisher or author, except as permitted by U.S. copyright law.

Cover Design: Kim Wilson of Kiwi Cover Design @kiwicoverdesign.com

Proofreading: Waugh Editing and Proofreading

# CONTENTS

| | |
|---|---:|
| Dedication | X |
| Preface | XI |
| Playlist | XIII |
| 1 | 1 |
|   Harry | |
| 2 | 14 |
|   Harry | |
| 3 | 26 |
|   Harry | |
| 4 | 40 |
|   Harry | |
| 5 | 60 |
|   Jack | |
| 6 | 67 |
|   Harry | |

| | |
|---|---|
| 7<br>  Harry | 81 |
| 8<br>  Harry | 94 |
| 9<br>  Harry | 104 |
| 10<br>  Harry | 114 |
| 11<br>  Harry | 121 |
| 12<br>  Harry | 132 |
| 13<br>  Harry | 143 |
| 14<br>  Wyatt | 153 |
| 15<br>  Harry | 165 |
| 16<br>  Harry | 177 |
| 17<br>  Jack | 188 |

| About Author | 432 |
| Also By | 433 |

To every Harry:
May you conquer your Marcus
and find your Wyatt, as I did.

# Preface

*Play Me False* is the book that almost wasn't. There will be an uber-lengthy list of acknowledgments at the end, but first, a word about the how and why it came about for those who want to know.

I began writing in 2020 and very quickly published ten novels, one right after the other, within 18 rapid-fire months. Even after an out-of-the-blue divorce and two moves, I made sure to hit my deadlines and get the books published. It wasn't until Covid hit in January of 2022 that everything fizzled and I published what would be my last book for a while, *Entropy*.

I tried to write.

Hell, I tried to read.

I'm not certain what was happening with my brain, other than utter fatigue and fog, but I simply couldn't hold on to a thought for longer than a few thousand words. It took until May of 2022 to grasp a tentative concept and begin making progress. It took until September to nurture and refine that progress into an actual book.

Covid took something from us. Even after we "recovered" from it, I think we're finding places we're still healing, still filling in the gaps. This book has nothing to do with Covid, and yet it's the hallmark of my victory. My 42.

# Playlist

*Two and a half hours of angsty, romantic music. This playlist is available on Spotify.*

*Malibu Nights* – LANY
*You Wreck Me* - Tom Petty
*Closer to Fine* - Indigo Girls
*Strong Enough* – Sheryl Crow
*Only If For a Night* - Florence + The Machine
*I Can't Outrun You* - Home Free
*Sex on Fire* – Kings of Leon
*exile* (feat. Bon Iver) - Taylor Swift, Bon Iver
*Friday I'm In Love* – The Cure
*Breakfast At Tiffany's* – Deep Blue Something
*I'll Stand By You* – Pretenders
*Parachute* – Chris Stapleton
*The Night We Met* - Lord Huron
*This Kind of Love* – Sister Hazel
*Let Him Fly* - Patty Griffin

*abcdefu* -GAYLE
*Here On Out* – Dave Matthews Band
*Let Me Hold You* – Josh Krajcik
*Tell Her You Belong To Me* - Beth Hart
*Can't Help Falling In Love* - Haley Reinhart
*She Used to Be Mine* – Sara Bareilles
*Praying* – Kesha
*You Are the Reason* – Calum Scott
*More Hearts Than Mine* – Ingrid Andress
*Landslide* - Dixie Chicks
*Sanctuary* – Nashville Cast
*Glitter in the Air* – Pink
*Falling Slowly* – Glen Hansard, Marketa Irglova
*A Safe Place to Land* – Sara Bareilles, John Legend
*I Just Want You* – Ozzy Osbourne
*A Little Bit Stronger* - Sara Evans
*Let It Be Me* – Ray LaMontagne
*Fix You* - Coldplay
*Give In To Me* – Garrett Hedlund
*Tin Man* – Miranda Lambert
*You & Me* – Dave Matthews Band
*Mrs. Robinson* -Simon & Garfunkel
*iris* – Grace Davies
*Mine Forever* – Lord Huron

# One

## Harry

*Present Day*

Life can change in an instant. I learn this lesson in the most crippling of ways one late November evening, to the accompaniment of piped-in Christmas music and the high refrain of childish voices echoing in a Richmond mall.

It's not my scene, the mall thing. I can feel the crowd and the noise polluting every pore and twist the silver Medic-Alert bracelet around my wrist. God willing, the lights and noise won't trigger one of my seizures. I have a splitting headache, though, and that's never good.

At my side, Sugar, my golden lab, whines low in her throat and presses closer to my thigh. She doesn't like the mall, either, even if she does love people. I scratch behind her ears, and she sits, panting softly. "Good girl, Sugar," I croon.

I'm here for my brother and his little girl, my sweet niece Ava. I straighten the Baby Gap beret that I had to get for her, even though it had only been marked down a single time. I have a slight online shopping addiction where my only niece is concerned, and I'm not even sorry. It's what happens when you don't have any rug rats of your own to spend money on.

Plus, I'm her only auntie, so it's required that I spoil her.

Tonight is the first time she'll visit Santa when she's old enough to understand who the big man is, and I have to be here to see whether she'll scream with joy or terror when she's sat on his knee. I'm voting for cool indifference, personally. She's a little on the different side, like her auntie.

I never did care about things like that when I was growing up. I was more about pondering the meaning of life than what I wanted from the fat man in the red suit. I thought it made me seem older and cool to be all existential and meta about things. "Why do we have to learn algebra, anyway?" one of my friends once asked. It was meant to be a joke, a universal complaint uttered by just about every kid forced to take the class. I considered the question very seriously, though, and then answered, "because 42."

My friend didn't get it, of course. No one ever did, except a select few other nerds who had some familiarity with arcane literature, and I wasn't going to explain *The Hitchhiker's Guide to the Galaxy* to those who didn't. So, the closest I ever got to a corporate understanding of the meaning of life, one that was accessible to my peers, was that life was a rank bitch and then you died.

These are the thoughts that cross my mind when I glance up from adjusting the pretty but impractical beret that refuses to stay on Ava's head and see my husband waiting in line to see Santa around ten people ahead of us. That he's in the line is in and of itself curious, but stranger still, he is supposed to be some eight hundred miles away, in Chicago. What's even odder is that there's an unfamiliar child who looks to be around Ava's age attached octopus-style to his pants leg.

My fingers go still on the hat, and I tilt my head, considering. I will stay calm and manage my stress. I will use the scientific method to figure this out. I will not lose my shit.

"Ammie Harry—" Ava pats my face with both little hands, and I shush her absently.

"Just a minute, baby girl. Owen, do you see that?" I direct the question quietly to my brother, who's engaged in conversation with the woman behind us in line.

*Observe*: one husband out of place, out of time. *Ask a question*: What possible explanation could said husband have for being here, when he's supposed to be at a sales meeting?

*Form a hypothesis*: he's back in town unexpectedly and accompanying a friend's family. Maybe? That doesn't quite seem to fit, though...

"Ammie—"

There's a blonde woman standing beside him, busty with what I'm positive are implants and pretty, if a bit Regina George-ish in her dress and manner. She is fussing over a baby in a stroller, and as I watch, she bends and picks the baby up. I blink, willing the vision to dissipate.

"He's in Chicago," I mutter, grasping one of Ava's hands. "It's just someone who looks like him." Everyone has a doppelgänger, right?

"Markie," Ava says, pointing.

*Experiment to test the hypothesis.*

"Fuck." The woman ahead of me shoots me a dirty look, which I return. "Double-fuck," I add, just for good measure. Is that her husband up ahead in line for Santa with a Regina George lookalike and a strange kid? No. I don't need your judgment, lady. Oh, holy night, there's another kid. How many is that, already?

"Damn," my brother adds, finally turning from his conversation and looking to where my attention is directed. "Is that...?"

My stomach sinks to the tiled floor of the mall and the gaily strung Christmas lights around Santa's workshop swing and blur. The scent of peppermint blends with pretzels from a vendor and I feel sick. What the hell is happening?

Boosting Ava onto my hip, I step out of line and close my eyes, conscious of the jostle and glide of bodies flowing around me like a school of fish parting around a stationary reef risen in their midst.

With my eyes closed, I feel the night. A Salvation Army bell jingle-jangling, discordant over the piped in "Do You Hear What I Hear?" carol. Ava's soft hand tangled in the hair at the nape of my neck, the scent of her, Johnson's & Johnson's underlaid with the Cheerios she'd eaten earlier in the car. The essence of holiday cedar and excited children, glowing lights and tolerant parents... it pulses in my veins with a reminder of our purpose here this evening. I'm here, in this too-loud and too-busy plaza, to make memories for Ava. To snap a photo of her looking confused and irritable on jolly St. Nick's lap so our entire family can look back and laugh over it every Christmas in the future.

Something Marcus and I can dream about for our own children.

It's been seven years, but it's not an impossible dream.

I am not here to discover anything horrible about my husband.

*Analyze the data.*

I'm not here for Jerry Springer-esque surprises, for the brand of drama that upsets carefully planned futures and happy homes. *Except your home isn't that happy*, a little voice whispers in my head. I ignore it. Thoughts like that are depressing.

I didn't see what I thought I just did.

No...when I open my eyes, it'll be someone else entirely. Someone else's husband, someone else's daddy, someone else—

"I thought Marcus was in Chicago? And who the hell is Fertile Myrtle?" Owen's question has an unwilling half-laugh springing from me.

"Oh, fu—Harriet?"

My eyes spring open, and there he is.

He's a handsome man, my Marcus. Dark hair that sweeps in a perfect wave back from the classic curve of his forehead, the ever-inquiring arch of his eyebrows and hazel eyes. They're looking at me now, wide and confused and panicky.

*Were you supposed to be here tonight,* he's wondering, *or did I mis-read the schedule?* That's my Marcus. So caught up in schedules and routines.

Is he though? Mine, I mean. The blonde woman standing just behind him and to his right doesn't seem to think so, judging from the possessive hold she has on his arm.

The arm that's not being used to hold an infant, wrapped in a creamy knit blanket with candy canes dancing across its swaddled expanse. Sleepy eyes blink out at me, and a pang knots my womb. They're the same hazel as Marcus's.

"Hi, Markie," Ava says, leaning forward. It's odd, given he's never paid much attention to her, but she adores her uncle. My spaghetti arms make no effort to stop her, and Marcus is forced to catch her, wrangling the arm attached to the blonde free just in time to swoop her to his chest in an awkward hold.

"Hey, there, kiddo, my favorite girl—"

"I thought I was your favorite, Daddy?" a small voice pipes, and as one our gazes lower to the little girl who hovers with elfin curiosity behind the blonde.

*Draw conclusions.*

The look-alike similarities in appearance. The proximity. *Daddy.* Her mother. *Her father.* I might puke. *42, babe. Life's a bitch, and then you die.*

The woman looks sharply at Marcus now and reaches for the baby. "Yes, *Daddy*," she says, placing cutting emphasis on the word. "I was under the same impression. Along with Trevor, and Jolie, and Barrett—"

It's then I notice two other children, both boys, standing to the side. They're roughly ten and eight, give or take a few years, and the dark cowlicks waving back from their foreheads make my throat tighten. Their arms are crossed in identical defensive postures across their chests and as my eyes fall upon them, they shift, looking from one adult to the next.

Owen steps forward. "What the hell, man?" I touch his arm, a silent plea to let me handle this. He's always been my protector, but I have to take care of some things on my own.

"Marcus… I don't…you said you were in Chicago this weekend? Who are these people? Who is… she?" The words fall from my lips into a vacuum and numbly I realize a crowd is gathering. A chill chases the numbness, making me want to shiver. I'm frozen in this moment, this dreadful blink of discovery.

These kids…they're close to a decade old. Much older than my own marriage. The thought stabs, something about it creating a nagging urgency to stop and process. But Ava whines, and my eyes skitter around to find people pulling their phones out, prepared for a gathering spectacle as readily as they were for a visit with Santa. "Harriet—" Marcus starts.

"I'm his wife." The blonde interrupts whatever he was about to say, shooting him a look I can't interpret. "Who the hell are you?"

*I'm a block of ice. Nice to meet you.* Owen takes his daughter from Marcus. "Well, this is awkward." He looks at the blonde. "She's also his wife. Which makes him a douchebag of the highest power."

The voices in the crowd are starting to settle in my consciousness and I look around to see phones and avid expressions. Damnit, that's all I need… to become the latest TikTok sensation. I'll be the campus laughingstock. Anxiety rising, I struggle to find my voice. Sugar whines again and paws at my hand, and my grip tightens on her leash. "Maybe we should talk about this at home, Marcus."

The blonde could care less about public spectacles. "Oh, hell, no." Handing the baby in her arms to one of the older boys, she's between us before Marcus can reply. "If you think for one second my husband will be going 'home' to discuss anything with you, you have another think coming." Her blue eyes hard on me, she reaches up and removes an earring.

Still frozen. I am arctic tundra, unable to move or shift from the reality staring me in the face. I'm dreaming, and any minute now I'm going to wake up. That's the only possible explanation for this insane turn of events that has my husband committing bigamy with this mean girl to end all mean girls, who apparently wants to fight me for him.

"Gina—" Marcus's voice is a whine in the background, accompanied by a growing hum of excitement from the group of spectators.

*And her name is Gina. Guess I wasn't too far off the mark with my Regina George assessment. My life is complete.*

"Gina? Is that short for Regina?" Dimly I realize I should probably be questioning her use of the word husband rather than her name, but I can't think about that right now.

I snort a laugh and lift the back of my hand to my nose. I can't help it. It's not amusement. It's a mix of nerves and confusion and fear and every other raw feeling I've felt for the past ten minutes begging for recognition and resolution. It infuriates Gina, though, and she launches herself at me, her hands landing solidly in my hair. I feel her nails sink into my scalp, scraping against the skin and tearing, and a screech rises up in my throat.

"What's so fucking funny, bitch?" *Yank.* "Not so funny now, huh?" *Pull.*

There's a metallic taste in my mouth and I toss a desperate look at my brother. He interprets it immediately.

"Oh, my God—let her go—" A hand grabs at us. Dimly, I register it as Owen's, but it's ineffectual with Ava in his arms. "Marcus, a little help with your crazy bitch, here..."

*This isn't happening.*

I've never fought with another person in my life. I'm a college professor, for God's sake, a food chemist. I wear glasses and a white coat, work in a lab with petri dishes and spectrometers and computers. I've never taken my earrings off in preparation for a girl fight in my life. I don't *throw down*. I don't *rumble*.

I'm not Ronda-fucking-Rousey and we're in a mall, feet away from Santa's workshop, with children standing open-mouthed all around us...she is insane. This woman is certifiable.

But for the sake of my wounded pride and my stinging scalp, I gather all the aggression I can muster, and wrap both hands around Gina's throat. She's significantly taller than I am, and to get more leverage I monkey-climb her torso, latching my legs around her hips until we both fall to the ground in a tangle of thrashing limbs and grunted curses.

"Nothing funny," I mutter. "You should watch your fucking language."

"I'll fucking watch you eat tile, fucking cunt." She releases one hand from my hair to claw at one of the hands around her throat. "Let go!"

My ears roar with the rush of blood and the din of bystanders shouting. My brother's voice rises above it all and when I break my focus to look for him, I find him pressing Ava's face against his chest while he yells something at Marcus.

"I'll let go when you let go of my hair!"

"I'll rip your fucking hair out!"

"I'll tear those fake boobs off!" I shouldn't go there. I could care less if a woman elects to surgically enhance her assets, but if Blondie tears one strand of my hair from my head, I will separate a nip. I swear I will.

"They're not fake—"

Just then I feel a pair of arms slide around my waist and pull me clear of Gina with an authority I can't shimmy free of. I try, though, kicking and sliding desperately until my foe hefts me upward with a grunt, banding one arm with painful pressure beneath my breasts and wrapping the other securely across my windmilling hips.

"Do I need to Taser you, ma'am?" a low voice asks, close to my ear, and I sag, my gaze searching for my attacker. She's receiving similar treatment from a guy whose carriage and general look scream cop, even though he's not wearing a uniform. An abandoned paper bag of Chicken King is scattered at his feet, along with a distinctive black jewelry store bag. Gina's thrashing foot kicks it across the tiled floor, her scarlet mouth drawing wide in a snarl, and I close my eyes in disbelief. *This isn't happening.*

As if discovering my husband apparently has a second life and another wife wasn't bad enough, now I get to find out what it's like to be arrested. I've officially descended to convict status.

"Holy shit," the man's voice comes again, and he holds me out a fraction, twisting me away from him. There's something familiar this time about his voice and I squirm to get a better look at him.

My jaw sags. No freaking way.

"Holy shit," I echo. "Jack."

"Harry."

At that moment, my vision dims and blurs, and everything around me begins to spin. I squeeze my eyes closed, fighting against what I know is coming. *Not now, God, please, not now...* It's no use. I can feel everything stiffening and know this one is going to be bad.

Commotion breaks out a few feet away and a flurry of movement registers in the corner of my eye. With one arm, Jack tussles briefly with someone, simultaneously holding me back with the other, until from nowhere a fist heavy with rings flies into my cheekbone. A flare of pain erupts, but I have no time to process it, as an instant later my body goes rigid against Jack and starts to twitch. My conscious yields one final thought as Jack curses and begins to lower me to the floor.

*Fuck.*

# Two

## Harry

*Ninth Grade*

*The tug on my braid comes as it always does, approximately thirty-three seconds after I take my seat in the third row behind the bus driver. It doesn't matter that I'm basically right under his nose; where discipline and Johnny Lee Jamison are concerned, the man is deaf, dumb, and blind. Most adults are, I've discovered.*

*"Hey, Harriet Maybe. You dork. What color are your panties today, dork?"*

*I sigh and look down at the book I just pulled from my backpack in preparation for the lengthy bus ride. It's a drive to virtually anywhere in Lucy Falls, Virginia, and I try to come prepared. I hate being bored more than anything, and riding around the winding roads of my little country town is not my idea of excitement.*

*But anyway.* Here we go. *I could try to read my copy of* Brave New World *in an attempt to ignore him, but I'd tried that before. Johnny Lee doesn't like being ignored. The one time I'd attempted it, on the advice of my momma, he'd snatched* The Once and Future King *from my hands and torn the paperback spine clean in half.*

*I'd cried like a baby in front of the entire bus.*

*As if in echo to my thoughts, Johnny Lee's voice slithers into my ear, a sibilant whisper.*

"Dork. You ain't ignoring me, are ya?"

*With careful deliberation, I close the book on my tasseled bookmark and tuck it away into my backpack before twisting to face him. His fingers are still in my braid, causing another painful pull of several strands. Gently, I tug it from his grasp.*

"What do you want, Johnny Lee?"

"Well, I asked you a question, didn't I?" *Hard blue eyes glitter down at me from where he leans over the seat behind mine.* "Inquiring minds want to know. What color are they?"

*I swallow and look around. The county bus is packed full of kids of all ages—ninth graders like us on down to the itty bitties, whom us girls try to watch out for in their mommas' absence. There's even the occasional senior, like Jack Brady two seats over, who rides the bus instead of driving. The little kids chatter amongst themselves, oblivious. Most of the older ones either stare openly or pretend not to watch while hanging on every word exchanged.*

*I'm not sure which I hate more.*

*Cheeks heating, I glare at Johnny Lee.* "Why do you have to be such an asshole?" *Asshole. The word is foreign on my tongue, and Momma would die if she knew I'd said it. All the more reason to use it.*

"Oh, you know. 'Cause I secretly like you or some bullshit." *He pauses, looks around to gauge his audience.* "You don't want to tell me, I'll just find out for—"

"That's enough."

*There's that moment in a movie when the hero steps in to save the day and makes some grand statement. All heads swivel to look at him, mingled admiration and anticipation coupled with fear for his safety in their gazes.*

Yippee-ki-yay-mother-fucker.

Hey, you guyyyys!

I'm Batman.

*That's what happens now, when Jack Brady's quiet voice pierces Johnny Lee's braying noise and silences the bus. I look at him in wonder.*

*Until now, I would have said he didn't know I existed. Hell, maybe he doesn't. Maybe his jaw would be doing that sexy clenching thing if Johnny Lee were messing with any girl, maybe he just feels a sense of injustice...maybe...*

"What did you say to me?" *Johnny Lee's hand releases my hair and he half-rises in his seat.*

"I wasn't speaking Portuguese." *Jack's eyes flick to me.* "You all right?" *I nod, not trusting myself to speak.*

*"Oh, Portuguese."* Johnny Lee says it like por-chu-gee-see, *and part of me wants to snicker, but that would just bring his attention back to me and I don't want that.* "Aren't we fancy this fine morning. Why don't you just Portugue-see yourself on out of this conversation, eh? This doesn't concern you."

"Yeah, I don't think I will. Leave her alone, Jamison. Hell, leave all these kids alone. Stop being a little punk."

*I watch in awe as a dull flush of red creeps up Johnny Lee's neck and cheeks. His fists open and close, and he stands to his full height.* "Sit down please, young man," *the bus driver calls. I'm impressed in spite of myself. Maybe he's feeling bold because he has Jack for back-up.*

*Johnny Lee ignores him and steps over to Jack, who remains calmly sitting in his seat.*

"He's gonna get his ass whupped," *the kid sitting next to me whispers.* "This is cray-zay."

*I'm not sure who he's referring to. I know most people would probably lay odds on Johnny Lee being the victor in any sort of physical altercation, simply because that's his thing. It's what he does, and grudgingly, I have to admit he does it well. All the Jamisons do.*

*I guess when you get a lot of practice at something, you're bound to excel at some point.*

*And yet there's a presence about Jack Brady, a relaxed confidence that suggests I'd be just fine placing my faith in him.*

*So, I do.*

*"He's going to be just fine," I say aloud, my gaze fixed on Jack as he rises slowly to stand a full head taller than Johnny Lee, so tall his neck bends at the peak of the bus's roof. He places a hand at the juncture of Johnny Lee's neck and shoulder and squeezes lightly, bending to speak softly to him. I can't hear what he's saying.*

*Whatever it is, Johnny Lee doesn't like it. His eyes narrow, and his mouth pinches, and at length he jerks his shoulder out of Jack's grip. Expression ugly, he pivots on his heel and storms back to his seat, pausing to look at me hard. "Bitch."*

*I don't reply, shifting in my seat to keep my back to him and my face forward. I'll take 'bitch' over 'what color are your panties' any day. Pulling out my book, I open it.*

*I can't help the furtive look I slide Jack Brady over the top of the bookmark I tap against my lip, though. Can't help the very real smile that forms on my mouth when I find him looking back. Can't help the words that I shyly mouth.*

My hero.

I come to slowly, aware only of shushed voices and a blinding headache. I'm exhausted, every muscle in my body screaming in protest as I open my eyes and shift positions.

I'm on the sofa in my living room, I realize after a glance to my side that has my neck protesting. *How did I...?* Sugar, beside my thigh, lifts her head and gives my hand a lick. The mall. I was at the mall. There were crowds and that tinny elevator music and Marcus... Marcus was there.

Memory returns in fits and starts. There was a woman. She was blonde, and there was something else...

"Look who's awake." Owen comes to squat beside me and smooths my hair out of my face. I wince. That hurts. "Hey, kiddo. How're you feeling?"

He helps me up to a sitting position and I take a minute to get my bearings. The metallic taste in my mouth... blood. "I had a seizure?" I look at Owen for confirmation and he nods.

"Sure did. A doozy, but nothing too out of the ordinary."

"How long did it last?" If I'm back home, it must not have been too lengthy. Anything over five minutes would put me in the hospital. It's a black hole, though, as far as me remembering it.

"Just over a minute. You bit the hell out of your tongue. You came to at the mall, but just for a few minutes...long enough for us to get you to the car. Then you sacked out."

Lifting a hand to my face, I wince again. "Did I hit my head? It's killing me."

"No." Owen looks uncomfortable. "That would be because you took a punch to the face."

I stare at him dully. "Someone punched me?"

"I figured your memory might be spotty." Owen sighs and presses his fingers to his eye sockets.

"It usually is." Slowly, the fog is starting to lift. "We were at the mall so Ava could see Santa. Oh, God—did I screw that up?" I hated my epilepsy most when it messed with my family. There had been so many interruptions to our best laid plans over the years…some minor that we were able to move on from, others more significant that had taken some time to recover from. If I had messed up Ava's ability to see Santa, I would never forgive myself.

"No…not you. Do you remember seeing Marcus?"

"Vaguely."

"He was there with…some other people."

"I remember a blonde…" Thinking is hurting my head. "Just tell me, whatever it is. And can I have some water, please? My mouth is gross."

"I'll get it." With the statement, I become aware of another man standing in the doorway, broad shoulders filling out a gray tee shirt that stretches across a nice set of pecs. With a slight twist of his lips that could be construed as a smile, he turns and walks away.

"Jack." His name comes to me, and with it an impression of strong arms holding me. "That was Jack."

"You remember Jack?"

I return my attention to my brother. "It's the last hour that's spotty, not my entire past."

It's been close to two decades since I've seen him, but Jack isn't someone you forget. He was my hero in high school, my biggest crush. My first experience with the pain of unrequited love.

I'd know him anywhere, no matter how much time had passed or how much he had changed. But Jack hasn't changed too much, physically. He's still damned good-looking, all the promise of that tall, sturdy senior fulfilled in a strong, solid hunk of man.

Owen stands from where he's squatting against the sofa and takes a seat beside me. "Right. Well, here's the thing. Marcus is married to someone else, apparently. A real bitch—that blonde you remember. He has an entire other family. We discovered this fact at the mall when he was also taking his kids to see Santa."

I blink. "That was so not what I expected you to say." Jack returns and hands me a glass of water. "Thank you," I say, taking a sip and regarding him over the rim. "Long time no see, Jack Brady. So, my husband is a bigamist, and he has children. Where do you come in?"

"I—"

Despite my prosaic words, my head is spinning. Marcus is married? To someone else? That means... I choke on another sip of water and interrupt Jack's attempt at an explanation. "Wait. This means my marriage isn't legal?"

"Let me take this." Owen removes the water from my hand. "We're still processing everything, but yeah. That's the way it looks."

"Oh my God." A thought strikes me and I clutch Owen's shirt. "Oh, my God, Momma is going to freak out!"

"You're going to freak out once you're feeling better," Owen mutters. "You're being pretty calm so far."

"Well, I did just have a seizure. Tends to put things in perspective."

A throat clears. "I'm going to get going," Jack says. "I just wanted to stay and make sure you came out of that seizure all right, Harry. If you're feeling up to it, your brother is going to bring you to the station to talk to me tomorrow."

I'm still so confused. "The station?" I repeat.

He taps the palm of his hand against the doorjamb. "I'm a detective with Lucy Falls. I just happened to be in the right place at the right time tonight. If you're able to recall anything leading up to when you seized, we need to add it to our report."

"Oh. Okay. It was nice to see you, I guess? And I'll see you tomorrow." I look at Owen for confirmation, as he'll be the one driving me, and he nods. As an epileptic, I'm not permitted by law to drive myself for six months after any seizure activity. My family—Owen in particular—has grown accustomed to chauffeuring me around.

"Take it easy, Harry. Get some rest." He pauses and gives me a serious look. "In spite of the circumstances, it is very nice seeing you again." With a final wave, Jack leaves.

Getting rest won't be a problem. I'm so tired. It's normal after a seizure. A doctor once told me that all of the electrical activity in the brain and the muscle work involved is like completing a day-long marathon in a matter of seconds.

"Help me to bed?" I ask Owen and begin to push up from the couch.

"Your wish, milady."

We start the arduous journey down the hall to my bedroom. It hits me that Marcus won't be coming home—not to sleep, anyway. Not tonight, not ever again. "You're staying tonight?"

"As long as you need. Ava's already snoozing away in her room."

The thought makes me smile. Ava has her own room at my house, her own stash of toys, her own toothbrush... it's her second home.

Another thought strikes.

"And you didn't say anything to Momma or Daddy, right?"

"Of course, I didn't. I knew you wouldn't be up to to dealing with that tonight, and I'm sure as hell not dealing with it."

"Thank you...you really are the best, you know. I wouldn't trade you except for maybe a sister."

"Promises, promises... So, have you been taking your meds like you're supposed to?"

"Yes, Owen. If you can grab my pill organizer from the bathroom, I need to take some now, before I pass out again."

In my bedroom, Owen helps me navigate the high, king-sized bed Marcus and I have shared for the past seven years. Sugar jumps up beside me, circles twice, and lies down near my feet. She must know Marcus isn't coming home, because she never sleeps on the bed when he's around.

God. If what Jack and Owen said is true, I'm going to have a mess to sort out tomorrow. I can't wrap my brain around it now, though. I don't even want to think about it.

Right now, I want to sleep.

Owen brings my pills to me, and I pluck out the ones for tonight and swallow them down with the water he hands me, then return the glass to him. "I'm going to have to start sorting my pills on my own, I guess." I laugh without humor and slide down in bed. Marcus always sorted my various prescriptions for me, making sure I took the right ones in the morning, after meals, and in the evening.

Tugging the comforter to my chin, I roll on to my side. Marcus's empty pillow stares back at me, and I smooth my left hand lightly over its surface. The gleam of platinum winks.

My wedding ring.

God. I can't look at it and close my eyes. Maybe when I open them, I'll find this has all been a dream.

"Night, kid." The light flicks out with a quiet click, and Owen's footfalls lessen in volume as he walks away.

Somehow, though, I think I may have moved beyond dreams.

I'm in a nightmare.

# Three

## Harry

The police station isn't what I expected. Having never been, my expectations lie somewhere between Mayberry's courthouse with its two cells sitting companionably beside Sheriff Andy's desk, and the large, impersonal city structures I see on television, where I might get beaten up—again—if I look at the wrong person.

The station in Lucy Falls is in a compact mid-century brick building, its utilitarian exterior echoed inside by neutral gray walls and a subdued stream of uniform-clad humanity. Owen drops me off and I enter, giving my name to a woman manning the courtesy desk when she asks.

Jack appears within minutes and leads me and Sugar through a series of corridors, all identical with more gray paint and random, unmarked doors. He's quiet, and suddenly I'm nervous.

"Um. Jack?" I wait until he looks at me. "Am I being arrested or something?"

A quick grin, easy to miss, flashes across his face. "No, Harry."

"Whew. Because I was starting to feel like I was being led to the guillotine. Or, you know, a jail cell."

"No need to worry. Just wait here, while I get a few things sorted for our interview." He opens a door and ushers me into what looks like the classic television interview room, complete with a steel table bolted to the floor and a darkened mirror that I know is actually a window to an observation room.

The walls and tile floor are, again, gray. I sit down, Sugar settling beside me, and look at the mirror-window. "You guys really need a new decorator."

After a while, I grow uncomfortable and sit forward in the chair to lower my head to the table, resting it within the circle of my arms. I still cannot believe this is happening to me. Every ugly detail of our trip to the mall had returned when I awoke this morning, bringing with them a faint feeling of nausea and anger and sadness.

My husband is married to someone else.

He's a bigamist.

The word is ugly, frightening. Do his actions mean I'm at fault, also? What happens now? Do I divorce him, or can I even do that, if our marriage has never been legal?

A dull headache starts to throb behind my forehead, and I groan. Everything hurts and fatigue dogs me. I want to go home.

Standing, I check the time on my phone. It feels like I've been in here for hours, but in reality, it's only been ten minutes. Wrapping my arms around my chest, I start to pace. I'm still doing so when the door opens and Jack pokes his head in.

"Ready?"

"I've been ready." My response emerges tartly, and I press my lips together. *I will not be rude.*

Beyond a twitch of his lips, Jack ignores it. "Come on."

He leads Sugar and me to a tiny cubicle with frosted fiberglass walls and tells me to sit. Or, at least, he points to the chair across from the business side of a messy metal desk, and without a word of protest, I take the plain metal chair situated there.

He sits across from me after shrugging out of the fleece-lined parka he was wearing, resting his hands on a flat mid-section and leaning back in the ancient wooden desk chair. It squeaks but he pays it no mind, choosing instead to focus every unnerving bit of his attention on me.

I shift restlessly, eyeing the utilitarian nameplate on the desk before looking around curiously. *Detective J. Brady.* It feels fitting that he's a detective now. A cop. He always did have that sense of justice that set him apart from others.

His office cubicle is tiny, and designed for function over appearance, but it is infinitely better than the sterile interrogation room he took me to at first. There's at least the mess on his desk that shows his humanity, his creaky chair, and the noise from the rest of the small department.

I frown, my tongue worrying a space between my bottom canine and its companion tooth. Detective Jack is as hunky as he was in school, maybe more so, with hair an indeterminate shade of blonde-brown and a squarish jaw covered with a bit more than just a five o'clock shadow. Everything about him is thick and solid-appearing: his eyebrows, the strong slash of his nose, his full, well-shaped lips. Not to mention his body.

With difficulty, I pull my gaze away. Why am I even looking?

I don't know what Jack wants, exactly. Why isn't he arresting me for creating a public disturbance or whatever it's called? Why is he just sitting there staring at me? Is he waiting for me to spill my secrets? Tell him where the body's hidden? Is this a game of who breaks first?

Is that really a thing?

Maybe he wants to catch up on old times? I feel heat flushing my face at the thought, memories of how I chased him unmercifully as a kid rising with the heat.

*Lord.* Talk about wrong time, wrong place. Straightening in the seat, I clear my throat and attempt to look professional. Best to keep things all business. "Should I call my lawyer?"

His lips thin as he takes the hint and leans forward a little. "Well, hello, Jack, it's nice to see you, too. It's been, what, twenty years?"

My eyes roll, all by themselves. "I said hello last night."

"Maybe I was hoping for a little more than *long time no see*."

"Are you kidding me right now? You're lucky you got even that, with the way I was feeling."

"Damnit." His chair creaks as he sits back in it with a frustrated fling of the pen he was holding. It skitters across the desk, coming to rest against a picture frame turned away from me. "Sorry," he mutters. "Long fucking day and it's not even lunchtime yet. You're right, of course. You feeling okay today?"

I lift my chin in a nod, then repeat my earlier question softly. "Do I need a lawyer, Jack?"

"That depends. Do you want to press charges?"

"Press charges?"

"We've already done enough witness interviews and seen enough cell phone footage to have a pretty good idea of what took place. We also have Mr. and Mrs. Lane's statements, which are wildly different from bystander accounts, naturally. Bystanders are in accord that Mrs. Lane was the assaulting party, and you were simply trying to...er...extricate yourself."

"Mrs. Lane."

He narrows his eyes. "The woman with her hands in your hair. The one who punched you in the face."

"I always thought I was Mrs. Lane."

"Mm. One second, please." While I wait, he pulls a legal pad across the cluttered surface of the desk and scrapes a spot clear. "I need to take notes, if you don't mind."

"Do what you have to do, Jack."

His eyes pinch. "It's my job, Harry. If it makes you more comfortable, I can pass it off to someone else, though." He waits, pen poised over the legal pad, while I think.

It's so weird, discussing all my secrets and truths with my former crush, laying bare every hurt and deception. But would it be any less awkward, or any less painful, with a stranger? I don't know.

It's that uncertainty that makes me sigh and wave a hand in defeat. "It's fine. Better you than anyone else."

He wastes no time, jumping right back to his questions. "So, what you're telling me is that you're also Mrs. Marcus Lane?"

"Correct."

"Please state your full legal name and occupation."

"You know my name, Jack."

"For the record, please."

"Full, legal name is Harriet Maelynn Bee-Lane." I speak the word *hyphen* as though it is its own presence within the confines of my name. Technically, it is.

He smiles a little. "Harriet Maelynn—"

"Harry still, of course. No one needs to know I was a sacrifice to grandmotherly pride." I spell my middle name, in case he's forgotten, and then clear my throat. "I'm a food chemist and professor at the university in Charlottesville and retained my maiden name after my marriage to Marcus Lane seven years ago. I continue to go by Professor Bee, so it looks as though I won't have to make that change." My finger is going numb, and a glance down reveals that I've managed to wind a loose thread from my sweater around its circumference, as though I were going to floss with it. Disgusted, I yank it free. "Thank God for small miracles."

"So, you married Marcus Lane." Jack's pen pauses on the paper, and he looks at me from beneath his brow.

"Yes."

"Like, in a church. With a pastor, and a license, and all that jazz."

"I did, yes. Well, technically we were married on my family's property, but we had a pastor."

Jack nods, scribbling the information down as I speak. "The same Marcus Lane who is already married to Gina Lane."

"That appears to be the case, yes."

He lets the pen fall to the pad and sits back once again, templing his fingers beneath his chin. They're long, I notice. Piano player fingers. I never noticed that when we were kids.

"So."

The breath I pull in is shaky. It's the first time I've qualified the situation in so many words, admitted the truth aloud. It's ugly, and I can feel that sensation thickening the base of my throat and burning my nose, the warning signals that tears are imminent if I don't divert. "You've said that a few times."

"You had no idea?"

The question is gentle, not accusatory, but he's not going to let me divert. Placing my elbow on the arm of the chair, I raise my hand so it covers my mouth, my index finger resting beneath my nose. It's my go-to when I feel myself getting emotional and need a physical anchor to keep from crying. Fingers crossed it will work here, in this cluttered, dusty police station, in front of this man who sees too much already.

"No," I say. "I had no idea until last night. At the meet Santa thing."

"At which time his wife…the first wife, according to the license of record, assaulted you. So, we have two issues. Two—"

"When were they married?" I interrupt. He raises an eyebrow, surprised. "Sorry. I need to know."

"I…of course. Um…" He flips through his notebook. "The license on record… Pennsylvania, looks like… let's see. It shows they were married twelve years past."

"Five years before us, then. He had all these kids—"

"Yes." He runs a hand around his jaw, eyes resting on me for a second. "Jesus, Harry. I'm so sorry."

"My God, I was oblivious. I don't understand why he even did it. Obviously, he had everything he needed already. I couldn't even give him kids." I feel a tickle on my cheek and realize, horrified, that a tear has escaped and is trickling free. I brush it impatiently aside. I've held up well emotionally so far. I don't need to break down in the police station, in front of Jack. "I was completely fucking useless. And clueless. How does that even happen, Jack? I'm fucking Mensa and somehow, I wind up married to a bigamist for seven years, just...ignorant."

"Harry..."

"I can't divorce him, right? I can't sue for alimony, or anything like that? I built a life with that asshole...shit, around him...but I'm going to walk away with nothing."

"Not nothing, Harry. I'm sure there are things—"

"This is bullshit."

"You're right. It is. But it's going to be shit for him, too. No, you can't technically divorce him since you weren't technically married. But that means he has no ground to stand on as far as division of assets. And we can bring him, and his wife, up on a few charges. One is assault. The other is the bigamy. I'm going to recommend that you seek council, naturally."

Charges. Jail time? I closed my eyes, my hands curling into fists. Part of me is screaming. Lock the bastard up! Put him under the jail. The other part of me...the part I sometimes despised for its ability to reason and remain clearheaded, was shaking her head. Did I want those children's momma and daddy to go to jail? To have a record? The adults deserved it; that was not in question. The children did not. They were innocents in all this.

"Wait—" Jack pauses at my answer, his hand already on the phone on his desk, and lifts an eyebrow. "It's just that everything's moving so fast. What if I don't want to press charges?"

Jack's chair is one of the old-fashioned wooden office varieties that rocks and swivels. He had been rocking the slightest bit in his chair but comes to a stop when I ask the question, tugging at his earlobe. "Any reason why you wouldn't?"

I look down at my lap as though it might answer for me. It seems silly. I brush at a bit of dog hair on my jeans. "It's the kids, I guess." Somehow, I know their faces will be forever ingrained in my memory, marked with confusion and defensiveness. He is their father, regardless of whether he's grade-A Nickelodeon slime.

And then there's Gina. Defending her man, literal tooth and nail, while I stood there and tried to pull my tattered dignity around me. Maybe she deserves him.

Before I can attempt to explain any of this to Jack, a tall, thin woman with olive-toned skin and close-cropped dark hair taps a brief knock on the divider and walks in. "Hey, Jack. This the vic?"

Jack nods. "Harry, this is—"

Her hand juts into my face. "I'm Officer Katy, that's my real last name, thank you very much. And look at this pretty girl..." She bends and croons to Sugar, asking with a raised eyebrow if she can give her a pat.

I nod and open my mouth to reply but Jack speaks first. "She has you beat in the weird name department. Her name's Bee." Our eyes meet, exchanging memories of long-ago introductions that weren't really necessary. *My name's Harriet, but if you call me that I'll kick you in the nuts. Call me Bee.* Laughter, and then: *All-righty then. Harry it is.*

"Oh, that is a good one. I'm just stopping in to introduce myself. I'm Jack's partner, so if you can't get him for whatever reason, just call me." She sets a card down on the desk in front of me. "There's my number."

"Okay. Thank you. Hopefully this will be done after today, though."

Officer Katy scrunches her nose. "I wouldn't bet on it. Are you going to press charges?"

Reality sluices over me like the icy blast of winter rain. "We were just discussing that. I don't think I need to press charges. I just want him...them...out of my life."

They exchange a long, considering glance before Jack speaks. "I feel I have to warn you that such a decision comes with risks." I cock my head in question and he continues. "First, there's the public perception if you don't press charges. If you don't stand up and say, this was wrong and I want it punished, people wonder why. Did she know about it? Condone it?"

I scoff. "That's ridiculous."

"Just the way people are, unfortunately. And second, to an extent, there's only so much control you and I have over the situation."

"What does that mean?"

"First, the mall episode happened outside the city of Richmond, not in Lucy Falls. As a courtesy, since I was the first responding officer and it involves a bigger crime of bigamy in a different area, the precinct this would go before is granting me jurisdiction. But since you're not pressing charges, it will have to go before the county's DA. Whether or not she presses charges is ultimately her decision. Usually stuff like this is misdemeanor-ed out, but you never know."

"Stuff like this?"

"Non-violent crime. Crime considered relatively minor in the big book of crime."

I close and reopen my eyes in a long blink. "Minor."

He clears his throat. "You know what I mean."

"Yeah. I think I understand. So, he won't have to go to jail or anything like that until the DA makes a decision?" I rub at my forehead. "This is all a little confusing. I think my brain is scrambled from yesterday."

"I'd feel a lot better about that seizure if you got looked at by a doctor," Jack says.

"I'm used to them," I explain. "I honestly don't need to see a doctor unless it's a long one."

"When did that even start? I don't remember you having seizures when we were kids."

"They didn't start until I was seventeen. I suffered a blow to the head and developed PTE."

"PTE?"

"Post traumatic epilepsy. Took a hard hit from a soccer ball."

"That's crazy." Jack eyes me like it's me that's crazy, rather than my story, and I look away, to the messy surface of his desk. A paper catches my eye. Up in the corner, the name Lane is scrawled in red ink and circled. Beneath it are demographic details, including a Charlottesville address and telephone number, and then lines of notes. Marcus or Gina's interview, I guess.

*3423 Mulberry Lane.* That's where they live when Marcus wasn't with me. *Is it nice? As nice as our house is?* Marcus had insisted on settling in one of Lucy Falls' fancier neighborhoods.

"Well, all this memory lane stuff is great, but I have work to do," Officer Katy breaks in, catching my attention. "Harry, Jack is right about all of this, so definitely something to consider. That said, he'll be bonded out, so he'll be free to go. Same for the wife. Bigamy is honestly seldom prosecuted unless it can be proven it was for intent to profit or some felonious scheme. This should be the end of it."

"Okay." I stand, gather the jacket that he placed on the back of the chair when we entered. "Am I free to leave?" I hold my breath, praying neither of them noticed my perusal of the paperwork. *3423 Mulberry Lane.*

Jack and his partner exchange another look before Officer Katy nods, a quick tip of her chin, and steps out of the cubicle. "Of course." Jack rises, as well, blocking my exit. Intentionally, I'm certain. I hold still and stare at the row of clear buttons on the pale blue shirt in my field of vision, breathing in shallow breaths to avoid inhaling his scent. *3423 Mulberry Lane.* "But I have to know why you really don't want to press charges, first. You gotta give me more than just 'the kids.' Why don't you want to nail this motherfucker? It's not right, what he did to you, Harry."

Without moving my head, I lift my eyes to his. I've avoided looking too closely and for too long up to this point, but they're the same stony lichen I remember, full of shadows and light. "Does there really need to be a reason?" I ask. He doesn't reply, just waits, and I shrug into my jacket. "How about forty-fucking-two for a reason."

His lips part, the tip of his tongue darting out to lick his full bottom lip before retreating. "I never did understand that shit," he replies, and steps back to let me pass.

I do so, shoving my hands in the pockets of my jacket to hide their sudden tremble.

# Four

## Harry

***Before Marriage***

*The afternoon sun glints off the windshield as I turn to look for Marcus, making me shield my eyes. Instead of walking with me, he has paused to study the house I grew up in, but there's something more than simple admiration or curiosity in his gaze. It's a blend of calculation and... recollection if I read the distance in his eyes accurately. It's like he's been here before, has memories set aside.*

*There's no way, though. Marcus is only seven years older than I am, and I've lived here all my life. This is literally the house that built me, grew me into the woman I am today. It's a century and a half year-old farmhouse, and I know every brick and board that comprise it, inside and out.*

*Even after it was renovated a bit over a decade ago, it retained the comforting familiarity of my growing-up years. I played hide-and-seek everywhere from the barn to the attic, named every kitten born in the hayloft each season. I would remember a visit from a handsome boy, older than me by just enough to make him exciting. I would have crushed hard in my silly girl days.*

*I must be mistaken. It's not remembrance I see, but perhaps...anticipation.*

A breeze blows a piece of my hair across my face, and with a frown I push it back, the wind's herald of approaching fall giving me goosebumps even though the day is pleasant.

"Marcus?"

He shakes himself like Sugar does when she gets wet and claps his hands briskly together. "I'm here. Let's do this, babe. Why didn't you tell me how stunning this place was?"

A frown accompanies my response. "Because it wasn't relevant? This is my parents' house, not mine."

"Since when is being rich irrelevant?" He pokes me in the side for good measure as we walk around toward the back of the house, where my parents are hosting a late summer barbecue in celebration of the engagement we just announced. "Maybe I don't want to be with a rich girl."

"I'm not rich, Marcus." Discomfort makes me defensive. People don't talk about money around here. It's considered rude. "Just like the house, it's my parents' money, not mine. And they were as poor as anyone until I was a teenager."

"What happened then?"

*"Someone died and left Momma a lot of money, that's what happened. It gave my parents what they needed to fix the house up properly and pay off the mortgage. Until that time, it was a fixer-upper fixing to fall apart."*

*"Oh." His hand finds mine and swings it up, up to his lips for a kiss. "Well, that just proves my point. It'll be yours one day, and that makes you rich. Did you say they're having steak? Something smells good."*

After my interview at the police station, I can't face the idea of returning home. I send a protesting Owen on his way, then call for an Uber and ask him to drive me to the neighborhood indicated on Jack's paperwork.

Mulberry Lane is as cute and picturesque as the name suggests. Houses are moderately sized with neatly kept lawns. Most of them are trimmed with bright strings of multi-color Christmas lights and the occasional yard decoration. The house Marcus lives in, if I read the paperwork correctly, is a brick ranch painted a pale gray with black trim and cedarwood accents. A giant inflatable snowman sways in the middle of the expanse of browning lawn, buffeted by a chilly breeze.

Marcus never would allow me to place one of those on our yard. Nothing except a tasteful white manger scene. He always claimed the inflatables were tacky.

The driver waits with a blank sort of patience while, in the back seat of his car, I dig my fingers into Sugar's fur and let out a low, anguished groan.

"How is this fucking happening," I mutter.

"Ma'am?"

In the mirror, I see the driver's eyebrow arch. "Are you married..." I trail off, realizing I don't know his name. "What's your name?"

"Chad."

"Chad. Are you married?"

"Uh...yeah. Two years now."

I nod, eyes trained outside the window once again. "That's great. Or, at least, I hope it's great. I've been married for seven years now."

"Um...okay." He shifts in the driver's seat, and part of me feels badly for making him uncomfortable, this stranger who's listening so politely to me word-vomit all over him.

"Sorry." Sugar gives my chin an encouraging lick and it sparks something inside me. "Actually, I have nothing to be sorry for. You see that house right there?" I point, and Chad nods. "That's where my husband lives. But not with me." I look to see his reaction and catch a frown line between his eyes. "That's right. That's where he lives with his *other* wife."

"I don't—"

"His first wife. His real wife. He's a *bigamist*, Chad. Can you believe that shit?" I shake my head. Chad's mouth is open a little, and he has turned around now in the seat so he can stare. "I'm a freaking college professor. I have a doctorate. I'm considered a genius in most circles. And yet...I missed it."

"Holy...I am so sorry, ma'am. That's some shit."

I laugh a little. "Hell, yeah, it's some shit. How did I fucking miss something like this, Chad?"

His face is pinched, uncomfortable. "I'm sure he hid it really well."

"I'm sure you're right." Silence falls after that, and he lets me sit without speaking for a while. "You don't mind sitting with me, do you, Chad? I just need a little time, I think. To wrap my head around all of this."

"I don't mind. Take as long as you need."

A few minutes later he clears his throat, getting my attention and meeting my eyes in the rearview mirror. "Um, I don't want to be presuming or anything, but if you want him, ah...well, I know a guy, that's all." He arches an eyebrow meaningfully.

My lips part, and for the first time in days I feel like laughing. Instead, I lift my chin. "I will definitely keep that in mind. Thank you."

The door opens and the older boy emerges from the house, pausing on the stoop to pull a knit stocking cap over his head. He starts jogging down the sidewalk to the road, halting when the door opens again, and the blonde woman pokes her head out. I can just barely make out the baby on her hip.

She calls something to the boy, and he nods before turning and loping off down the street.

Maybe he's going to a friend's house to play.

The blonde watches him go, then glances around the street. I hold my breath as her gaze slides over the car, pauses briefly, and then keeps going. I don't release it until she retreats, closing the door behind her.

*God. What am I doing?* The icky sensation of shame creeps over me, and I press the heels of my hands into my eye sockets.

This is a woman with children. There's no way she had anything to do with Marcus' decision to be a liar and a cheat…no way she knew what was happening. No doubt she is in as much pain and turmoil as I am. Inside that house, she's probably staring blankly at family portraits, wondering what the hell she's going to do now that she knows.

Maybe I should talk to her.

My hand is on the door handle, my chest rising and falling with nervous breaths, when the phone in my pocket buzzes. I rouse and pull it free to read the notification.

**Owen:** *your dick husband-not-husband is here*

**Me:** *Please don't punch him and get yourself arrested. Ava and I need you.*

**Owen:** *okay, but that's a big ask*

**Owen:** *where the hell are you anyway?*

I ignore the last message. "I'm ready, now," I tell Chad, plugging my address into the app. I've seen everything I need to see. It's just over half an hour back to Lucy Falls, and another ten minutes to my home, and that, combined with the two-plus hours we've spent sitting in this quiet little neighborhood, means Chad will be getting a nice payout.

The rapidly falling darkness is a blessed shroud when Chad pulls to a stop in front of the house I shared with Marcus. It hides the utter agony of awareness I'm certain is etched into every line of my face. I fumble with his payment, calculating a hefty tip to compensate him for his time, and climb out.

Marcus's vehicle is nowhere to be seen, but Owen is waiting for me. Inside the foyer, he pulls me into a hug before I can shimmy from my coat, holding me until the tension melts a few degrees before releasing me.

It returns, though, companion to the irritation that has me jerking my scarf from around my neck and tossing it down to the antique table. "He didn't stay for the big confrontation?" I say, keeping my tone deliberately light as I scratch Sugar around the ears, and then head for the kitchen. I need a beer.

Except... *fuck*. I just had a seizure, so alcohol is out for a while. I shouldn't have been drinking it at all, but the cider beer I like is mild. I didn't figure it would be an issue. Or, at least, I was hoping it wouldn't be.

"Grabbed some clothes and then he ran out like he left his dick in the car and he was afraid someone was gonna steal that precious thing," Owen drawls, accepting the beer I pass him and watching as I pull a water for myself from the refrigerator.

I laugh unwillingly and look at the time. It's just after eight. "Douche. Did Ava go down okay?" Owen told me this morning he and Ava would be staying until things calmed down a bit. I'm glad. I don't like being on my own so close to a seizure episode.

"Like an angel. She was fine."

"Oh, good. Did she...ask any questions about the stuff at the mall?"

"Nah. Went right over her head, thank God. She wanted to tell you goodnight, but she crashed. Apparently, today was an exhausting day at preschool." He mimics Ava's drama queen routine, letting his wrist flop forward and giving me wide eyes as he imitates her attempt to pronounce 'exhausting.'

"Cute."

"She's a mess. So, how was the interview? And Officer Hottie? Did he give you a cavity search?"

I wag my finger at him. "Funny guy, you are."

In my living room, I bypass the light switch, leaving the room in darkness save for the light filtering in from the hall. I flop without grace onto the oversized couch and fold my feet beneath me, sans the shoes I toed off in the hallway. Owen crashes on the open length of sofa, bouncing me airborne for a split second and spilling water on the knuckles wrapped around the plastic bottle. I lick them and glare without malice as he puts his feet in my lap.

"Grace," I tell him mildly.

"Turd."

"Francis."

"Ooh, savage." Owen's middle name is Francis and is approximately as despised as Harriet is to me. "Talk to me."

"It was...surprisingly okay. Jack and his very cute female partner were helpful." Owen snorts, clearly not impressed. "Obviously, I'm not under arrest. There were plenty of bystander accounts and cell phone videos to show that Gina Lane assaulted me. I elected not to press charges."

"What?"

"She was really cute." I deliberately misinterpret his question. "Maybe five-six, one of those pixie cuts. Looked like Tinkerbell, except with black hair—"

"Harry."

"Didn't you have a thing for Tinkerbell when you were a kid? I think—"

"Harriet."

I stop and sip my water, taking my time to reply. "There are so many kids, Owen. I couldn't do it. Can you imagine those babies waking up in the morning and their momma isn't there?"

Owen shakes his head emphatically. "No. Just no. That's on them, Harry, not you. You don't get to be soft about this. They fucked up, and it's up to them to teach their children that mistakes have consequences."

I don't answer, and the only sound is the tone of a distant windchime from the neighbor's house. Sometime later, Owen speaks, his voice slurred and sleepy. "What are you gonna do, Harry?"

"In a few minutes, I'm going to get up, wash my face, and go to bed."

"Don't be smart."

I side-eye him and set my empty bottle down on the coffee table before answering. "I'd have to work really fucking hard to fake stupid." I say the words, but they feel empty. I was duped, and on a pretty spectacular level. "I was pretty fucking stupid, though. Wasn't I?"

"No, babe, you weren't. He was cunning and he knew how to hide who he really is. That doesn't make you stupid."

"Seven years, Owen. And I feel like I always had this sense that something wasn't exactly right. I thought about leaving, you know. More than once." I shake my head, disgusted with my own stupidity. "I don't know why I didn't."

"You didn't leave because you, like me, are the product of two amazing parents who have shown us what you can have if you're willing to work at it. To take the bad with the good, and not expect perfection from imperfect humans. There's nothing wrong with that."

I make a sound. It's not agreement, but it's not an argument, either. Owen is still talking.

"... and a criminal, Harry. Hell, he's probably a sociopath. You have to be to do something like this. We don't think the same way people like that do. It would never occur to us to be suspicious that he was up to something of this magnitude...that's how he was able to get away with it. It has nothing to do with your intelligence or perception."

It was eerie, the way he knew how much it bothered me to have been duped. How much I blamed myself for it.

"Yeah, but...still."

"No 'still' about it. Get that out of your damn head, hear?"

"Yeah, yeah."

"So back to the plan. You need action."

"I don't have a plan. I mean, obviously there will be a dramatic moment where I bust the window in his car, and I'll probably cut all his favorite ties in half."

Marcus is a certified dandy and loves his wardrobe far more than is healthy. The idea of destroying it makes me smile, but it doesn't satisfy Owen.

"Super cliché. You're better than such mediocrity, kid."

"Mmm. I'll also invent a recipe or ten and bake three hundred cookies. Maybe it'll go viral and I'll become an overnight cookie sensation and get filthy rich. And Marcus will get none of it."

Owen is still unimpressed. "Hmpf. I'll think of something diabolical for you."

"I think that's why he did it, Owen."

"What's that?"

"I think he married me because he thought I was rich."

"Hmm."

We're quiet after that until his deep, even breaths tell me he's fallen asleep, and then I speak low to the deaf ears of the midnight room. "I'd just rather it all be over, you know? I don't want to think about it. I don't want to wonder if I was some kind of weird challenge to him, or if his other...wife...supplied something I couldn't give him." *Maybe he did only want you because he thought you were rich,* the little voice in my head murmurs. "No..."

I peek over to make sure I haven't disturbed my brother. His eyes are shuttered, breath still relaxed and steady. I talk softly out loud, pretending I'm talking to him, telling him all the vulnerable things I can't say when he's listening. "I know I'm going to be thinking every day for the next six months about what I'm losing. Another person in my bed. Someone to talk to when I come home from work. Someone to text stupid memes to, to eat with, to watch Saturday morning cartoons with. Not that he ever did that, but...anyway. I'm not ready to start thinking about all that right now, though."

I lift my hand to find my cheek wet, exactly what I wanted to avoid. I didn't want to contemplate any plans of action, first moves, then secondary ones. Didn't want to acknowledge the fact that I was going to have to get my own lawyer, start itemizing remnants of a life spent together like they were nothing more than assets.

Start dividing physical memories into Discard, His, Hers, and Goodwill piles. Determine what once-precious items could be rolled out to the curb with the rest of Tuesday's garbage.

"I'm not ready."

The words are a whisper but drop like a bomb in the silence of the living room. Tomorrow, what I want and don't want isn't going to matter. Tomorrow, I'm going to have to handle my shit, ready or not. Put my money where my mouth is and acknowledge my brokenness so I can begin the process of moving past it.

Sniffling, I yank the throw from the back of the couch and stretch out opposite my brother, sticking my feet between his backside and the sofa cushions for extra warmth. Weekends found us camping out like this as kids for marathon cartoon sessions that stretched into black and white sitcom nights. We need more of those, I think. Ava would love it, especially as she got a little older. Somehow life and adulting always managed to get in the way.

I snuggle into the throw and close my eyes, and after a few minutes, feel Sugar's weight settle on my hip as she joins the pile. For these last few hours before tomorrow comes, I allow myself grace. Here, in the darkness of my living room, with my sleeping brother to stand guard, I'll cry if I want, and be pathetic if I need to be.

And then I'll wake in the morning, put on some lipstick, and be just fine.

As it happens, the next morning I don't have time to wallow, or slice through any ties, or even apply some damn lipstick. The door opens at the ungodly hour of seven A.M., when Ava and I are sharing a bowl of Cheerios and bananas. Owen moved to the guest room at some point during the night, so it's Ammie Harry who stands in front of her at the kitchen counter while Daddy sleeps. We alternate bites, me holding her securely in place as I trade off my own portion with gulps of black coffee. Sugar, snoozing at my feet, lifts her head and growls before lowering her head back to the floor with a tired sigh.

The sound of the front door unlatching has me pausing mid-swallow.

"Harriet? Harriet, it's me. I come in peace." Marcus appears in the doorway to the kitchen, fresh and pressed-looking in his Monday suit. Pride keeps me from looking down at my rumpled tee shirt and knee socks, one of which has slid down to my ankle, but I'm painfully aware of the contrast in our appearances.

Maybe Gina looks better in the morning. Maybe she wakes up without raccoon eyes because she remembers to wash her face before bed each night, and maybe her hair doesn't end up in fucking Los Angeles even though she lives on the east coast. Maybe she's born with it.

"Maybe it's Maybelline," I say, grinning at my own cleverness.

"What?"

"Shit. Nothing. What do you want, Marcus?"

"*Sit*. Ammie Harry said *sit*. Hi, Markie."

Marcus gives me a look and reaches for Ava, so I hand her over after a kiss on the forehead and a roll of my eyes. "Ammie Harry did say a wordy dird, baby. Sorry. I'll give your daddy a dollar for your piggy bank, and you'll be rich."

"K, Harry. Hi, Markie." Ava reaches for Marcus's cheeks and he deftly dodges.

"Whoa-ho, hey, there sticky fingers. Harriet, can you pass me a paper towel?"

I don't move. "They're right behind you, where they always are."

"But my hands—"

"Have two opposable thumbs, just like mine. I think you can handle Ava and a paper towel at the same time, Marcus. I'll be in the living room."

In the living room, I busy myself folding the throw I used the night before and smoothing out the wrinkled sofa. A contrary part of me wishes my brother were awake to act as buffer to the unpleasantness I know is coming, but I refuse to go upstairs and interrupt his sleep. As a single dad and an independent business owner, I know he doesn't get much, even with me and our parents helping as much as we're able.

Marcus enters, his expression stiff, a few minutes later. Ava follows after him and beelines for the corner where I keep a collection of toys for her piled in a basket, giving us relative privacy to face each other. My erstwhile husband stares at me for several silent moments, until I break, shifting my weight from one foot to the other and crossing my arms over my chest.

"So? What are you doing here? Have you come to apologize? Explain? Get your stuff?"

He runs a hand over his head, ruffling his perfect hair. "I—"

"How about all three?" I'm deliberately goading him now, unable to stop the bitterness from pouring forth like the coffee I just drank. "Why, Marcus? How could you?" I can feel the pinch covering everything: the question, the set of my mouth, my eyes... even that point where my neck and shoulders intersect. Everything squeezes uncomfortably, waiting for his answer.

I'm doomed to further disappointment. His features lose any animation he walked in with, any potential regret or sorrow. "I don't actually have time for a lengthy heart-to-heart this morning. I have an eight o'clock meeting. I just wanted to stop in and make sure you were okay. Make sure you weren't going to do anything...crazy."

I squint. "Crazy?"

He shifts, a sign of his discomfort. "Obviously there's a lot I need to talk to you about. I was just visiting my children last night. There's nothing there...damnit, I really don't have time for this right now. We'll talk, okay? Just don't do anything crazy."

"Again with that word. I'm not going to jump off a cliff, Marcus."

"No, that's not what I mean. I just want a chance to explain. Things aren't what they seem. I'm glad you know...this is good. It's better this way."

My lips part, shock at his blasé attitude rendering me speechless. "Better? How is this better, Marcus? You just decimated a seven-year marriage overnight. And who knows...maybe you sank the other one, too. What do you think is going to happen now, exactly?"

"I just meant that—"

"You just meant that it's better for you. You're tired of living a double life, and now you have an out. Well, I don't know that it's going to be that simple."

"What does that mean?" Alarm etches his face, momentarily disrupting his mask. It's not the first time I've seen it. Marcus has always been good at concealing the truth of who he is beneath the surface. It is the first time, though, that I've seen it as a woman who is *done*. I'm done with lies, done with being the only one trying, the only one who cares.

I have no desire anymore to keep fighting to hold on to something that should have been discarded years earlier, and that's what colors my perception of the man standing before me.

Up to this point, I wanted to believe we could do it, that maybe I was mistaken about the man beneath the mask. Now...I'm ready to see the truth. And that truth...it's ugly. Marcus has been playing me false from the start.

"I don't know yet."

"Harry—"

"You don't get to call me that any longer. My name is Harriet."

He straightens and places both hands on my biceps, his fingers kneading and squeezing in a pleading manner. I close my eyes. This isn't genuine, honest affection. It never was. Marcus was always distant, a little uptight, cold, even. Sure, he could turn it on when the situation called for it, but I see it now. He wants something. It's so obvious.

He's still talking, oblivious that I'm not listening. I open my eyes. "Harriet, then. Don't be like this. I made a mistake, and I'll do what it takes to correct it. I love—"

I scoff, startling him enough that he stops mid-sentence. "Marcus."

"What?"

"I think you should leave now."

"Excuse me?"

"You heard me. Leave."

His fingers tighten on my biceps, and if I hadn't been watching his expression closely, I might have missed the nerve ticking at the corner of his right eye. "I'm not finished."

I pull back, but his hands don't loosen. "You're not hearing me," I hiss. "I'm finished. Do we have some shit to work out? Maybe. For now, you keep paying your share of the bills and when I'm ready to talk, we'll talk. But that's not today. Leave—"

"I don't think—"

"Now, Marcus. Let go of me." *Tick, tick, tick.* His mouth tightens.

Slowly he removes his hands and steps back, retrieving his coat from the back of the chair where he tossed it. "Fine. But I'll be back later. We're not done."

"Oh, we're done. Don't come back." I stand also and begin to walk him backwards toward the door. I cannot hear another word. I will scream. Or throw something; I'm not certain.

"Harriet, this is important..."

Avoiding assault charges are very important; he should know. "I'll have my lawyer contact you about picking up your things."

"Are you fucking kidding me?"

There he is. There's the beast beneath the pressed suit, prowling to be let loose. I open the door and gesture toward the gray December morning that waits outside. "Be glad I haven't thrown everything out on the front lawn. As of last night, we are officially over, and since by virtue of your first fucking legal *marriage* we aren't actually married, I don't have to do anything more than tell you just that and nothing more: *we're over.* Done. Finis. Kaput. And we are never, under any circumstances, ever getting back together."

For what feels like an eternity he regards me with mute astonishment. "What? You're letting the heat out, Marcus," I finally snap.

"Are you going to press charges?"

Door open, one foot in and one on the stoop, he blurts the question in such a way that it's obvious it was the reason for his visit—the only thing keeping him civil. My spine stiffens. *Yes*, I want to hiss. *I'm going to make sure they throw every book in the freaking Library of Congress at you.* Instead, I push him gently, inexorably over the threshold.

And then I shut the door in his face.

# Five

## Jack

From behind the kitchen window of my carriage house apartment, I take a pull on my beer and stare outside. It's just past midnight and I've been home for maybe twenty-minutes, just long enough to toss a load of laundry in the wash, toe my shoes off, and give Kota, my dog, some overdue dinner.

Like every other day this week, it's been a long one. Leaning against the cold porcelain of the kitchen sink now, I can't stop thinking about the woman who had her life turned topsy-turvy. *Harriet-Motherfucking-Bee.* What an absolute clusterfuck.

I haven't seen Harry since her first and my last year of high school.

A reluctant smile tugs at my mouth at the memory of what Daniel and I had walked up on in the mall. We'd been there after a long workday, Daniel wanting input on an engagement ring for his girl. We'd just gotten his ring and grabbed some chicken for dinner when our attention was caught by an altercation unfurling in front of Santa's Workshop. In a matter of seconds, it had gone from words exchanged to a curvy, pocket-sized redhead clinging to a statuesque blond for dear life, expletives rolling off both their lips like they'd spent time in the Navy.

"You get the blonde," I'd drawled to Daniel. "I'll take the firecracker."

The Harry I'd pulled off the blonde had changed considerably from the kid I knew years ago. In her youth, Harry carried the remnants of baby fat and was self-conscious and shy. She's an absolute bombshell now, all wildly curling red hair and lethal curves on a slender, petite frame. The woman who had sat across the desk from me earlier was no longer shy and retiring. She was all tightly held control and self-possession, even as her marriage was crumbling around her.

She didn't crumple, though, even after a brutal epileptic seizure.

My chest squeezes at the memory.

Moonlight is minimal, but the outline of the house across the expanse of yard is perfectly clear. Perfectly familiar. The old brick colonial with its interesting additions and choppy roofline has sat empty for the past seventeen months, three weeks, and two days. I've looked at it every one of those days, forced myself to meet the eyes of its windows without blinking.

Usually houses that sit empty that long a time have problems. Leaky roofs. Windows swollen with moisture. Insects. Mice and other infestations. Not this one, though. I've been a faithful caretaker during these past seventeen months. I've tended the flower beds, mowed the grass, controlled the climate inside the house and run water in the pipes to keep them from freezing in cold winter months.

It seemed the appropriate thing to do, after the woman who lived there passed. *Rose.* She loved her house, loved the quiet neighborhood it was situated in.

I take another pull on my beer, squinting at the ivy that creeps up the brick of the house across the lawn. Rose loved that damn ivy, but it's always been a pain in my ass.

I don't know why, but I can't think of Rose without Harry's face rising to the surface. Except for their old-fashioned names, they're two entirely different creatures. Harry isn't sweet and soft and vulnerable the way Rose was. Harry...she's all sharp, jagged glass around the edges. She's a warning wrapped in soft female skin, held together with yellow caution tape. *Crime Scene: Do not cross.*

She'd caught me off guard. Maybe it was because I'd known her when we were kids, known she had a godawful crush on me, even, but something about her tugged at me, caution tape be damned. It made me want to promise to keep her safe, slay her monsters, lock away the one who had hurt her.

All I could do, though, was work on putting Marcus Lane away. Despite how Harry felt about it, that's what needed to happen. The entire situation stank of lies and rottenness. Who's to say Lane wasn't running a similar scheme elsewhere, with other women?

It was why I'd decided to watch him tomorrow...just hours from now. I'd find something and make sure he ended up where he belonged—in jail.

I didn't normally find myself feeling like that about cases, about the people involved. It was unsettling. Led to drinking Guinness inside a dark room in what was basically a garage, staring out a window at a house I used to live in, with a woman I used to love.

A house where ghosts walked nowadays.

---

I fucking hate stakeouts. There's not even a purpose to this one...not really, anyway. Nothing except my gut talking to me like we had bad tex-mex for lunch. Something's telling me to keep an eye on Marcus Lane, though, and when instinct talks, I listen.

So, I sit at the curve of a nice little cul-de-sac—nothing near as nice as where he lived with Harry Bee, mind—but more than acceptable. I have a good view of the Lane's front door from where I'm parked, as well as all the neighborhood comings and goings.

Of course, there's not much going on this early in the morning. A couple of people have left for work, some of the keener ones sending me curious stares on their way out but most failing to notice me at all.

It's how I see the two of them—Marcus and Gina—when they step out onto the small porch.

They're arguing. It's obvious in the way she pokes his chest with a fierce finger, chin jutting as words I can't hear tumble from her mouth. He listens, meek save for the fist that opens and closes at his hip, then gives a single curt nod. Then he opens that fist and grabs a handful of Gina's hair, yanking hard and slamming her bodily into the door. My hand is on the handle until I see that she's grinning, and I ease back, watching as he leans into her and kisses her hard.

I grimace. They're crazy, and not the good kind. Obviously, passion exists between them. It makes everything that much more confusing. Why would a man with a relationship like this—passionate, if nothing else—risk it for a bigamous one with another woman? It doesn't make any sense.

After a lengthy and stomach-turning kiss, Marcus opens the door behind Gina and shoves her lightly inside with a slap on the butt, then turns and strides to his car.

I wait until he's pulled out of his driveway and down the cul-de-sac before following at a sedate pace.

It's soon obvious where he's headed. I hang back when he pulls into Harry's driveway and climbs from the vehicle, straightening his clothing as if he's headed in for a business meeting instead of seeing a woman he was intimate with for seven years. Why is he here, especially at the ass crack of morning? The hair on the back of my neck stands at attention.

I watch, mouth sour, as he uses his key to open the door and walk in like he still lives in the place. Technically, I guess he still does. She probably hasn't had an opportunity to officially kick him out, yet.

She has to kick his ass out. She'd be an idiot to…what? Try to play sister-wives? I scoff at my own imagination, which clearly needs eight hours of uninterrupted sleep. My gaze sweeps the neighborhood, still relatively quiet at seven in the morning. It's the epitome of genteel southern class: spacious homes set back off a tree-lined street, framed by meticulous landscaping and flaunting matching mailboxes. It's without a doubt one of the nicest streets in Lucy Falls, where all the wealthy people settle. It's the polar opposite of the comfortable, cozy middle class house Marcus shares with Gina.

It doesn't really reconcile with the Harry of my past, but maybe she chose this place. Maybe this kind of thing is important to her now. Didn't seem like it yesterday, but maybe she's too brainwashed by all the obvious trappings of wealth to consider giving it up.

Maybe this is why she didn't want to press charges.

The idea doesn't sit well, and I reach for my coffee to wash it down, only to find it cold and bitter.

Fuck.

Harry and her family were humble, down-to-earth people, though. It doesn't jibe.

I'm turning the engine over, done with monitoring Marcus—done with my own self, if I'm being honest—when the door opens once again. This time both Marcus and Harriet are clearly framed in its opening, and as I watch, she places a hand on his chest and pushes him out before closing the door in his face. He stands there, obviously stunned, before turning on his heel and stalking away, muttering and gesticulating to himself.

I can't help but laugh a little as I pull away from the curb and head toward the station, a thousand times lighter than I was sixty seconds earlier.

I don't know why I was worried. She's still the Harry I remember.

## Six

**Harry**

Owen and Ava stay at the house with me for the next four nights, Owen claiming I needed the company and the chauffeur.

I've never been a fan of being by myself. There was always the possibility of having a seizure while I was alone, and the need to call for constant Ubers since I'm not medically allowed to drive. It wasn't so much about security or being afraid to be alone. One of the contentious points of our marriage was that Marcus was always traveling, so I had become accustomed to the comfort of knowing I had a security system, a baseball bat in the closet by my bed, and having been raised in the country, a gun I kept locked securely away in my bathroom.

I guess I always figured if someone broke in, I'd run for the bathroom and lock myself in.

It was more an abstract sense of how helpless I could truly be, both on my own and if I were at the whim of someone who wanted to harm me. I didn't like that feeling.

So, I didn't argue when Owen took the guest room next to the one I'd decorated for Ava and any other children that might come along in the future, and told me he was staying for a while. Marcus's impromptu appearance showed me I needed to change the locks, and besides—there was something comforting about my brother's presence those days. Something that reminded me of home.

Shelter.

Especially since I still hadn't told our parents about Marcus. I should have called them that same evening, or at least, that's what Momma was going to say when I finally did come clean. Keeping it from them was starting to feel like a lie, but the longer I held on to it, the less I knew how to broach the subject. Now, as I lie in bed and stare at the ceiling, I try to imagine how the conversation might go.

*"Momma, Daddy, I have something I need to tell you. Can we turn off the game for a sec?"*

*"Oh, my Lord, she's finally pregnant. Praise—"*

*"No, that's not it. I—"*

*"Oh." (Deflated sounding.) "Oh, I know! Marcus got a new job and is going to be home more often."*

*"No—"*

*"Well, I just don't know what could possibly be so important, then—"*

*"If you could possibly be quiet for a split second, I'd tell you and you'd know."*

*"Why, Harriet Maelynn. That was disrespectful as all get-out."*

Yeah. I was not looking forward to this conversation.

On the fourth night, the house has been steeped in slumber for what feels like hours when I give up my own feeble efforts to fall asleep. I haven't gotten a good night's sleep since the mall incident. I see no point in lying here any longer.

Maybe a walk will clear the cobwebs.

Sugar whines as I get up and I scratch behind her ears and croon to reassure her. "I'll be right back, Sugar baby." I'm not going to take her, even though I should. Where I'm going isn't a great place for a protective animal.

She resettles with moody eyes as I dress swiftly and warmly, conscious of the thirty-degree temps. I pull a beanie over my ears, letting my hair snake out from beneath it with its typical temper, and then, in a small act of defiance, grab a Bold Rock from the fridge. I hate the restrictions on me because of my health, hate not being able to have a beer when I want without feeling guilty. I need to be normal tonight, if only for a few minutes.

Quietly, I let myself out and begin to walk down the street with purpose.

I know exactly where to go.

There's a bridge nearby, an old railroad one that overlooks the river. At one time, Lucy Falls, Virginia was a busy railway station, and the bridge was a vital thoroughfare from one place to the next. The railroads died out decades ago, though, and now Lucy Falls is merely a testament to the past, a stopover between towns where travelers shake off the dust and gas up. In the summertime, the iron trelliswork that spans the structure is covered in a lush blanket of wisteria, the town namesake's, Lucy Van Hollister, favorite flower. The lavender blossoms hang low and fragrant, providing shade for pedestrians.

The bridge will be black and formless at this time of night, but I'll walk there anyway. Listen to the chop and gurgle of water as it moves inexorably downstream. Drink my beer and let the night sounds wash everything else away, if only for the few hours that remain of the night.

Maybe then I'll be able to sleep.

*I'm so angry.*

The thought stays with me, keeps me warm as I near the bridge.

I don't think I've ever been as full of rage and bitterness over anything as I have been the past several days. The anger fills me, fills the cold and reckless emptiness present since the big reveal, but I don't like it. It's not that good feeling of satiety. Not a good warmth. It's that blend of icy-hot that plagues when a fever strikes. The steamy shiver in your cells. That nauseous sense of discomfort when you've eaten something bad.

I don't like being angry. Some people thrive on the emotion, revel in righteous indignation. They look for things to get upset about. Waitress brought unsweet tea instead of sweet? Gasp! Make sure she knows about it. Been waiting on hold twelve minutes? Oh, hell no, Mary. Let me speak to your manager.

Not me. Anger has always made me faintly ill, to the point where I'd find myself tucked in a bathroom stall or some other private place, waiting it out. I can't wait this one out, though. It's not going away. This hurt...this fury...it just keeps getting bigger, swelling inside me until it feels like my skin's going to burst. I can't make it stop.

A little sob escapes, and I look up to see the bridge's framework looming above me, one more black shadow in the night against a black sky studded with moon and faint pinpricks of starlight. I'm here. I pull my glove off and run my palm against the chest-high beam of the railing, the rough grit of century-old wood doing something to begin settling my nerves. The wooden structure of the bridge proper rests behind a modern metal security rail but it's a simple matter to climb over. Or at least, I think it still is.

It's been years since I've been here. Far too long since I've given myself space to simply be, to stand as I'm doing now and breathe in the sweet air, fragrant with cold and the rush of river.

I walk to the center, pop the top on my beer with a quick smack against the rail, and after a long pull, lean against the supports and stare, transfixed by the muted gleam of moonshine on the rapids beneath me. A street or two over a car rolls past, music and muffler pollution overlaying the sounds nearer me for a brief space of time. Then it's peaceful again, just me, a river, and a midnight bridge.

After a while, I tire of standing and climb to the top of the security rail, then carefully over to the thick wooden rail to sit, instead. This is why Sugar couldn't come. She'd have been going crazy to get up here to me, to join me on the narrow plank.

I perch with my back to the bridge, feet dangling above the black water below, and because I'm not entirely reckless, curl my left arm around the vertical post beside me that rises and connects to a canopy rising over the bridge. Leaning my head against the post, I relax back with my beer and allow my thoughts to wander.

It's only been four days, but I feel like I've been floating in limbo for an eternity. All I've done is sit around in my pajamas and watch the murder channel on television, taking perverse pleasure in deciphering how the murdering parties could have gotten away with their crimes if they'd done something just a little different. Today was the first day I showered, and only then because Ava refused to play with me, saying "Ammie Harry stink." I have to *do* something, make some changes. Otherwise, it's going to be too easy for this funk to simply stick. To sit, and wallow. Feel sorry for myself. Be angry all the time. And—

"Whoa! Lady! Easy there—oh, holy shit—"

The shock of another human makes me startle and my balance shifts, forcing me to twine both arms around the support beam if I don't want to tumble. My beer drops to the river below and I squeak in dismay. "W-who the hell are you?" I twist my neck to catch a glimpse of the man behind me, getting a vague impression of height and athleticism before I turn my face back to face the beam.

"Look, I know things may look bad right now, but everything's going to be all right."

I want to laugh as I realize what he's thinking, but my beer fucking fell, and I'm in a super awkward position that could turn dangerous really fast, and I should probably cry, instead. "What? No—"

"Ah...so, hey. Did you ever hear the one about the man who had a job crushing cans all day long?"

I blink at his change of subject. "Huh?"

"Yeah, he quit because it was soda pressing."

I shake my head. "That was terrible."

"Yeah? Give me another shot. Did you know when you die, your pupils are the last part to stop working?"

My silence is my response.

He grins and a dimple flashes in the scruff covering his cheek. "They dilate. Get it? Die late?"

I laugh and quickly turn it into a cough. "That was the worst. And in very poor taste considering you think I'm about to kill myself."

He cocks his head to the side, that dimple makes another appearance. "It was pretty bad. Listen, why don't you come down from there? We can talk, and..."

His voice fades as I ponder his request. I wouldn't mind climbing down if I'm honest. It's getting cold, my position is uncomfortable, and I'm not at all certain I can hold it for too much longer. But...stranger danger and all that. My brain flashes the warning in big red blinking lights. "I don't know you," I manage, cold and fear making my teeth chatter a little.

The man, tall and lanky, with what looks like dark hair tucked under a beanie like mine, holds his hands out in a placating way. "I'm not here to hurt you, I swear." He laughs a little, as if the idea is absurd. "I'm trying to help you. What's your name? I'm Wyatt."

"As in...Earp?"

"Just like. My mom had a thing for the wild west."

"Huh. Could be worse." I start to shrug but realize that's going to make me lose my tenuous grip. Below, the current seems to swirl and heave with greater insistence. My stomach heaves in countermeasure and I go still, pressing my forehead hard into the vertical beam. *You picked a fine time to decide you don't like heights, dummy.* "Um. I'm not sure I can move."

A moment later his arms come around me from behind, holding me steady, and despite my fear, I sag back against him. There's a height differential, putting my butt closer to his face, but it doesn't seem to bother him. Then he's climbing, holding me securely between himself and the bridge. "Oh, yeah? What's your name, hmm?"

"Harry," I breathe, and let him pry my stiffened fingers from the beam with one hand while he keeps the other securely around me. There's a second's pause before he continues, folding my arms carefully across my chest.

"Harry, huh?"

"Told you it could be worse."

"Oh, I don't know." With one arm holding mine in place and the other across my hips, he begins to pull me backwards and down. "Okay, coming back with me now...nice and easy. I kind of like Harry. It's different."

I snort. "Sure."

As his feet hit the ground and my ass clears the metal security rail his voice rumbles in my ear, deep and kind of growly. "What were you doing up there, Harry?" He pulls me clear until we're a few feet away, but instead of letting me go as I expect, continues to hold me to him with a strange and brutal intimacy, my back to his chest.

I let him, grateful that he's not looking at me, glad that he can't see the shame certain to be visible on my face. Have I sunk so far that I'd stand in the embrace of a stranger—be so greedy for that kind of contact, even—in lieu of a person...a man...I thought I mattered to?

*Yes. Yes, I would.*

I hang my head, exhausted all at once. "I'm not suicidal," I say. "I just couldn't sleep, and I came out to look at the river."

"Mmm."

For a reason I can't identify, his response bothers me. I don't know why, but it matters that he believes me. "I'm not," I insist. "I've got a lot on my mind right now, and I used to come out here all the time…to walk, and think, and look at the river while I sipped a beer. I just thought, maybe if I had a little of that tonight, I might be able to sleep when I went back home. Might be able to let everything go for a little while."

There's nothing at first. No response, verbal or otherwise, and then his hands begin to rotate me until I'm facing him. "Look at me?" He requests, and I lift my eyes. His gaze is burnt amber in the weak illumination, his eyes faintly tilted at the corners, studying me intently.

Whatever he sees must satisfy him, because he turns my biceps loose and secures my right hand in his left. Our skin is covered by thin gloves, but his heat seeps through, electric, and it feels a little like my stomach is caving in on itself. I flinch, and he grips me tighter. "Let me walk you home."

"Ah…okay." Our footsteps clomp on the wooden trestle as we move in the direction we came from. "You going to hold my hand the whole way?"

"Was thinking about it."

"Okay."

"That's quite a shiner."

"Yes." I know what he wants to know, and because he's a stranger and I'm unlikely to ever see him again, I give it to him. "My ex–not really–husband's actual legal wife gave it to me at the mall the other night when I discovered her existence."

"Oh…"

"Yeah. Oh."

"I guess you needed that beer, then."

"I guess I did."

"Sorry for interrupting." His hand squeezes mine, and I shrug.

"I'll be okay." And somehow, I know I will.

It's the weirdest, most strangely wonderful night I've had in ever. It reminds me of an old Patsy Cline song Momma used to sing to with the radio, "Walkin' After Midnight." As we stroll toward my house, Wyatt talks with desultory lightness about random topics: a retired baseball pitcher, a fast-food restaurant's strawberry lemonade, his family's Christmas traditions. He holds my hand like an afterthought, and I allow it, aware that he's a stranger but too enthralled by the sensation to say anything. His hand holding mine is large and warm, giving me a sense of safety and innocent pleasure.

It's been so long since someone held my hand. So long since someone stroked their thumb over my knuckles with absent tenderness, as if unaware they're even doing it.

I can't help feeling mildly guilty when we reach my house. It's only been days since my marriage fell apart, and already I'm having feels when a man touches my hand. There's obviously something wrong with me.

Wyatt drops my hand when we reach the front stoop and casts an awkward glance around. "Nice place."

I look, too, seeing it through a stranger's eyes. It's big and imposing, three stories of creamy gray masonry and black shutters. "I'm selling it," I say now, making the decision on the fly. It feels right. "It's never been home."

He looks at me curiously, a question on his lips. Instead of asking it, though, he lifts his chin in acknowledgment and turns to leave. "Forty-two," he says with a small, careless wave. "Sweet dreams, Harry."

My jaw gapes, and in a dizzying spin of every lucid thought in my brain, I know: this stranger is my soulmate. He has to be. There's no other explanation for him showing up to offer calm and comfort when I needed it most. No other possible way he could know my fascination with the number forty-two.

The concept of soulmates has always held allure for me. There's this theory in quantum mechanics known as quantum entanglement. It is a crazy, counterintuitive phenomenon where if two particles have interacted, connected to the point where they vibrate in unison, they'll always be intimately entangled thusly. Even if separated by millions of light-years, what happens to one particle will affect the other.

The idea struck my fancy and lingered, long after I moved on from the intricate abstraction of quantum mechanics and settled into chemistry. Before recorded time, we were all simply particles. What if, in that blank canvas of time and space, there were other particles with whom we became entangled? Even now, unimaginable eons after the universe expanded and particles were separated and flung into the far reaches of the universe, we are still enmeshed. The particles that make up our human composite recognize their kindred, the ones with which they once vibrated, the ones with which they were once one.

It's why we recognize some people immediately. Our particles call, sing, reach...whatever...to one another. One soul recognizes another soul.

He's halfway down the sidewalk when I shut my mouth and grab the courage to take three steps in his direction. "Wait!" He stops and turns, eyebrows lifted in question. "What did you just say?"

"Sweet dreams?"

"Before that."

He thinks. "Oh. Forty-two."

"What did you mean?" I hold my breath.

He shakes his head a little, looking at the sidewalk before casting a sideways glance in my direction. "Ah. Well," he answers, "if you know, you know."

My quiet exhalation is the only sign I understand what he references. "Yes. I guess you do. Goodnight, Wyatt."

"Goodnight, Harry."

Opening the door quietly, I slip inside and shut it behind me before I slide down its surface to the floor. Forty-two, he said.

It's the number from which all meaning can be derived, according to *The Hitchhiker's Guide to the Galaxy*. It's the answer to everything, from something as incomprehensible as the meaning of life to something as simple as the explanation for why I like ketchup on my fried potatoes. It's nothing more than a joke created by a genius, but somehow...it's exactly what I need.

And yet, I let him walk away, without so much as asking for a phone number. He might be my soulmate, but he's gone, now. *Way to go, Harry.*

I huff a breath of laughter into the foyer. I mean...it's not like I just discovered my husband was a bigamist a few days ago, or anything. I don't know why I wasn't thinking about hooking up with someone new.

I stare into the dark hallway for a long time. I can feel things changing, shifting, cracking open inside me. I don't know whether I like it or not.

# Seven

## Harry

I NEED TO PAINT the inside of the door to the garage. It's a boring color, a dull beige-y hue that doesn't really say anything. Like "have a good day at work, bish. I'll be here when you get back, ready for you to stare at. Now, git!"

I lift my hand, place it on the doorknob, and wait. One-Mississippi, two-Mississippi, three-Mississippi...

*Fuck*.

Growling in frustration, I let my forehead fall against the door. I can't do it. To all appearances, I'm ready. I'm dressed and made-up; my hair is done, and I have matching shoes on my feet. Hell, I'm even wearing pants for the first time in nearly two weeks.

But I'm not ready. The thought of turning that knob, of walking outside and climbing into my car and going to class... facing the stares of hundreds of curious students and faculty... no. The thought makes bile burn the back of my throat.

Just... no.

Turning, I slide down the door to sit on the floor and pull my phone from my purse. The calendar app taunts me. It's early December and our one month break between semesters is looming. Early December is exam time—professors are slammed with a seemingly never ending carousel of review, administration, and grading—along with calculation of final semester grades. There couldn't be worse timing.

Mentally, I roll my eyes. As if there's ever a good time for one to discover their spouse is a bigamist and then have the mother of all seizures. *Excuse me, dear... could we move the big reveal to July, please? I'll be on sabbatical then...*

I have a feeling I can kiss tenure goodbye. But I can't teach. Not yet.

Each morning, there's this moment in the space between sleeping and waking where I forget that it happened. There's a calm, blissful moment where everything is as it was. There's no betrayal. No collapse of everything I've known for nearly a decade.

Then I open my eyes, and memory floods me, buries me in an avalanche of stinging ice and arctic rock, and I'm heavy. Weighted down with the gravitas of everything real.

Heaving a sigh, I fire off a message to my department head, apprising her of the status change, and then follow it up with an email to all my students, letting them off the hook for class today. I attach the exam review guide I was going to give them and congratulate myself on having that prepared, at least.

I'm not a complete failure.

Before I can rise from my position on the floor, the phone rings. It's my department head, Sharon. Sighing, I answer.

"Hello."

"Harriet. I just received your email." This is typical Sharon, always rushing headlong into a conversation with no preamble.

"Good morning to you, Sharon."

"Oh, stuff it. Harriet, for the sake of your career, you have to pull yourself together and get to class. I can't keep covering for you forever."

I groan. "I know. I am, I promise. I just need another day or two."

"I can give you until Monday, and not a day more. And I'm appointing a TA to your classes. That should help, right?"

"I don't want a TA, Sharon. It's not the workload. It's...damnit, it's hard to explain. I feel like I'm suffocating when I think about going back. Standing there and lecturing like nothing's changed."

"I do understand, Harry." Sharon's voice softens. "And I feel for you, I do. But it's the end of term, we have to get these exams done properly, and there's only so much I can do. See a therapist. Talk it out...vent. Do whatever it takes to move on and get your ass to work." There's a beat of silence in which she waits for my response, then her own sigh when I say nothing.

There's nothing I can say. She's right. About everything.

Another breath, then a weary. "Monday, Harry. Please." The line clicks, and she's gone.

Disgusted with myself, I stand and kick off my shoes, then unbutton and shimmy out of my dress slacks. If I'm staying home, there will be no pants worn. But I'm damn well going to be productive. No more of this sitting around feeling sorry for myself.

There's a bake sale coming up at my parents' church, a fundraiser to provide a Christmas for families in the area. I'll make cookies for that. Lots and lots of cookies. Maybe cookies will soften the blow when I tell Momma I am, for all intents and purposes, a divorcee.

Plan in place, I head for the kitchen in a more settled mood. There, I pull my hair back into a low ponytail and turn on some music, flipping through my library. Lana Del Rey...not today. Dave Matthews...nah. Red Hot Chili Peppers...yesss.

To Anthony Kiedis's raunchy vibe, I clear my workspace, then set out my tools and ingredients with precision, as if working through a lab. Really, completing a recipe start to finish is a bit like a science experiment. You begin with a hypothesis of what the end product will be. Follow the steps, perhaps change a variable. If you've been careful, and followed the recipe with accuracy, the outcome will prove the hypothesis.

It's one of the things I always liked about cooking—baking, in particular—how it synced with the science of chemistry. It basically is chemistry. Measure this, mix that. Experimentation with the expectation of a desired result. Knowing, based on the chemical makeup of this or that ingredient, what should take place when a variable such as heat is added to the equation.

There shouldn't be any big surprises. No wow moment, such as discovering your husband has another wife. An entire other family.

*No. Focus on the cookies.*

My hand shakes as I crack the first egg. A fine tremble, causing a bit of shell to drop alongside the egg white into the bowl. It's a variable. I stare into the bit of white floating in clear goo. It changes everything. Mucks it up. Holding another bit of shell over the offending piece, I pause before scooping it free, and then retreat without doing so.

The variable stays.

The whistling feedback from Daddy's hearing aid has to be the most annoying sound I've ever heard. I stare at the scenery whizzing by the passenger side window, my attention split between the high-pitched whine to my left and the low hum of chatter from the back seat, where Momma sits with Ava. She talks to her about everything and anything she can think of, pointing out things we pass that she's pointed out every Sunday for as long as I can remember. Ava doesn't mind. She listens with wide, patient eyes, mostly silent but sometimes uttering a little giggle or sigh.

"Did you see that cow, Ava? What's the cow say?" Ava side-eyes her as if to ask, *really, lady*? and disdains to respond. Every three-year-old knows cows go moo. "What are you going to have to eat when we get to the restaurant? I bet I can guess. Hot chocolate with whipped cream and smiley-face pancakes." Ava smiles, a tiny smile that I catch in the visor mirror. She gets the same thing every time we brunch with my parents.

My hands twist in my lap. I felt the best course of action would be to break the news about Marcus at Sunday brunch, now right around two weeks since the big reveal took place, and Owen reluctantly agreed to keep it quiet until then. Every second Sunday of the month, Owen and I meet Momma and Daddy for our obligatory church appearance, and then journey to the IHOP the next town over for pancakes. Owen takes his car and Ava and I ride with my parents, a decision I'm regretting by the mile as the hearing aid whines and Momma coos.

"Oh, my Lord, those cookies smell divine, Harriet. It was so sweet of you to make them for the fundraiser."

"Oh, um, sure. I was making cookies, anyway." All two hundred and forty of them, one of them with a special eggshell prize.

I try to focus on the plan. We'll be in a public place, so Momma will have to think twice about dramatics. Ava will be there as a little mini buffer, so that should grant me even greater protection. And Owen has sworn to help me should Daddy go off the deep end and have apoplexy right there in the blue pleather booth.

Cowardly? Maybe a little. Anyone with parents like ours would view it as strategic, though.

As if on cue, Momma's voice rises from the back seat. "Where did you say Marcus was this morning? He never misses pancakes."

*Shit.* "He...ah...had a thing," I reply, my voice weak. From beside me, I feel Daddy shoot me a sharp look, but I stay focused on the fields flashing by out the window.

"A thing." Disapproval is heavy in her tone. "Now, he knows better than that. Nothing's more important than family. Especially this close to the holidays. I wanted to take a few family photos outside the IHOP when we finished eating, too. For the Christmas cards, you know."

The thought of photos is distracting. Outside the car, the sky is steel and spitting angry tears. "Momma, it's been raining off and on all morning."

"Pssh. We can use the foyer if we need to. Now I'll have to wait until next week and my cards might be late."

Heaven forbid. "Why don't you just send digital cards like everyone else nowadays?"

"Harriet Maelynn! Speak no evil in this car, child!"

She might as well have collapsed to the ground, holding her hand theatrically over her forehead. Ava giggles.

"Let's just do the photo today. Use that one, just in case Marcus can't make it next week, either." In the visor mirror, I see a frown wrinkle her forehead and cast about for a subject change. "When are we doing the Christmas buffet?"

"That'll be the sixteenth, and I'm glad you brought it up, actually..."

I let the subject of ham biscuits versus turkey and who should be assigned which side dish—critical when Aunt Bernice's corn pudding isn't quite as good as Great-Aunt Ginger's and it would be a tragedy if she made it, 'specially when everyone knows it—lull me into a state of quietude.

It doesn't last long.

"Honey, something is off with Miss Ava. What do you think? Is it my imagination or is she quieter than usual?"

I groan and let my head fall against the cold glass of the window. "Momma, she's three years old. She talks when she wants to. She jibber-jabbers all the time. Ask her father." *And if she is quiet, it's because you've talked nonstop the entire drive.*

"Jibber jabber. It's not jibber jabber, is it, doll baby? Every word you say is extremely important." Mom leans into Ava's car seat and boops her nose with her stuffed sloth.

"I didn't mean—"

Dad interrupts me, his voice low.

"You may be able to fool your momma, but you can't fool me. What's going on with you and that boy?"

It's the first time my father has spoken since I climbed in the car and the depth of anger in his voice stops my mother in her conversational tracks. I swallow into the sudden silence and look desperately out the window. There's the Food Lion, and the furniture store. We're maybe a mile from the IHOP. Just a few more minutes.

"I'll explain everything shortly, Daddy."

"What is he talking about?"

"This is really not the time or place to discuss the matter," I reply. Dad shifts in his seat irritably, and the feedback from the hearing aid whines more volubly. "Jesus, could you get that fixed, please? It's like a fucking dog whistle."

"Harriet! Language!" Ava's giggle accompanies Mom's shocked gasp. "Oh, my Lord, the baby is laughing. Why is she laughing? Doll baby, your Ammie Harriet's mouth is not funny…"

"I can hear you just fine," Dad claims, tone defensive.

"I'm sure you can. I can hear you, too. You're whistling, Daddy. It needs adjusting, trust me."

"You're letting her sidetrack you, sweetheart. Harriet, what is going on with you and Marcus? Are you having problems? Because if you're having problems, I know a good therapist we can get you in to see."

"We will talk about it later, I promise. And please stop calling me Harriet."

"Stop calling you Harriet! For the love of—! Young lady, you should be ashamed! Your grandmother Harriet would roll over in her grave, *her grave*, I say." Momma fans herself, shifting forward and then back again in agitation. "Donald, did you hear that? They've split up. Dear God, I can hear Bessie Chambers now. Harriet, why don't you move back in with us temporarily, honey? We have plenty of room, and it would be good for you. You could come to early service with us every Sunday!"

I groan. "Momma. I am not moving back home."

"But—"

"Look, we're here."

I seize upon the distraction of pulling into the IHOP's parking lot and am out of the car as soon as my father parks. Across the lot, I see Owen climbing from his own vehicle. He gives a half-wave and begins making his way to us.

"Hey, kid. Why do you look like a cat in a room full of rocking chairs?"

"She wants me to move back in," I mutter, watching as Dad unhooks Ava from the car seat.

"Oof. Did you tell her already?"

"No! She has some kind of sixth freaking sense."

"Harriet, I know what you're trying to do and it's not going to work. You can't avoid this conversation forever, and your brother is not going to save you, you know." Ignoring Owen, Momma comes to stand in front of me, her hand reaching out with automatic authority to straighten my scarf.

"I'll go get us a table."

Owen begins to follow Daddy and Ava, but I quickly, desperately reach out and grab his sleeve. "Daddy's got it. Help me."

"How is he going to help you? Your marriage is in trouble, Harriet. You have work to do that your big brother can't help you with. You're going to have to wipe those tears and put on your big girl panties and be the bigger person."

*Big girl panties.* Moisture spits against my face, the sky deciding to let go, and I swipe at it, restraining the urge to laugh with difficulty. If I start, I won't stop. I'll stand in this parking lot and laugh like a loon until someone comes to carry me away. "I don't think you completely appreciate the situation, Momma," I say after a moment in which we stare at each other, her impassioned, me full of frustrated longing for her approval.

"Of course, I don't understand." Her face, lined and lovely, is a study in frowning exasperation. "You haven't told me anything so I *can* understand, honey. I'm assuming he's made a mistake, though, like most men do at some point."

"A mistake?" Owen squeezes the hand that still grips his arm. Warning.

"Well, yes..."

"Momma...he committed bigamy." She stares at me blankly, and memory of all the times I tried and failed to explain some scientific concept rises within me in a wave of irritation. "You realize what that is, right? He's married. Or he was already, when he married me. He already had a wife." My breath accompanies each word rapid fire, until I'm panting in sync with each syllable, each raindrop that hits my skin. "I found out when I stumbled upon him with his other wife...his other family. At the mall, of all places. It was the most humiliating experience—" I break off, stifling a rising sob.

Momma is silent for a second, then huffs in affront. "I'm not stupid; of course, I know what bigamy is. I'm just shocked. I figured he had cheated or spent too much or something. That maybe you needed a loan to get back on track."

"There's not going to be any reconciliation, Momma."

She snorts a little and clutches her pocketbook closer to her ample chest. "A bigamist. Naturally not." She stares across the parking lot. "But we don't need to make a scene, either. We'll handle this the proper way. Quiet-like. Not give anyone fodder for gossip."

Owen's fingers tighten on my arm. "Mom, if anyone deserves to give Lucy Falls a little something to talk about, it's Harry—"

"I don't plan on doing anything crazy, Momma, sheesh. I haven't decided whether or not I'll be pressing charges. The police said the DA may do it whether I do, or not."

She's quiet for a second before brushing past me with a gentle pat on the cheek. Her scent, Beautiful by Estee Lauder, wraps me in a familiar fragrance hug. "I understand. For what it's worth, I think you should bury the bastard under the jail."

Owen follows her, raising his eyebrows in a 'what the fuck' look back at me before he disappears inside. I remain standing, waiting for my breath to return to normal. I'm still waiting when the gray skies burst open with a vengeance, and the rain comes pouring down.

# Eight

## Harry

My morning handful of pills stick in my throat, and I drink more water, staring at my wan reflection in the mirror.

Today officially sucks. I don't want to go to work today any more than I did last week, but I'm feeling moderately stronger, at least. I can't come up with a good-enough reason to stay home. Sharon was able to give me just enough time off to get to the end of the semester, but I still have a week to go before winter break, when I'll have a real opportunity to deal with the chaos I've been thrust into.

Every time I turn around, though, reminders of him trip me up. Of us.

The mirrored medicine cabinet over the sink reveals a dulled razor and a bottle of aftershave I gave him Christmas a year ago. I flick the razor in the trash impatiently, following it with the aftershave, but his shampoo-conditioner blend and body wash crowd me in the massive marble-tiled shower. I find myself turning the water off with a snap of my wrist, ignoring the soap that streams down my naked flesh and the fact that I didn't wash my hair.

I can't deal with the reminders today.

Instead, I dress like one of my students in a pair of jeans, a Rolling Stones tee shirt, and a blazer in a half-hearted nod to decorum. Inwardly, I direct the energy produced by an extra cup of coffee toward erecting walls against all the little reminders. I cultivate my anger, stoke the simmer supplied by the sight of his things. I have a terrible feeling if I don't, if I let myself sniff his aftershave or stare too long at the beard hairs in his razor... I'll fall apart. I'll crawl back between the bedsheets and refuse to emerge. I'll succumb to self-pity, taking selfie after selfie of my own tear-stained cheeks and posting dramatic micro poems on social media about finding myself and emerging stronger after the storm.

Outside, a horn toots twice. Owen is here to drive me to work. Resigned, I take Sugar's harness in hand and gather my bag.

"Morning," I say as I open the car door and settle Sugar in the backseat, then situate myself in the front. Owen hands me a paper cup of coffee and a bag emblazoned with the Karla's Cuppa logo. "God bless you."

Chuckling a little, he pulls out of the driveway. "You ready for this?"

With a low hum of response, I look out of the window to contemplate the question. "Honestly, I don't know. I'm exhausted."

"Maybe you should just take a leave of absence for a while."

"I can't. I've been told I need to get my ass back to work, or else."

Owen taps his fingers against the steering wheel. "Technically, you don't even need that job. I'd call the bluff."

He's right. I could sell the house, live with him and Ava, or my parents, for that matter. I could conduct my own private research, and still publish. But... "The school gives my research weight and credibility it wouldn't otherwise possess," I explain. "I need to stay, at least until I decide research no longer matters to me, you know?"

"I get it. It's not worth the expense of your health, though."

"Owen..."

"I'm just telling you like it is."

"Can you just...not, though? I appreciate everything you've done, but I need to get my head straight before I walk into that classroom."

The remainder of the ride is made in silence.

When he pulls up to the building where my classes are located, I climb out and bend back to peer in at him. "Thank you, Francis."

He grunts, then watches as I wait for Sugar to climb from the car. "I'll be back this afternoon."

"I'll be the one with the dog..."

"Harry." He is unamused. "Call me if you need anything."

"I will. Love you."

"Bye, kid."

I'm a hundred years older than my thirty-five years when I enter my lecture hall one minute and thirty-seven seconds after class is supposed to begin and navigate the stepped rows down to my podium, the focus of sixty-plus pairs of student eyeballs.

"Apologies for being late," I say as I get myself sorted. "It's been a morning."

There are a few murmured replies, but overall, the class seems distracted, and none too concerned with my tardiness. They whisper among themselves, some of them passing cell phones discreetly between their seats. Clearing my throat, I choose to ignore it and launch with no further preamble into the lesson.

"Okay, so we have roughly a week before mid-terms. We're going to spend today..."

I trail off as the door opens and a young man swaggers in, a telltale slip of yellow carbon paper clutched in one hand. That yellow indicates TA status. Sharon followed through on her threat and appointed one, even after I stated unequivocally that I didn't need or want one shadowing me.

Worse...it's *him*.

Or maybe it's good? God, I don't know. I was kicking myself for letting him get away the other night, but I don't know that I want him *here*, intersecting with my class. My job.

Everything goes still as he makes his way to the front of the room. A few brave souls shout a welcome and he raises a hand lazily in greeting without once shifting his gaze from me. "Dr. Bee—" he begins, holding the yellow paper out.

It takes me a minute, but eventually I come back to myself and reach out a shaking hand to take it from his hand. *It was dark. Am I mistaken? Maybe I'm wrong.* As I often do when I'm upset or anxious, I take refuge in sarcasm. "Let me guess. You're my new TA, come to save me loads of work one whole week before the end of the semester. Great. That's fantastic. Have a seat."

He blinks at me. "Actually—"

"I need to start class, Mr.—"

"Granger. Wyatt Granger."

Wyatt. Yep. It's definitely him. I nod infinitesimally and scratch the side of my neck. He waits, and after a second, I realize it's not just him, but the entire class that's waiting—almost as if they're expecting me to give him some kind of acknowledgment. But that's crazy. They don't know that we know each other. Not unless he went around telling people about our encounter, which would be...surely, he wouldn't have done that. I level a look at him over the rims of my eyeglasses. "Yes? Am I supposed to recognize you, or something?" Someone snorts, and a smile plays around his mouth.

I look at him openly now that I have the chance to do so in the light of day. He's tall—but then, most men are to my five-feet-two—and lean to the point of lanky. He boasts a well-defined chest, though, beneath the thin hoodie he's wearing, as well as a sculpted pair of biceps. Good quality tennis shoes peek out from the hem of a pair of running pants, and everything looks, even to my untrained eye, as if it's worn for function rather than mere comfort or looks. He must be an athlete, then, which explains the class's reaction. I don't do sports.

Wyatt squints at my question but answers smoothly. "No, ma'am. Not at all. Where should I sit?"

"It's Doctor, and there will be fine." I point to the first row.

He turns to seat himself and as he does, I draw in my first deep breath since he'd come to stand before me. His cologne wafts my way, something bright with citrus and woodsy tones that makes me lick my bottom lip involuntarily. I shuffle my laptop and books on the desk, annoyed. Why couldn't he stink?

As a chemist, and a food chemist in particular, my senses have always played a heightened role in processing data. Smell is especially potent, not only in helping me identify ideal qualities in different dishes and foods, but also in how scents might translate to or trigger emotion in an individual.

Vanilla, for example. It's a warm, sweet fragrance, embodying familiarity and comfort. The scent of licorice has a snap, a bite that's just the opposite.

And then there's peppermint. Peppermint will forevermore be burned in my memory as the scent of candy canes. I'll connect it henceforth to Christmas and visits to Santa and the bitter tang of betrayal.

The thought of peppermint helps pull my thoughts away from citrus and wood aftershave, and I manage to get my lecture going. When it's time to collect experimental data from last week's assignment, I'm surprised when Wyatt rises without prompting and begins moving from row to row, gathering them for me. I'm even more surprised when he waits as students begin to file out and then approaches, papers in hand.

"If you'll set me up with your rubric, I'll score these over the weekend," he says.

My tongue darts out to lick my lower lip as I shut down my laptop. "What are you doing here, Wyatt?"

A line appears between his brows. "I was hired as your TA, Dr. Bee."

"I'm supposed to believe that? Do you even have any experience with the kind of experiments we're doing...?"

"Dr. Bee, if you look at that form I handed you, you'll see that I already have a degree in biochemistry and am nearly finished with my master's. The TA position is for a few extra credits that I need to finish early, and for some additional income. And I'll be here for the remainder of the year…not just the rest of this semester."

The classroom is silent as I consider his words. "This has nothing to do with the bridge?"

"Not a thing."

Even though his tone is polite, I feel myself flush. I'm going to have to apologize, damnit. Irritated, I tap my fingers on the desk. I hate apologizing.

He laughs, a low chuckle to himself, and my gaze flashes to his to find caramel brown eyes filled with humor. "No apology necessary."

"What?"

"You said 'I'm going to have to apologize, damnit.' It's not necessary. I took you by surprise… I get it."

"Oh. I didn't realize—"

Now he laughs out loud. "That you talk to yourself? It's all right. I won't tell anyone."

I look at him doubtfully. "I'm not sure I like you, Granger. I definitely wouldn't like you before coffee. You're too…talky. And smiley."

He runs a finger in a zipper motion across his mouth. "Quiet before coffee: got it. And tone down the smiles."

"Exactly. Okay, so I'll see you next time, I guess—"

"I do have one question, if you don't mind answering." He tips his chin toward Sugar, who's taking a nap beside my chair. "What's with the dog?"

"Oh. Yeah, I guess you should be aware of that. Sugar's my service dog. Medical alert and response, more specifically." I watch his face closely for signs of distaste or discomfort when I continue. "I have epilepsy. Sugar is trained to recognize when preliminary seizure activity is taking place, and then help protect me during the seizure."

His expression shows nothing other than sympathy and interest. "That's incredible. How does she know?"

I lift one shoulder in a shrug. "Honestly, I'm not certain. Some say they sense the electrical activity in the epileptic's body. Others say it's a change in scent that their more acute noses pick up on. Whatever it is, I'm thankful for it. I know when she whines, and paws my hand, that a seizure is coming, and I need to find a safe place to lie down."

As if understanding our conversation, Sugar picks that moment to stretch and rise to stand beside me. Her tongue lolls out of her mouth, and I scratch her flanks affectionately. "So, I need to ask—and I completely understand if the answer isn't 'yes'—but are you okay with helping me if I have a seizure in your presence? Getting the class away, making sure I don't hit my head, timing the seizure, calling for medical assistance, if necessary...? Oh, and I might pee myself. That's always fun." I grimace, a little embarrassed even though there's nothing I can do to prevent it.

"God, yes! Of course." He shifts his weight from one foot to the other. "I appreciate you trusting me with that information."

Rolling my eyes, I turn and start collecting my things. "Don't get too excited. I tell all my students at the beginning of the year, so they don't freak out if I seize."

"Very logical. So, we're good? You'll email the rubric?"

I study him, my lips twisted in thought. A TA isn't a bad thing. Less grading might free me up to spend more time dealing with my crap and give me more time for my personal research. I wasn't used to having someone following me around all the time and asking questions about my work, but I could work with it if he could keep his mouth shut. "Sure, Granger. We're good. I'll email the rubric. Just have those done by Monday."

"No problem. Have a good weekend, Prof." With a wink, he spins and walks away.

I shake my head at the wink. Something tells me second semester is going to be very interesting.

# Nine

## Harry

Weekly trips to the local Food Mart are always exciting. Sugar inspects every foreign object on the floor, snuffling her way through fallen produce and crumbs. People stare, because holy moly, there's a dog. Usually, I cannot wait to collect the few items I came in for and get out.

Today is no different.

Owen waits for me in the car, saying he needed to make a few phone calls. Even though he gave me strict instructions to *not take all damned day, please,* I can't help myself from dawdling over the pitiful winter selection of avocadoes in our produce section, anyway, picking each one up that looks the least little bit promising. I inspect them carefully, thumbing off the little brown caps to check for ripeness and squeezing the sides gently before either returning it to the bin or placing it gently in my cart. Some are far too gone, almost total mush. Others are green bricks, unlikely to ripen before spring.

"I don't think I've ever seen anyone scrutinize an avocado so carefully before," a voice rumbles from across the span of the produce bin. My head jerks up and I see Jack, an empty hand basket in his grip.

"Jack," I say. "Hi."

"How are you, Harry?"

"I'm doing well, thanks. Do you live around here, too?" My head tilts, kind of like Sugar's does when she's bemused about something. Lucy Falls has two grocery stores, this market-style one that a lot of people in my neighborhood use, and a perpetually smelly Food Lion on the other side of town. I've never noticed Jack Brady here before.

His smile turns sheepish, and he rubs the back of his neck. "No, I live over on Kennedy Avenue. I just happened to be here, I guess. I'm glad I ran into you, actually."

"Oh, yeah?"

"Uh, yeah." His voice deepens, turning official-sounding. "I was going to wait until after the holidays, but you should be expecting a phone call from the department. Since you elected not to press charges, it looks like the DA is going to do so."

For some reason, I feel inexplicably deflated. "Oh. Sure, yeah, that makes sense. I haven't completely made up my mind, though. I've been talking to an attorney. It's just taking a little time, with everything happening at once."

"I see." He shifts, and in the shadowy gap formed between shirt and jacket I catch a glimpse of his holster and gun. "For what it's worth, I think you should."

"More than you know."

He frowns. "What?"

"You said 'for what it's worth.' Your opinion is worth more than you know. I think I'd like to talk to you about things sometime, Jack, now that I've had a chance to calm down and gain some perspective." His eyes flare in response, but before he can reply, my phone rings. When I answer it defaults automatically to speaker.

"Hello?"

"Hello, may I speak with Ms. Harriet Lane, please?"

"This is she."

"This is James with Certitude Home Financing. I'm calling because the December mortgage payment for the property at—" Belatedly I realize this is a conversation I do not want broadcast over speaker, and fumble to switch it over. I'm not fast enough, though, and catch a frown demarcating the space between Jack's brows as he pretends not to pay attention.

"One moment, please," I say into the phone. To Jack, I wave the phone and begin pushing the cart toward the nearby self-checkout stations. "I'm sorry... I have to go. I guess you know how to catch up with me, right?"

"Of course, yeah..." He waves me on, and I plant myself at a nearby self-checkout register, feverishly beginning to swipe my groceries as I bring the phone back to my ear.

"I'm so sorry, I'm in the grocery store. Could you repeat that please?" Frowning, I finish the checkout process as quickly as I can, shoving my groceries haphazardly into my tote bags as I listen to the voice on the other line.

"Yes, Ms. Lane, not a problem. We're calling because your December mortgage payment is overdue, and we were concerned."

"It's what... uh... one second, please." I have to pause again, this time because I don't trust myself to speak without my voice wavering.

"Certainly."

*Shit. Shitdamnfuckmotherfuckbitch. What the hell, Marcus?*

I push the cart through the double glass doors, hoping my expression doesn't betray the sting of turmoil and betrayal making it difficult to function. I need to make it to the car. Cross the parking lot first but wait... look both ways. Wouldn't do to get run over on top of everything else. Keep it together as I throw the bags in the cargo space and usher Sugar into the back, and then drop into the passenger seat.

Owen gives me a curious look and starts the engine.

I give myself a moment to draw in a deep breath, and then bring the phone back to my ear. "Thank you for waiting. I was unaware of the late payment. My... husband... always makes those, so I will need to contact him and find out what has gone amiss." I stumble over the word 'husband.' I don't want to lie, but I don't think confessing the truth of our situation would work to our benefit at the moment.

"I understand. Sometimes things happen, especially during these busy times of the year. We do need to arrange a payment to keep things from falling further behind. Are you able to do that now, or at a future date?"

I do some rapid calculations. If something happened and Marcus refused to pay the mortgage, I would have the funds by mid-month. Our mortgage is high and paying it would leave me tight, but it would prevent a blow to my credit. I had thought it strange at the time that Marcus had insisted on putting the house in my name, but I guess it makes sense now. He was supporting two households. Even with a salary as healthy as his apparently was, being approved for a mortgage for two houses might have been a bit of a stretch.

I don't understand why he insisted on such an expensive house, given what I know now. He had to have one of the nicest homes in Lucy Falls, when I would have been content with something small and cozy.

"Ah... let me discuss this with my husband first. If he is unable to make the payment for whatever reason, I will call back and schedule a payment for the middle of the month."

"Okay." The man's voice is cooler than it had been before. "I am notating the account. I have to alert you that these phone calls will continue until a payment is made or scheduled, however."

"I understand. Thank you."

Owen begins to pull out of our parking place as I hang up. "Everything okay?"

"No. Not even a little. Can you take me to Marcus's office, please?" He nods and makes the turn that will take us there without comment. "Thank you," I add. "I'll explain everything later."

"I think I have the general idea," he replies grimly. "Fucking asswipe."

I don't reply, instead resting my arm on the window ledge and worrying a strand of my hair as we drive.

At Marcus's office, by some twist of fate we just manage to catch him as he's leaving for lunch. Owen pulls to a stop behind his car, blocking him in, and I step out and lean against the hood, arms crossed over my chest to hide the fact that my hands are shaking. He stops in mid-stride, eyebrows arched in surprise, with his key fob extended toward his vehicle. "Harriet. What are you doing here?"

"I received an interesting phone call a few minutes ago, Marcus."

His gaze flits to the side and he frowns. "From whom?"

"The mortgage company. They say our December payment wasn't made."

His expression blanks and he opens his door. "That's your house now, Harriet. Your responsibility. Take care of it."

I make my voice strong, remind myself that he can't hurt me. "Are you kidding me right now? We were technically, if not legally, married for seven years, during which time you had to have the most expensive house you could get your hands on. You paid the mortgage every month, took care of every bill. And now you decide to just stop, without so much as a heads up, knowing I can do nothing about it." I shake my head. "As if the bigamy wasn't enough. This is unbelievable, even for you."

"Sell it, Harriet. Consider it your alimony."

"Oh, don't worry. It'll be sold. I just... I just don't understand how you can do this to someone. Especially someone you professed to love." His face is so neutral, so devoid of feeling. "I don't even know who you are anymore, Marcus. Make me understand. Why are you doing this to me?"

We stare at each other, and somehow, he knows I'm not asking about the mortgage. Behind me, the driver's side door opens and I stiffen.

"He's a narcissistic prick, Harry. That's who he is." Owen's voice rings out, loud enough to be heard across the parking lot.

"Mind your own business," Marcus says, pointing a finger at my brother. He continues, speaking over top of Owen's reply. "It was never about you, Harriet. Not really."

"What the hell is that supposed to mean?" Owen exclaims, coming to stand beside me and throwing his arms out. I lay a calming hand on his forearm.

"So, what was it about, if it didn't have anything to do with me? Did Gina know about me?" I have to force the words through clenched teeth. He stares at me, stares through me, considering.

"It's nothing you'd ever understand," he finally answers. "You're a bit of an odd duck, Harriet, but you're a good girl. And I feel sorry for you, you know. With the epilepsy and all. I think we should just leave things there."

*A good girl.* So good I let him treat me like a doormat. A bitter wind blusters through on the heels of his words and I shiver. Words fumble over themselves before I can stop them, and I hate myself for the vulnerability they reveal. "I...that's...really shitty. You owe me more than that."

"Come on, Harry," Owen says, tugging on my sleeve. "You tried. He's not worth it."

Marcus's features grow taut. "Owe you? *I* owe *you*?" He takes a step into my personal space and I back up. "That's rich. You have no idea what it means to owe someone, and yet you owe me more than you can imagine." His finger stabs the air in front of my face. "You're going to find out, though, real fucking soon."

"What are you talking about? I don't owe you anything. I gave you everything I had. My family, my love, my affection. But I'm pretty sure that you never loved me." I don't mean it to be a question, but it comes out that way, the pause after the words leave my mouth hanging between us, asking for truth.

He shrugs. "As much as I can love anyone, I guess."

My forehead pinches. "What does that even mean? What about Gina? Do you love her? It doesn't even make sense—"

A muscle ticks in his jaw and I can tell he's losing patience. "It never will." He looks past me, his blue eyes distant. "I guess if I had to frame it, to give it a reason, it would be very simply because I could." His gaze returns to me then, and what I see in them is chilling. They're cold—completely devoid of any feeling. Reptilian. "You were a means to an end." He glances down at my involuntary inhalation, brushing off an imaginary spot on his suit jacket.

The cold wind blows stiffly, pushing my hair into my face and providing a convenient excuse for the tears that sting my eyes. I push it behind my ears and study the man I gave seven years to. The man I lived on tenterhooks around, never knowing if I'd be welcoming Jekyll or Hyde into my bed. The man I would've given a lifetime to, because that's what you did when you got married.

He's right. I'll never understand such madness. Something about his explanation doesn't ring true, but I'm not going to get truth from him. Truth isn't in him; neither is the capacity to feel shame. This is fruitless.

This is the moment I realize two things. First—part of me harbored hope. Hope that maybe one day I would be able to attach meaning to the incomprehensible. I hadn't understood, not until now, how desperately I needed this to make some kind of sense.

Second—this is the moment hope dies, in this blink in time it becomes clear there will be no meaning. No apprehension. Nothing about this will ever make sense.

I straighten from my position on the car hood and walk around to the passenger side door. "Okay, then. Goodbye, Marcus."

He looks at me in question. "Goodbye?"

"Yes. Goodbye. I got what I came for. I'm done."

I climb into the car and watch as Owen says something indistinguishable, then slides behind the wheel. I cast one last look and a faint nod in Marcus's direction as Owen puts the car into drive and pulls away. Then I look resolutely forward, heading into a future that's frightening and unknown, but infinitely better than what stands behind me.

# Ten

## Harry

The house hums with activity, Owen and my parents all present to help me pack everything I can in preparation for putting the house up for sale. The realtor explained that the house needed to essentially be a blank slate, with all personal items tucked out of sight so people could imagine their own possessions making it a home. From outside, Owen's voice floats in, directing the moving company on the pile of boxes that belong to Marcus.

I'll be glad to see the back of them.

Momma straightens from the painted hutch in the dining room, holding a gallon-sized zipper bag aloft. "What in the world...is this something you need to keep, honey? It's something broken." Doubt underscores her voice and I look up from the box I'm packing to see familiar shards of blue and white china through the plastic bag.

"Yes, that needs to be packed. Let me see it, please... I can put it in with this stuff."

She hands the bag to me, and I open it, withdrawing a piece of shattered porcelain. I run it between my fingers for a few contemplative moments before I hold it up for her. "You don't recognize it?"

Squinting, she studies it hard. "Oh, my goodness! That's my momma's vase! And I was going to throw it out! How on earth did it get broken?"

I place the fragment carefully back in the bag. "The same way everything was broken. Marcus." The memory of the occasion makes me wince with shame. How did I stay with him as long as I did? How did I not realize what was happening to me—no, not what was happening to me...what he was doing to me. What I was allowing to take place. I am a smart woman. I have a doctorate, for god's sake. How did I become this meek, mild, yes-woman when I was with him? Afraid of upsetting him, afraid of his anger, his bile?

How am I just now realizing that entangled with my embarrassment, my shock, my shame...there is this immense feeling of *relief* to no longer be with Marcus Lane? And why does that make me want to cry?

Momma regards me quietly, the plate she was wrapping forgotten in her lap. I can't tell her any of this, but somehow, she knows. I can see it on her face. "We'll fix it, honey. We'll put it all back together."

Standing, I place the bag in the cardboard packing box and cross the floor, resting my hand gently on her soft hair as I go. "I know, Momma."

*Summer, Six Years Earlier*

*I hum as I arrange the pretty purple flowers in my grandma's antique flow blue pitcher. They're only weeds, both stem and blossoms spiny and sturdy and a study in contrast to the delicate, gold rimmed china I've seated them in, but I like the look. I tilt my head, considering, and add a little forsythia from the bush alongside the back fence.* Perfect.

*Grandma's pitcher is lovely sitting on our kitchen table, a shaft of afternoon sunlight illuminating the delicate tracery of fragile blue and white. She passed it along to her daughter at her marriage, and Momma handed it down to me at mine. It's one of my very favorite objects.*

*I found the thistle growing along our fence line near the forsythia when I went out to get some cuttings, and despite knowing it was no more than a nuisance, was delighted to add the common blossom to my bouquet. It reminds me of the farm where Owen and I had grown up, acre on acre of beautiful rolling pasture abutting the foothills of Blue Ridge Mountains. Daddy had always hated the flower because he had to dig it out from around the fences so the cows wouldn't eat it and, since it was an invasive species, so it wouldn't take over the fence lines altogether and create a tangled mess.*

*"But it'd be a super pretty tangled mess," I remember telling him. Owen just rolled his eyes. Since he was a boy, and older, he had to go help Daddy dig that thistle, and he despised it with every slash of the shovel and drop of sweat he shed.*

*Especially since it was a job never finished. The damn stuff always came back, and next summer found them out there again, digging once more.*

*When I saw the weed, I snapped a photo and sent it immediately to Owen, of course. "Sending you a cutting," I texted. "A little bit of home sweet home."*

*"Do it and die," he texts back now, prompting a giggle.*

*"What's so funny?" Marcus asks, coming in the kitchen and wrapping his arms around my waist. "What's this?"*

*"Just some flowers for the table. Aren't they pretty?"*

*He straightens. "Harriet... those are weeds, dear." His upper lip curls and he scratches just above his right eyebrow.*

*"You mean the thistle? I know. It's pretty, though."*

*"We don't need weeds in the house. God, the things I put up with..." Rolling his eyes as though I've personally offended him, he grabs the vase and opens the door to the back yard, stepping through to the patio. "Come here, Harriet." Already feeling chastised, I follow. He begins to gesture from one spot in the yard to another. "You have rose bushes back here! Peonies. All sorts of flowers you can make legitimate arrangements with, and yet you pick a weed." To emphasize his point, he grabs the flowers and flings them to*

*my feet. "What do I need to do, Harriet? Do I need to buy you fucking flowers?"*

*I'm silent, having learned in only a single year of marriage it's better to keep my mouth shut in most instances than to give him the wrong answer.*

*This is not one of those times, though. The vase, my precious flow blue vase, follows the weeds to the concrete patio. A scream of pain and protest, swiftly held prisoner by one fist to my belly and another to my mouth, tries to break loose.* Hold it together. Hold it in. I can't let it escape. I can't let him see—

*"Answer me!" The demand is a bellow, and I flinch.*

*Oh, my God, it hurts.*

*I try to answer him. "I—"*

*"Fucking impossible. You know what? I'm not going to buy you flowers. Flowers are expensive, and then they fucking die, Harriet, which is why I had gardeners plant this beautiful garden right here. If you want flowers, pick them. More will grow. But don't pick fucking weeds. That's an insult." He's pacing back and forth, spittle flying from his mouth. "It's a personal insult to me." He stops in front of me, and I struggle to remain composed. "I know you don't mean to insult me."*

*My eyes are riveted on the broken porcelain at my feet. "No, of course not."*

*"Get rid of the weeds, Harriet."*

*Maybe I can put it back together...* "I will."

*"Where's the bush?"*

*Maybe some kind of clear glue...* "What?"

"The bush. Where's the bush with the weeds on it?"

I point to the fence at the rear of the property. "It's over there."

"Show me." We walk across the lawn, him in his dress shoes and slacks and me in my rubber house shoes and yoga pants from earlier today. Mute, I show him the small patch of thistle. "Shovel." When my face registers a question, he shoves past me impatiently to the small garden shed a few yards past, entering and exiting a moment later with a sharp-pointed spade. He pushes it into my startled hand. "Dig."

"Me?"

"No, Harriet, the landscaper. Dig the fucking weed out of the ground."

I think for approximately ten seconds about turning and walking back into the house. Something stops me, though—a look in his eyes that's weirdly devoid of any true emotion. It's a look that shows his commitment to his task, to his end-goal.

I start to dig.

It's a laughable task. I'm not an athlete, not strong or particularly adept with tools of any sort. I'm wearing rubbery house shoes, which slip and slide on my bare feet when I plant the tip of the shovel in the soil and step on the edge, trying to use my body weight to push it into the ground. Marcus watches, arms crossed over his chest, lips pressed *together in irritation as I try and stumble off the shovel, try again and fail again.*

*The third time, when I cut my ankle on the side of the shovel, he jerks it from my hands with a muttered curse. "Ridiculous. Can't do anything."*

*He doesn't stop me when I flee inside to clean the cut, to watch him from the windows above the kitchen sink. I observe, swallowing down my instinctive fear and hurt, as he digs and digs and fights that thistle, and a lifetime later, drags it triumphantly from the ground.*

*I observe and hide a grim smile as I separate each stem of thistle from the broken china I swept up from the patio and set it carefully in the trash.*

*It'll be back, stronger and more lovely than ever. The damn stuff always comes back.*

# Eleven

## Harry

Ava catches her lower lip between her teeth as she counts the chocolate chips into the mixing bowl rotating slowly on the stand. "Firty-free. Firty-seven. Firty-hunnan." With a flourish, she dumps the rest. "All dem. Turn it up, Ammie Harry."

"Oh, no. That's good for pancakes, baby." We really don't need the mixer, but Ava loves to watch it spin, and I love to indulge her when Owen lets me babysit. "Ready to put them in the pan?"

Pretending that she's gotten super heavy all of a sudden to make her giggle, I lift her from the counter to her seat and turn the mixer off before moving the pancake mix to the stove. I've made a stack of six when the doorbell rings and Sugar sets up a deafening blend of barking and howling. I widen my eyes dramatically at Ava. "Who is that, Ava-Bell? Who did you invite for breakfast?"

She giggles and I grab a dishtowel to wipe my hands as I head for the door. Through the frosted glass panes, I can make out a male outline and frown. *Better not be Marcus.* I swing the door open on the tail end of the thought to see Jack Brady, hands in his back pockets. He's dressed casually in a flannel and jeans over a pair of work boots, a ball cap pulled over his brownish-blond hair.

"Jack."

"Morning."

"Ah, sure. Good morning." I open the door wider, stepping back. "Please come in." I'm awkwardly conscious of my messy morning hair and bare feet, the toys all over the hallway floor, and Sugar, sniffing Jack's pants leg like he's a delicious new dessert. "I'm so sorry... everything's a mess..."

"Please," he returns mildly. "I'm completely barging in." He sniffs the air. "Is something burning?"

"Oh, shit." Turning, I run. "Forgot the pancakes!" I yell over my shoulder.

In the kitchen, Ava offers Jack a toothy smile smeared with chocolate, then turns back to the small television mounted under the cabinet, where cartoons play. I race to the stove, grab the handle of the cast-iron fry pan, and tip it up over the sink. Three charred pancakes drop out and I sigh, then use the dishtowel to wipe the pan. At least nothing caught on fire this time.

"Strike one," I say. "Let me just try this again…"

Cartoons change to a commercial, and a few seconds later, a news break. I watch idly while I hover over the pancakes, waiting for that moment when the surface begins to bubble.

"In today's news, another coed has gone missing from the Charlottesville campus. Amber Derrickson, twenty-two years old, was last seen leaving an area bar at twelve-forty-five A.M. to begin a brief walk home. When her roommate arrived at three A.M. and checked on her, it was discovered that she had never arrived. Police are canvassing—"

"Hey," Jack says, and flips the volume down. "Whatcha got there?" Ava flicks wide eyes from the screen and Jack engages her in animated conversation about how delicious chocolate chip pancakes are.

I give myself a little shake, mentally berating myself for not noticing Ava's interest, and pour more batter in the pan.

When I glance over a minute later, I find him looking at me with a disconcerting intensity. Self-conscious, I lift a hand to push my hair out of my face. "What?"

"Are you worried about that?"

"The missing girls?" I mouth the words. "Yeah, of course. That's happening right around where I teach. One of the girls…the one from six weeks back?" He nods to indicate his knowledge of who I'm talking about. "She was a student of mine."

"Damn. I'm sorry."

"I just want them to be safe, you know. Their poor parents."

"Yeah. I know."

"Pawents?" Ava echoes, poking a finger in a pancake.

Jack's eyebrow raises and he grins at her. "I saw the For Sale sign out front," he says, changing the subject.

I turn back to the stove to flip a pancake. "Yeah. The place is too much for me. In more ways than one."

"I get that. Any bites yet?"

"One or two families have shown some interest. I guess time will tell. Want some?"

Jack looks surprised. "Sure. If you have enough. I promise I didn't come over here to steal your food, though."

"There's plenty. Coffee, too." I nod toward the pot. "Cups in the cabinet right above."

He opens the cabinet and extracts a mug, the one that says *that was sodium funny ... I slapped my neon that one*. "This is your brother's kid, right?"

"Yeah, Ava. More pancakes, baby?" She shakes her head, mouth full. "Every now and then she gets to stay with Ammie Harry overnight while her daddy has an adult evening."

Jack nods, a smile playing around his lips. "Nice of you."

I shrug. "I'm lucky. She's kind of amazing." *And since I've never managed to have kids of my own, it's nice to pretend—just for a little while—that she's mine.* I shrug the morose thought away.

I wait until he's settled at the table beside Ava with a cup of coffee and a plate of pancakes and I'm seated beside them before asking the question I've been wondering about since he showed up. "So...not that I begrudge your visit, but to what do I owe the honor, Jack?"

He glances at Ava. "It's several things."

"Go on."

"Are you sure?"

"Yeah. Looks like she's finished, so Ava's going to play with Sugar now, aren't you, baby?"

"Sug." She scrambles down from her chair and wanders off to find the dog, and I grin into Jack's bemused face.

"Nice trick." He takes a bite of pancake and I watch as his face transforms. "Holy shit."

"Madagascar vanilla, maple syrup, and a pinch of sea salt," I tell him, forking my own bite into my mouth. "The contradicting flavors enhance one another. So, spill."

"You should use that fancy ass degree for cooking instead of chemistry. No offense."

"None taken. And I don't want to turn a passion into a job, you know?"

He takes his time, chewing slowly before setting his fork on his plate and resting both elbows on the table. "Yeah, sure. Makes sense. Listen, in the grocery store the other day."

"That's not for the police to worry about."

"I'm not here in any official capacity."

"Then why are you here?"

He works his jaw. "Because I care what happens to you?"

I close my eyes briefly. "Sometimes it's better not to care, Jack. I'm a mess right now."

"I guess that's a polite way of telling me to mind my own business?"

My smile is tight. "Pretty much."

His smile is apologetic as he shakes his head. "I can't do that, Harry."

"Well, I don't need a hero these days, Jack."

"That's not—" He lifts his eyes heavenward, exasperated. "I take it Lane has bailed and left you holding the bag on the bills?" I sit back in the chair and cross my arms over my chest. "Damnit, Harry, I'm not the enemy here."

"I know that!"

"Then why won't you talk to me? Let me help you?"

"Because it's humiliating, that's why." I stand and walk quickly to the French doors that lead out to the backyard. Leaning my forehead against one of the cold glass panes, I stare out at the yard rather than look at him, at the look of pity I'm certain to see in his expression. His hands on my shoulders a minute later are a shock and I jump, meeting his eyes in the glass. He squeezes lightly and drops his hands, but his eyes hold mine.

"You have nothing to be embarrassed about, Harry. And there's no shame in accepting help. So, here's what we're going to do. I'm going to tell you about some next steps you can take, some things to think about that you might not know about. Because there's no precedent for things like this. How would you know what comes next? What to do next?"

"I... but..."

"No more buts. No more excuses. Turn around, Harry."

Something in me responds to the command in his voice, and I find myself turning and lifting my face to look up at him.

"Do you trust me?"

"I...yes?"

He laughs a little. "I'll take it. Come on. Let's go sit down where that niece of yours is playing so you won't worry about her, and we'll talk. Deal?"

I draw in a deep breath, feeling oddly soothed and optimistic for the first time in days. "Sure. Deal."

After topping off our coffees, we follow the sound of Ava's chortling to the t.v. room. The only seats in here now are a couple of giant-sized bean bags that unfurl into floor mattresses, and we lower ourselves to a couple.

"So, the way I see it, there are two separate issues," Jack begins. "First and foremost is making sure you have what you need to take care of yourself." I start to speak, and he holds up a hand. "Just facts, Harry. You've lost what looks to be an essential component of your income, right?"

I hate admitting it, but he's right. College professors don't make big money. "Yes. But I just need to downsize. I never wanted all of this, anyway. It was all Marcus." I wave the hand not holding the coffee mug to indicate the house. "Once it sells, I'll be fine. More than fine."

"I'm glad that you're not especially tied to it, and obviously you've already put things into motion. That's good. It makes things easier. But you know that's not going to happen overnight."

"I know. I'll just have to manage in the meantime." I tug at the sleeve of my sweatshirt, pushing it up and then pulling it back down again. "I'll be fine." Lucy Falls is a small town, but my family did a pretty solid job of keeping their financial status a secret. Jack probably has no idea my parents are wealthy. Wealth came to them late in life, when a distant relative died childless and left a massive estate to my mother. As it was out of state and she had no personal connection to it, she had an attorney liquidate the assets and put most of the proceeds into stocks and bonds. My parents were never flamboyant about their fortune, and most of the town never even realized it had come their way.

A healthy portion had been put into trust for Owen and me. So far, I hadn't needed to touch it, but if necessary, I can always draw on it.

"That's good, Harry. That's a good start. If you're interested, I know of a house that would be great for you. It's a little farther from the Charlottesville campus than this one is, because it's farther up the mountain, but it's inexpensive and in a really safe neighborhood, and..." He trails away when I just stare at him.

"Did you search out real estate for me, Jack?"

"No! No...I live there...in the neighborhood, I mean. So, extra safe, right?"

"Oh." I tuck my chin and breathe in my coffee, considering. Still in Lucy Falls, near to my family. House in a neighborhood with a cop. Cheap rent. I'd be foolish not to consider it. "It sounds too good to be true."

"Maybe we could go take a look one day this week? If you like it, great. Problem solved. If not, no big deal."

"Well...yeah. Okay." Ava chooses that moment to sashay over on chubby legs, an offering of plastic broccoli in her hands. "Oh, my goodness. Thank you so much! Just what I needed with my coffee." Beaming, she goes back for more. "What was the other thing?"

"Hmm?"

"You said there were two issues. What's the second?"

"Oh, right. Harry. I don't want to tell you what to do, but I really wish you'd go ahead and press charges. The DA's making her case to do it, anyway, like I told you, but it'll make you look considerably better if it comes from you."

"What do you mean?"

"I mean if you don't press charges, it looks like you're in collusion with him."

"Damnit." I set my coffee mug down on the floor, choosing a spot Ava's not likely to run into it. Then I flop back into the bean bag and close my eyes. "You know that's not the case, Jack."

"Of course, I do. But in a case like this, it's all about perception."

"Tell me why," I demand softly. "The only person he hurt is me. Convince me why putting him in jail...separating a father from four kids...is a good idea, and I'll go sign the papers today."

When he answers, his voice is a low rumble strained with uncertainty. "Have you considered that you may not be the only one?"

My breath catches.

"What if he's done this before? What if he'll do it again? What if, in uncovering his fiction, you've stumbled on something much bigger than just that one lie, Harry? People don't just do stuff like this in a vacuum. And his wife...something's been nagging at me. She put on a good act, but I don't believe she was all that surprised by you. That bothers me. If she knew about you and the marriage, why would she have gone along with it? What if it's his reason for doing it that we need to be paying closer attention to, instead of the bigamy itself?" My eyes are open now, fixed on his, caught unwillingly in the scenario he poses. "What if all this... what if it's just the edge of a bone, peeking out of a shallow grave that was never meant to be disturbed?"

We stare at each other. His gaze is pleading. Mine, I'm sure, is merely confused.

The possibility of Marcus's bigamy being a part of something bigger, something worse than what it seemed on the surface, had never occurred to me. I remember our conversation in the parking lot, his dreadful blankness and puzzling non-answers. Hadn't I thought at the time there was something I was missing?

After the silence stretches a beat too long, he shakes his head and looks away. "Sorry. I know that sounds dramatic. I guess I've been reading too many thrillers lately—"

"No." I stop him with a hand on his. "You're right. I'll do it. I'll press charges."

# Twelve

## Harry

I DO NOT NEED Wyatt Granger's eyeballs on me today, and that is an incontrovertible fact. He's always looking at me with that whiskey gold stare of his. It sees right through me. It makes me nervous.

I've decided he's definitely not my soul mate. That fanciful thought the night of the bridge, as I've taken to calling it, was just that...a passing fancy. After all, how could my soul mate be more than a decade younger than I am? How could he appear on the heels of the worst romantic disaster I've ever experienced, when I need time to work through things and find who I even am, again?

Easy. He wouldn't. A soul mate appears when you're ready for them. Maybe you're not looking, but you're open, receptive, ready to engage. That's not me, so he's not my soul mate. He's just a student I need to ignore.

I fumble through my introduction to triglycerides and fatty acids, looking up once to confirm that yes, the big guy in the front row is still watching me with those eyes, following my every movement.

It's unsettling. If he hadn't been proving himself to be helpful, I might even take steps to have him removed as my TA. But he has been helpful, anticipating my needs before I voice them, grading assignments, even proctoring an exam I couldn't make because it interfered with an interview with the DA.

With a mental shake, I push the clicker on my slide show and force myself to focus. It's an introductory level class, and the material is less than scintillating. "Fatty acids. The name suggests something bad, right? Fat. Acid. Doesn't really sound like something we'd want in our bodies. But fatty acids are actually the foundation for many critical functions in our bodies. Who can tell me, from the reading I requested, why they're important?"

Several hands go up, and the next few minutes pass with some semblance of my brain being where it's supposed to be.

"But in looking at food chemistry, we need to be aware of the different types of fatty acids, right? There are both saturated and unsaturated acids, and one type is better than the other. Which is the one we want to ensure is present in the majority of the food we consume…?"

"Definitely the one you're eating." A voice pipes up from somewhere in the middle of the room to the accompaniment of a few scattered laughs. Alton Roberts, wannabe class clown. I rub my forehead with my forefinger.

Burnt sugar eyes meet mine from the first row, intent and unsmiling from beneath dark brows. He doesn't look happy. I shake my head a tiny bit, a warning not to interfere. "Mr. Roberts. Enlighten the class, please, as you seem to want to participate."

A smile curls the student's lips beneath a ruddy mustache as he stands and inwardly, I cringe. *Danger, Will Robinson*. Should've just ignored him. "It'd be my pleasure, Miz Bee."

"That's Doctor Bee, Mr. Roberts."

"Apologies, ma'am."

"Doctor."

"Yes, ma'am—*Doctor*. Anyway, I just meant, whatever fatty acids you're eating, those are the ones everyone should be eating."

*Leave it alone, Harriet.*

*I can't. He's such a tool.* "And why is that?" It's obvious where he's headed. His delivery is brash and devoid of subtlety. A product of his arrogance.

"Because those fatty acids are clearly working. You're a beautiful woman." He changes his arrogant smirk to something resembling calf-eyed adoration.

Even expecting something of the kind, I find myself snorting a laugh. "Ah, okay...let's stick to the specifics, Mr. Roberts, as failing to do so could get you slapped with a harassment charge. What are the polyunsaturated fatty acids—that's omega-3s and omega-6s, class—doing to improve my appearance?" As I wait for a response, my gaze flickers to Wyatt. He watches me from the front row, a little smile now playing around his lips. When he catches my eyes on him, his smile grows wider, and he shifts to a more comfortable position in his seat.

Alton Roberts transfers his weight from one foot to the other. Sitting on my stool behind the podium, I motion for him to speak.

"Um...I'm not real sure, to be honest. You just look good—"

"Sit down, man." It's Wyatt. He doesn't turn around, or raise his voice, but Alton scrambles to do as he says. The class is quiet. His interference annoys me. What is it with every man I meet wanting to play hero? I'm not some defenseless damsel in distress, damnit. And more than being able to, I *need* to take care of myself.

"Did you have something to contribute, Mr. Granger?"

He lifts his eyes from the text in his lap. "You're how old? Thirties?"

Thinning my lips, I nod. "Correct."

"I think what Mr. Roberts meant to say was fatty acids are responsible for the hydrated, supple quality, and overall healthy appearance of your skin. We're obviously not studying it under a microscope, and I feel confident in saying that lack of overexposure to the sun plays a big part, but your skin looks much younger than some of the women in this class, and I'm pretty sure you don't wear make-up to conceal flaws." There's scattered grumbling, along with some audible agreement. "Your hair is the same, which can also be contributed the same properties of fatty acids."

I have to clear my throat. "Thank you for that assessment, Mr. Granger."

"Sure."

I give him a brisk nod and resume my lecture. If my gaze strays in his direction a few too many times for the remainder of class, that's probably more my fault than it is his.

If he winks at me and completely disrupts my train of thought, forcing me to end class a few minutes early... well, that's his fault and all the more reason he needs to sit in the back next time.

The way back.

---

After back-to-back classes, I make my way, Sugar trotting alongside me, to a small campus coffee shop for a midday pick-me-up. It's busy as usual this time of day and I take my place in a long line, casting a quick glance over the other patrons around me. All the usuals, a mix of students and professors here for their own fix.

We creep forward, one debit card transaction at a time, until the buzz of a text pauses me. I pull my phone from my bag, frowning at the unfamiliar number. It doesn't take me long to decipher the sender's identity.

**Unknown:** Marcus was just arrested thanks to you. That was a mistake. Big mistake.

Though the café is cool, my cheeks flush hot. I pat them with my free hand as I study the message. I can feel my mouth twist into a scowl, forming voiceless words of response. *Whoa, Nelly.* Is it my fault he committed a crime and has now been arrested for it? These people are certifiable.

My nose wrinkles as Jack's words echo. Did Gina know? When Marcus started courting me, when he proposed and gave me a ring, when we married...did she close her eyes to it all? How does a woman even do that? And more significantly, *why* would she?

My finger hovers over the keypad, and I chew my bottom lip. I can't decide how to respond.

I have questions. I don't really want the answers, but eventually curiosity will eat me from the inside out. It'll destroy me, the not knowing.

"Ma'am?"

I start to reply.

"Ma'am? What can I get for you?" The barista waits politely, a hand on her hip.

With a start, I realize it's my turn to order. Blinking, I look up, the menu board blurring after staring so long at the phone. I can't even remember what I usually get. I rattle off some words. "Uh. A large venti Americano with oat milk, double shot, lots of sugar, extra whip, and sugar free caramel. And skim."

"You want a—" Her expression is doubtful, and I cut her off.

"Yes. Thanks."

Swiping my card, I turn my attention back to my phone.

Please don't contact me.

That's weak. *Delete.* I muse over options for my reply, discarding them as quickly as they appear. It needs to be succinct, to put an end to this absurdity so I can move on, but the small, hurt side of me doesn't mind the idea of twisting a knife in the process.

My mother, that icon of southern grace, wouldn't like it, but what she doesn't know won't hurt her.

Your perspective is skewed…

A finger pokes my side, startling me into dropping my phone. Turning with a glare, I find Wyatt smiling at me. "You. Did you follow me here?"

"Of course not." His even response has me feeling shrew-like.

"I think you're supposed to wait over there." He indicates the end of the counter, where another customer waits, and belatedly I realize I'm holding the line up again.

*Damnit.*

"Sorry," I mumble to the barista. She rolls her eyes and I stomp to the end of counter, taking my place in the waiting queue. I try once again to focus on my phone but give up as Wyatt finishes his own order and comes to stand beside me.

"It was a simple mistake," he begins.

"Don't."

"No, really. You're obviously distracted, and—"

"Why are you stalking me?" I snap at last, whirling on my heel. "And what the hell was all that in class? I indicated I had it covered."

"One, I'm just here for my afternoon energy drink, and two, I was tired of his crap—"

"Skinny oat milk latte with sugar and *real* milk —" The barista's tone is sardonic, and a few snickers go up.

"Who the hell ordered that ridiculous concoction?" I murmur to myself. "Okay, if that's truly the case, I need you to stay back five feet and leave me —"

"You."

"What?"

Wyatt nudges me in the direction of the counter. "I promise, I'm not stalking you, but that's your ridiculous concoction."

"Shit." I jerk the drink off the counter and leave the building in a cloud of pique that follows like Pigpen's dust, ignoring the coffee that sloshes through the lid and onto my wrist. "Sorry, baby," I mutter to Sugar. Dimly I'm aware of the door opening and closing behind me several seconds later, and then I feel him, his presence large and undeniable behind me. I cast a look over my shoulder as he tails me along the sidewalk.

He raises an eyebrow and takes a sip of his energy-whatever drink. "Just happen to be going in the same direction, ma'am."

Ma'am.

My back teeth grind together, my last nerve thoroughly, officially plucked. It's *Doctor*. I'm going to tell him so. He's going to know, once and for all...I whirl around, Sugar circling with me, my free hand extended in a *stop-right-there* gesture.

"I earned that doctorate, damn—"

I stop.

My hand is on his chest, halted by delicious planes of muscle packed beneath a jersey hoodie. His heart beats into the pulse of my palm, making my fingers curl against the soft fabric.

He's so close there are only scant inches dividing his carbon monoxide from my oxygen, so close his body heat blocks the winter chill and warms me through.

So close my eyes are level with chest and I have to look up, up, up to find patient eyes glittering down at me with a quiet sort of intensity.

*Ma'am* suddenly takes on new meaning.

*I can't breathe.*

He doesn't speak; just looks at me, a universe of understanding in his regard. It makes me want to kiss him and punch him, that understanding.

The thought of doing either rocks me back on my heels. "God, what is—I don't understand—?" I lift a hand to rub my forehead, grimacing when he plucks the coffee from my grip before it makes contact with my face.

"It's all right, Harriet. Here, let me take this for you."

"You just used my given name." As he steps back a few inches, the Wyatt haze starts to clear, and with it, things begin to crystallize. I'm standing in the dell, and my ovaries are visibly sighing over a student. An older one, sure, but a student, nonetheless. Any of the students or faculty milling around could notice us, could wonder at our proximity.

As attractive as his chest is, Wyatt Granger is professional suicide. I inch backwards.

"I did. You should get used to it." His hand on my elbow, Wyatt starts to turn me in the direction we were headed.

"You're just a kid with nice pheromones. Sexy, attractive pheromones," I tell him, resisting as imperceptibly as possible. It's terribly important that I make this point, that I not let this go unsaid. "I don't know what you think this is—" Pointedly, I look down at his hand on my arm. "But that's all it is. Biology."

"One, I'm not a kid. I'm a man, and you're a woman. A few years older than me, sure, but I can promise you it's nothing to worry about. And two, I'm surprisingly into biology, Harriet."

Dammit. I stare up at him helplessly. "You're not hearing me, Wyatt."

"I hear you just fine," he returns. "I have sexy pheromones and your pheromones like them. Seems like a solid start."

"No, that's exactly the opposite—"

"Am I interrupting something?"

Turning, I face unpleasant surprise of the day number seventeen.

Marcus.

# Thirteen

## Harry

*Am I interrupting?* I can't help but startle, the little hop I make guilty feeling for some reason. "Marcus—I... I thought you—"

"Were in jail?" Marcus is unkempt in a pair of jeans and a plain tee shirt beneath a striped overshirt. He's usually so finicky about his clothing, so intent on perpetuating the right look. His polished veneer is gone, replaced with an ugliness I was fortunate to only see a time or two when we were married. I learned how to avoid it, became a master in diverting it before it showed itself.

But here it is.

Sugar sees it and growls low in her throat. Paying her no heed, Marcus takes a step closer, and she snaps at him. He jumps back, then steadies.

"Control that damned dog. And let's talk about why that would be, hmm? Maybe because you put me there?" Despite the foot or so that separates us, he manages to hiss his final few words in my face, spittle flying from his mouth as he leans his upper half closer to me.

I tighten my fingers around Sugar's leash, preventing her from moving against Marcus. She's not a violent animal, but he's obviously triggered her protective instincts. I won't have him calling animal control over something he instigated.

It's only the calming presence of the hand Wyatt sets casually on my shoulder that keeps me from backing away altogether. I hate confrontation, have always struggled to stand up for myself if it meant an argument or unpleasant scene. It's probably why Marcus was able to manipulate me so well for so long. Now is no different, and I struggle for a reply.

"Hey, now—" Wyatt starts, seeing my effort.

"Who the hell is this?" Marcus rears back, his gaze raking up and down the man standing slightly behind and to my right. "Looks a little young for you, Harry, babe. I'd aim a little older if I were you."

"He's not...we're not—" I stop and shake my head to clear it. "What are you doing here, Marcus?"

Instead of answering, he laughs. "You're a damned hypocrite. Getting your panties all in a wad over another woman when you've probably been two-timing me all along." A sneer twists his face. "Maybe he can teach you a few things, because you always were a shit lay."

Something snaps inside me. It breaks wide open, and I react, my palm flying out and landing with a crack of sound against his cheek.

"You...you asshole! Getting my panties in a wad? Please." Despite my intuitive caution where Marcus is concerned, Wyatt's presence behind me lends me courage and my voice shrills. Sugar shifts uneasily at my hip and Wyatt's fingers tighten on my shoulder, a subtle reminder of where we stand. When I look around there are small signs that we are not going unnoticed—a couple stopped to stare, a girl looking up over the edge of her phone, furtive glances from students and faculty rushing by. Oh, my God. This is my job. My workplace. I pull away from Wyatt's hand, just the tiniest of movements, but he hears what I don't say out loud and drops his hand.

Swallowing, I lower my voice. "You were married to someone else when you married me, Marcus. That's a crime, one you implicated me in. I guess I did get a little upset."

Marcus waves his hand in a dismissive gesture. "Don't you worry. When this goes to court, I think you'll find that it was an error. Mis-filed paperwork. I won't serve five minutes."

A brief, abruptly cut-off laugh escapes. "You are unbelievable. Even now, you can't just admit that you fucked up, you got careless, and you got caught. There's something wrong with you if you can't look at what you've done over the past seven years and see that it was wrong. Fuck being illegal. It was just wrong, Marcus. On so many levels—"

"Boo fucking hoo, babe." He leans in again after a quick glance at the dog, speaking quietly into my face. Somehow his control is more chilling than his open anger. "You messed up when you decided to press charges, Harriet. You don't even know. All I can tell you is, you better watch yourself. You better—"

"That's enough," Wyatt's voice cuts in, silencing him. When I glance up, all I see is a muscle ticking at the base of his jaw. His gaze flickers briefly to mine, reflecting my own simmering emotion, before it shifts back to Marcus. That quick look, though, does something to me. For the first time in weeks, warmth spears through me, softening the ice that's slowly stolen any desire to feel anything. I'm not alone. Numbness morphs to a swirling sense of being off-balance, being out of control—

"Yeah?" Marcus sneers. "Maybe I'm not finished yet, Captain America. What are you going to do about it?"

"The very last thing you want me to do, old man. I'm not going to kick your ass, although that would be fun." He raises a hand to reveal his cell phone, the screen clearly displaying nine-one-one. His finger is poised to press 'call.' "One call, and you're back where you started from. No get out of jail free card this time, because I'm pretty sure one of your bond provisions is that you keep your nose clean. How about it, Lane? What's it gonna be?"

I hold my breath as Marcus visibly wages war with himself. Finally, he directs his attention to me, pressing a finger hard into my chest for a couple of seconds. "I'm done, anyway. You remember what I said."

Content to get the last word in, he pivots and stalks back the way he came.

"Damnit," I murmur, adrenaline levels plummeting as suddenly as they flooded through my system. I swipe at a tear on my cheek as surreptitiously as possible. "Just...fuck. Fuck."

Wyatt doesn't allow me any time to brood. "Come on," he says, pressing my coffee back into my hand and steering me down the sidewalk. "You're done for the day and have..." He checks his phone, where I know he has my schedule loaded and synced with his. "Nothing pressing this afternoon, correct?"

"Yes, but—"

"No buts. You need to shake that off."

Somehow, I find myself and Sugar in his truck and driven across campus to the sports complex, where Wyatt leads us into a massive cave-like gym with a series of batting cages at the far end. It's empty, our footsteps ringing in the hollow space as he marches me toward them. I start shaking my head. "No. One hundred percent, this is not happening. Thanks, anyway."

He laughs and pulls me into one of the cages, dropping an athletic bag on the floor before moving to the side and inspecting a rack of helmets. Sugar lies down just outside the cage. "It's happening, and trust me, you'll feel so much better after you pop a few. Just pretend like the ball is your ex-husband." He pulls a helmet from the rack and plops it on my head.

I tilt my head and the helmet slides, covering one eye, as I contemplate his advice. *Tempting.* But... "You don't understand. Sports and I just don't mix. My P.E. teacher passed me just to get me away from her. I'm a klutz. I'll end up kneecapping you or something, even if you're standing ten feet away." *Not to mention it's how I ended up an epileptic.*

"Oh, ye of little faith. You have a good teacher, now. Standing before you is the Baseball King." I watch doubtfully as he strikes a pose, balancing a bat on the toe of one shoe. He raises an eyebrow. "Nothing?"

I shake my head. "No clue."

"Huh. How 'bout that. That's cool." Springing into action, he places the bat in my lax grip, then stands back a few feet and eyes me up and down. "All right, let's see it."

"See what?"

"Your stance, Red."

"I really don't want to do this." Facing him, I lift the bat in front of me like a sword.

"Oh, boy." With a grin hidden behind his hand, Wyatt steps in to adjust how I'm standing, turning my body so I'm angled toward the machine that spits the balls out, moving one foot a fractional distance in front of the other, pulling my hips back, shoulders forward, elbows up…

"How am I supposed to remember all of this?" I whine.

"It'll become second nature, don't worry. Now, I'm going to bump the speed down way low. All you have to do is keep your eye on the ball and swing away. Okay?"

"Right. Okay. Keep my eye on the ball and…what's the other part?"

"Swing, Red. Swing."

"Right."

Wyatt walks out of the way and a minute later a ball sails my way, heralded by a *thwap*. I close my eyes and swing. When I open them, I'm facing the rear of the cage, and the ball is rolling on the floor at my feet. I drop the bat. "Told you."

"Oh, no…you just need a little practice. Here, let me help." After nitpicking my stance once again, Wyatt moves in behind me and curves his body around mine. I allow the stiffness in my form to relax, melted by the protective warmth of his frame. It reminds me of the bridge. I didn't know who he was then, and it felt so perfect at the time.

It still does. It's just complicated now by the fact that he's my student. Well, technically not my student. He's my TA. Are there rules against that? I should look that up. I should—

"Stop thinking." Fitting his hands atop mine on the bat, he moves my body in a practice swing, coming back to rest in a waiting position. There's something visceral about it, the imperfect alignment of his taller, leaner musculature against my softness. I find myself wanting to dwell there, if only for a few minutes, meditate on each sensation like my breath in a held yoga pose. *In. Hold. Release.* Feel each muscle give, every tiny, incremental submission allowing for deeper parlance.

His cheek brushes mine and he uses the contact to nudge a piece of hair out of the way, whispering in my ear as he does, "And keep your eyes open this time."

*Thwap.* Neither of us move, and the first ball lands harmlessly behind us.

"Ready?"

*No.* "Uh-huh."

The machine hums, a precursor to the ball's release. Wyatt moves, a fluid shift rippling through the lift and step of his foot, the rapid twist of his core, and the twist and crank of his forearm and wrist. I can't help but move with him, a lesser copy trying to apprehend his grace and power.

I giggle at what I must look like, the sound abruptly seizing in my throat. *Contact.*

We fucking smash the ball. It cracks like lightning, the reverberation echoing along the wooden bat and coursing like chaos into every cell. It's instant gratification, an adrenaline high I know I'll never forget. I drop the bat and whirl around, flinging my arms around Wyatt's neck. "I did it! I mean, we did it! I hit a baseball! And it felt amazing! Do you have any idea—"

My question is cut off by Wyatt's mouth landing on mine: hard, hungry, and utterly unapologetic. He kisses me like there is no choice, like not doing so right now, right this very moment—is inconceivable. His mouth finds mine like we're the opposite poles of magnets in a science experiment, like we're particles of glitter and glue, feng and shui, bugs and windshields...all inescapably drawn to one another.

Kind of like a soul to its mate.

Panic washes through me, leaving me pale and shaken. *No.* This can't happen. It can't. I obviously have crap discernment—*hello, Marcus*—so I need to back my truck up. And then there's Jack. Sweet Jack, who has done so much for me already and maybe there's something there? Maybe, after all these years, there could be something more than a just a one-sided crush. And I know I can trust him. He's still the same person he was more than a decade ago—solid, dependable, worthy.

When I break away, though, breathing hard and holding Wyatt at bay with a wary hand, I feel as though a piece of that magnet has stayed behind. As though I'm making a mistake. "I...I have to go," I stammer. "Take me back."

"Harry—"

"Doctor. It's Doctor, damnit. Take me back *now*." Panicky, I exit through the gate of the batting cage and grab for Sugar's leash, making for the exit to the cavernous gym space. I spare him a look over my shoulder as I half-run, half-walk away. I can't fall for him. It's just not a risk I'm willing to take. "This didn't happen, Wyatt."

Half a gym separates us, but it's not so great a distance that I don't see the tightening of his mouth as he bends to scoop up his bag. "Right," he mutters, loudly enough that I hear. "Never happened."

# Fourteen

## Wyatt

*Never fucking happened. That's fine*, except it did happen, and it was fucking brilliant.

My fingers dance on the steering wheel in tune to Ozzy's "I Just Want You," and a low string of curses rolls from my lips. She's all I've wanted since I saw her at the bridge and figured out shortly thereafter who she was. It hit me as I was walking her home and she made the comment about her ex-not-really-husband's-actual-legal-wife giving her a shiner.

A TikTok hashtagged with our campus name, hot-professor, and mall-mom-girl-fight had gone viral a couple of days earlier, actually making the news in Lucy Falls and cancelling out, for a brief moment, the awful headlines about the missing girls and *is Lucy Falls a serial killer's hunting ground* crap. Curious about the shell-shocked woman who'd obviously discovered the worst thing imaginable about her husband—and then been assaulted by the other woman—I'd done my research.

What I found left me a little moony-eyed.

Dr. Harriet Maelynn Bee was nothing short of brilliant. She'd graduated from high school at sixteen, gone on to complete her bachelor's in three years, and had earned her doctorate in chemistry by the time she was twenty-two-years-old. Now an ancient—and smoking hot—thirty-five-year-old, she is the recipient of several distinguished awards for her research in the field of food-based chemistry. I'd been fascinated by a recent interview in which she'd discussed her latest pursuit—work involving an enzyme responsible for the modulation of the brain's signaling pathway that controls binge eating. It was something she felt strongly about, she said, having been overweight as a child.

Aside from her intelligence and devotion to her work, her perseverance called to me. To go through what she'd gone through and respond by taking a walk and having a beer at midnight...that was my kind of girl.

But I'd moved too fast. I knew she was skittish. Who the hell wouldn't be, with all the shit that she'd been through in recent weeks? And that jackass's visit to campus earlier... the things he'd said... I've never wanted to punch someone as badly as I did Marcus Lane in that moment. I knew, though, that it would be the absolute worst thing

I could do, for Harry and myself. People were already looking. I could kiss goodbye the possibility of any future in baseball.

My fingers tighten on the steering wheel, and I take the turn for the middle-class neighborhood where I live with my mom. I stopped living on campus in my sophomore year, when life changed in huge, never-go-back kind of ways.

I can't shake the events of the afternoon. I made an error in kissing her. Now I have to prove that my wanting her isn't a sexy professor thing, either, though she's plenty sexy. She's actually kind of quirky—classic nerd girl with black glasses she wears for reading, crazy curly red hair, and skin that looks like it's afraid of daylight. She's always wearing band tee shirts and Docs, and I've never, ever seen even a minuscule amount of make-up on her face. She's not the typical girl that hangs out around the ball field in cut-offs and ponytails.

But she appeals to me in some weird way. When she talks centrifuges and chemical reactions, her face loses its careful, polite distance. It grows animated and vibrant.

I want to make her come alive like that, but under my hands and my mouth.

Sighing, I pull into the garage that houses my mom's white station wagon-looking SUV and turn the ignition off. I'm exhausted. The season hasn't started yet, but it's never truly off season...there's always cardio and training to be done, and today was no exception. I was up before the sun to run this morning, and had weights done before classes.

It's physically and mentally grueling, taken alongside the home stretch of my master's, but I can't slow down now. I'm so close to regaining what I gave up a few years ago—being drafted. There's even talk that I could receive an invitation to spring training from the Phillies.

Just thinking about it makes my gut clench. That kind of thing doesn't happen every day. The honor of it…it's overwhelming to even dream about.

It's so far removed from my current situation that I try not to think about it too much. Instead, I focus on the fact that in just a few months, I'll be done with school for good. I've done the extra time, worked my ass off for the master's in science, and after May, I'll finally have it. Maybe it sounds dumb when my alternate plan is playing pro-baseball, but the degree has always been important to me. Something to fall back on if anything ever happened with the sport, if I didn't make a team, or if I ended up permanently injured.

Maybe it was stupid.

I glance in the backseat, at the toddler seat stained with apple juice and crumbed-over with Cheerios, and climb out and shut the door. *No. Not stupid at all.* Career-ending injuries happen in the blink of an eye. One day I could be playing ball, reveling in a seven-figure contract. The next I could be recovering from a torn rotator cuff, looking at a high school coaching position.

The degree is insurance.

Plus, I love it. Baseball came late to me, when I was a high school freshman and required to play a sport. Up until that point, I'd been a bona fide nerd, thrilled by everything tech and chemistry and all things biology, in particular. Biochemistry was a no-brainer, an extension of who I really was inside.

I chuckle to myself as I push the button to close the garage door, recalling Harry's blank look when I tried to hint at my baseball career. She didn't have a clue that I could—maybe—be going pro soon. Hell, she'd probably be just as dismissive if she did know. Harry couldn't give a shit less about baseball. It's refreshing, considering my face plastered on posters scattered all over campus generates a lot of attention.

From inside, I hear a high-pitched squeal, followed by my mother's lower tones. "Noah Tyler, put that hammer down this minute and come wash up!"

*Oh, well. Back to the real world.* Grinning, I slip in through the mudroom door, just in time to catch the whirling dervish that is my nearly four-year-old son. Conceived early freshman year, he was born just before my sophomore year, the year I red-shirted. His mother, a friendly hook-up, wasn't interested in being a mom but was willing to include me on the decision-making process, something I will be eternally grateful for. She allowed me to pay for her medical expenses and signed full custody of Noah over to me at birth, and together we managed to ensure that she was able to continue her coursework and not miss any time from her studies.

We made it work. Together.

Now she's in New York, chasing her dream of fashion design and living the high life. I send regular updates on Noah, she oohs and ahhs over the life we created, and we remain friends.

"Noah! What the H-E-double-hockey-sticks is that in your hand?"

He peers up at me with mischief and mayhem sparkling in equal measure from his eyes. "It's a hammer, Daddy. I's a building."

"Whatcha building? Give me the hammer and show me."

He hands it over with no further argument and I slip it to my mom with a wink and a kiss on the cheek. "I'll get him washed up." I sniff. Mixed with the ever-present scent of *urushi* from her *kintsugi* practice, I smell something else. Chicken? "Did you make dinner?"

"Chicken and dumplings. I need to finish a repair, so probably thirty minutes."

"I'll keep him busy. It smells delicious."

"Thank you, love."

Mom wanders back to her studio, where she spends her spare time repairing broken pottery using the traditional Japanese art of *kintsugi*. It's a beautiful and unique pastime that allows her to work wherever she chooses. From the beginning, she has adamantly refused to allow anyone but herself care for Noah, and keeps him busy with playdates, preschool, and toddler sports.

A lump forms in my throat as I watch her walk the length of the hall and disappear. I'm lucky to have her. Turning, I grab Noah and zoom him, Superman-style, in the opposite direction. "Come on, bud. Let's go play."

Down the hall of our sprawling ranch-style home, Noah and I spend a few minutes together inspecting the wooden block structure he's spent the last hour building. I'm not certain what the hammer was for, or where he got it from, but he's a rascal. Where there's a will, there's a way.

The irony echoes as we make our way from blocks to bath to dinner. If my three-going-on-four-year-old can figure out how to steal a hammer, I can find a way with Harry. I have the will. I just need to figure out the how.

---

After a sleepless night of going over my next move, I decide the 'how' is to change tactics altogether and do exactly as Harry said—forget it ever happened. Instead of pushing forward, my best course of action would be to retreat and act uninterested. Harry is too nervous for anything else, too burned by her past. So, I'll call her Doctor, be courteous but distant, and become just another student.

When she's ready, I'll know.

It's harder than I realize, though.

When she arrives, Sugar in tow and arms full of her books and laptop, I have to curb my natural inclination to jump up and help her. Instead, I remain slouched in my seat, pretending to play a game on my phone. From beneath my brows, I see her flinch of surprise.

"Wyatt?"

I don't look up. "Mornin', Doctor Bee." My tone is the epitome of professional disinterest.

"I...um." She stumbles over her words, and I finally glance up at her. Her troubled eyes lock on mine. They hold questions and a pinch of hurt that weakens my resolve, and I have to look down again. "Everything okay this morning?"

"Right as rain."

"Good...ah...maybe you could set the laptop up for my lecture, please?" It's the first time she's had to make a request of me. Usually, I predict her needs and see to them without direction.

I rise without haste and stretch, allowing the hem of my shirt to rise above my jeans. Her gaze dips, lingers, and when I chuckle low, she quickly averts her head.

Not before I see the pink rising from her throat to color her face, though. *Score one for me.* She's far from immune.

"Sure thing, Doctor."

While she fiddles with something useless at her desk, I set up her computer and sync its Bluetooth with the audiovisual system. A slideshow is minimized on her home screen, and I set it to play on auto whenever she clicks to start.

"This slide show, right?"

"Yes, that's what I need." She hesitates. "Thanks. You know I suck at that techie stuff."

I stifle a smile and refrain from responding. Her observation is one hundred percent accurate. In my brief tenure as Harry's TA, I've witnessed her manage to corrupt three programs, forget her password to two school sites, and somehow manage to blow the power in her classroom just by plugging in a smart board.

She also drops things. Expensive, computery things. It's better for everyone if she stays far away.

Students are beginning to arrive and settle. Finished with setting up her system, I start to return to my seat.

"Wyatt, wait." Turning, I lift an eyebrow, inviting her to continue. She takes a step toward me and then stops, looking around. Her lips thin. "Never mind."

*Damn.* With a small shrug, I sit, and after a few minutes she opens class.

"Good morning, everyone. Please take your seats so we can get started." Chatter slowly dies away as the class of predominantly sophomores gives her their attention. "I've spent the past several days identifying what I believe to be a few gaps in your knowledge bank. Prior to the exam, here are a few areas I'd encourage you to take another look at it." She dims the lights and clicks to the first slide. "The first thing I've observed is...what in the world?"

Whispers and gasps and the sound of barely concealed panic make me look up from my phone. Splashed across the foundation information on the slide, in bright red lettering, is the word CUNT.

I half stand, intent on getting to the laptop and shutting it down. Even in the dimness of the room, shock is clear on Harry's face. She clicks to the next slide. Immediately the sound of moaning fills the room. A few hoots sound as the class gets a good look at what appears to be a porn clip playing.

"That's enough!" Stalking over to the laptop, Harry yanks at the power cord. That won't do it, though—it's synced through Bluetooth.

"Let me," I say. Quickly I remove the computer from her grasp and start disconnecting.

"Who's responsible for this?" She stands in front of the class with hands on hips, anger making her breath come fast and choppy.

Silence answers, accompanied by a few shrugs and shared glances. Harry lifts a hand to her brow and closes her eyes. I move rapidly through each slide. There are twelve total, and each one is defiled in some way. All are variations on a theme. One has been changed to a photo of Harry with her eyes blacked out. It's captioned 'whore.' Another has a nude female body with Harry's head photoshopped to it. It's poorly done and obviously fake, but it still makes me want to take my bat to the culprit.

"I'm sorry," Harry says after a lengthy moment where she visibly gathers her composure. "I'm sorry you had to see that, and even sorrier that my first impulse was to accuse. Class is dismissed."

As the class files out, Harry sinks down in her desk and puts her head in her hands. "I can't believe that just happened. Wyatt, please tell me what just happened."

I lift my hands and let them drop. "I don't fucking know. Who had access to your computer?"

"No one!" She wails. "Yesterday it was in my office when we were...when I went to get coffee. My office was locked. I know I locked it. I always..." Her voice dies away, and she chews on her lip, forehead creased.

"What is it?"

"He couldn't have possibly..."

*Marcus.* The rightness of it sets my blood to thrumming in my veins. "He was on campus yesterday."

"I never requested my keys back from him. I just changed the locks on the house. He has one to my office. We figured it might be necessary if I had a seizure."

I close the lid on the laptop and return it to its padded sheath. "You need to report this. See if someone can do some cyber-investigating."

She nods, her eyes distant. "My brother can do that, but you're right. I need to report it."

"And let the police, not your brother, do the digging."

Harry bristles. "Why? I trust him implicitly."

"No, not because he's not trustworthy. Because if anything is there, it needs to go through the proper chain of command." Her expression is devastated. Forgetting my resolve, I nudge her shoulder with mine. "Don't you watch television?" She attempts a wobbly smile before it crumples. "Shit." I put an arm around her shoulders. "You're not going to cry, right? Because I'm not sure I wouldn't do something awful like kiss you again."

"Aargh. That's not happening, Wyatt." She pulls away and reaches for the laptop case. "I'm going to my office to call the police and my brother. Could you take this stuff to the lab for me?" Without waiting for a response, she picks up Sugar's leash and begins to walk away.

Back to distance. "Happy to, Doctor."

Her gait hitches with the barest of pauses, but she doesn't look back. "Thank you. I'll see you next time."

"Right."

I salute the door as it closes in her wake; then kick her chair, sending it flying across the front of the room.

One step forward. Two steps back.

It's the story of my fucking life.

# Fifteen

## Harry

In my office, I drop everything on the desk and sag into my swivel chair. Sugar lays her head on my knee, looking up at me with worried brown eyes. She has the most expressive face. Sometimes I feel talking to her is like communicating with a particularly empathic human. "I know, baby. That was bad."

I lower my head to my desk, the wood surface cool against my forehead. I'm having trouble processing what just took place. I've never been so embarrassed, so humiliated. Felt so violated.

But I can't dwell on those aspects. I have to pull myself together. Acknowledge, move on…isn't that what Owen's football coach used to tell him when he made a shitty pass?

It seemed like such a simple concept when he explained it to me as a teenager struggling with weight and self-esteem issues. It's so much more difficult in practice, though, than in theory. To accept that the past isn't going to change—that it's not up for a re-do—and move forward from that place of weakness or inadequacy… that's always been my battle.

I want to move forward from a place of perfection, and somehow, attain even greater perfection.

The illogic of that isn't something I can defend, even to myself. Lifting my head, I pick up my phone and call Jack.

He arrives within twenty minutes.

"Let me see it." Without preamble, he takes the second chair at my desk and pulls the laptop to him.

When he opens the computer, it prompts for a password, and he eyes me over the top of the screen. "I take it the computer has always been password-protected?"

"Definitely." Rising from my own chair, I circle the desk and enter the passcode, then gesture to the bottom of the screen, where the slide show has been minimized. "It's that one."

I sit back down while he clicks through the document. I don't want or need to see it again, or even know what's present in the slides I didn't look at. I watch Jack's face, instead, seeing through his carefully neutral mask to the little micro-expressions that reveal his emotions.

Jack is angry.

Fury is evident in the flare of his nostrils and the slight pinch of the muscles around his eyes. It warms me, makes me feel so not alone.

After just a few minutes, Jack closes the computer and exhales heavily through his nose. "Any ideas who might have done this?"

"Wyatt—that's my TA—and I were talking about that," I say, picking a pencil up from the desk to give my hands something to do. "My computer was locked in my office after I worked on this yesterday. There's only one person, other than my department head and maintenance, who has a key."

Jack lifts an eyebrow. "And who is that?"

"Marcus." I tap the pencil on the desk a few times, then let it fall. "He was on campus yesterday. He came to…I don't know. Yell at me? Threaten me? He wasn't happy about me pressing charges."

"Gotcha." He sits back in his chair and temples his fingers in front of his mouth. "Okay, this is what we're going to do. You're going to say nothing about this to anyone. I'm sure people will find out about it because you had…what? A hundred kids see it?"

"Something like that."

"Right. But we're going to attempt to keep it on the down low anyway. I'm going to take your computer in for analysis. We have people that can look at a lot of different things that I'm clueless about and come up with a profile of sorts."

"A profile?"

"Yes. A profile that will help us identify and prosecute the individual who did this."

"Okay, that sounds good." I hand him my laptop sleeve and after placing the computer inside a plastic evidence bag and scrawling the passcode on a sticky note, he slides the laptop into it. "When will I get it back?"

"I can't say. I'll keep you posted on the progress, though." Jack stands and I do, as well. Extending a hand, he takes one of mine in his warm grip, fingers stroking lightly over my knuckles. "And in the meantime, why don't you come over tonight or tomorrow and take a look at the house? Might get your mind off things."

"I'll see if Owen can drive me." Jack frowns and I roll my eyes. "I can't drive right now...not until I've been seizure free for six months."

He lifts his chin in apprehension and doesn't release my hand. "Oh, right. Just give me a call if it works out. I'll turn the heat on." He shifts his weight from one foot to the other. "I hate that this is happening to you, Harry. I promise I'm going to do everything I can to fix it."

I nod, not trusting myself to speak.

With a single quick squeeze of his hand, he releases me and walks away.

Whether I want him to or not, Jack is turning playing hero into a routine thing where I'm concerned.

The house is straight out of a dream. Old and a bit creaky in places, with painted radiators, wide wooden windowsills one can perch in, and heart pine floors that Jack says are every bit of a hundred years old.

"The closets are kind of small," Jack says, lips twisted in a doubtful scowl as he opens the door to one. I peek in behind him.

"It's fine. There are plenty of them, after all, and it's just me living here. I can put winter clothes in one room, summer clothes in another." I nudge the dog. "What do you think, Sugar? Do you approve?" She pants softly, unconcerned.

"True." We move to the upstairs bathroom, shared by several small bedrooms. He flicks the knob on the sink. "Fixtures could use some updating."

I smile and keep moving to the rooms on the other side of the hall.

Ideas begin to bloom as I look around. I can use one as an office—maybe the one overlooking the back garden. This one could be Ava's room for when she visits, and the one next to it a guest room. The morning sun would be lovely through a set of sheers, and maybe... "Would it be okay, do you think, if I painted? Nothing crazy, of course."

"Oh, sure. If you tell me the colors, I'll take care of it."

I pause and frown over my shoulder at him. "Jack. I'm not helpless. I can paint."

His eyes are calm as he looks around the room, but there's something there...a flicker of disquiet. "I'm not saying you can't do it. As your landlord, though, I should do it, and—"

"My landlord?"

"I didn't mention that?" He inspects a window sashing.

"No, Jack. You said you lived in the neighborhood." His generosity takes on new meaning and I can't help but wonder where, exactly, he lives. What he expects. God, have I been a complete fool, thinking he's been such a good friend, that I could trust him entirely? When am I going to learn...?

I worry my lower lip, wrapping my arms around my torso. "This changes things."

"How so?" Jack faces me. "You need a place. I have one. What's the problem, Harry?"

"The problem is, this doesn't feel right! It doesn't feel like landlord and lessee...it feels like..." I pull at my hair, agitated.

"More," he finishes.

"Maybe? I don't know. Things are really confusing right now, Jack. I'm not sure I'm ready for more."

He stands across the room, but I can feel the weight of his hands on me, the comfort of a hug as he theoretically draws me in. He smiles, a small, crooked smile that tugs at the corner of his mouth. It reminds me of a long-ago day on a bus, and I feel myself settling. I'm being paranoid. "It's just a house, Harry."

"Just a house," I mutter. "Here, have a couple hundred thou. No big deal."

"Well, I'm not giving it to you. Not technically. And it really is a great neighborhood. Mostly older people, except for this one youngish teacher that lives cattycorner." He points in the vague direction.

"Right." Shoving my hands in the pockets of my jeans, I inhale deeply and puff it back out. "Okay."

Cocking his head to the side, Jack motions to the door. "C'mon. I have something that might help."

I follow him across a well-kept, traditionally southern backyard to a carriage house tucked away behind a row of tall holly bushes. A curious glance reveals hibernating azaleas, forsythia, and wisteria climbing an iron trellis atop a stone patio. My heart sighs wistfully. I bet it will be lovely in the summertime, all scented shade, a peaceful little hideaway.

At the carriage house, Jack opens a sliding door into a tastefully converted apartment. A German shepherd raises its head from where it's napping on the floor, and I realize right away this is Jack's home. I hover in the doorway, Sugar's leash held firmly, until Jack motions me in impatiently. "You're letting the heat out."

"Is it okay for Sugar to come in?"

"Absolutely. This is Kota. Retired K-9 and very well-behaved. Coffee?" Without waiting for an answer, he moves into the open kitchen and begins fiddling with a Keurig.

"Sure."

Kota comes to sniff, and I hold my hand out, palm up, then introduce him to Sugar. When both of their tails begin to wag, I relax a fraction. Sugar is very sociable, but I always worry about other dogs.

"Have a seat." He nods toward a leather couch that demarcates the living room from the kitchen and I sit, my gaze roving around the small space with unabashed curiosity. It's undeniably a bachelor's space, with framed Marvel comic posters and Atlanta Braves artwork decorating the space. A massive television dominates the room. A digital photo frame sits on an ottoman-style coffee table in front of me, and without thought I pick it up, interested to see who might take center stage in his life to warrant photos.

It's a woman. She's beautiful, ethereally so, with shoulder-length dark hair and almond-colored eyes. She's also pregnant.

"That's Rose."

Jack takes the frame from my hand and uses a finger to swipe to the next photo. "I'm sorry. I didn't mean—"

"That's what I was going to show you. Sit."

I follow suit as he sinks into the leather sofa, our weights naturally drawing us thigh to thigh in the soft cushions. "Oof...sorry," I mutter, pushing myself upright.

"Don't be. Anyway... Rose was my wife. We married straight out of college, well over a decade ago. Lived in that house." He shows me a photo of the brick colonial, dressed for Christmas. Rose is mugging for the camera in front of the fireplace I admired earlier. She's dressed in a pair of plaid flannel pajamas, her pretty face bare of make-up, her hair a mess.

"She's so lovely."

"She was, yes." He clears his throat, sets the photo frame down.

"What happened, Jack? Why are you telling me this?"

"My house has been empty for the past eighteen months. Plus two weeks and two days, but who's counting, right?" His laugh is harsh and self-condemning. "She had metastatic breast cancer that went undetected until she was three months along. She refused treatment, wanted to carry the baby to term."

"Oh, my God...and the baby?" Gaze fixed on the floor, he shakes his head. "Jack, I'm so, so sorry."

"So, I'd really, really like it if you'd agree to move into my house, if you don't have any major issues with it. The house needs people, Harry. I know that sounds weird, but it's true. I can't live in it. Not now, anyway. There are too many memories. I stare out at it at night, and it's all dark and silent and still...it's like its heart is broken."

"But I..." I break off. I'm not even sure what it is I want to say. My own heart hurts for him, my old hero Jack and his broken-hearted house. His own broken heart, too. It pulses from behind his stone and water eyes with such raw grief—it makes my own hurt seem childish by comparison. "I don't know if I have what it takes to heal your house's broken heart, Jack," I finish softly. "I can't even mend my own, and it's nowhere near...I mean, my struggle is nothing compared to yours." Both of us know it's not just the house I'm talking about.

Jack clears his throat roughly. "We can't hold our pain up for comparison," he replies. "Pain is pain. My scale of seven might be your scale of three. Or someone else's scale of ten. So, it's just fucking pain, you know? We all hurt the same, so it's up to us to help each other feel better, however that happens."

"God, Jack..." I'm crying. When did I start crying? "Damn you."

Jack doesn't respond in words. He lifts me sideways onto his lap, instead, tucking me securely into the cradle of his arms. Then he tips my chin up, settles his mouth on mine, and kisses me.

I have just enough time to take a breath before his lips are there, slanting with surety and stealing away my ability to think. All I know is sensation. Where Wyatt was flash and thunder, taking what he was sure we both wanted,

Jack is all sweetness and temptation. Every stroke of his tongue at the seam of my mouth is a question, every brush of his beard against my skin a brusque tease.

His fingers cup the bones of my face, rough fingers wiping at the tears I can't help but weep for a woman I never knew, and this man's simple perspective on suffering. Not content to wipe them away, he trails kisses across each salty track, lingering on my eyes. Then his hands delve into the thickness of my hair, using it to direct my mouth back to his for another lingering kiss that has us both breathing hard.

At length I break away. "Jack... wait."

He lets me scramble off his lap and waits, that steady, infernal patience of his holding him motionless on the sofa while I pace a few feet away.

"I'm sorry," I manage. "I did not mean to lead you on. This just started moving super-fast, and—"

"Harry, it's okay. I didn't plan on doing that, especially not when I'm trying to get you to come rent my house."

"No, it's not okay! I kissed you just now, and I kissed someone else, just the other day. I don't know who I am anymore, Jack, I don't know—"

"Hey, hey, now..." Jack stands and takes hold of my upper arms, then pulls me into a tight hug. He begins to croon to me, something I can't really understand, but it doesn't matter. It's not the words that matter, if I recall the science of hugging correctly. It's the swaddling sensation, coupled with the tonal sensation of any humming or singing.

All I know is that I'm babbling, and he doesn't seem like he's mad, and this hug feels incredible, and without conscious thought, I shut up and allow myself to relax against him. We stand there for what feels like centuries, until Jack's vague crooning becomes distinguishable words. "You're okay, baby."

*I'm about to go to sleep*, I think. Rip Van Winkle kind of stuff. I let my head fall back on my shoulders and look him in the eye. "Will you come over and do that if I'm having a bad night and can't find my melatonin?"

I feel the rumble of a chuckle in his chest, and he nods. "Sure. Does this mean you'll be my renter and heal my broken house?"

I offer him a hand for a shake. "It does. As long as you're okay with me kissing who I want until I decide who I want."

He takes my hand in his but doesn't shake it. Instead, his thumb trails lazy circles around the flesh of my knuckles, making me feel even that simplest of touches. His eyes crinkle at the corners, gauging my reaction. "I can deal with that. As long as you make me one of the recipients of those kisses." He leans forward, brushes a bit of hair off my cheek, and kisses me one last time, briefly and sweet. "You take your time, Harry... I'm not going anywhere."

# Sixteen

**Harry**

I MOVE INTO JACK'S house two weeks after he walked me through it. It's a good time—we've finished up for winter break, Christmas is right around the corner, and I'm more than ready to get out of my current house. An army is present to help, including Wyatt, Jack, my parents, Owen, and a moving company, and it's no time before my new home is filled with boxes, haphazardly placed furniture, and people.

Momma stops unpacking a kitchen box to blow a pouf of graying hair from her forehead and regard me with something less than affection. "I wish you'd given me more warning. Everything is so disorganized!"

"Sorry, Momma. The buyer made an offer on mine with the stipulation that I be out before Christmas. I had to get moving." I look around at the chaos that surrounds me. "I didn't really expect to get it done this fast, though."

She looks at me from beneath her brows. "You know you didn't have to move."

I kiss her cheek and walk past her, into the living room. We had already spent a full day discussing why I wouldn't draw on my trust fund and simply purchase the house outright, so I wouldn't have a mortgage. I love her, but this is not an argument I want to repeat. "No," I say simply. "I really did. It wasn't home." Her *hmpf* follows me.

The day is spent moving boxes into their appropriate rooms and putting the big furniture pieces in a rough approximation of where they should be. I'll fine tune things as I settle in, take my time making this into a cozy retreat that offers comfort and peace.

Later in the evening my family leaves and Wyatt picks up his coat and follows them to the door. "I need to head out, too," he says, but hovers in the doorway, his eyes narrowing on where Jack has just flung himself down on the couch with a weary-sounding sigh. "You want me to stay?" he asks.

"No. I appreciate you coming to help," I say, leaning on the edge of the door. "I wasn't expecting you to be here."

"You and the cop have something going on?" He asks in a low voice, not commenting on the tension that still exists between us.

*Damnit.* With a sigh, I step over the threshold and pull the door closed behind me. "We are not dating, if that's what you're asking," I reply, crossing my arms over my chest.

"But you're something."

"No! I just mean…we—you and I—we're not dating, Wyatt. We're not involved. I told you, that kiss—"

"Never happened. I got the memo," he says, and looks out over the lawn. For what feels like forever, we're silent, captive of a tense standoff where neither of us know quite what to say. Then he speaks. "Just for the record, Harry…we may not be dating or involved—" He makes air quotes. "—while you wrap your head around stuff, but we're not nothing, either." He leans in close, and I swallow, my mouth suddenly gone dry. His breath coasts warm against my face when he continues. "We're *something*. You just aren't ready to hear it, yet."

"I…I have to go. Goodnight, Wyatt." I twist the doorknob behind me and open the door.

With a last pointed look, he leaves.

Sugar and Kota snooze in one of the few empty spaces in front of the fireplace, worn out from dodging movers and being super helpful all day. Jack looks back as I come in. "Everything okay?"

"Oh, yeah. He was just nervous about leaving me alone, I think. Would you like a cup of coffee?"

"That'd be great, thanks."

I bring Jack a cup of coffee and sit down opposite him on my sofa with my own mug, suddenly nervous now that we're alone.

It's because he kissed me and made it clear that he was going to pursue things if I left that door open. Now I'm conflicted. Do I let him in, or keep him at arm's length? I decide to keep things friendly for the moment.

"So, tell me, Jack—"

"I feel like we—"

We both start talking at the same time and share an awkward laugh. "You go first," Jack says.

"I was just wondering what you'd been up to since high school. You kind of fell off the map."

"That's because I went into the military straight out of high school. Marines. I did my time, came back, decided I wanted to become a cop, and that's what I did. I ended up getting lucky, if that's the right word?" He makes a face. "...when there was that bombing in Richmond. It propelled me up the ranks very fast."

"I remember that. The one at that outdoor festival thing. All those people killed, except for one teenage girl, if I recall correctly." I shake my head at the memory. It had been, hands down, the most terrible thing to ever happen in our state's history, an act of domestic terrorism committed by an unknown individual approximately fifteen years back.

"Right. I'll never take credit for saving her, but I found her in the wreckage."

"Oh, my God. That's…incredible, Jack."

He shrugs, his face broadcasting the horrors he witnessed. "I just happened to be in the right place at the right time. I often wonder whatever happened to her."

We're both quiet for a few minutes, lost in our thoughts. "And you got married somewhere in all of that. Did you know Rose in high school? Is that why…" I make a face. "I don't know why I brought that up. You can ignore that question."

"Why I didn't take you up on your offer?" Jack finishes, his voice mild. "Not at all. I met Rose around a decade ago, after I was working as a cop. We were in our late twenties when we married."

"Oh."

"Hey."

"Hey, yourself."

He grins at my tart response.

"I didn't take your virginity—" I groan, setting my coffee cup down and burying my face in my hands. It's a memory I'd rather forget, but Jack doesn't seem inclined to let me.

*"I can't believe I'm doing this." My hands are shaking, and I curl them tightly into the front pocket of my hoodie. Lilah, my best friend, giggles and shoves me forward, further into the shadows created by the row of evergreens at the base of Jack Brady's lawn.*

*"I'm so proud of you, bish. Tonight is your night, bro," she sing-songs.*

*"What if he laughs at me?"*

*Lilah smooths my hair around my shoulders. "Why would he do that? You're utterly adorable."*

*"Ugh." I start to walk away, back toward the street where Lilah's car is waiting. "I'm four years younger than him...he doesn't care about me. I'm not doing this."*

*She grabs my shoulders and turns me back to face the trees and the back of his house. "You sure as hell are. We did not get you all gussied up to wuss out." Her palm smacks smartly across my bottom, covered in a short, flippy skirt, and I yelp, jumping forward. "Now get your ass in there!"*

*Grimly, as though I'm walking toward my execution rather than a hot night with a hot guy, I start walking forward. Behind me, Lilah waits for a minute to make sure I'm going to follow through, and then her receding footsteps tell me she's returning to her car.*

*Leaving me here.*

*At the edge of the evergreens, I take a minute to check my pockets. Condoms...check. Chapstick...check. Cell phone...check.*

*I take a deep breath, and then begin to cross the yard to the ground-floor window I know belongs to Jack's bedroom. It's two A.M., so he has to be home...probably sound asleep by now. All I need to do, according to Lilah, is get into his room and slip (naked, of course) into his bed. He won't be able to resist.*

*At the window, I shake out my still-trembling hands, and then place them on the sash and push up. With an agonizing* screeee *of sound, the window moves.*

"Shit!" *I jump back from the stupid-loud window as a light flicks to life inside. Turning, I take a step away, then stutter step back...should I run? Gah!*

"Harry Bee?" *Jack's outline fills the window, and he pushes it the rest of the way up.* "What the hell are you doing here? Is everything all right?" *His gaze roves behind me, searching for whatever imagined danger brought me to his home in the middle of the night.*

*I can't process thought quickly enough to respond, and stand, staring dumbly at the expanse of naked boy torso on display for me. Naked* man *torso, I correct myself. Because Jack Brady is a man, and he is delicious. Ripped. I—*

"Harry?"

"Um. Hi, Jack."

What now?

"What are you doing here?"

Oh, nothing much. Just came over to see if you'd be willing to take my pesky v-card and fuck my brains out.

"Excuse me?"

Oh, fucking ABCDEFG. *I just said that out-fucking-loud. I am such an idiot.* "I mean..." *I bite my lip, decide to grab life by the balls, as Lilah would say.* "Yeah. That's what I meant. I want to have sex, and you seem like a good candidate." *I look at him from beneath my lashes, doing my best to channel raunchy sex goddess.*

*It doesn't work. Instead, Jack laughs. Hand to stomach, belly-clenching kind of laughter. It's my worst nightmare, come true, the one thing I was most afraid would happen.*

*Turning, I walk back the way I came.*

*"Harry, wait!"*

*I ignore him and keep walking. It's a long walk home, but no matter. Thankfully, school is out, and I'll never, ever have to see him again.*

"Oh, my God, stop!" I slap my palms over my eyes. I can't look at him and remember that humiliating night.

"No…the elephant is standing here in the room, and we might as well get rid of it." Gently but insistently, he peels my hands from my face. "I didn't sleep with you because you were a child, Harry. You were fifteen years old, and I was a man, about to go into the military. It would have been wrong on so many levels. I thought of you as my little sister."

"That's even worse."

"Well, I definitely don't think of you like my little sister now."

"Fabulous." I eye him from beneath hooded lids. He's so earnest, so intent on making the past right. But… "You laughed at me, Jack. I can't help thinking that if we were meant to be or whatever, you wouldn't have done that. Age wouldn't have made a difference."

Jack squints, the lines around his eyes crinkling. "First, I'm sorry I laughed. You were just so earnest. And second…I don't follow."

"Do you believe in soulmates?" I settle myself more comfortably in the corner of the sofa, pulling one of my legs beneath me and twisting so I'm facing him.

"Soulmates?" He runs a hand along his jawline. "I've never really thought about it, to be honest with you. I guess…if I had to make a decision…I think it's possible to have more than one over the course of a life. Same with a 'true love.' I don't think we're meant to love only one person in our lives."

I nod slowly and take another sip of my coffee. "I agree with that. I think souls recognize one another, though. Whether one is a child and the other is an adult, soulmates call to one another."

"Hmm. Do you think you have to be someone's soulmate in order to love them?"

"Not at all."

"Then I'm not clear on where this is going."

Smiling, I reach forward and pat his thigh, then sit back. "Poor, practical Jack. So uncomfortable with all this talk of love and destiny. I'm not going anywhere in particular with it. I just think it's an interesting discussion."

"Okay, I'll grant you that."

"But here's the thing. For me…I don't plan on settling for less than a soulmate next time. Life's too short. Too unexpected. Next time—if there is a next time—I want it all."

Jack doesn't reply in words. Instead, he sets his cup down and slides along the length of the couch until our knees are touching; then takes my own coffee and sets it on a nearby box. His gaze locked on mine, he takes my face in his hands and cups my cheeks and jaw, his thumbs brushing the contours of my cheeks before he moves them to the base of my skull. For a long moment, he simply touches me, exploring the line of my neck and spine and head in lazy caresses of his fingertips. I push the thought of Wyatt, standing close to me on my doorstep, away and roll my head forward in response. He reaches upward and tugs the rubber band from my hair, and it cascades in tangled skeins, draping itself around us like a shield when he leans his forehead against mine.

The kiss hangs between us, only breath separating us. But Jack is unmoving before me, a statue except for his fingers tunneling through my hair. "Are you going to kiss me?" I finally ask, the question a whisper.

He rolls his forehead against mine, then removes his hands and eases back, his gaze flitting around the room and resting for a second here, on the fireplace, and there, on the window overlooking the front yard. His eyes, when they return to mine, are haunted. "I was going to," he answers. "And then I remembered where I was. I—" He closes his eyes, takes a breath. "I can't."

I understand immediately. "It's okay. We'll just have to remember that for next time." I attempt a laugh to ease the tension. "You're just as haunted as your house, I guess."

He blinks a few times, then rubs his hands briskly over his face. "Fuck. I've gotta go." Without another word, he stands, clicks his tongue at Kota, and strides away. Seconds later I hear the back door opening. "Set the alarm behind me, Harry."

The door closes, and he's gone.

Tired all at once, I let Sugar out to use the bathroom and then head for bed. The mattresses lay on the floor, the bed frame not yet assembled. It's no matter. After a quick search, I find the box containing my linens and make the bed up, then give my face a quick splash with water in the small, attached bathroom. Through the open door, I see Sugar turning a circle at the foot of the bed.

Jack's face floats behind my eyelids as I lie down. He's such a good man. Quiet and steady and handsome and dependable. I like the way he looks at me, and the way he likes me, even if he's not quite ready to do so just yet. And yet, as sleep overtakes me, I'm plagued by a vague sense of guilt.

Why can't I like him the same, just a little bit more?

# Seventeen

## Jack

My eyes are gritty with the three hours of sleep I managed to steal last night. Well, this morning, really. After leaving Harry's house, I'd put Kota up and gone straight to work out the remainder of the night shift. There was no way I was sleeping after making such a fool of myself.

*Are you going to kiss me?*

I had a warm, sexy woman practically in my lap. One I liked and had a history with we could build on. And yet, all I could think as I sat there with my hands in her hair was that she wasn't Rose.

*Such a fucking sap.*

On shift, it had been one call after another in sleepy little Lucy Falls for some reason. Full moon, maybe. After a night involving one runaway nursing home citizen, a wannabe graffiti artiste, a skinny-dipping couple who got a little more than they bargained for with the frigid river temperatures, and an attempted robbery at the town's humble jewelry store, I got home around six and fell face first onto my bed. I was awakened hours later by Kota's vigorous tongue letting me know he needed to go outside.

Now I'm back at the station, yawning and waiting impatiently for the coffee maker to finish plinking its way, one miserly drop at a time, through its brew cycle. The break room is too bright with its yellow-white cabinetry and fluorescent track lights, one of which needs a new ballast, judging from the annoying buzz overhead. Leaning against the counter, I roll my mug between my palms and stare down the coffee machine, willing it to work faster. The first pot had been drained, so now I have to wait on a fresh brew.

I need caffeine.

There was a time when three hours wouldn't have made me blink. I'd have gone all night and been up with the birds. Shit, I'd have sung in the shower. Now I feel like I was tied to the bumper while my blind Aunt Bess drove to the station with Vaseline on her hands.

Fuck it. With equal parts skill and desperation, I pull the pot from beneath the drip and replace it hastily with my mug, letting it fill three-quarters of the way full before switching them again. I'm drinking it down and ignoring the burn as I turn to leave, almost running into Officer Katy.

"I totally saw that," she grumbles, stumbling toward the counter with her own mug. She looks as though she had her own rough evening, her normal neat boyish hairstyle standing up as though she forgot to smooth it.

I pause. "And?"

"And one hundred percent respect your ingenuity. Carry on." She pauses and gives me a curious look. "What are you doing here, anyway? Didn't you work last night—on your night off, I might add?"

"Yeah. I have reports to finish up."

"Damn."

Instead of heading toward my cubicle, I eye her closely. "Everything good?"

"Yep. Everything's fine."

I know from experience when a woman says everything's fine that everything is one hundred percent not fine, but there's not much I can do if she doesn't offer anything up. I linger for a second, until she sticks her tongue out at me and flicks me off.

I've finished my coffee and a follow-up traffic report from last night and am contemplating a return to the coffee pot when Katy appears around the corner, a steaming paper cup in hand. "Figured you could use another, as big a hurry you were in."

"Damn straight." I accept the offering with gratitude and motion her into the seat across from me. The coffee's not the only reason she's here. "What's up?"

"Call just came in. I thought you might be interested."

"Oh, yeah? Why is that?"

"Because it's from a woman who lives on your street."

I stand from my chair immediately. "Who?" I take a big gulp of the coffee and reach for my coat. "And what's the call?"

"Shiloh Brookings?"

I have to think for a second. "Teacher. Lives cattycorner from me."

"Yes. Jonas and I were out there a week or so ago...she was freaked out over some call. Jonas was pretty dismissive, but I think there's something there. The call today is over some devices Twiggy Gentry was able to find in her house."

Some of my urgency ratchets down a notch at hearing that it's not precisely an emergency, but I'm concerned, all the same. "Twiggy Gentry, huh? I don't like hearing that stuff's been happening on my street and I'm just now finding out about it."

"I know. Jonas really thought it was nothing. Over-active imagination, maybe. But I'm not convinced."

"All right, well, let's go."

Katy grins. "I figured you'd say that. The techs are already en route."

Shiloh Brookings' house is an older, well-preserved Craftsman. The yard is neatly kept, with shrubbery and stone lining the porch and walkway. As we park and climb out of the car, a young woman opens the door to let us in.

"I knew there was more to this," Katy starts, sending an apologetic grimace her way. "Apologies for my associate the other day."

"Thank you." She stands to the side to let us in, and I hold my hand out.

"Ma'am. I'm Detective Brady. I understand we're neighbors."

"Oh? That could be handy." She offers me a shy smile and gestures to the living room. "Please have a seat."

I sit on the couch, while Katy makes a beeline for a spread of electronics on a coffee table, speaking in a low voice to Twiggy Gentry. I give her a nod in greeting and she tips her chin my way.

Twiggy is a fascinating creature. Tiny, young—not even out of her teens, I don't think—and a genius, especially when it comes to anything electronic or internet-related. She could be an incredible asset, even with her youth, to law enforcement, but her family is tangled up with the Irish mob. Despite her criminal connections, we've used Twiggy—under the radar, of course—for a job or two that required a sophisticated skillset. She's working on Harry's computer issue at the moment, along with Shiloh Brookings' problem, it appears.

Pulling out my notepad and pressing the record function on my phone, I eye Shiloh with as much encouragement as I can muster.

"Just start at the beginning," I tell her.

Shiloh fidgets from her seat in the armchair across from me. "Are you sure I need to repeat all of this? Officer Katy should have a record."

"I'm sorry, but yes. I'll be working with Katy on this, but I prefer to get my own picture of events. And I'm sorry they weren't able to give you more help when you called before. I am a detective with the department, though, and have access to more resources to dive into this further than the beat officers do. We'll do our best to find this guy. Now, tell me what happened. Try not to leave anything out."

Shiloh closes her eyes briefly and then focuses on her lap. "Okay. The first thing that happened was the phone call. I was baking cinnamon rolls, the phone rang, and it was an unknown number. I answered, and the caller spoke as if he were there, in my house.

"How so?"

"He said those cinnamon rolls sure smelled good and asked me to save him one."

"And I take it this wasn't a normal, routine activity that any Joe Schmo would have known about?"

"Not at all. I like to bake, but it's something different all the time. And his voice was mechanically disguised."

"Keep going."

"That's when your officers came. They did a walk through but didn't see anything to worry them. The man—"

"Jonas."

"Yes. He thought it was a prank."

"But obviously more has happened that makes you believe otherwise?"

"Well, yeah. Even if that wasn't enough—which it is, for me—the other night at work something happened." She stops, her cheeks turning a brilliant red beneath their light sprinkling of freckles. She looks a lot like Harry, now that I think about it. Both have red hair, although Shiloh's is sleek and an almost russet tone. Harry's is bright—carroty, she used to call it—and curly. "I work at Kendrick's," she says in a whisper. "And I didn't call right away because I was worried about my teaching position—"

"It's okay, Miss Brookings." I reach across and pat her shoulder awkwardly, my pen still caught between my fingers. "What you do in your time off is your own business—although it may certainly have something to do with what's going on. Stripping is considered a high-risk profession. You're more likely to come in contact with individuals who target you because of your vulnerability."

Shiloh pinches the bridge of her nose, shoving her glasses down a smidge. "I wouldn't be doing it if I had any other choice. Believe me. And I prefer 'dancing.'"

"Not my business, ma'am."

She pulls in a deep breath and releases it. I wait patiently, seeing her nerves for what they are—fear. Finally, she goes on. "I was dancing a peep."

"That's when you're in the enclosure and you have a single viewer?"

"Yes."

I nod for her to continue.

"The client was a little pushier than usual. He asked me to tell him that I loved him, and when I refused, he dropped this through the tip slot." Reaching in her pocket, she pulls out a handmade string of colorful beads. I take it and turn it over in my palm, studying it. The center bead is white with a black S.

"S for Shiloh, I assume?"

"My younger brother made this for me years ago. It's...precious to me. He was in a car accident around two years ago, one in which our mother died, and he suffered terrible injuries. He's still recuperating."

Out of the corner of my eye, I watch as Twiggy leads Katy deeper into the house, murmuring something about showing her where the pile of listening devices and such had been located. I watch them go, pondering Shiloh's statement.

I remember the accident she's referring to. It was big news at the time—a truck driver taking a quick peek at a text message cost this girl her mother and put her brother in a hospital. "I'm sorry for your loss, Ms. Brookings."

"I had the bracelet hanging from my rearview mirror since Sammy gave it to me. This client, whoever he is, broke into my car and stole it."

"And then returned it to you to mess with you."

She nods. "And then, because it didn't seem like the police were going to do anything, I got Twiggy to come and take a look at everything. See if she could figure out how the man on the phone had known what I was doing. She found all of that stuff." She gestures toward the group of electronics, then turns back to me with a challenging look. "Do you believe me now?"

Flipping my notepad closed, I stand up and pocket it. "One hundred percent. Shiloh, I want you to know, we will be doing everything within our power to figure out who this guy is. And I live right over there..." I point out the window. "Anything feels off, you get scared, whatever...I want you to come to me. I'll be keeping an eye on things, too."

Her lips tremble but she firms them and nods a few times, blinking rapidly. "Thank you. Is that...it? Are we finished?"

She looks like she's on the brink of a meltdown. "Yes. Why don't you sit back and relax while we finish our walk-through?" She sinks down to the couch, pulling a knapsack over to her and tugging some thread and stuff from it. Knitting? My grandmother used to do that. "Just trust us to help, okay?"

Without answering, she gives another faint nod. I guess I can't blame her for being a bit gun shy when it comes to trusting cops, not after Jonas' shitty job.

But I'm not Jonas, and when I tell a woman I'll protect her, I mean it.

I leave to find Katy, determined to get all the information I can to find this creep.

---

The day goes straight to the shitter from that point on.

As soon as we get back to the station and I settle back into my desk to do paperwork, Katy comes to find me again.

"Call just came in," she says, echoing her earlier words.

"Another one?" I swivel in my chair to look at her.

Her expression... the hair stands at attention on the back of my neck. Normally goofy and amiable, Katy looks troubled and more serious than I've ever seen her. Whatever call she caught wind of—it's big.

"Mm-hmm," she says, watching me closely. "Suicide off the old railway bridge."

"Suicide?" My heart sinks. Suicides are messy and heartrending. The notifications, searching for a potential last message, motivation, ruling out foul play... they're terrible. I definitely don't want to deal with one when I ought to be sleeping, and sleep is long overdue. "I appreciate the thought, Katy, but I really don't want to deal with—"

"No, trust me, you'll want this one." Her eyes, an intense dark blue, continue to bore into mine. She's trying to say something without coming out and saying it. "Tied to one of your other cases. White male. Approximate age early forties. Dark hair."

I lean back in my chair, my gaze flitting to the mess on my desk. "No positive i.d.?"

"A potential, based on the driver's license in the vehicle. They're waiting on an i.d. from the wife in a few hours after the medical examiner gets him ready. Get this. He set himself on fire, Jack."

I rock forward in my chair, releasing a low whistle. "Why the fuck would you do that if you were taking a sail off the bridge anyway?"

Katy gives me a smug smile. "Exactly. There are things here that don't make sense, Jack."

"And we don't like that, do we." It's not a question. "Who has the case?"

"Dave Fisher. But I feel certain he wouldn't care if chief gave it to us. He's so close to retirement and this feels like a doozy."

I stand, grab my coat from the hook where I'd slung it just a few minutes earlier. "I agree. I'll go talk to chief now."

Katy's mouth thins with satisfaction. "I knew you would." She stands, too, tilts her head to the side. "You banging her yet?"

I stop, one arm half in, half out of my coat, and stare, frowning. She shrugs, her olive-toned cheeks with just a hint of winter's pallor reddening. "The scorned wife, I mean. Ex-wife?"

I continue to stare.

"Unwife?"

Shoving my arm through its sleeve, I shove my cell and keys into my pocket and walk past her.

"Damn, dude. Why so touchy? Forget I asked!"

Fucking Katy. She should know better than that. I stew the entire brief distance to the chief's office, unclear why her comment bothers me so much. We tease each other all the time here in the station — the single ones, at least. We give each other hell with raunchy humor and locker room jokes. God help you if you take someone new out on a date and a fellow cop sees you, or you get laid and someone finds out about it. You're liable to come to work and find your cubicle decked out in condoms and lube.

Everyone knows, though, that you don't make fun of anything involving the wives. Or the husbands, if the cop is a woman. That shit is sacrosanct. They're our backbone. Our sanity. Our glue.

The thought stops me fucking cold outside Chief's office. I stand, breathing hard, staring at the brass nameplate on the frosted glass of the door. That's not how I'm thinking of Harry, not even subconsciously.

I shake my head, just a little, to clear the thought. It's foreign. Wrong. That's what Rose had been for me—my glue. The thing that held me together. And goddamn, if

I don't hate being alone, but fuck if I'm going to replace the best thing that ever happened to me with just anyone.

Harry... she's amazing, but she doesn't seem to have a clue what she wants—not that she should. It's only been a blip since she found out about Marcus. She needs time.

Apparently, so do I.

It doesn't help my patience level any to know this.

I give myself another ten seconds to chill the sweat that's broken out cold across my skin and then knock on the door.

"Enter."

Ten minutes later, the chief agrees to put me on the case. The contents of the wallet point to the jumper being Marcus Lane; thus, there's potential for intersection with my current case. She also sees the guy setting himself on fire prior to the jump as suspect.

I have to move quickly.

The medical examiner has already removed the body from the scene and taken it to the morgue. It is slated for next of kin identification in two hours, so I visit the bridge first to get a feel for the scene.

The spot where a death took place is always notable. There's a miasma that hangs over everything, a kind of gloom that the casual passerby might dismiss as mere cloud cover or a weak sun. But it's more. It's the pall of death, whether it occurs with the blessing of old age and a willing spirit or be it unnatural and painfully fought with every step.

This death was not an easy one.

Marcus Lane's vehicle, a black Navigator, is parked in the gravel on the side of the road, just before the entrance of the sidewalk that lines either side of the railway bridge. The bridge has been closed to automobile traffic for years, and Lane's suicide occurred before dawn, so the scene was thankfully pristine when an early morning jogger stumbled across the grim tableau.

There are scuff marks leading from the Navigator to the bridge railing, already marked for evidence. I study them closely, trying to fit them into a story that makes sense. They could be that of a man dragging his feet on his way to his own self-execution, but I'm skeptical.

The scuffs are deeper, longer...they look like something was dragged through the gravel.

I continue to the bridge, using the various evidence markers to tally Lane's last moments. Nothing stands out. In many—most—suicides, there are signs that the individual wrestled with him or herself. Pacing. The mark of sweaty fingerprints in multiple locations. This scene is straightforward, cut, dried.

Almost too straightforward.

There...the swash of oily black marring the wood...that's where he climbed the security rail, stood on the wood trestle, and lit himself on fire before dropping to the river below. The question raises its head again. Why the hell would a person set himself on fire before jumping into a river? Was he worried the drop wouldn't kill him? That he'd somehow survive the fall? I stand, my gaze riveted by the incongruency of the peacefully rushing river and the lab techs milling around like ants, busily searching for whatever evidence they could scout out.

He would have screamed. He wouldn't have been able to help himself. Fire isn't a merciful death, regardless of whether or not it was chosen. I look around, searching for nearby houses or businesses whose inhabitants might have heard him. There. Through the trees.

At the glimpse of pale siding, I beckon to a youngish deputy.

"Sir?"

"See that structure?" I point.

"Yessir."

"I want you to canvas that neighborhood. Interview the inhabitants of the houses, particularly this side of the street, and see if anyone heard anything early this morning...a man screaming, that sort of thing. He would have screamed."

Comprehension clears the confusion on his face and he nods. "Yessir. Will do, sir."

"Report on my desk."

With another nod, he leaves.

I comb through the collected evidence for a while longer, and then leave, satisfied I have a complete picture of this morning's events. Complete enough, anyway, for an interview with Mrs. Marcus Lane.

The morgue is, conveniently enough, attached to the station in a small red brick building that was once used as a dentistry. Inside, the odor of formaldehyde assaults my nostrils, an immediate and pungent irritation. I breathe through my mouth and repress a shiver. It's colder in here than it is outside, a necessity for the preservation of dead flesh.

"Daniels?"

Footsteps sound on the creaky wooden floors and the medical examiner appears, wiping his hands on a cloth. He's a slight man, balding, with wire-frame glasses hiding sharp, intelligent brown eyes. "Jack. Long time no see, man. Whatcha been up to?"

"Nothing good. Hear you have a body for me?"

"Yeah, come on back. The wife is on the way."

"Great." He returns the way he came, waving me along, and I follow.

Inside the examination room, a sheeted form laid upon a table grabs my attention. Daniels hands me a tub of Vicks and I rub a healthy bit beneath my nose to block the noxious scents of death, then turn on a recording app and speak into my phone.

"Preliminary morgue report for Marcus Lane, alleged suicide victim. Provided by Medical Examiner Frederick Daniels, December 11, 2021, 11:58 A.M."

I give a brief nod and Daniels folds the sheet back and begins to speak.

"Male, approximate age forty-two. Time and cause of death to be determined definitively, but appears to be 4:45 A.M. Burns along the right periphery..."

I listen with half my attention. I'll go back later and listen to the recording, notate the key points. Right now, I'm riveted by the horror of the body before me on the stainless-steel table.

As much as I don't personally care for the woman, I can't imagine putting Gina Lane near this monstrosity and asking her to produce a positive or negative identification. The skin—what's left of it—maps a confusing topography: some parts black char, other parts shiny and stretched, like the flames had only just begun to lick and lash before water snuffed them out. The body tells a grim tale, every pained twist and contorted tendon exposing the agony it suffered on the bridge before it plummeted into the waters of the river, sending steam billowing into the December air.

What it doesn't convey, as far as I can see, is identity. I can no more make out Marcus Lane in the twisted mass of burned, bloody flesh and bone before me than if he were to open his eyes and proclaim his name. All the maybe forty-two-year-old male form before me is, is death. Pitiful, painful, death.

"How tall was he?" I interrupt the medical examiner when the question occurs to me.

"Ah…" Daniels fumbles. "I haven't gotten that far yet. You can see the fire twisted his form and shrank his tendons, making it difficult to do a quick, accurate measurement. It'll take me some time." I nod, but he continues. "It's not quite as bad as, say, a house fire, because in lighting himself on fire and then jumping, he extinguished the flames fairly rapidly and his soft tissues were not as exposed for as long a period of time. There's not the same amount of extensive damage. It's why we can hope for a positive identification from his wife."

"Are there any identifying marks left? Obviously, he doesn't have hair anymore, but… eye color? Anything like that?"

"Well… we'll look at things like that. Dentals. We'd look at fingerprints, but he doesn't appear to have any."

"No fingerprints?"

Daniels glances up at me, expression bland. "No. They were burned off—I'm uncertain whether chemically or by the fire, but I would think we'd at least get a partial if by the fire."

I rub my jawline. "That's odd."

He raises his chin. "Quite."

"And you can't tell when that would've occurred?"

"Not yet."

In the main room, the door opens and closes, and heeled feet strike the aged hardwood like knives. "Hello? Damnit, why isn't anyone ever around in these places?"

"That'll be the lovely Mrs. Lane," I murmur.

Daniels recovers the body and peels off his gloves with a grunt. "Mm. Be right back. Don't touch anything."

When he returns, it's with Gina by his side. She's less irritable now, tears already tracking down each carefully made-up cheek. "Miz Lane," I drawl.

She stops in the doorway. "Detective Brady. I wasn't expecting to see you here."

"I'm sorry for your loss, ma'am."

Lifting her chin a fraction, she walks further into the room. "Thank you. It was a shock. I'm hoping this is just a big mistake, somehow."

She's a good liar, I'll give her that. Everything in me says that Marcus and Gina are so full of lies they don't know what truth is, anymore. But I play along. My tone oozes sympathy when I reply. "I surely hope so, ma'am." Placing a hand on her shoulder, I lead her to the examination table. "Whenever you're ready."

She inhales, releases it. "I'm ready."

Daniels pulls the drape down to waist level.

The breath she draws in this time is genuine. "Oh, my God."

"Take all the time you need."

She studies the body in silence for a while, tears streaking silently down her face. "I'm just not sure. Everything is so...wait. His hands. Can I see his hands?"

Daniels pulls his hands from beneath the sheet. On one hand is a detail, nearly buried in a fold of flesh, that I hadn't noticed. The gleam of gold, faint but unmistakable. When she sees it, Gina Lane begins to sob in earnest, great, gulping, loud cries of grief.

"It's him," she says. "Oh, my God, it's really him. He's dead."

# Eighteen

## Harry

For the first time in what feels like a small slice of eternity, it feels like a good day. It's cold, but sunny, and as I make my way to my lab on campus there's an extra boost in my step. I'm moving forward. Making progress. Moving into Jack's house was the right thing to do. Now, instead of memories and questions haunting every step I take, there's possibility around every corner, opportunity waiting with each new room I make my own.

Even if sadness lingers for Jack, happiness breathes there for me.

A new house gives me the chance to adjust to life without Marcus. I've never really been on my own. Never had the ability to worry solely about myself instead of another person. It's different. Freeing. I can eat a bowl of cereal for supper if that's what I feel like, and not be concerned that it's not good enough. I can leave the TV on all night and roll up like a burrito in the bedcovers without stealing them from someone. I can nap and work and visit my family at weird times and not fear messing up another person's schedule.

Now, with winter break nearly over, I'm ready to be back at work with a clean slate. It's a fresh semester, ripe with new possibilities.

Today I have lab work to get through before class starts in a few days. When I open the door, the first thing I see is Wyatt, sitting at a computer. He looks up, his eyes unfocused from whatever he's doing, and gives me a wave. "Hey. I got everything set up and ready to go for you."

"You're amazing. Thank you, Wyatt." I set my stuff down on an empty table, pull Sugar's dog bed from beneath my desk, and walk over to where he's set up all of the equipment needed. I want to work through an experiment that I'll have my classes do and iron out any bugs before setting them loose on it. "Everything looks perfect."

Picking up the instruction document I had Wyatt work on for me, I begin working through the experiment one step at a time, precisely as directed. Sugar snoozes beside me and the lab is almost eerily quiet as I do. Wyatt has a pair of ear buds in and is watching something play out on the computer screen. The corridors and surrounding classrooms are empty of humans and the silence is loud. It almost makes it harder to concentrate.

When I get to the lab's conclusion, I peel off the gloves I'm wearing to protect my hands and walk over to where Wyatt is sitting. Engrossed in what he's watching, which appears to be a ball game, he doesn't notice my approach and almost falls off the stool when I speak close to his ear. "Whatcha watching?"

"Damn, you're a fucking ninja. Wear a bell."

"Well, you are wearing ear buds. What's so fascinating?"

"I'm studying my pitch. Replays of last year's games, dissecting everything to see what I can do to improve."

"Oh." I turn my attention to the screen and watch as Baseball Wyatt gets ready to throw the ball. The camera zooms in on his face, revealing an intent, almost grim expression. He holds his glove close to his chest, his eyes focused on the hitter and his catcher, and gives a barely discernible shake of his head. "Are you and the catcher communicating with each other?" I ask.

"Yeah. He gives me signals for the pitch he wants, and I can either follow through or choose something different."

"How many different pitches are there?"

He turns to look at me. "How many different pitchers are there?"

"Got it. So...you're really serious about this baseball thing, aren't you?"

The side of his lips kick up in a grin. "My agent would say yes."

"You have an agent?"

"Yeah. He's looking into different opportunities, trying to find the best one to go after."

"You have so much to offer the science community, though. Both academic and commercial."

"You sound like my mother. She doesn't understand why I want to play a sport when I could be an academic. The science community doesn't pay in the millions per year like baseball does. I mean...that wouldn't happen straightaway. I'll probably end up on a minor league team, and they don't pay squat. I got the degree so I'd have something to fall back on if I needed it. So I'd have a marketable skill if baseball didn't work out. But I need to earn a good living."

I nod. "I understand that." For a few minutes longer, we both watch the screen. Wyatt jots something down a note on a legal pad sitting beside the keyboard. "What's the next step?"

He presses pause and swivels the stool around so he's facing me. We're so close I'm virtually within the vee formed by the spread of his thighs, and warning bells begin to chime. "You mean in baseball?" His voice is lower than it was. Husky.

I lick my bottom lip and take a half-step back, nervous all of a sudden. "Yes. Of course, baseball."

"Because I was kind of thinking I might have a next step right now." He eyes me with the same single-minded intensity he was just watching his tape, and it makes something flutter low in my belly.

"Huh?" I say dumbly.

"I want to kiss you, Harry Bee."

"B-but—"

"No buts, Red. You want this as much as I do." Placing his hands on my waist, he draws me slowly back into the circle of his body. "No more lies." Eyes locked on mine, he loops his hands together behind me, low at my tailbone, and I slowly raise my own to rest on his chest.

"No more lies…" I whisper, hypnotized by the dance of amber in his gaze.

"It's just a kiss…" he replies, and then his mouth descends, sealing to mine with a mind-numbing truth I can't ignore.

I want Wyatt Granger's kisses. Hard kisses, soft kisses, hungry kisses…I want them all.

The space between us detonates with my epiphany and I press closer to him, the room around us falling away to nothing. My heart misses a beat as his tongue sweeps out to taste me, and my hands, curling into his shirt and then climbing to grip his neck, cannot pull him close enough.

It feels like starving and satiety, all at once. Devouring and being devoured.

But then he's pushing me away, setting me a foot away from him and clearing his throat, and after a second of confusion I realize the door is opening.

We both look up to see Jack hovering on the threshold, another officer I don't recognize standing behind him. Jack's lips part, then he blinks and presses them firmly together. When he speaks, it's with a formality that distances us. "Dr. Bee? Sorry to interrupt, but may I have a moment of your time?"

"I—uh—yes, certainly. Wyatt, would you mind gathering that stuff...? The lab instructions were perfect, by the way. We'll be able to use them as-is next week."

"Great, and yes, of course."

Battling a sense of sudden doom, I follow Jack outside the classroom. "What's going on? Is it my family? Has something happened?"

"No...your family is fine. Harry, I don't know how to tell you this, so I'm just going to say it. We had a suicide call this morning. All signs point to it being Marcus Lane."

The corridor is an icebox. I don't understand why the hell maintenance can't keep it at a decent temperature. "Come again?"

Jack blinks. "Marcus killed himself, Harry."

I laugh. "You're joking."

"No... I'm sorry, Harry. I wish I was joking." His expression is sober. I search his face for the lie and find none.

"My God... Marcus..." The hallway spins and I reach out a hand to steady myself against the cold cinderblock wall.

"Are you okay?" Jack's voice is concerned but it's muted, as though it's coming from far away. "You want me to take you to your mother's?"

I shake my head. There's something…this is all wrong. "It doesn't feel right—" I manage, and then I'm slipping, sliding against the wall to the floor, Jack's hand clutched firmly around my elbow.

"Of course, it's not right, sweetheart." He squats down in front of me, stony eyes fixed steadily on me. "He was a relatively young man. He wasn't due to die yet. I guess he felt like he was just done? Or maybe there's some dark, ugly secret we'll all discover in a few days that he didn't want to face."

I cover my face with my hands. They're shaking. Damnit, I practically hated Marcus in recent days, but I can't help feeling terrible that he would do this to himself. "I can't do this."

"It's going to be okay, Harry. I need you to trust me. I—"

"What's going on?' The door opens and Wyatt steps out. His gaze sweeps over me, with Jack squatting in front of me, and a dull flush stains the high sweeps of his cheekbones. "Harry?"

"It's okay, Wyatt… I'm all right—"

"The hell you're okay. You're white as a sheet. What happened?"

"He said Marcus k-k-k—" I can't say the words and bury my face in my knees.

Jack continues for me. "Marcus Lane committed suicide this morning."

"Holy shit." I feel Wyatt's hand on the crown of my head, then air as he steps away. "I'll be right back."

"Jack, we need to leave." The second officer, the one I hadn't paid any attention to, picks this moment to assert his presence. "You gonna tell her about the note?"

"What note?" I lift my head. "Did Marcus leave a note?"

"Fuck it all, Dave." Jack shoots a disgusted glare in the direction of the other cop before looking back at me. "Yes. I'll bring it by later for you to look at, but right now it's part of the investigation—"

"Investigation?" I squint up at him. "For a suicide? Isn't everything pretty cut and dried?"

"I like to be thorough."

"I see. Of course."

"Anyway—I really do need to leave. I have work enough to last for a month and they have me running point on this. I'll check in with you later, but are you okay to get home and everything?"

"I...yes, of course." I wipe at my nose, at the small tickle there. "I'm so sorry. I'll be fine."

We both stand, Jack helping me to my feet. His hands linger on mine, squeezing gently. "I'm sorry, sweetheart. He was a bastard, but I know this isn't easy."

I nod without speaking, and then he's gone, striding down the hall alongside his partner with a single worried glance tossed over his shoulder.

I sink back to my haunches after Jack leaves, the strength leaving me in a rush of spent adrenaline. My hands are still shaking, I note, and curl them into fists in my pockets.

Marcus is dead.

I'm not sure what to feel. Should I cry? Because there are no tears. Not yet, anyway. If I cried right now, it would be for the young woman who stood opposite a handsome, charming son of a bitch in her family's church, stars in her gullible eyes, and pledged to give him every fragile piece of who she was until death itself separated them.

Well, here we are. And isn't it ironic?

The classic nineties tune starts a chorus in my consciousness, giving me a half-hearted longing for a cigarette, even though I've never smoked. I feel certain there's a No Smoking sign around here somewhere.

"What are you mumbling about? You want a cigarette?" Wyatt's in front of me suddenly, his face close to mine. Sugar waits obediently beside him, and my bag is looped over his chest by the strap. He pushes it out of the way as he reaches for my hands, cupping my fists in his palms and squeezing gently without comment before sliding them up to my biceps and pulling me easily to my feet. "Up you go." One arm goes around my shoulders.

"Think you'll be okay to walk out to the parking lot, or would you like a piggyback ride?"

His question almost makes me laugh; then I realize he's serious. "I'll be fine," I answer. "I'm not crippled." Then I realize he's walking me, leaving my lab behind. "Wait—we can't just leave—"

"We can and we are. You are officially on leave for the next two weeks. Everything's picked up and the lab is straight and locked, so don't drive yourself crazy over that."

My head is spinning. "You did all that...in there...while I was out here having a mental breakdown?"

He gives me a slanting smile as we exit the building and cross the dell toward the parking lot. "When are you going to realize... I'm kind of a badass."

"I guess so." I'm a little unnerved by how smoothly everything seems to have been handled. "So, there's nothing for me to do?"

Wyatt steers me to his vehicle, opening the passenger door for me and smoothly ushering Sugar into the backseat before he answers. He leans down in my open door, ostensibly to place my bag at my feet, but I don't know if that's actually what he does. My senses are too full of Wyatt. Wyatt's aftershave. Wyatt's eyes, like burnt sugar, only inches away from mine. His skin, perfect and winter pale but with an underlying olive tone that's at odds with the slight tilt to his eyes and dark, brownish-black hue of his hair. I've never been able to identify his nationality, but it doesn't matter. He's simply a handsome man.

I remain looking at him, feeling ridiculous, until he glances at me, then my mouth.

"Seatbelt." His voice is husky as he straightens and closes my door, then comes around to the driver's side and climbs in.

"Right." I buckle and look out the window as we pull away. With each passing mile, I feel the anger that's never too far from the surface making its presence known. Marcus is dead. I shouldn't be angry with him, still. His demons, whatever they were, won in the end. He succumbed to them, cut his own life short because he couldn't conquer them.

While that isn't cause for celebration, by any means, I shouldn't be feeling this incomprehensible fury. What am I even mad about? That I no longer have a target to direct my rage toward?

No. It's more than that.

All of this...our less than perfect union, my horrid discovery of his secret, the legal and criminal implications, his life cut short... all of it is such a fucking waste. If he'd just left me alone, stayed faithful to Gina...every disastrous turn of this story could have been avoided.

Things could have been so very different.

That's what makes me angry.

For some reason, I remember a visit to the doctor several years ago. We were both undergoing a battery of tests to find out why I wasn't conceiving. He sat beside me on a small sofa in the doctor's office, both of his hands gripping one of mine as the doctor informed us that I would very likely never be able to get pregnant.

It was a hormone issue, he said. I had abnormal levels of ovarian and pituitary hormones, and the incidence of women conceiving with it was approximately five percent.

Although later it would all go to hell, that day Marcus held me while I cried. Later, in moments where he wanted to hurt me, or make me feel less, it would be "my fault." My failure as a woman. That day, though, he was patient, and tender.

Some miles later amidst the blur of scenery, I hear Wyatt's voice.

"Harry?"

"Hmm?"

"You don't have to hide. It's perfectly normal to cry, let it all out. He was terrible but he was, for all intents and purposes, your husband."

"No, I –" I stop, surprised. My voice is thick and wet, the glass before me fogged with the breath of the tears I hadn't realized were streaming silently down my cheeks. I wipe at them and straighten resolutely in my seat. "I'm fine."

"Harry." He brakes and turns, the car yielding smoothing to his control of the wheel, and my new old house rises before us. The entire ride had escaped my notice, lost to automaton sadness and memories of better days. I unbuckle and start to open the door but am halted by Wyatt's hand on my left arm. "Wait a minute."

As I turn to look at him in question, I see that he's shifted his seat back. Twisting, he grasps me firmly beneath my arms and in a move that I resolve to wonder at later, plucks me up like I weigh nothing and pulls me over the armrest and into his lap. "What are you doing? Wyatt, you can't just—"

"Shut up and cry, damnit," he says, and pulls my face into the crook of his neck.

"I'm done now," I protest, lifting my head. "I cried a few tears, got it out of my system. Now I'm done." I'm too conscious of our bodies, aligned where my legs straddle his hips in the narrow seat, where our chests are pressed, breath to breath, together.

"You're all done, huh?" he mutters, glaring into my face. Outside the car, it starts to rain. Momentarily distracted, I look at the window where the raindrops beat and slither, cold and wet, obscuring the world. Obscuring us.

"Yes. I couldn't cry now if...if..." I search for something big enough, something bad enough. He pokes me. In my shoulder, hard enough to annoy but not hurt. "Hey!"

"Does that make you mad?" He does it again. Sugar gives a sharp bark but doesn't move. It's as if she knows Wyatt has no ill intent toward me. It just makes me angrier.

"Yes! What the hell, Wyatt?"

"Do you cry when you get mad?" He pokes me a third time, a bit harder. This time I swat back at him. I do cry when I get mad, and I hate that somehow he knows that about me. Hate that he sees me.

"Stop it, damn you!"

"What about this?" He tugs on my hair, secured in a knot on top of my hair, and I feel it loosen.

"Wyatt Granger, I swear to my momma if you don't quit it now, I'm—"

He tugs again, and it starts to fall. "You're gonna what, Red? You gonna cry, or what?"

My damn lip starts to tremble. Damn him. "You know what, Wyatt? Fuck you." Wrenching open the door, I push against his chest and heave myself off of his lap and out of the car.

I didn't count on my left leg going numb, though, while I straddled him.

Didn't count on thirty-five-year-old hips that forgot how to work when I needed them most.

Didn't count on face planting in the driveway like some supine Wyatt worshipper.

The worst of it?

When it's all said and done, I lie there in the rain and cry like a baby.

# Nineteen

## Wyatt

Shit. Shit. Shit.

That didn't go as planned. It only takes a microsecond, or so it seems, for Harry to go completely off the rails and jump from the car into the pouring rain. Except her leg gets hung up and before I can catch her, she's sprawled out on the driveway, sobbing as if her heart is broken.

Maybe it is. I have yet to ask how she really felt about Marcus Lane. Maybe she still loves the bastard. But that's neither here nor there.

"Fuck, Harry..." I jump after her and scoop her up and into my chest. "That is not what I meant when I told you to cry—" At a glance, I can see a few mild abrasions on her face, as if she used her forehead to catch herself, and several brutal ones on her hands. I wince. Those are going to hurt.

She punches me ineffectually in the neck and cries harder. "Fuck you."

I let Sugar out and then kick the car door closed, hitching her closer to me with one arm beneath her knees and the other around her back so I can hold her close. "Yeah, definitely fuck me, and not the fun way. I deserve that."

We're getting soaked, the cold rain uncaring that neither of us are wearing coats. Steps brisk, I carry her to the front door, pausing while she gives me a six-digit code to unlock the modern keypad that's at complete odds with the house's old-fashioned colonialism, and then take her inside. The dog follows closely, watching me with a keen, too-human gaze. I like this house Harry's moved into since the bridge, even if it does belong to that Jack guy. It's a more modest, time-worn model on the other side of town, and feels more like Harry. Even in the pouring rain, I can appreciate the obvious craftsmanship of the build.

Inside, the house is dim and quiet, shadows draping heart pine flooring, high ceilings, and walls the color of old cream. Boxes are piled here and there among random pieces of furniture; it's clear Harry's still settling in.

"Bathroom?" I was here, helping her move in, but damned if I remember where everything is. She points without speaking and after navigating a darkened bedroom with more piles of boxes, I find the master bath.

The vanity light is bright after the lack of sun and general gloom of the empty house. Harry blinks as I flick it on and set her on the sink counter, then regards me soberly as I brush her hair out of her face and inspect her more carefully than I was able to outside. I shake my head. "You're a mess, Red." She's sopping wet and covered in tiny bits of gravel from the driveway, the skin on her forehead and palms angry and abraded.

"Your fault," she mutters.

Picking up a washcloth sitting beside the sink, I wet it and then begin to clean her cuts. "I'm sorry."

Her tears are mostly done, but her eyes remain wet and accusatory. "You were being an asshole."

"I was," I agree. Her lip is puffy, and I blot it carefully. She shivers a little, then stiffens on the countertop. "I really felt like you needed to let out all those emotions. I could see you struggling with them." I move to her hand, guiding it to the sink after a brief look to let running water help move the gravel from where it has embedded in her skin. Her flesh is raw and oozing; she winces as the water hits it. "I thought I was helping."

She jerks her hand from mine. "I don't need your help."

"Fair enough." I raise both hands, palms turned outward—a white flag.

She cleans both hands slowly, taking care as she lets the water remove the gravel. Finished, she turns the water off, then shifts on the counter. "Well?"

Helplessness hits me. I'm just standing here, soaking in her anger. What does she need... bandages? A clean shirt?

"How can I help?"

"Move!"

Oh. I move to the side and watch as she climbs from the counter. "Would you...ah...like some dry clothes?"

She throws me an exasperated look over her shoulder as she walks stiffly toward the bedroom. "I think I can take it from here, Wyatt. Tell you what, get me something hot to drink and I might forgive you for being a jerk. I'll be out in a few minutes."

"Done." Relieved to have a purpose, I move past her.

On the way I tug my own shirt off. I'll drape it over a towel rack or toss it in the dryer. The damn thing is too wet and uncomfortable to sit around in, though, and I'm not comfortable leaving Harry just yet.

I'm pulling a jug of apple cider from the refrigerator when I hear a faint moan from the bedroom and then a string of curses. Setting it down, I return and push open the door after tapping on it. "Harry? Everything all right?"

My breath stalls. She stands in the middle of the floor, frustration etching her features and damp hair tumbling around her pale face. Her feet and legs are bare, pants puddled on the floor beside her, and the blouse she's wearing just skims the tops of her thighs. "Damnit, I'm sorry—" I close my eyes and begin to back out, the image of all that curvy, firm flesh permanently seared into my visual memory.

"Wait. I need your help."

Her statement, soft and grumpy, stops me. I open my eyes and look at her. She holds out her hands and I wince at the open wounds on her palms.

"I can't...I thought I could, but it hurts to move my hands. I managed to push my pants off with the backs and my fingertips, but I just can't—"

"Oh." I regard her from across the room. Is she asking...?

"My buttons, Wyatt! Can you help with my shirt or is it too much to ask?"

"Yes! Of course..." I move to her and take the top button of her shirt in hand. "I just wanted to be sure I understood you properly." She doesn't reply and I begin unbuttoning her blouse. "We need to bandage those."

"I want the air to get to them...help them scab over."

I nod. "Might be better to do that tomorrow, though."

"I appreciate the expert assessment, Dr. Granger."

My fingers are rough against the soft fabric, hot against the coolness of her flesh when I inadvertently graze the swell of one breast. "Sorry," I mutter gruffly.

"It's fine," she returns, a trace of breathlessness in her voice. Her pulse flutters in her throat.

My fingers still, and then continue the path of buttons southward slowly. Prior to her response I would have hurried just to have the task finished, to be able to walk away with some shred of dignity intact. But there was that catch in her breath, that pulse beating in the hollow of her throat. I'm an idiot for doing it, but now I torment myself with my own leisurely pace, my eyes tracking the strip of skin revealed with each loosened gap of fabric.

If I can torment her a little, too, it's worth it.

Maybe it'll take her mind off things.

When I reach the last button I wait, my fingers rolling it between them before releasing it. The shirt placket hangs, moving slightly with each of her inhales, a temptation to my hovering hand. I can see the line of her underwear, something pale peach with a band of lace. Raising my eyes to hers, I see the same need I feel reflected back at me.

At least, that's what I think I see. Maybe it's something else. She's skittish, I remind myself, remembering how she fled when I kissed her. She needs slow. She requires patience. Gentling, like a wounded animal.

Restraint.

I don't know if I can be restrained. My hand trembles with the need to touch. To reach out and grab…haul her to me and not let go.

"Finish what you started," she whispers, and I close my eyes, balling my hand into a fist. God, if only she knew how close she came to finishing me with those words. How near I was to *done*, my control snapping, patience be damned—

"I don't think I can touch you right now and not kiss you, Harry," I admit, the words gravel in my throat. "Not do more than just finish this last button. I need—I want—" *Tell me to leave. Tell me to go…that you've got it. You can take your own damn shirt off.*

A weight settles on my shoulder, and I turn my head, opening my eyes to see her arm stretched across and resting, palm up, on my shoulder. My gaze travels the length of her arm, traversing the fabric of her shirt, caressing every mile-long inch, until I reach her face. Her eyes are clear. Steady, even with an open vulnerability that threatens my control. Her arm is a bridge. An invitation. As are her next words.

"Wyatt. Finish me."

# Twenty

## Harry

Once upon a time, I loved my husband. I did. After a meet-cute for the books where he literally rear-ended my car before inviting me to dinner, we had a whirlwind courtship my friends were envious of, culminating in a beautiful, fairy-tale wedding on my parents' property.

There was teasing, and heated looks, and enjoying each other's body virtually every night and every morning.

I don't remember when things began to change. Maybe it was after the first business trip, which was approximately three months into our marriage. He came home tired. Distant. Or maybe it was later that same year when he slowly grew critical and cutting.

*I wouldn't eat that second donut if I were you. Wouldn't want you to end up like you were as a kid.*

*For God's sake, Harry...is it too much to ask that my pants not have hanger wrinkles?*

*What the hell have you been doing all day? Wait...let me guess. Grading papers? I guess I'll get takeout. Again.*

*I hope you know how lucky you are to have me. No other man would put up with this shit.*

Whenever it happened, it happened. And it slowly, insidiously destroyed my confidence in myself, in my abilities. I was stupid. I was lazy. I was going to end up overweight again, like I was as a child.

No one would ever want me like Marcus did.

It's why, even when he never lifted a physical hand against me, I tolerated the things I now see—courtesy of distance and clear vision— were abusive behaviors. I didn't want to be alone. Marcus was good-looking, smart, successful...it was like he said: I *was* lucky to have him. I was a freak, a nerd, an appallingly non-domestic female that no sane guy would want to tether himself to.

And yet, here was this beautiful man standing before me, fingers shaking with the need to touch me.

And dear God, did I need to be touched.

I feel that need rising within me with each eternal second Wyatt lingers before me, his hands making my skin sing with their proximity alone as he moves from button to button. Desire wars within me. There's so much to consider—my fascination with not just Wyatt, but Jack, as well, uppermost in my mind. There's my job. My apparent idiocy where men are concerned and worry that

I'll screw up again. My awareness that I'm fucking broken right now, and the fear that I'll never be whole again.

And then there's Marcus, dead for mere hours. It makes me feel oddly unfaithful to be standing here, mostly nude, practically begging another man to make love to me. Even if technically it was Marcus who cheated, Marcus who broke our vows to one another, it's difficult to shake the ingrained instincts of seven years.

I still feel the weight of the ring on my finger. I still feel married, a fact that pisses me off anew.

But I can't think about any of that right now.

Wyatt's so intent upon his task, upon keeping the control I sense him struggling with so firmly in check, that he doesn't notice my own quickened breathing or trembling awareness. He doesn't see my need warring with anger, clashing with common sense, until it duct tapes that part of my brain and all that remains is longing.

He pauses, his hands going still on the final button. I open my mouth, intent upon salvaging what shred of dignity I have left. I'll tell him I've got it...tell him to go...

Instead, I whisper doom to dignity. "Finish me."

There's no ambiguity in my request. Wyatt's eyes flash to mine, seeking something. Reassurance, maybe, that this won't be ending in a "never happened." Whatever he sees written on my face must provide the answer he needs, because it's only a breath of time, a gasp in the space between us, before his hands are moving, unbuttoning the final clasp and spreading the plackets of my shirt wide, baring me to his gaze without preamble. His palms slip inside the cavern of the shirt to settle on my hips, his fingers digging briefly into my giving flesh before relaxing into a firm hold.

"Finish you," he murmurs, and then pulls me into him. His chest sears my own overheated flesh as our skin kisses a greeting and he pushes the shirt off me altogether, his hands following its descent from shoulder to hip once again, then back up to tunnel beneath my hair and cup my jaw. My breath stutters in my throat as he dips his head, blotting out the light from the hallway, and presses his mouth to mine.

It's different from the kiss in the batting cage. Softer. His kiss is balm to every wound my body and soul has suffered recently. When his tongue parts my lips to slip between them and explore, it's easy to forget the sting of abraded flesh and rejected love; instead, I feel his need, as deep as my own, drowning every hurting defense, every instinctive protest.

I close my eyes, answer the sweep of his tongue with mine, and embrace impulse for once in my life. I will not think tonight, not about tomorrow, not about the right or wrong of things. I don't want to consider things like my job or his role as my TA, don't want thoughts of my unsettled personal life to intrude. It's just me and Wyatt, strong and slim and tall against me

I'll think about all of that later. Right now, this is all I want, even if it's just for tonight.

He lowers a hand, pulling slightly away as he does, to trace the tendon in my neck down to my collarbone and lower, finding and covering my breast. "So pretty," he says, his voice thick. My nipple pebbles, as much at the open desire in his voice as at his touch, and I find myself arching more fully into his palm. More, I beg silently, my lips parting in a soundless gasp. I need more.

He gives it to me, bending his head to suckle hard, first at the breast he holds within his grasp and then at the other. "Oh, God," I mutter. "Yes..."

My encouragement seems to inflame him, and he lifts me, his hands greedy on the globes of my ass. I curl my legs around him as he half-turns, seeking the bed, and then he's lowering me to its rumpled surface, following me down in a tangle of limbs and roving mouths. "I want to touch you—" I tell him, frustrated with the state of my hands.

"Mm—" he responds, busy working his way down my torso. "Plenty of time for that later, Red."

"Later..." I echo. My brain tries to compute. Will there be a later? I don't know that I want that. This is for now. It's not something I'll deny later, pretend it never happened as I did with the batting cage, but I'm not planning on a repeat, either. That would be foolish.

Resolving to sort it out later, I touch the top of his head with the back of my hand, silently urging him to continue.

Wyatt has stilled, though, alerted maybe by the sudden tension I tried to banish seconds earlier. "Yeah. Later," he confirms, his eyes glittering up at me from the vicinity of my bellybutton. "As in days, and weeks, and months down the road. Maybe more. That work for you?"

I stare at him, a feeling of something like helplessness seizing me. "That's—" My voice is gritty, and I clear my throat. "It's just…it's early days and—"

Wyatt closes his eyes for a long second and I know. I fucked up.

He levers himself up and off me until he's sitting beside my hip. For a long moment we stare at each other, the air thick with everything we're not saying. Then he sighs and runs a hand through his hair. "I think we might be operating at cross-purposes, Red."

"I don't understand."

Leaning forward, he kisses me lightly on the lips. "Just that you obviously need one thing, and I want something very different. And that's okay. I shouldn't have jumped at your invitation…should've known." He shakes his head a little and pinches the bridge of his nose.

"Wait—" I protest and sit upright, using the backs of my hands to push myself up.

"It's all right. I get it. You've had a shock, plus the adrenaline…sex seems like a good idea."

Is he patronizing me? I can't tell. He seems completely sincere, and I respond warily. "Is that a problem?"

Reaching out, he brushes a piece of my hair behind my ear and then my shoulder. "Only if I want more than a one-night stand brought on by shock and adrenaline." He pauses, then stands. "I'm not a one-night kind of guy, Harry, and you're not ready for what I want, but that's okay. I'm a patient man."

He doesn't need to say more. I wrap my arms around my chest, chilled suddenly. How on earth did I pick the one college guy uninterested in a night of hot sex, no strings attached? "Isn't it ironic..." I mutter, mostly to myself.

"Don't you think," he finishes with a wry quirk of his lips. "Why don't you get some rest? I'll stay...make something for you to eat later."

Nodding, I sink back into the pillows and allow Wyatt to pull the covers over me. His eyes linger as he does, revealing a mix of regret and appreciation, and I smile a little as he turns to leave. He's being a gentleman, but it's not an easy choice. He wants me.

"Wyatt."

He pauses to look back, one hand resting on the doorjamb. "Yeah?"

"Thank you."

He shakes his head a little and disappears into the hall. I can hear him muttering to himself. "Yep. You're welcome. You're a fucking idiot, Wyatt Granger. Fucking. Idiot."

I close my eyes, feeling lighter than I have since getting the news about Marcus.

I am wanted. For now, it's enough.

# Twenty-One

## Harry

THE NEXT DAY I sit across from Jack at my kitchen table. I'm still in my pajamas—boxers and a tee shirt— but he doesn't seem to notice, his attention fixed on my hands rather than my attire.

"What the hell happened to your hands between yesterday and today?"

I look down at my hands, free of bandages now but still a bit rough-looking, and turn them face-down. I'm reluctant to tell him how Wyatt prodded me and I flung myself out of the car like an idiot. "I fell in the driveway," I finally answer. "I'm fine." I nod toward the plastic sleeve containing a piece of white paper. "Is that Marcus's note for me?"

He frowns. "Yes. Listen, Harry...it's not a nice little fond farewell. And reading it isn't going to change anything. I really think—"

"Give it to me." He hesitates and I lift an eyebrow. "It's okay. I'm a big girl, Jack. I can take it."

"Don't say I didn't warn you," he grumbles, and passes Marcus' final words across the table to me.

I hold the letter for a moment. It's separated from my skin by the plastic sheath, but I fancy I can feel Marcus just the same, the strength of his emotions imbuing the paper and ink with a near tangible sensation. Then, taking a deep breath, I begin to read.

*Harriet,*

*You always did have to win, you know that? Didn't matter what I did, you were always better. Calm. Collected. In control. You'll be in control right now, as you're reading this. I can almost hear you— "well, Marcus...what did you expect me to do?"*

*Fuck you, you fucking bitch.*

*I just want you to know—this is for you. It's because of you. You ruined everything, and I need you to understand that. You lit a match and set everything on fire when you decided to press charges...and now there's nothing left to do except to finish the job you started.*

*So, when they tell you about me, make sure you think about that. You could have just kept your stupid mouth shut. Could've just let me walk away.*

*I hope you're happy.*

My hands tremble as I set the note down on my kitchen table. Across from me, Jack watches me, a little line of concern between his eyebrows. "He really hated me," I say. The words are thick, sticking a bit in my throat.

"He was angry," Jack answers. "And obviously, he needed help. This wasn't about you."

"Actually, I kind of think it was."

Jack curses beneath his breath. "This is why I didn't even want to show you the note. There's no good in it, Harry. He was a bitter, resentful narcissist. There's nothing you could have done to make this situation any better."

I nod. "I understand that, intellectually. Emotionally..." I lift my coffee mug with careful fingertips and take a long sip of the steaming brew. "He lit himself on fire, Jack. To make a point."

"I'm sure a psychiatrist would have a field day with that, too. You can't dwell on this, Harry. He wins if you do."

I snort out a laugh. "Since I always have to be the one who wins, we can't have that, can we?"

Jack pinches the bridge of his nose. "Poor choice of words." Standing, he pushes his chair in. "I hate to leave you, but I have to get back to it. Listen...we'll be releasing the body to next of kin in the next couple of days. The autopsy is complete; we're just waiting on a couple of things to come back for final confirmation. Dental records, stuff like that."

I nod. I'm not sure why he's telling me all of this. I'm no longer next of kin.

"If you want to attend the funeral, you might think about keeping a low profile. I'll go with you, if you like."

"I hadn't even thought about it..." He's right, of course. I hadn't considered any of the hundred things that come after a person's death. The funeral, the visitation...it's hard to think about, but I don't guess I'd be particularly welcome. And yet, Marcus was my husband, as far as I knew, anyway. I wouldn't feel right about not closing out that chapter in some way, some respectful sort of nod to his life. I rise, as well, and meet Jack's eyes. "Yes. I think I'll take you up on that."

"Okay, then. I'll keep you informed, and we'll make a plan." Jack reaches out and touches the top of my hand. "Until then...please don't take Marcus' note to heart, Harry. He just wanted to hurt you."

I nod. "I know. I'll try."

After a second's hesitation, he leans forward and kisses the corner of my mouth. I'm startled. Is he moving past his guilt and sorrow where Rose is concerned? Do I even want him to, anymore? I hold my breath when he lingers there, his cheek warming mine, and then he turns his head a fraction until his lips brush against mine.

Another moment's uncertainty, and then he's kissing me in earnest, winding his arms around me and pressing me back against the counter. His tongue teases the seam of my mouth, requesting entrance, and I open to allow it, tilting my head to grant him better access.

Inside, though, I'm screaming at myself to *stop*. What is wrong with me, that I would jump from Wyatt to Jack in less than twenty-four hours? Am I that desperate? That lonely? I can't—

I break away, gasping.

"God…" Taking my action for a simple need for air, Jack presses his forehead against mine. "I really do have to go." He presses tiny, nipping kisses against my temple and down the line of my jaw, forcing my head back.

"Go, then." My hands grab at his waist to keep myself steady, twinging with an angry flare of pain. Even up against the hard surface of the counter, I feel off balance. *Control.* I have to gain control.

"Right. I'm going…" With an effort I can feel, he pulls himself several inches away. He regards me for a second, his expression hungry, then leaves without another word.

As soon as the door closes behind him, I fumble for my phone and call the one person I can think of. I need to talk. I need advice. "Owen?"

"What's up, kid?"

"I need you."

His voice changes. "I'll be right there."

"Wait…" I need air. Distance from this house, with its echoes of Wyatt's hands and Jack's hungry, haunted eyes. "Can we go to Karla's?"

"Yeah, okay. I'll be there in twenty minutes."

While I wait for Owen to arrive, I engage myself in mindless tasks. I empty the garbage and take it out to the curb for the ten A.M. pick up, then return and lock the door carefully behind me. I wash my coffee cup in the sink, then dry it and pour another cup. I wipe the already-clean counters and rearrange the wooden spoons in the crock near the stove, then dress simply in a pair of sweatpants that are easy to pull on and pull a thick sweater over my tee shirt.

All the while, I can't shake the sense that someone is watching me. It's Marcus' letter, I suppose. It left its presence behind, angry and full of hate.

A knock comes on the door, and I look over to see Owen standing outside. He rattles the knob until I let him in.

"Why do you have the door locked, kid? You knew I was coming, and you were standing right there." Putting his arm around me, he hugs me to him.

I shrug. "I'm feeling paranoid, I think. I keep feeling like someone's watching me. Anyway...let's go."

"What the hell happened to your hands?" he asks.

"Long story. I'll get there, I promise. Just let me get there my way."

He nods, opens the car door for me and Sugar and closes it after we settle, then jogs around to the driver's side. "I can do that." He puts the car in gear, and we start to drive.

"Jack came over this morning. He brought a letter from Marcus."

"A letter? Like a suicide note?" I had called Owen late last night after sleeping most of the afternoon to tell him about Marcus and ask him to let Momma and Daddy know. I wasn't ready to discuss it to the degree Momma would've demanded.

I nod now. "Yes. It was awful, Owen. He said it was my fault...that the reason he chose the way he did—" I stumble over the words. I can't speak the terrible truth just yet—that Marcus lit himself on fire, choosing drama and pain, because of me.

"Harry—"

"It's the truth. I could have not pressed charges. Could've let things settle however they were going to. If the DA wanted to charge him, it would've been her decision. Not mine. It wouldn't have been so personal, you know?"

"But you can't blame yourself over that. He committed a crime, for God's sake. And Jack was right when he said they really didn't know anything about him. He could have been running some kind of scam in ten different states, for all we know. You did the right thing, Harry. You did the only responsible thing you could."

"I know this, but it doesn't make me feel any better."

"Give it time."

Karla's Cuppa appears, the parking lot full even on a weekday morning when most people are busy making their way to work. Owen pulls into the parking lot, and we park and make our way into the popular little hole-in-the-wall donut shop.

Everyone in Lucy Falls must have had a mid-morning craving for donuts, judging from the length of the line. Digging into my purse, I pull out a wad of cash and hand it to Owen. "I'll grab us a table."

"Coffee and a Boston cream, right?" He pushes the money back in my purse.

With an eye roll I turn to find a table. "Yup."

Lucking out, I grab a booth as two people get up to leave and slide in. The wait is interminable. When Owen finally brings our coffees and pastries, I'm more centered and ready to continue our talk. I take a sip of the steaming brew, then set the cup down. "So, my never-ending drama. That's not all."

"I didn't doubt it... What else has you all bent out of shape?"

"Jack kissed me. He just landed one on my cheek and I—"

Owen is grinning. "I don't see the problem."

"The problem is that yesterday I was this close to going to bed with Wyatt." I hold up a pinch of donut as an example.

He grimaces. "Explain yourself."

So, I do. I tell him about Wyatt taunting me into losing my cool, trying to get me to express the emotion I always kept so tightly shuttered. I tell him about my graceless trip and show him my hands. Tell him about Wyatt helping me with my shirt, and how I wanted him like I've never wanted anyone before. Owen takes it all in silently, head bent over his mug, fingers steepled before him.

"So?" I finish. "What the hell is wrong with me? And what do I do with these guys?"

"There's not a damn thing wrong with you, kid. I mean, aside from the fact that I'm your big brother and I do not need to hear about some dude taking your clothes off..."

"Oh, please. I babysit your kid when you want to bust a nut."

He grins. "I'm regretting ever having taught you that expression. But seriously. I'm a computer guy, not a psychiatrist, but it seems like you're responding to things on a physical and emotional level at the moment, instead of a logic-based level. You've been rejected, so emotionally, you're looking for the opposite."

I chew thoughtfully. "You mean I'm subconsciously looking for someone to reject?"

He nods. "Maybe? I think it's more that you need to get laid, though. Speaking of which..."

His gaze drifts past me, eyes hooding, and I know before I turn that I'm going to have to save some poor girl. Ever since Ava's mother, Owen has become something of a playboy, keeping his heart carefully locked away while letting everything else have a good time.

"Owen..."

"Hold on a sec." His expression shifts, sharpens. "Hi, there."

A young woman pauses in mid-stride beside our table, glances uncertainly at me, and offers a crooked, awkward smile. She's a bit younger than Owen's usual type, with dark reddish hair and pale skin. She looks oddly familiar; she may be a student on campus. "Hi?"

"Please ignore him—" I begin, but Owen cuts in smoothly, speaking over top of me.

"Are your legs tired?"

I groan and drop my head to the table. "Owen, noooo. Leave the poor girl alone."

The woman frowns. "I'm sorry, I don't under—"

"I just thought your legs might be tired, because they've been running through my mind all day."

I thump my head on the table, once, twice. I can't even look at the woman's reaction, but if that choking noise is any indication, it's not good. Lifting my head, I glare at Owen and then cast my gaze at the girl. "I apologize most sincerely for my brother. He knows not what he does. Let me buy you coffee and a donut to make up for his dumb ass."

"Oh, no, that's not necessary. I already paid; I was just looking for a place to sit, actually..." Her eyes rove around the crowded café and mine follow. There are no seats open; she would have to wait.

"Problem solved," I say. "Sit with us if you don't mind putting up with his flirting. I promise to kick him every time he gets out of hand, and you can sit beside me."

"Oh..." She looks uncertain. "Are you sure? I don't want to intrude..."

"Very sure," Owen answers.

"You shut up," I tell him. "Let me just put Sugar over there with him..." Rising, I shift the dog to the other side of the booth to make room for our new friend, then sit back down. "I'm Harry, and this is my brother Owen." I hold out my hand for a shake and the woman grasps it as she slides into the booth.

"Shiloh Brookings," she says. "Is that Boston Cream? That is my absolute favorite."

"It is! My favorite, too. You look super familiar, Shiloh. Do you maybe go to school around here?" I can't shake the sense that I've seen her somewhere.

Shiloh shakes her head. "No. I teach at the high school. I live over on Kennedy...maybe you're familiar with that neighborhood?"

Owen snorts and takes a sip of his coffee. "She lives there."

I stare open-mouthed. "No way! I do live there! Which house is yours?"

"It's an old Craftsman bungalow...low stone wall around the porch, red metal roof."

"Shiloh, I'm pretty sure I'm right across the road from you. I just moved into Jack Brady's brick Colonial."

"The cop?"

"Yes!"

"Oh, my God...this is so cool. I feel like everyone in that neighborhood is ancient. It'll be nice to have a friend."

"Very true. Please come by anytime. I'm actually a teacher, too...I'm a chemistry professor at the Charlottesville campus. We can commiserate about students and admin."

The barista calls Shiloh's order and she hops up to retrieve it. "She seems nice," I say.

Owen lifts an eyebrow. "Looks nice, too."

"Keep your hands to yourself," I warn him. "She is way too young for you. And too sweet."

"Eh," he says. "You're probably right. But back to your problem...you need to just make sure you're up front with both these dudes. But don't get yourself involved in any kind of serious relationship just because you don't want to hurt someone. You need to worry about yourself right now."

"So, your advice is to kiss as many people as I need to...?"

Owen rolls his eyes to the ceiling. "No, Harry. My advice is to do what you gotta do to feel like you again, and don't feel guilty about it. If that means taking your time while you decide which dude you want to screw, or screwing multiple guys, then you do you. Everyone heals in different ways."

"But I shouldn't just use them for my own healing. They're people, too, and—"

"And if you're up front with them, like I said, you're not using them." He pauses. "Besides. I don't think there's a red-blooded guy around that wouldn't want to be used in that way, if it came down to it." He clutches his chest. "Use me and abuse me, baby. Please." He pauses. "Not you. But you get it."

"You're a Neanderthal."

"Most men are."

"True enough, I guess." I pluck another donut from the box between us. "I did tell Jack, a couple of weeks ago, that he wasn't the only one I was interested in."

"Okay, so you're halfway there. Why haven't you told Wyatt yet?"

I've been asking myself the same question. "I don't know?" I offer.

"Lame. Look at me, Harry." I look at my brother. "Why haven't you said something to Wyatt?"

I force myself to consider the question without shying away from it. The truth is plain. "Because I'm afraid. I'm afraid he'll walk away."

"And yet you said something to Jack. What is that telling you, Harry?"

I shove the donut in my mouth instead of answering, smiling up at Shiloh as she returns and settles back in the booth beside me.

That's a truth I'm not ready to admit. Not yet.

# Twenty-Two

## Harry

*Eight years earlier.*

*Dinner had been nice. He'd taken me to a fancy Italian place in Richmond, not quite an hour from Lucy Falls, and I was stuffed after eating my way through countless breadsticks accompanied by a bottle of wine. Now we were strolling down a cobbled path near the restaurant, lit with romantic string lights hung from the branches of Bradford pear trees.*

*I watched him out of the corner of my eye as he talked about something he was doing for his job. His expression was animated, his hands gesturing with contagious enthusiasm as he described some new account he'd landed.*

*"It's a good one," he was saying. "One of the biggest group practices in this part of the state. It will, not even kidding, establish me in medical sales around here." He paused*

*suddenly and reached for my hand. "But enough about me...oh—is this okay?" He indicated the handholding with a small squeeze.*

*I nodded. With anyone else, it wouldn't have been. It would have been moving too fast for my comfort and I'd have moved my hand, probably with a great deal of awkwardness.*

*But this felt nice. Safe and comfortable but just the tiniest bit daring. "It's good," I said. "More than okay."*

*He flashed a smile at me, his teeth even and white in his movie-star handsome face. I was staring, I realized, ducking my head to hide my suddenly red cheeks. Probably drooling. Lord, I was acting like I'd never been on a date. I didn't go on many, Lord knew. I wasn't sure why this handsome man had chosen me...why he'd wanted to spend time with me.*

*"Anyway," Marcus was saying. "I'd love to know more about what makes Harriet Bee tick, aside from her passion for chemistry. What do you normally do on Saturday nights?"*

*Um. Laundry? That was so the wrong answer. So boring and blech. That was me, though. Boring.*

*As I searched for a suitable response, my heel caught in a crack between cobblestones. Off balance, I tilted, arms flailing for something to hold on to. Marcus grabbed me just as I fell completely against him, strong arms encircling me and keeping me from hitting the ground. "Oof—"*

*"Oh, no—"*

*"I've got you. Here, hold on to my shoulder and I'll try to get you loose."* Marcus squatted beside me, glancing up at me with a reassuring grin as my dress blew against his face in the evening breeze. I held on as his hands encircled my ankle and carefully undid the strap holding the shoe on my foot. *"It looks like the heel snapped."*

*"I felt it,"* I murmured.

He straightened, holding the broken shoe out to me. *"Well, that's no good. You can't walk around with only one shoe. Here, hop up."* Turning, he presented me with his back. I stared at it, dumbfounded. Was he suggesting...?

As I debated, he looked back at me. *"Come on, then. Your steed awaits."*

He was suggesting it—a piggyback ride. I hadn't had a piggyback ride since I was a child.

*"Are you sure...? I'm heavy—"*

*"Nonsense. You're a tiny thing; I could carry you all day."*

Gingerly, I placed my hands on his shoulders, the shoe dangling down his chest, and hopped awkwardly onto his back. His hands came around to hold my hamstrings. *"Hold on,"* he said, and took off at a brisk walk toward the distant parking area.

Tiny. He'd called me tiny, even though I was anything but. I was short but a curvy, solid handful. If that's genuinely how he saw me...a little thrill ran through me and looping my arms more securely around his neck, I held on. I didn't think I wanted to let this one get away.

\*\*\*

I'd held on, all right. I'd held on past the point of madness, even when it was obvious Marcus and I never should have married.

From my vantage point under an oak tree a hundred yards away, I watch the funeral with a distant kind of sadness. Jack stands beside me, an umbrella held over us both to protect against the icy rain sleeting down. It's such a small gathering. How did I never realize Marcus had no friends, no one he spent time with on a regular basis? No one he golfed with or had a beer with on Fridays after work? The only attendees are Marcus' family—his real family, his first family—and a man I recognize as his employer. As I observe, he lifts his arm discreetly, checking his watch.

Even from the large expanse that divides us, Gina's sobs are noisy and grating. It's a dramatic scene: the closed casket shiny in black lacquer, a pile of white flowers atop its surface. The grieving widow in her figure-skimming black dress and wispy veil, one hand holding a handkerchief. The children sit beside her beneath the canopy, the older ones stoic of expression, while the toddler squirms in another woman's hold.

I don't know why, given the funereal perfection of the tableau, but something about it rings false.

"There's something…" I bite my lip, uncertain of what I want to say.

Beside me, Jack hums a tuneless sound and shifts his weight from one foot to the other. "I know."

The funny thing is, I know that he does know. Without any explanation or clarification of what I mean, he understands the feeling the scene before us evokes in me. Like a lightbulb blinking on, it strikes me.

"That's it. It's like this elaborately crafted scene, like something from a movie."

"Like it's lacking authenticity."

"Exactly. Everything's too perfect. Too much as it's expected to be." I hug myself against the bitter chill. "Maybe she's just a perfectionist or something."

"Could be."

We stand a few minutes longer, until it looks as though the pastor has finished speaking and Gina rises. Then I turn to leave, stepping resolutely from beneath the shielding umbrella. The rain chills me through instantly, but something about it makes me feel clean, and I linger before I reach Jack's car, lifting my face to the sky and closing my eyes. I've mourned enough for this man who never loved me.

"Harry?" Opening my eyes, I see Jack is standing with the door open, looking at me with a question on his lips. I blink and slide into the front seat. I have no desire for any kind of confrontation with the woman he did, apparently, have real feelings for. I'll leave her, and their children, to their own grief.

Even if I never understand the why and wherefore of Marcus Lane's actions, it's time to move on.

Back at my house, a crowd has gathered. My parents, Owen and Ava, Sharon, my department head, and several other friends from the life I once shared with Marcus. This is what was missing, I think, as I walk into the too-warm kitchen and begin removing my jacket. The bustle and presence of people that care. There are more gathered here to support me than there were gathered at the gravesite.

The kitchen counters and table are laden with Tupperware and assorted dishes. I lift an eyebrow. "I'll never eat all this, not in a lifetime."

Jack, entering behind me, makes an appreciative sound. "Send some my way. I'll happily take it off your hands."

"I'll do that. Who's it all from? I haven't even told anyone about Marcus."

Momma approaches and pulls me into a hug. "News travels fast, sweet girl. I made your favorite," she whispers in my ear.

I draw back, smiling as Daddy thumps me on the back and moves past us, into the other room. He'll find the one quiet spot in the entire house, I know, and camp there until it's time to leave. "Chicken pot pie?"

Momma nods, tucking a stray curl back into the twist I struggled with this morning. "And mashed potatoes to go with."

"You might be my favorite mother ever."

She snorts. "Funny girl. Go. Talk to your guests. I'll take care of the kitchen and pack some stuff up for your young man, here."

Jack and I look at each other. "He's not—"

"Thank you, ma'am." He winks at me, unabashed humor lurking in his gaze as he makes zero effort to correct my mother.

"Lord," I mutter, rolling my eyes. "Just what I need."

"Pretending I didn't hear that, you being a fresh widow and all," Momma singsongs. She peels the top off a Tupperware and sniffs. "Whew. That cheese is rank."

"Please don't say that. I'm not a widow."

"Might as well be," she returns.

I swivel on my black pumps and exit the room. "Owen, I need you!"

My brother emerges from the living room, Ava on his hip. She squeals when she sees me and squirms to get down, and I feel the first authentic stirring of happiness I've experienced in days. This kid. She's balm to my wounded soul.

"What's up, kid?" Owen gives me a squeeze and tweaks my nose.

"Momma's just being full of herself today, that's all. Thanks for doing all this." Owen was the one that organized the 'wake,' saying that it would help me find closure if nothing else. He's right. I can already see the door on that part of my life closing. This gathering is a peaceful kind of farewell, a nod toward saying goodbye and turning from the past.

"You needed it. Come on, let me find you a beer. Have I told you how much I really like this house, by the way? It's much more you than that other monstrosity."

"Isn't it? I'm kind of falling in love with it."

"What about the dudes? You any further along in figuring that shit out?" Pressing a glass of iced tea into my hand, he arches an eyebrow toward Jack, who's stopped in the doorway to talk to Sharon.

"No. I think right now I just need Jack to be my friend, though." Hearing his name, Jack glances away from his conversation, meeting my eyes as he tips his beer in acknowledgment.

"Mmhmm. Whatever you say."

"Owen. It's only been a little over a month since everything happened. The last thing I need is to be looking for a guy."

"Yeah, well, sometimes the thing you're not looking for finds you whether you're ready or not." Owen's gaze rests on his daughter, his expression faintly brooding. I have no response. It's true, especially in his case, where he discovered a girlfriend had found herself pregnant but had neglected to tell him. She'd ended up dying in a car accident around eighteen months ago and Owen had been notified that he had a child after her funeral. It was a shock—the good kind, thankfully, but still a shock.

From the front door, a discordant screech rises. "What the—?"

Owen and I turn to see Gina Lane attempting to enter, her path blocked by my father. "A fucking party?" She hollers, neck on a swivel as she takes in the gathering. From her spot by the fireplace, Sugar lifts her head and growls. "Marcus not in the grave for an hour and you're having a party?" She shoves past Daddy, making her way toward me.

Jack pushes his way forward to cut her off. "Ms. Lane. I'm not sure why you're here, but I can guarantee you weren't invited." Taking her arm, he begins to inexorably pull her back, toward the door.

"Wait."

He stops at the word that pushes its way past lips gone numb, looking at me in question.

"I want to know why you're here," I continue, moving to stand face to face with Gina. "Why aren't you home, grieving with your children? They just lost their father."

She narrows her eyes at me and juts her chin pugnaciously. "I want my ring."

I shake my head, confused. "What ring?"

"The engagement ring he gave you. It's mine. I want it back."

A headache is starting to pound viciously within my skull, and I lift my fingers to my temples, closing my eyes briefly. "I don't under—"

"You don't understand," Gina mocks. "That's all you can say, isn't it?" I regard her in silence, remembering my confusion when I discovered her existence. I didn't understand then, and I don't understand now. "Marcus gave you my mother's engagement ring. I want it back."

"Did you...did you know about me? From the beginning?" She had to have, right? If she knew he had given me her mother's ring, she knew about me.

"Of course, I knew about you." She echoes my internal war.

*I don't understand.* I clamp my lips against the statement, but the rest bursts out, unable to be contained. "Why? Why would you allow him to do that to another woman? To you! To your family—"

"You stupid fool. One didn't allow Marcus to do something. Marcus did what Marcus wanted. If I—" She starts to say something else, seems to change her mind, and presses her lips together, instead. It's the first time I've seen her exhibit anything like uncertainty, and it's fascinating.

"So, if you wanted him to stay, you let him go his own way," I finish softly. "Even if it took him away from you."

"I'd like my ring, now," she answers. It's answer enough.

I nod. "Wait here a minute."

Ignoring the incredulous hum of voices, I go upstairs and to the small wooden box I placed on my nightstand. Inside is the ring Marcus gave me when he proposed, a ring I now understand doesn't belong to me. It never did.

And that's fine. Good, even. I want no reminders of him.

Removing the vintage gold band, I stare at the diamond before closing my fist around it and returning downstairs. Gina has moved to stand before the built-in bookcase, a picture frame in her hand. It's a photo of me and Owen with our parents, back when we were teenagers. She sets it down when I approach and turns my way.

I hold the ring out to Gina. "Here."

She takes the ring, studies it for a moment before offering a stiff, "Thank you," and moving toward the door.

I shrug. "It's yours. Gina?"

She pauses. "What?"

"For what it's worth, I'm sorry for your loss."

Her chin comes up and her shoulders square. "Okay." Another step, and my father opens the door for her. She stops again, a dark silhouette against a pale January day. "For what it's worth? I don't hate you, either."

# Twenty-Three

## Harry

After the funeral, I settle gradually into Jack's broken-hearted house, unpacking slowly and with deliberation. Everything matters—where I put this chair, or place that knickknack. I want... no, I need... everything to be perfect. To have meaning, even if only for me. To provide comfort and peace.

Everything stutters to a stop when I open a box and see a Ziploc bag on top of my china cabinet contents, shards of blue and white porcelain glinting up at me through the plastic. Grandma's vase. Opening the bag, I upend the broken pieces into my tee-shirt. My fingers travel slowly, carefully, through the pile.

Of all the memories I have of Marcus, this is the one I struggle most to reconcile with who I am. How did I lose my confidence, my sense of self, so completely that

I allowed this treatment? How did I never say, *no more*? *Not again. I'm worth more than this.* I ducked my head and learned to avoid, deflect, mute... I ignored the crumbling of my spirit, the breaking apart of who I'd always perceived myself to be. Somehow, I have to find my way back to who I was before the shattering of myself.

I have to unbreak me.

The doorbell rings. Climbing to my feet, I hold the broken vase carefully in the swaddle made of my tee shirt and go to open the door. It's Wyatt, here for what have become nearly daily check-ins. After my last-minute leave of absence, he's been tasked with leading course lectures at my direction. I feel stupid for ever arguing against a TA. He's been an unbelievable asset.

"Hey," he greets me, pulling off his beanie as he comes inside. "What's up?"

"Same old," I say. "Still unpacking." I glance around. "I don't think I'll ever be done."

He holds up a familiar flat box. "Well, time for a break. I brought takeout."

As he says the words, my stomach grumbles. I cover it self-consciously with my hand, the broken pottery clinking a little. "I guess I can't argue that I'm not hungry."

"Not even a little," he returns, moving past me to the kitchen. "What's that?" He gestures to where I have my tee shirt balled around the glass.

I empty it into a wooden bowl on the kitchen counter. "Just something broken I need to fix."

He peers over at it as he places the pizza box on the counter and the scents of cheese and pepperoni waft my way. "Yeah? I might be able to help with that. My mother is a *kintsugi* artist."

"Kint- what?" I pull plates from the cabinet I stored them inside and open the refrigerator. "Beer or water?"

"Water, please. *Kintsugi* is an ancient Japanese art form where the artist puts broken pottery back together, but with gold."

"Gold?"

"It's like a gold leaf mixed with a bonding element. It seals the cracks and when it's finished, it's this broken thing made even more beautiful than it once was. It's pretty cool... I can introduce you to my mother and she can tell you all about it."

The idea is intriguing. I look at the bowl containing my vase and try to imagine it whole, with a webwork of gold spun throughout.

"Veins of gold..." I murmur and pick up the plate Wyatt has fixed for me. "I'd like that, I think."

Wyatt collects his own plate and we settle in the living room, each of us taking a corner of the couch. I tuck my feet up beneath me and sit facing Wyatt. "Great," he says. "I'll let her know and find a time that suits."

I take a bite of my pizza. "So, your mother is this cool artist. What other secrets have you been keeping, Wyatt?" In all the times Wyatt has visited, we haven't spent a lot of time talking. Not about anything personal, anyway. He goes over the classwork, and I provide the new lecture. I show him my progress on a couple of articles I'm writing for a scientific journal, he provides his thoughts. We talk about his thesis project, and I give advice, and then we dance. Tiptoe as gracefully as possible around our interlude of a couple of weeks ago. He refuses to allow me to feel embarrassed about it, and I can't look at him without feeling the heat of his skin against mine.

I want him, but I have to respect that he wants more than what I'm prepared to offer.

He chokes a little and takes a sip of his water before replying. "Um...well, it's not really a secret, but I may be getting an invitation to spring training."

What does that even mean? It's something to do with his baseball, I know, but I'm clueless when it comes to sports. "I don't know what that means," I finally say.

He laughs and turns to an imaginary audience, gesturing at me. "Have y'all met her?" Sobering, he looks at me. "No, really, that's one of the reasons I like you. You couldn't care less about my baseball. It just means that I have a pro team looking at me to see if I'd be a good fit for them. It's a big opportunity."

"Oh. So, this going pro thing is a distinct possibility." I'm pretty sure that's the right phrase. *Go pro.* It sounds right.

He nods. "Thinking about it. I had the chance several years ago, but decided I wanted to get my degree first. So, there's always the possibility that I screwed myself."

"That's..." I struggle to find the right response. "That's really cool, I guess. And if they wanted you years ago, I can't imagine they wouldn't want you now." Something niggles at me. "I guess being on a pro team is super-involved, right? As in travel and commitments, things like that." I can't help thinking about Marcus, how he was never home in the past several years.

"Yes. I'd be gone a great deal. Major league teams play a hundred and sixty-two games in a year. But I could be sent to a farm team. They play a bit less, but it's still a significant commitment." He sets his plate on the table beside the couch. "Which brings me to another kind of secret."

I raise an eyebrow. He sounds so serious. "Okay..."

"I have a son. I'm really not sure I want to be gone that much."

*A son.* I set my own plate down, my head spinning. "You have a child."

He nods. "I do. He's three...almost four years old and absolutely amazing."

"But you're so young—"

He frowns a little. "I'm twenty-four, Harry. Plenty old enough to have a kid."

"Biologically, of course. But...isn't it difficult, with you still being in school and such?"

"Sure. Nothing about having a kid is easy. But my mother helps, and we make it work." He pauses. "Does it bother you?"

"No!" The response comes swiftly. "It doesn't bother me. It's just...a surprise." My voice is shaky, and I laugh a little to conceal it. "I'm sure you're an incredible father."

"I'm trying," he answers. "What about you, Harry? Any deep, dark secrets you want to share?"

*I'm a broken mess.*

*I'm glad I'm not with Marcus anymore.*

*I think I really like you and it scares the hell out of me.*

Things I could say—secrets I could reveal—flit through my head in the second before I blurt the truth farthest from what I was thinking in my mind. "I can't have children."

He blinks. "That's... I'm sorry, Harry."

The sincerity in his voice almost undoes me and I shrug to combat it. "I've dealt with it. But you're very, very lucky."

"Believe me, I know." He looks away, the corners of his eyes crinkling in the ghost of a smile, and I know he's thinking of his son.

"Tell me about him?"

He does, filling the quiet with stories of a funny, stubborn little boy who likes building blocks and superheroes and sugar cookies. "Would you like to meet him?"

"I—Wyatt, that's kind of a big deal. I'm not sure..." I roll my water bottle between my hands, the condensation anchoring me.

Leaning forward on the couch, Wyatt takes the bottle and sets it beside my plate. Giving me time to move if that's what I want to do, he closes the distance between us, lifting my chin with a single finger to place a slow, sweet kiss upon my mouth. My eyes drift closed of their accord, opening only when I feel him move back. He studies me with the patient watchfulness I've come to expect, letting the quiet stretch between us before he answers.

"I'm sure enough for both of us."

---

An hour or so later, Wyatt has no sooner left than a sharp rap comes on the back door. Jack. Sighing a little, I let him in. It's after ten and I'm tired, ready for bed.

"Hi, Jack."

"Harry. I'm sorry to show up so late." Jack's gaze roves the kitchen as he pushes the door closed behind him.

"It's okay. Can I get you something to drink?" At the negative shake of his head, I lean against the counter and cross my arms over my chest. "What's up?"

"I came to give you an update." He pauses. "I saw that guy leaving...Wyatt, I think?"

"That's right."

"So...you and him?"

"There's no me and him. He's half my age and a student." I don't know why I lie. Maybe because there is something between Wyatt and me, but I'm not ready to label it. Not ready to explore it, I don't think.

Jack reaches out a finger and touches the leaf of a potted African violet I have sitting on the kitchen table. "He's only...what? Less than a decade younger than you are, Harry. That's nothing. And your TA, if I remember right. Not a student."

"What's your point, Jack?"

He spreads his hands wide. "Nothing. Just...damnit. This isn't what I came over here for."

"I told you I was confused, Jack. That I hadn't made—"

"—up your mind. Yeah, I know. It's fine." He stares at me, frustration etched plainly on his features. I can't help the mixed feelings of guilt and defensiveness that make me want to simultaneously beg for forgiveness and argue my innocence. He takes the choice away from me. "Anyway. We had some results come back from the autopsy we conducted before Marcus was buried. The dentals don't match."

"You mean—"

"They belong to someone named Heinrich Richter. Ever heard the name?"

I shake my head and glance at the photo he produces and sets on the table in front of me. "No. I've never seen him before. But Jack...that means..." I reach for the back of the chair in front of me, pull it out from the table, and sink down until I'm sitting.

Jack's voice is grim when he finishes my thought. "That the man Gina buried isn't Marcus Lane."

# Twenty-Four

## Harry

I have so many questions.

I lie awake, unable to sleep after Jack's revelation. My brain won't stop; it churns without ceasing long after the melatonin should have kicked in.

Does Gina know? How could she not? Why would Marcus fake his death? Who is Heinrich? Was his death natural, or did Marcus kill him?

*What the hell is going on?*
*Am I losing my mind?*

Down the hall in the living room, the mantel clock chimes two A.M. I turn onto my side, kicking at the covers restlessly until they pool around my thighs. It's stuffy in here, the old radiators somehow so much warmer than electric heat.

And then there's Wyatt. My thoughts won't stop returning to his own confessions. He has a child. He's a father. Everything makes sense now—his reticence in having a one-night stand, that sense of gravity that clings to him.

Knowing what he went through to keep his child makes me like him even more. He had told me how he red-shirted his sophomore year after learning about the baby—and had, of course, explained what it meant to red-shirt—knowing that it could irrevocably damage his chances of making a major league team.

For those teams to be looking at him again, giving him a second chance...it's huge. I feel with a certainty like dread that he will be picked up. He will join a pro team. And that's when whatever this fledgling thing I feel for him will die, because I know I won't be able to handle another man being gone all the time. Even if I trust him, I need someone I can depend on. All the time, at weird times, random times. I need someone there for me if I have a seizure, ready to call for paramedics if necessary.

Selfish? Maybe. But I can't help it.

Determined to sleep, I close my eyes. Sleepy thoughts. Sheep. Kenny G. Ninety-nine bottles of beer on the wall.

Eventually, I must doze off. I wake to the scent of Clive Christian and the certainty that I am not alone. Outside my bedroom, the floor creaks. I go rigid, listening. At the foot of the bed, Sugar lifts her head. I can faintly make out the hair on her spine standing up. A low growl sounds in her throat. Before me, a shaft of moonlight illuminates the collection of small, gold-framed silhouettes on the opposite wall. I fix on one of a young girl with her hair in a ponytail, trying to steady my breathing against a sudden rush of adrenaline. Everything seems to tunnel into that single space outside the closed door. It's perfectly quiet again, and yet the atmosphere vibrates with expectancy.

With presence.

*Someone is in my house.*

Common sense wars with fear. I locked the door and set the alarm after I took the trash to the curb. Right? No one could have gotten in the house without setting it off. No one is here. The sound was my imagination, or simply the house settling. Old houses do that. They settle, to the tune of creaks and shuffles and groans, and always, always do so at night when it's guaranteed to scare you.

That's all it is.

But Sugar...and the smell...you don't smell things in dreams.

I am lying on my side, facing away from the door, as is my habit. Although my body goes rigid, I try to remain still and calm...feign sleep so I can attempt to assess the situation.

It's hard, though, when my heart wants to beat out of my chest. Drawing in a deep breath, I hold and release, praying if someone is there, he'll attribute it to disturbed sleep and nothing more.

It's quiet and still for so long I begin to doubt myself. Maybe I am dreaming. Experimentally, I sniff. The scent of cologne — that expensive brand I'd recognize anywhere, in any crowd — is still strong. Real. I don't think I'm imagining things.

*God, I really wish it was just my imagination.*

Panic starts a low, steady throb in the region of my heart and my lungs tighten. I don't know what to do. There's no scientific method for this, no means of talking myself out a blind terror. Why is he here? To fuck with me, to scare me senseless, or...something worse? *Ohmygodhe'sgoingtokillme...* I'm not ready. I need to see Ava grow up, go to her first school dance. I need to tell Wyatt—

What? What do I need to tell Wyatt? I squeeze my eyes tightly closed instead of answering my own question. A tear edges from between my lashes, dropping onto the pillowcase.

Beneath the covers, my fingers twitch. My phone lies two feet away, two feet that may as well be two miles. I could fake a sleepy sprawl and reach for the phone then, but something tells me my intruder is as aware of me as I am of him. Or her. Whoever it is has registered every minute change I'm struggling to contain: every choppy, panicky breath, the tension in my body beneath the blankets.

I can't conceal my awareness. It tethers us, stretches between us like an invisible cable, pulsing with electricity.

A low chuckle sounds, galvanizing me into jerking upright in the bed. In the pitch dark of the room, I can just barely discern a form, standing a foot inside the doorway. He's nothing more than one more shadow amongst shadows, a deeper black than the rest.

My fingers clutch the blanket. "Marcus?" The word emerges as a rasp, my throat to dry for anything more.

"Boo!" The figure...apparition...shouts in guttural response. I scream and Sugar erupts into a cacophony of barking and growling, and then he is gone, fading backward into the deeper dark of the hall behind him. Sugar continues to bark, standing up on the bed with her legs straddling me and her body positioned protectively in front of me, even though she's never been trained as a guard dog.

I dig my fingers into her fur and stare until my eyes burn, but the figure doesn't reappear. Tension holds my muscles in a vise. I have to move.

Reaching out, I curl my fingers around the phone and bring it to me. My fingers have fumbled a number and pressed send when it happens: shrill and discordant, the alarm begins to scream. Sugar erupts into another violent frenzy of barking and jumps from the bed to run to the door.

I don't wait. With a scream of my own clutching my throat in a stranglehold, I leap from the bed and grab for her collar, then stumble for the bathroom, slamming and locking the door behind us. I'll wait here. The alarm company will call the police and Jack—Jack will come. He'll hear the alarm; he's probably already running across the lawn.

I lift the phone, belatedly recalling it in my hand. The line is open, courtesy of the number I dialed in a panic. A male voice shouts my name over the connection, his own voice hoarse.

"Jack?" I force the word past lips gone dry. "Someone's in my house. Someone—"

"Are you okay? Harry, are you safe?"

"I'm okay... I'm in the bathroom with the door locked—"

"Stay there. I'm on the way. Don't open that door, Harry, not until I'm there."

"Okay."

I sink down to the floor, unheeding of the cold ceramic tile against my skin. The dog lies down beside me, lending me her warmth. The phone stays in my hand, the voice on the other end speaking continuously, the sound a soothing hum against the jangling alarm.

I remember the gun I keep in the cabinet beneath the sink and pull it from its hiding spot, holding it to my chest.

It isn't until a few minutes later, when I hear a fist sound against the door and Jack's voice yelling for me that I realize it's not him on the phone at all.

It's Wyatt.

It was Wyatt's number my fingers dialed, Wyatt my subconscious called, completely disregarding the cop next door who could've been here in under a minute.

I drop the gun to the floor and open the door, grabbing Jack's biceps and hanging on when he appears.

It's Jack I cling to, Jack I try to explain events to, my words tumbling over one another.

But it's Wyatt I called.

Jack holds me away from him, peering into my face. "I'm going to check the house, Harry. Stay right here...close and lock the door and don't open it until I come back."

I nod and close the door, then pick the gun back up. Its weight makes me feel better.

Wyatt arrives while Jack is doing his walk-through, making the twenty-minute drive in fourteen minutes flat. "I'm here now, Harry. I'm going to hang up, okay? I'll come get you in a minute."

Again, I nod. "Okay, yes..."

I hear their voices, rising and falling as they check everything. It feels like eons pass before a knock comes on the door and I open it to find both men waiting.

Wyatt reaches for me and I move forward into his arms, sinking into a hug that restores and bolsters.

"Whoa... Let's put that down." Jack reaches for the gun in my hand, and I surrender it willingly. I know how to shoot it, but I can't imagine doing so. He checks the chamber and clip, frowning when he sees there are no bullets, and then tucks the weapon into his waist band.

"Did you get him?" I ask, unable to disguise the hope in my voice. I pull away from Wyatt to look more fully at Jack. "It was Marcus, I know it was. I smelled his cologne."

"Unfortunately, no one was here by the time we got here," Jack answers. "Come on...let's go sit down and go through everything." He pauses. "Let's grab your blanket, first."

Suddenly aware of my clothing — or the lack thereof — I cross my arms over my chest. I'm wearing a tee shirt, my normal sleep attire, and nothing else.

Wyatt pulls the blanket from my bed and wraps it around me, his expression inscrutable. Holding the blanket to me, I make my way down the hall and into the living room, Jack in front and Wyatt bringing up the rear.

Every light in the house is on. My eyes dart everywhere, confirming that Marcus is, in fact, not there. I sit on the sofa and Wyatt drops down beside me. Jack positions himself on the sturdy wooden coffee table in front of us.

"Okay. Start from the beginning and tell me what happened. I'm going to record this so I can put it in your file." He presses a button on his phone and sets it on the table beside his hip.

"Something woke me up and...I just smelled him, I guess. His cologne. Clive Christian. Sugar went on alert. I knew I wasn't alone."

"How did you know you weren't just having a bad dream?" He lifts his hands when I shoot him a wounded look. "I'm sorry. I have to ask. Especially after our earlier conversation."

Beneath the blanket, I cross my arms. I get it. He's thinking his announcement that Marcus is likely not dead influenced a hallucination or something. It's not out of the realm of possibility, but he heard the alarm.

"Aside from the dog barking her head off and the alarm going off," I say dryly, "it's very rare to experience the olfactory sense while you're asleep — less than one percent of individuals and sleep studies report any kind of scent. But it was there, strong. There was a moment when I was asleep, then another when I knew I was completely awake and aware of my surroundings." Wyatt places a hand on the back of my neck, squeezing lightly.

Jack glances at Wyatt, his lips thinning. "Good enough. But the alarm didn't go off upon entry, correct? Just as he was leaving?"

"Right. Somehow, he got into the house without my knowing."

Jack rubs his scruff. "It's possible that he knew the code, and although he was able to take the time to use it on entry, was in too much of a hurry when he ran out."

"That makes sense," Wyatt says.

"Okay, so you were awake, smelling this cologne. What happened next?"

"I tried to fake being asleep. I didn't know what to do. I think I was hoping he would just go away."

"Keep going."

"It seems like hours that I just laid there, but then he laughed." I shiver. "It was evil sounding. He laughed and shouted *BOO*. Wait...I sat up first and saw him. He was just this black shadow...not really recognizable. I said, *Marcus?* And that's how he answered me. *Boo*." I bury my face in my hands. "Then he just sort of disappeared. I watched for him to return for a minute or two, and when the alarm sounded, I grabbed my phone and ran for the bathroom."

"And called your TA, here, instead of the police?" Jack shifts, irritation plain.

"I—"

"What's your point, Jack?" Wyatt interrupts, his fingers continuing to soothe the tension in my neck.

"Just getting a full accounting, that's all. You're damn lucky I heard the alarm."

He was wounded I hadn't called him first. "Habit," I mutter. "I call my TA all the time."

"Good enough," he says again. He looks down at his phone, his expression weary. "Okay. I think it's safe to assume that it's Marcus, but I don't like doing that. I'm not trying to scare you, but there's a woman just down the street whose house was broken into recently...and then all this business with these young women being abducted."

Panic flares through me. "I'm totally different from those girls, though…not a coed, not young…and whose house was broken into?"

"Until we know for sure who it is, I'd rather err on the side of caution. I'm going to get a report written up for this first thing in the morning. In the meantime, I don't want you here alone. Do you have someone that can stay with you?"

"I'm staying," Wyatt answers.

Jack nods, the gesture clipped. "And let's get that lock changed tomorrow, as well. I don't like that your code is out there."

"Whose house was broken into, Jack?"

"I can't comment on that, Harry."

"Dammit." I close my eyes and flop against the back of the sofa. I'll have to call Shiloh tomorrow, make sure she's okay, that it wasn't her.

Jack stands, picking up his phone as he does and turning the record feature off. "Okay, then. Looks like you are in capable hands, so I'm going to try to get a few more hours of sleep." He glances around, releases a heavy sigh. "Try not to touch anything. I don't have a lot of hope that they'll turn up anything, but I'll bring in our forensics unit tomorrow and have them dust for prints." He turns to leave. "Good night, Harry. Granger."

I stand, as well. "Jack…"

He pauses, back to us but head turned in our direction. "Yeah?"

I fight the urge to apologize. "Just — thank you."
"Just doing my job." With that, he leaves.

# Twenty-Five

## Harry

Silence settles after Jack leaves, ripe with everything unsaid between us. Biting my lip, I fight the urge to follow Jack. I hurt him. It's obvious from how short he was with me. I didn't mean to and have no idea how to go about fixing it.

Or even if I want to fix it, to be honest. I can't help that my subconscious chose Wyatt to call, rather than Jack. Maybe I need to pay attention to it and focus more about Wyatt's feelings than Jack's.

Or maybe I need to stop worrying about both of them and focus on dealing with the ghost that showed himself tonight.

"You okay?" Wyatt's question breaks the spin cycle of my thoughts, and I give him an over-bright smile.

"I'm fine," I say. "Thank you for coming so fast. And for staying. I know I wouldn't sleep a wink if you weren't here." I scrunch up my nose. "But I don't have the guest bed unpacked and set up yet —"

"Not a problem. I'll take the couch." He tosses a throw pillow into the corner and tips his chin in the general direction of the back door. "What was that all about?"

"The sofa won't work." I answer. "You're too long. You can have my bed, and I'll sleep out here." *Drop it*, I urge him silently. My complicated relationship with both men is not something I want to discuss at three in the morning. I can't help my gaze from flickering to the foyer and the front door. I'd rather have Bodie between me and the door, but I guess just knowing he's here will help.

"That's not happening," Wyatt replies when it becomes obvious I'm not going to discuss Jack. "The couch is plenty comfortable. Go on to bed, Red. I'll be right here."

I look at him for a long moment. I could debate the issue, but it hardly seems worth it. It's late. I'm tired. "I won't argue with you," I say and stand. "Good night, Wyatt."

"Night, Harry." I walk to the hall and glance back to see him toeing off his shoes and then grabbing the hem of his sweatshirt. His eyes burn into me from across the room a second before he pulls the shirt over his head and tosses it to the floor. Without speaking, he watches and waits as my gaze dips involuntarily to his lean, sculpted chest and strong arms.

There's a challenge there. One I can't answer, not yet. Something tells me Wyatt Granger would be too much for me under normal circumstances, let alone right now when everything inside me is in such turmoil.

Swallowing hard, I flee. Inside my room, I cut off the light and stand beside the bed. The bathroom light is still on, but I leave it. I'm not ready for darkness.

I climb into bed and close my eyes. Instantly I'm plunged back into the waking nightmare from earlier. The scent of cologne, acrid and strong, fills my nostrils.

"No one's here," I whisper. "Just you. Just Wyatt."

Knowing it's only my imagination doesn't help. Like an ear worm, I hear the man's low rasp again, crawling like a spider over my skittering nerves. *Marcus is dead.*

I try to sleep. I lie there, closing my eyes and rolling over so my back is to the door. I won't allow this jackass and his sick games to settle permanently into my psyche. *I'm stronger than that.*

That's what I tell myself, over and over, for the half hour I lie statue-still, trying to convince my brain to shut down and allow me to sleep. *I'm stronger than my fear.*

At last, I give up, acknowledging it for the lie it is, and get out of bed. Sugar follows as I pad down the hall.

The living room is dark when I stop to hover uncertainly in the doorway, only a faint trace of moonlight limning the contours of the man asleep on the couch. *This is stupid. A mistake. I don't want to wake him up.* I pivot to return to my bed.

"What is it, Harry?"

His voice cuts through the darkness, stopping me. "I can't sleep," I say, one hand braced against the doorjamb. "I've been trying, but I keep smelling that damn cologne. I shut my eyes and see him in the door—" My voice breaks.

"Come here."

"No — I'm sorry I woke you. I'll be fine."

"Harry. Shut up and get your ass over here."

I don't need any more urging. As I cross the room, Wyatt lifts the corner of the blanket he's covered with, revealing the bare skin of his chest. Suddenly, I can't wait to be curled up next to him, surrounded by his warmth and steady presence. I crawl onto the sofa beside him and snuggle into him as he folds the blanket around me. One arm goes around his waist, while the other rests against his chest. I press my face against his sternum and listen for the sound of his heartbeat.

There it is. A soft thud beneath his skin.

His hand curls into my hair, gripping lightly and holding me secure against him. His other arm winds around me and rests lightly on the lower curve of my butt. I think I feel his lips touch my forehead. I sense Sugar settling beside the couch, hear her soft huff as she goes back to sleep.

Cocooned against Wyatt, I close my eyes to the sound of his heart and sleep.

Someone set the thermostat way too high. Either that, or I have a fever. Heat surrounds me, sinking into every muscle and making me think of hot tubs and saunas. It feels divine, if just a bit too warm. Stretching my leg, I search for the edge of the blanket to poke my foot out.

"What're you doing?"

A sleepy voice rumbles next to my ear and an arm tightens around me, a hand on my butt pulling me closer.

*Closer.*

Awareness sets in slowly. The heat source isn't my thermostat, or a fever. It's Wyatt, his limbs tangled with mine, our bodies pressed so close together in spots I couldn't squeeze a piece of paper in between us.

It feels natural. Kind of perfect, if there exists such a thing as perfection, to be lying here with him like this. If I close my eyes, I can imagine hundreds of mornings just like this, stretching out before me.

I have to move, before I do something stupid.

Like lick him.

Super slowly, I start trying to extricate my limbs from his without disturbing him. It's like playing pick-up sticks. Hold your breath, stick out your tongue, and concentrate.

My elbow connects with a rib, provoking the hand on my ass to grip harder. Wyatt's eyes open, fixing on me with a sleepy sort of intensity.

*I never was good at pick-up sticks.*

"'S'alright. You can be good at other things."

I blink. There I go thinking out loud again. I do that a lot when Wyatt is involved.

"Good morning," I finally say. "I was just about to get up."

"Don't."

"W-what are you talking about?"

"Stay."

"I need…" I don't know what I need, and the words trail away. Why had I started getting up? Oh, yeah. "It's hot. I'm hot."

With his foot, Wyatt draws the blanket down until it only covers us from the knees down. "Better?"

I can see almost all of him now. All those inches of olive-hued skin, firm with lean muscle and mapped with interesting veins. Flat stomach bisected with a perfect vee, disappearing into the elasticized waist of a pair of gray sweatpants.

I close my eyes and channel Momma. "Sweet lord, have mercy."

Wyatt's laugh is low and dirty-sounding. "That's no fun."

"Wasn't talking to you."

"I figured I'd let you know my intentions, anyway. I'm going to kiss you now, Red, unless you say no. I'm going to kiss you, and I'm liable not to stop for a good, long while."

I stare at his face, transfixed. He's beautiful, in a spare, masculine kind of way. I can stop what's about to happen. I can say 'no,' and stand up, and he won't stop me. Won't be upset, won't throw a fit that I don't want him.

But the truth is...I do want him.

Want this.

I'm not sure what changed between last night and this morning, but I'm ready for this man to help me mend the last of the cracks created by Marcus's betrayal. Ready to feel desired again, ready to trust that maybe, just maybe, I can offer up the most vulnerable pieces of me without fearing they'll be crushed.

"Wyatt." He lifts an eyebrow, waiting, but doesn't speak. I breathe deeply, then let it out. "I'm not saying no."

The amber of Wyatt's eyes flares and deepens, and the tense set of his mouth relaxes. He reaches out a finger and traces a straight line down the center of my forehead and nose, stopping on my bottom lip. "Something changed between last night and this morning. What was it?"

There's no pretense here, no hiding from him. Anyone else would be kissing me right now, content with my agreement. Wyatt wants more. He wants it all. He wants to know what happened to shift us from an unspoken invitation, one I chose to flee, to a complete reversal.

I'd like to know what happened, too. When did I choose Wyatt? And why?

Reaching up, I wind my fingers through his, twisting his hand so I can press a kiss to it as I struggle to give voice to something I'm only just realizing.

"Last night I upset a good man because when trouble came knocking, I ran to you. He was my hero when I was a kid, and I guess we both kind of figured he would be, again. But—subconsciously, at least—I chose you when I called you instead of him."

"Mm." His eyes are steady on me as I work through my thoughts.

"I think there was too much spinning in my head last night to be worthy of…this." I gesture between us with our linked fingers. "I didn't want to feel conflicted, or for anything to be tainted by fear, or guilt, or…" I pause to kiss the sensitive skin on the back of his wrist. "Maybe I just needed to feel sure."

His expression, sober and intent, doesn't change. His eyes are flames, though, singeing me with their warmth. "And are you? Sure?"

Lowering our entwined hands to my heart, I regard him seriously. "I'm not going to lie and say I don't have fears… but I'll work on them."

"I'm really glad to hear that," Wyatt says.

He lowers his face to kiss me, but I dip my head and disentangle myself from him, rising to stand beside the couch. Without speaking, I pull my shirt over my head, my hair tickling my bare shoulders as it drapes around them. His indrawn breath is loud in the quiet of the living room as he looks at me, bare except for a pair of pale blue panties.

He reaches out to touch me, but I turn and walk toward the hall. On the threshold, I stop and look back for a brief second before continuing. It's all it takes to send him scrambling from the sofa to follow me, and a heady rush of feminine power infuses me.

He catches up to me as I enter the bedroom and grabs hold of my waist, whirling me around to face him. Lifting me against him, his mouth descends upon mine, and he kisses me with an undeniable hunger. I raise my hands to his cheeks and hold his mouth against mine, opening for his tongue to sweep in and decimate the last of my control.

Wyatt tears his mouth from mine and walks me backwards until the bed hits the back of my legs and I fall. He comes over top of me to kiss a hot trail along my jaw and neck and further, paying reverent homage to the slope of one breast with his lips. His hand covers its twin, his thumb working my stiffened nipple. He sighs against me before he takes my breast into his mouth and sucks, hard. "You are so perfect, Harry. So fucking beautiful it hurts."

A sweet, aching pressure rises in my chest. God, the feels...I haven't had feels like this since I was a young girl, swept away by the romance of my momma's forbidden novels. And my stomach... "*Butterflies*. You give me butterflies, Wyatt."

I whisper the words. They're more for myself than for him, a final explanation for why I feel the way I do. And yet he hears me and lifts his head from my breast.

"I want to give you everything, Red. Butterflies..." He lowers his head, moving to tease the skin of my stomach with lips and splayed fingertips. "...tacos and orgasms..." I giggle, a breathless sound cut off abruptly as he moves lower and fingers the lacy band of my underwear, then nuzzles into the vee between my legs. A gasp leaves me, my hands coming out to grip his thick dark hair and pull. "...all the things you deserve."

"Oh, my God..."

It's all I can manage as his mouth finds me through my panties. He raises up to help me kick them loose, then shoves his face between my thighs once more. My eyes roll back in my head as his tongue licks a line of fire along my pussy, stopping to tug my clit between his lips in with lethal suction at the same he sinks a finger inside me. When I shudder and lift my hips helplessly against him, he looks up at me, a wicked grin twisting his lips. "Ah...you like me to play with your pussy, hmm?" *Oh my God. He's a dirty talker, thank you, Jesus.* His voice is deep and rougher than usual, sending shivers down my spine as he pushes my legs farther apart and returns to his task.

I can't speak to answer him. I moan, instead, and encourage him the only way I can.

I fuck his face.

I grip his hair tightly, hold his face to me, and revel in the feel of his tongue and fingers working me over fiercely as I buck and grind against them.

His tongue lashes my swollen clit, rapid and relentless, while his finger presses upward in a rhythmic motion against a spot inside my pussy that makes me whimper. His perpetual scruff scrapes deliciously against my tender skin, abrading and heightening every sensation. As tension—familiar and yet somehow different— coils within me, all I can do is flex my fingers in his hair and hold on.

Marcus never did this. It was depraved, he said, disgusting. I always felt mildly ashamed for secretly resenting his prudishness.

But there is no shame here. No depravity, no disgust. It's all beautiful, limitless feeling, infinite numbers and ancient eons and light years of pure, transcendent feeling.

When the orgasm breaks, I shake and shudder and sob incoherent prayers to the god between my legs. He rises over me and fastens his mouth to mine, and I feel him against me, hard and naked and nudging against the pulse between my legs.

It seems crazy, given how hard I just came, but I want...no, I need him to fill me. He restrains himself, though, the strain of his control evident in the tense lines of his body. My hands lift to grip his arms and I kiss him deeper, a silent plea with tongue and lips. I taste myself on his lips, the flavor fascinating and carnal and... "...please," I beg, lifting my legs to wrap around his waist and seat him more fully against me.

He thrusts a shallow inch into me, out, then in again. It's not enough and I push upwards and against him. His eyes close. "Fuck. I don't have anything with me—" he mutters. "I can't—" He starts to withdraw, and I lock my legs, preventing him from leaving me.

"I can't get pregnant," I remind him. Somehow, it's not as mournful a thought as it usually is.

"You sure?" He answers gruffly. "I wasn't thinking."

"Same. Yes."

"I'm clean. I don't want you to—"

"Wyatt! For the love of God, Stop talking and fuck me, please!"

His nostrils flare and he surges forward and into me. He's long and thick and so, so hard, and for a long, breathless moment he holds himself perfectly still against me, his hands clutching my hips in a near-painful grip. I rock helplessly against him in tiny gyrations, seeking more. More sensation, more depth, more movement...just more.

I do this until he rises to his knees and moves his hands to cup my ass. They're so big, his fingers so long, they cover nearly every inch of my cheeks as he pulls me up and impales me upon him in one fluid movement. Holding me open for him, he begins to pound into me in strong, forceful strokes. Reaching up, I grab on to his forearms and hold on. Each slam of his hips against mine sends a shock of pleasure-pain rocketing through me, the sensation erupting from my lips in a series of gasps and moans that have me moving the back of one hand to cover my mouth.

Wyatt shakes his head. "Don't you hide from me."

Slowly I move my hand, curling it into the sheet, instead. I've never been vocal during sex, but I can't help the sounds that break from me each time Wyatt fucks into me. I could be the soundtrack for a porn flick, and I don't even care. Every concern I have narrows to a single point, one Wyatt hits with unerring accuracy each time he pulls almost all the way out and then thrusts forcefully back in.

I'm no longer numb. No longer cold ash and banked embers. I feel. I burn.

Every inch of my body is alive in a way it hasn't been since long before I discovered the truth about Marcus. Every vein and artery and capillary from head-to-toe lights with electric sensation; every nerve ending fires exquisite thrills. I buzz with feeling.

Unbelievably, I can feel the wire stretching from that point low in my core to another one deep within my pussy, drawing impossibly tight. I'm going to come again. *Another first.*

I shake my head. "I can't..." It's too much. Too much sensory input after what feels like deprivation. It almost hurts. And yet...

I drop my hand between my legs, whether to work my clit or hold myself together, I'm not sure. Wyatt grunts and I look up to see the skin stretched taut over the high blades of his cheekbones, a look of intense pleasure on his face as he stares down at my hand. "That's so hot, baby. Touch yourself...ah...fuck—"

The wire draws impossibly tighter, and everything clenches a millisecond before it breaks altogether, and I explode in a wave of fierce, undulating pulsation. The rippling contractions of my climax trigger Wyatt's release, and he throws his head back with a guttural roar as he comes, his fingers bruising against my flesh as he spills himself into me.

Then he's slumping over me, gathering me tightly to him as he rocks us both through it. I clutch him back, arms wound around his shoulders and hands twining into his hair, sweaty and curling, at the base of his skull.

When our breathing slows and our hearts beat more calmly against our chests, I try to form words to express what I'm feeling. "That was...it was..."

"Everything," Wyatt finishes, his lips moving against my neck. "It was everything."

# Twenty-Six

## Wyatt

Something is licking my ear.

I bat it away, only partially conscious, and groan when it comes right back, wet and cold and accompanied by a snuffling sound. Opening my eyes, I see the pale-yellow underside of a dog's chin and a long tongue lolling out seconds before water...spit? ...drips down on my face.

*Sugar.*

Memory returns in a flash. Harry's stalker. The couch. This bed.

I turn my head and see her, sprawled on the other side of the bed, arms and legs akimbo. She breathes deeply, the slight flutter beneath her eyelids telling me she is deep in an REM cycle. Her hair is tangled around her face and the faintest snore sounds from between her parted lips.

She is stunning.

Smiling, I push Sugar off me and sit up, swinging my legs over the side of the bed. Twisting at the waist, I sit for a second and just watch her sleep behind me.

Last night...well, this morning, really...falls into the category of things I'll need to repeat a thousand times before I believe they're true. It was every wish come to fruition, every dream realized. I need her again, and start to reach for her, but Sugar noses into my crotch, reminding me of her presence.

*Shit.*

"Okay, okay. Give me a minute." Standing, I glance around and locate my sweats on the floor and pull them on, then pad into the living room for the rest of my clothes. I slip my feet into my shoes, still laced from where I kicked them off last night, and grab my shirt up from the floor, Sugar watching me balefully the entire time. "All right. C'mon."

Sugar trots behind me obediently, waiting while I disarm the alarm and then shouldering past me to beeline for the back yard. I follow, scratching my chest as I step out onto the patio and look around.

It's a pretty day, if cold. The sky is a brilliant, cloudless blue, the kind that usually follows a snowstorm. I tug my shirt over my head while Sugar pees and then starts sniffing around the various shrubs planted around the place. As I wait, a car pulls into the driveway at the back of the property, near the carriage house, and Jack emerges from the driver's seat.

"Morning," I call.

Even from across the yard, I can see his fingers tighten on the car door before he swings it closed. His face is neutral when he looks at me and nods a single time. "Good morning." After a quick survey of the yard, he starts toward me.

I wait, curious, until he stands a few feet in front of me. Even after only seeing him a couple of times, his attraction to Harry has been apparent. After last night, I've won a battle of sorts. I can't feel especially victorious about that, because I've never looked at Harry as a competition, but I can't bring myself to feel guilty or particularly sorry, either.

It's true what they say—all's fair in love and war.

Jack must realize a similar truth, because there's no resentment in the way he looks at me. "I take it the rest of the night was uneventful."

"You take it correctly," I answer.

"Good, good. I've arranged for some guys to come dust for prints in around an hour if that's okay?"

"I'm sure it is. I'll let Harry know, make sure she's up before I leave."

Finished with her business, Sugar chooses that moment to return and snuffle at Jack's hand in greeting. "Hey, Sugar Baby," he says, bending to scratch between her ears. "Appreciate you staying and keeping watch," he says, not looking at me.

The comment rubs at me, just a little. It's not his place to thank me for that, as if he has some stake in the matter. I could see it if it were Owen making the comment, but not a neighbor. "Forty-two," I answer, turning to head back inside. "Come on, Sugar."

"Did Harry explain that to you?"

"What are you talking about?" His question makes me pause on the threshold, and Sugar slides in around me.

"Forty-two. Harry has always said that, from the time she was a kid. I've never had any clue what it meant."

"Oh. No…it's just something I'm familiar with, I guess." His expression is disgruntled, and I take pity on him. "It's a book reference. *Hitchhiker's Guide to the Galaxy*."

"Ah. Thanks."

"Yeah, sure." We stand, looking at each other in awkward silence, until I slap my hand against the doorjamb. "Well, nice seeing you, Jack. I gotta go…stuff to do. Have a good one."

"Yeah. You, too. Ah, Wyatt?"

"Yeah?"

"Take care of her."

Without responding, I nod curtly and go inside. I'll get a pot of coffee started for Harry and then I'll have to throw on my clothes and leave. As much as I'd like to stay in bed, practice starts in under an hour.

Inside, I find the coffee grounds and figure out Harry's fancy ass coffee machine. As I start looking for a mug,

Sugar barks, a high, urgent sound coming from the back of the house. Dropping the mug, I run. Sugar doesn't bark unless there's a reason.

The reason is still in the bed I just left, in the throes of a seizure.

Sugar is stretched out at her side, preventing her from falling off the bed, and I take the other side. And then, one eye on the clock, I wait.

Watching Harry seize is one of the worst things I've ever had to do. She warned me it could—probably would—happen. Told me that with her anxiety and stress at an all-time high, her seizures could end up becoming more frequent occurrences.

Harry's pragmatic acceptance of her condition doesn't help my feeling of absolute, utter helplessness as I sit beside her. For one minute and thirty-two seconds after I start my watch, I can do nothing as she shakes and heaves. Blood pools at the corner of her mouth as she bites her tongue. I can't even help that. From the crash course I gave myself in epilepsy after her revelation, I know better than to attempt to place anything in her mouth.

Finally, the shaking subsides and she goes limp. Her eyelids flutter rapidly before her face goes lax and she appears to settle into sleep. Gently I wipe the blood from the corner of her mouth and smooth her hair, then reach out to stroke Sugar. "Good girl," I croon. "Such a good girl." Harry is mostly nude from the night before, having donned a sleep tank and a pair of underwear, and I pull the blanket up and over her to keep the chill away.

Then, phone in hand, I navigate to my contacts and call Harry's brother. Now that the seizure is past, I need to get someone here that knows what comes next.

"Hello." Owen's greeting is brusque, wary, I suppose, from not recognizing the caller.

"Owen Bee?"

"Speaking."

"Owen, this is Wyatt Granger, your sister's TA."

"Is Harry okay?" His voice changes, sharpens.

"She just had a seizure. It lasted a minute and thirty-two seconds—"

"I'm on my way. Are you in her classroom?"

"No. We're at her house. I'm not sure if she was even awake. I took Sugar out and when we came back in it started. She's sleeping now. Is there anything I should be doing?"

"No. I'll be there in a minute. Just keep her comfortable, and if she wakes and wants to get up, tell her not to stir about too much."

Owen ends the call and I ease into a more comfortable position beside Harry. I watch her closely, zoned in on the rise and fall of her chest with each breath and the slight flicker of her eyes beneath her eyelids. I'm loathe to glance away, even for a second, afraid if I do that something might happen.

Owen shouldn't be long, maybe half an hour. His office is near the campus. I think he's even been driving Harry to and from work since Marcus's disappearing act.

Reaching out, I push a curl from where it rests on Harry's face. She's different in slumber. Her face, normally telegraphing a mix of anxiety and curiosity, is relaxed and as close to peaceful as I've ever seen it. After a little while, her brow wrinkles and she begins to stir, moaning low as echoes of the seizure make themselves known.

The need to hold her claws at me. I pull her carefully upward until she's lying against my chest in the circle of my arms and wait for her to regain full consciousness. Around the same time I hear the back door open, she opens her eyes and blinks up at me. "Hey, you," I whisper.

"Hi," she returns. "Why are you looking at me like that?"

Owen's feet sound on the hardwood and he appears around the corner of the door. "Because you had a seizure, apparently, and scared the poor guy half to death," he answers. Her lips part in surprise. "How're you feeling?"

She struggles in my arms, and I help her to sit. "I'm all right, I guess. Tired. A little groggy." She sniffs. "Is that coffee I smell?"

I ease out from behind her and stand. Owen doesn't seem at all surprised or concerned to see me in his sister's bed, but it feels awkward all the same. "I was making a pot when Sugar alerted. Want a cup?"

"Please."

Happy to have something useful to do, I head to the kitchen to make her a cup. "Cream and sugar, right?"

"Yes." The low buzz of her and Owen's conversation pauses as she answers, then continues.

In the kitchen, the microwave clock catches my attention and I curse as I quickly prepare Harry's coffee and carry it back to her. I'm going to be late.

"Here you go."

Harry reaches to accept the mug with grabby fingers, casting me a swift smile. "Thank God for coffee."

"Ah...I really hate to do this, Harry, but I have to go. I have practice and I'm going to be late—"

She cuts me off with a wave of one hand. "It's fine. I'm fine now. Go, do your thing."

"Are you sure? Because I can try getting hold of Coach and letting him know—"

"Absolutely not." Her tone is firm and cheerful, but I swear I can see a dash of insecurity in her gaze as she looks at me. *Fuck.* I need more time.

Bending, I take her face in both hands and press a hard kiss to her mouth. "I'll be back in just a little while," I murmur. "I don't want to go. I..." There I falter. I have words I'd like to say, things I'm feeling, but it's not the time. "Rest."

She nods and licks her lips. "I will."

"Well, that escalated quickly," Owen quips, rising and leaving the room.

My attention is on Harry, though. "I'll see you later."

"Okay."

"Bye."

"Bye." I back slowly out of the room, holding her eyes with mine. Hers are still faintly shadowed, slightly worried. Am I leaving because her seizure scared me off? Am I coming back? I can see the questions in the tense set of her shoulders, as loudly and clearly as if she'd shouted them at me. "Don't worry," I say, and then force myself to walk away.

Owen stands beside the couch in the living room. A crease of worry separates the space between his eyes, his initial levity from the bedroom gone. Hands on hips, he surveys me as I enter. "I'm glad you were here," he says without preamble, his voice pitched low, so Harry doesn't hear. "They're coming more frequently now, and she needs someone."

"I wasn't sure what to do," I answer, curling one hand around the back of my neck. "I mean, I knew how to handle the seizure, even if was shit to basically just sit there. But after…I didn't know what she would need."

"What you did is all we can do, unless it lasts longer. Then she needs the hospital."

I lift my chin in a slow nod. "Got it. You're good here for a while? I need to go."

"Yeah, I'll stay, make sure everything's copacetic. She'll probably fall back asleep. Some of the rougher ones wear her out."

"All right, then." I pick up the hoodie I was wearing when I arrived last night and my keys and head toward the door. A niggling worry...something I hadn't yet allowed myself to think... hits me and I pause with my hand on the doorknob. "It wasn't because...she didn't seize because we—"

"Fucked?" Owen's interruption is brusque and filled with humor. "No, man. Go with God."

Releasing a short laugh, I leave. His words stay with me, though, following me through practice and beyond. *They're coming more frequently...she needs someone.*

What if I'm not capable of being that someone she needs? I'll destroy us both.

---

There are scouts at practice. They sit in the stands, their phones and clipboards in their laps, watching. I can't help my eyes from straying as I take the mound, can't shake the nerves that make me want to puke.

My first pitch is shit, at least six inches high and outside the box. Pinching my lips together, I blow a breath out from my nose and prepare to go again. A shrill whistle halts me.

Rob, my pitching coach, jogs across the field to stand before me. "What the fuck was that?"

"Fucking nerves," I answer. He knows what it was.

"Get rid of them. Now. Ignore those motherfuckers and do your job. Yeah?"

"Hell, yeah."

He slaps me lightly on my cheek and returns to the dugout.

I'm fine afterwards. For the remainder of practice, my pitches are consistent and top speed, my fielding is efficient, and my batting is strong. As I head to the locker room afterwards, tired and sweaty, I know I couldn't have performed much better than I did.

So, why then, don't I feel better about it? Mixed with my euphoria is a nagging sense of gloom. It doesn't make any sense. Brad, my agent, even stopped me before I left the field to tell me one of the scouts had asked if I was available for lunch. I *know* I did well.

I shower quickly and dress for a restaurant in a pair of khakis and a polo. I'm meeting Brad and the scout at one of the nicer spots near campus and my heart thumps erratically as I drive over. On the way, I call Mom to make sure she can pick Noah up from day care if I'm too late to do so. Then I call Harry.

"Hey." Her voice is soft and sleepy.

"Hey. I just wanted to call and let you know I'll be later than I had planned. There's a scout...he wants to have lunch with me and my agent."

"Oh. That's great, Wyatt. Really, really great. Right?"

"Well, yeah. I mean, it's not a commitment, but it's interest, and interest is good."

"I'm so happy for you."

The restaurant is ahead, and I'm quiet as I pull into the lot and park. Instead of getting out of the car immediately, I sit. "I really hate that I had to leave this morning, Harry. I want you to know that. I—"

"It's fine, Wyatt. Owen's still here. He's working from here today, so he's good. Just enjoy your lunch, and good luck."

"No, that's not it." My fingers grip the steering wheel tightly, frustration riding me hard. "I know you. I saw your face this morning, and I know what you're thinking, even if you're not saying it. I know you're worried that the seizure scared me off, that I don't want to deal with it. You're wrong, Harry. You couldn't be more wrong. I—"

"Wyatt. Don't."

"No, you don't. You don't get to withdraw and push me away before we've even really gotten started."

"That's not what I'm doing—"

A knock on my window startles me and I look up to see Brad and the scout standing a foot or so behind him. Brad gestures impatiently. "Damnit. I have to go, Harry. They're waiting on me. Just...I'm strong enough, okay? Strong enough for you, strong enough for your epilepsy, strong enough for anything you want to throw at me. Don't shut me out."

I hang up and climb out of the car. As I shake hands with the scout and we head inside the restaurant, I know I'm right. I am strong enough to deal with everything that makes Doctor Harry Bee my Harry.

The only question is whether or not she'll let me prove that to her.

---

The house is quiet when I get home for the afternoon. From the kitchen, the smell of chicken and vegetables drifts, fragrant with soy sauce and spices. Yakisoba, I bet.

Moving quietly, I peek in Noah's room and find him fast asleep, one arm pinning a stuffed tiger to the pillow beside him. I close his door with a soft snick and continue to Mom's workroom, knocking once before cracking the door.

"Hey. Okay to come in?"

She doesn't look up from where she's bent over a repair. "Of course, my son."

"What are you working on?"

"Hilda Thomas's Spode platter. Fell off the wall when her grandson slammed the back door."

I wince. Hilda Thomas is famous for the turkey she serves on that very platter every Thanksgiving. It wouldn't taste the same on anything else, I'm sure.

"I have no doubt it'll be good as new when you finish with it," I say. "Listen, Mom. I have news."

She turns to look at me now, her bright dark brown eyes casing me over the rims of her bifocals. "Last time you had news, you had gotten a girl pregnant."

I huff a laugh and run my hand down my face. "Nothing like that, I promise. It's good news."

"I'm waiting."

"I had lunch with a scout today. Brad thinks this is it."

She frowns a little and swivels back to her workstation. "I thought we were done with that."

I bite my tongue, holding back the knee-jerk reaction to say something rude. *Be respectful. She's your mother.*

It's an old argument, one I don't stand a chance of winning. Like the noodle dish in the kitchen, my mother is steeped in tradition. While she's proud of my accomplishments, it's not something she fully understands. Not when I could do something to help society with my degrees.

"It could be a big opportunity." I decide on a neutral response.

"What about your son? Your family? While you are off playing, what will Noah be doing? And me?"

"I want him with me as much as possible, of course, but I'll need you when that's not possible. I'll always need you. If it happens, we'll work out those details." I flick my fingers, restless. "It hasn't happened yet, though. Let's not get ahead of ourselves."

She sniffs. "I have done research, you know. It is not easy, this professional sportsman's life. All the travel. The spotlight. The pressure."

"But isn't it worth it? If I get on with the Phillies, that's...that's Noah's college fund, Mom. A nice house for you."

"I like my house."

"Security."

"Has your life not been secure enough?"

It's a loaded question, and I choose my words with care. "You were...are...an excellent provider."

"You always had everything you needed."

Except a father. That's not something we talk about, although a psychologist would undoubtedly link my desire for material security to having grown up without a father figure. He left when I was an infant, and to my knowledge, my mother never heard from him again.

It's part of the reason I fought to keep Noah, even if his mother wasn't interested in doing the mom thing. In some twisted way, I'm making amends to myself on my own father's behalf, healing my own scabbed-over wounds by doing everything in my power to be a good parent.

"Yes," I say now. "I did. And now I want to make sure my son has everything he needs, whether it's a pair of shoes or a trip to Disney, or something much bigger. Can you see that, Mom? Understand it?"

"Money is not everything, my son."

Frustration brings me to my feet. "It's not about money. It's about—"

"Hi, Daddy."

We both turn to find Noah standing in the doorway, one hand still clutching the tiger and the other rubbing his eye.

"Him," I finish, picking him up and nuzzling my face into his sweet-smelling neck. "It's about him."

Mom rises and touches my back softly before moving past me, into the hall. "I understand, my Wyatt. And I will help, however you need me to. Now, yakisoba is ready. Come, eat."

I bend my face to Noah's hair and breathe him in. "Thank you," I whisper. "Thank you."

# Twenty-Seven

## Harry

"What was that all about?"

From his position on the sofa, Owen eyes me over the edge of his laptop screen, eyebrows lifted in question.

"Nothing."

"Didn't sound like nothing."

*That's because it wasn't nothing.* I curl more deeply into my armchair and resolutely flick the volume on the remote. I'm in the middle of binging an incredible sci-fi series where a few people in a small town rise from the dead, perfectly restored. I don't have time to dissect my emotions or lay them bare for my brother to do so.

"Oh-kay. Just ignore me."

"Stop it, Francis. I had a rough night." He laughs, and at first, I don't understand why. When realization strikes

I feel my cheeks flushing. "Oh, my God. That is not what I meant—"

"Uh-huh. It was that good, huh?"

"You ass. Before that I had a break-in. That's the whole reason Wyatt was here in the first place."

He switches from mirthful to furious so fast I feel the room spin. "What! Why am I just now hearing about this? What the hell, Harry?"

"Chill. We got it taken care of. Jack and Wyatt were here—"

"So, you had a threesome. Awesome."

I groan. "Jack is a cop. He heard the alarm and got here before Wyatt. So, NO, we did not have a fucking threesome."

"Shame. You should try it sometime." He sobers. "Who broke in? Did Jack catch the guy? Start talking, kid, or I'm calling Mom."

"It was Marcus." Forehead wrinkled, Owen starts to say something, and I hold up my hand to ward off what I know is coming. "I know. Believe me, I know. But I smelled his cologne, so I know it was him." Resigned, I pause my show and tell him everything, up to the point I crawled onto the couch with Wyatt. I'm careful to downplay my terror. Still, I can feel his rage, his helplessness and frustration, vibrating through the room.

"This is not acceptable. You're not staying here alone anymore, Harry."

"What? I'm fine, Owen—"

"He. Broke. Into. Your. House. End of discussion."

I raise myself to a standing position and point a trembling finger at him. "No, it's not the end of discussion, you Neanderthal. This is my house, my life. I'll live it the way that I want to. If you think for a hot minute that I'm going to tuck tail and run to Mom and Dad's, you are so very mistaken. I—"

I don't know why, but it's imperative that I do this my way. That I handle my own business without leaning on anyone. I feel like I've been leaning on one person or another my entire life, taking as gospel that I have limitations, that I need help.

No more.

"Calm your tits, Harry. That's not what I was suggesting. Someone is going to be staying here with you from here on out, though, until they catch this guy. Either me, or the kid, or the cop—"

"Wyatt is not a kid! And he has a kid—he can't just abandon him to come stay with me. And neither can you, for that matter."

"We'll do what it takes, Harry, because we love you and want you to be safe."

I drop back in my chair, choosing to focus on the one battle I think I might win. Owen will be staying. That one is a skirmish lost before it even really got started.

But I don't need him thinking there's more to this thing with Wyatt than there is. "He doesn't love me."

Owen snorts. "Then he's doing a damn fine imitation."

"I scared him, Owen. The seizure...no one's ready for that. They think they are, and then it hits, and they realize the gravity of it and how difficult it would be, being with someone like me, and—"

"Harry. Slow down. Take a breath. When I got here, Wyatt was doing just fine. He was worried about you, but he wasn't unraveling or anything."

"He ran."

"What? No, he didn't."

"He got out of here as fast as he could. Probably left a trail of rubber on the road."

"He had ball practice, Harry. He had to leave. Was he in a hurry? Sure. I think events might've made him a little late, so he was hustling. But that doesn't mean that you scared him off."

"I guess we'll see."

"Yes, I reckon we will. Did you take your meds this morning?"

"No. I forgot, damnit. I took them last night, but with everything—"

"Just calm down. I'll go get them and you can take them now. It's all right, Harry. Just make sure you're generally taking them the way you're supposed to."

I nod. "I am, I swear."

"Okay, good. I think...hang on." Owen gets up and disappears into the back of the house, reemerging a few minutes later with my pill organizer and a glass of water. He hands them to me and continues talking as though he never stopped. "I think Ava and I should come and stay until things even out a bit. Until the police find Marcus and put him away, at any rate."

I swallow a capsule and quell my reflex to reject his offer. "I'll think about it."

He raises an eyebrow.

"I don't want to mess up your lifestyle or confuse things with Ava. Let me think about it."

"Right. Okay, you think, and while you're doing that, I'll be bringing supper and a few changes of clothes this evening." He begins to gather his computer and paperwork he was working from. "I'm going to go to the office for a few hours. Get some rest, make your decision. And make the right one, sis, or I will be calling in reinforcements."

---

The next twenty-four hours crawl by. I message Shiloh and learn that it was, in fact, her house that was broken into. Worse, she said it appears to be a stalker more than just a random burglar.

**ME:** This can't be coincidence.

**SHILOH:** It would certainly be a strange one, I agree. But what more can we do? The police are watching over everything and investigating.

**ME:** We need to keep an eye out for each other and make sure we let each other know if anything strange happens.

**SHILOH**: Done.

**ME**: And don't go anywhere alone.

**SHILOH**: Okay, Mom.

**ME**: Ha,ha.

Owen brought supper and Ava, and as I figured he would do, didn't leave until he took Ava to daycare the next morning. I finish the third season of my sci-fi series, and then struggle with a Netflix hangover as I sit on the couch and *blip* my way through option after option, never settling on any one thing. All those shows and absolutely nothing to watch.

So I watch the clock.

By nine P.M. the day following my seizure, my feelings are officially injured and my ass is up on my shoulders as I slam cabinet doors in the kitchen, as much for the satisfying sound they make as for trying to find the bowl I like to eat my ice cream in.

Wyatt never called again. Except for one brief text to ask how I was feeling and tell me things were weird with his mother and he needed to be home, I haven't heard from him.

I get it. I understand that he has things happening right now, important things he must be present for. I've never been the kind of woman to pine for a man or be resentful of my guy's interests or work. It kind of bit me in the ass where Marcus was concerned, but I'm independent, damnit.

Still, I can't help feeling just a smidge hurt that I don't warrant enough courtesy for a phone call or a conversation after having sex with this man, and as a consequence am very desirous of a half-gallon of moose tracks ice cream.

"What you doing, Ammie Harry?" Ava's sweet voice pipes through my irritation and I smooth my features before turning to look at her. She's wearing her Bubble Guppies jammies and it's an hour past her bedtime, but I shrug inwardly. Staying up a little late never hurt anyone.

"I'm just getting some ice cream. You want some?"

"Ice cream, yay!"

"Go ask your daddy."

Her face falls. "He's gonna say no."

"Why?"

"Cause. It's past my bedtime and I ain't brushed my teefs yet."

"Oh." The slump of her shoulders does me in. No sense in both of us being depressed. "You know what—never mind. Ammie Harry says it's okay."

Owen's groan from the next room is audible. "I will remember that." Ava giggles, the sound a balm to my bruised feelings.

Between Ava and the ice cream, I feel slightly better by the time I head to my bedroom to read for a while before going to sleep. I've almost convinced myself that

I'm fine, and it's no big deal, when my phone chimes with a notification. Just like that, every bit of anger and resentment returns in full measure.

*Wyatt.*

**WYATT:** hey

**ME:** ...

I start to type and then stop, unsure how or if I even want to reply. I'm pissed. Finally, I decide not to be juvenile. I'll tell him straight out how I feel and let him deal with it.

**ME**: I'm pissed at you.

**WYATT**: I was afraid you would be. I'm sorry.

**ME**: not good enough.

**WYATT**: I am. I fucked up. I didn't know—

His text cuts off abruptly, leaving me wondering exactly what he didn't know. A second later, he calls. I answer warily.

"Wyatt, let's just leave it as a never happened, and never happening again, okay? We shouldn't have—damnit, *I* shouldn't—have gone there. I knew it was a heartbreak in the making."

There's a swift intake of breath on the other end of the line. "Is that what this is? Heartbreak?"

*Fuck.*

Is it heartbreak? That would imply I was in love, and I'm not ready for that. Everything's moving too fast, coming too soon on the heels of my recent failure. I can't be in love. Won't be.

I scramble to backtrack over what I've mistakenly revealed. "No. It's just an expression. Mistake might be a better word."

"Right." There's a pause, then he speaks again, his voice challenging. "You sure about that? Want to think about for a minute?"

"I'm not doing this, Wyatt." I pluck at the blanket, pulling at a loose string.

"Not doing what? Talk to me, Harry."

"I'm not going to fight with you over whether I am or am not in love with you!" Growling, I fling a throw pillow to the floor.

"We're not fighting, Red. This is just a difference of opinion."

"Regardless, it's immaterial. We had sex and you didn't even bother to call me for nearly two days. And this was after telling me you didn't want a one-night thing, that you wanted more."

"I am sorry that I didn't call sooner. It has nothing to do with you—"

"Or perhaps 'disaster.' Yeah, I think that one works best."

"Yesterday and today both just ended up being insane, and by the time things calmed down, it was late."

I sigh. "Look, it's okay. I'm fine—"

"Harry—"

"—everything's fine. But whatever—"

"Would you just—"

"— that was the other night, I'm not up for a repeat."

"Damnit, Harry, stop talking and listen to me."

The urgency in his tone stops my ramble. "What, then?"

"That scout yesterday…there's a chance I'll be given a contract. Or invited to spring training. Or both, I don't know."

I wait, but he doesn't expand. "You know I have no concept of what that even means, Wyatt."

"It means it's happening, Harry! It's fucking happening for me, finally! And I'm sorry I didn't call earlier, but if this goes through, there are decisions to make for Noah, and paperwork, and—"

When I was a kid, my parents took me and Owen to the Outer Banks for vacation every summer. I remember sitting on the beach, a plastic sieve in my hands, watching the sand pour through the little holes with a sense of awe. Over and over, the sight mesmerizing for some reason, no matter how many times I repeated the experiment.

That's what this feels like. The anger and hurt are gone, slipping away like sand through a sieve at his announcement. Sadness and a certain resignation replace them. I thought we'd have longer. Thought I'd have more time before I was forced to say goodbye.

Because this is goodbye. I don't delude myself into thinking anything else.

"That's really...congratulations, Wyatt." Silence fills the line between us, as choked as my words. "I'm happy for you."

"You don't sound happy."

"I am. It's everything you've ever wanted. Your dream." I inject cheer I don't feel into my voice.

"Not everything," he says.

He means *you*, my brain shouts. He means that you're a part of that everything, He wants you, even after a seizure and seeing what a mess your life is. He wants you.

But...there's no way this can work. No way I can travel the way those baseball girlfriends do, and sure as hell no way I can take being left behind all the time, like I was with Marcus. I need more than that.

"Wyatt..." I let the word speak for me, trailing it into dust.

"I'm coming over." Whatever he hears in my voice, he doesn't like it.

"No!" I need to get off this phone and go back to wallowing, maybe with another bowl of moose tracks. I need to not hear his voice any longer. "There's no need. I was about to go to bed."

"You can wait a little while."

The line clicks as he hangs up and I growl before throwing the phone to the floor. The look Sugar gives me as she lifts her head in response chides and I flop back on the bed, my arm over my eyes. "I know, I know."

The dog licks my other hand. *It's okay*, she seems to say. Turning to my side, I bury my face in the soft fur of her flank and run my fingers over her silky head.

That's how Wyatt finds me when he appears in the door to my bedroom a short while later. There's no knock to announce his arrival; he knows the code and let himself in.

Without saying a word, he crosses the room, sits down beside me on the bed, and gathers me onto his lap. I lay my head against his chest and listen to the thump of his heart, loud in the quiet of the room. We sit like that for an interminable length of time, neither of us wanting to speak first and break the tentative truce touch has drawn.

But we both know what this is.

"When do you leave, if you get the invite?" I finally ask. *And you'll get the invite.* I finish the thought in my head.

"A week from today," he says. "But there's still a long way to go, Harry. Even if I did get invited to spring training, there's no guarantee I'll be given a spot on a team. I need at least a minor league contract, so I have a chance at moving up." His long fingers trace the bones and tendons in my forearm. "This doesn't mean we're done, Harry. It doesn't mean anything except I'll be gone for a little while. We'll talk, we'll text...video chat—"

"Wyatt." Reaching up, I cover his lips with my fingers. "I can't. I'm sorry."

"What do you mean, you can't? Can't what?"

I pull away a little and take hold of his face with both hands, forcing us both to look at each other. "I cannot be in another relationship where one person is absent all the time. I won't do it."

"You don't trust me."

"I don't trust myself." The words—the realization—surprises me. *Where did that come from?* The squinch of Wyatt's face communicates his lack of understanding, and I try to make this feeling comprehensible, even to myself. "I don't trust myself to have the kind of faith one needs to have for a long-distance relationship. To feel connected and...necessary...and to make you feel the same. I don't trust myself to be happy with what little time we get. To be satisfied."

"But, Harry, that's why we have to work together. I'm not saying it would be easy. I'm smarter than that. I'm saying it would be worth it—worth every bad day. Worth every minute that we're not together."

I shake my head. "I can't. I've done it before and look where it got me. Marcus was gone constantly, and I did all the kind of work you're talking about. I was never suspicious, never begrudged him his time at work. And I lost...I lost so big." Phantom pains of what I lost ache at the mention, low in my gut. "I wasted so much time with him."

"I'm not your fucking ex, Harry."

"I know that! But I'm still the same person, and I know myself too well. I cannot... I will not do it again."

"This is bullshit and you know it." Wyatt disengages from me and stands, raking his hand through his hair until it stands on end. He thrusts a finger in my direction. "You're scared, and the least you can do is own it. You're scared of everything about me. You're scared of how much younger I am. You're scared that I tempt you to be more than what you've settled for all these years. You're scared that I make you *feel* more than what you've ever felt before."

I shake my head. He's wrong. "You're wrong. If you're leaving, this is the only logical decision—"

He leans in close to where I'm kneeling on the bed, putting his face only inches from mine. "It scares you so much I can see it every time you look at me. I can taste it. You've had one foot out the door the whole time." His lips tease mine before he withdraws and stalks to the doorway. "I love you, Harry." He laughs, a bitter breath of sound. "I think I've loved you since I found you on that bridge. It was like something in you called to something in me, like we had known each other before."

I pinch the bridge of my nose hard against the tears that threaten. Particles. He's talking about particles and doesn't even know it. "I'm sorry, Wyatt. I'm so, so—"

His hand flies up and I stop. "Don't. Fucking. Apologize." His eyes sear into me, digging and finding every secret, every shortcoming. "We could have something incredible, if you would just stop being afraid."

He leaves the room, and a minute later the sound of the back door opening and closing registers. I sink back onto the bed, all of the energy spent fighting his convictions depleted. I quell the instinct to argue against my choices and curl into my pillows.

Tears burn at the back of my eyes, but I won't let them fall. I can't help wishing the pillows were a person, a person with all-seeing brown eyes and strong arms to wrap around me. But that person is gone, and no tears will change the sinking feeling that maybe...just maybe...he was right, and I was wrong.

# Twenty-Eight

## Harry

There is a dizzying array of pill bottles on the counter before me, each with its little folded packet of instructions and side effects. The realization that it's been years since I've paid attention to what I was taking, or why, or when…it's disturbing and faintly shaming. Marcus always did this, shooing me away and saying it was his job to take care of me. If he couldn't be present all the time, this was the very least he could do.

I loved it. He was so invested in my health, in making sure I took every medication and every recommended supplement and had no reason not to do so.

But now he's gone, and it's time—past time—for me to take care of myself.

I begin to read each accompanying pamphlet, sorting the pills into morning, midday, and evening doses as I do, when my phone chimes with a text.

**WYATT**: You going to be all right for class tomorrow?

The message surprises me after the way we parted yesterday. He was angry with me, and hurt by my rejection, and I wouldn't have blamed him if he had resigned as my TA and never spoke to me again.

That's not Wyatt, though, and I'm grateful for his maturity.

**ME**: Yes. I'm ready to be back. I'm surprised to hear from you. Are you planning on being there?

**WYATT**: Yes. I tried telling you; I don't even know if I'm going, yet.

**ME**: You're going to get an invite. Or a contract. I feel it.

There's no response at first, and I set the phone down. Then I pick it back up and begin typing again.

**ME**: I don't want things to be awkward between us. I hurt you and I know you're not happy with me right now. If you need space, take it.

**WYATT:** I'm fine.

**ME**: I'm not. I'm going to miss you.

**WYATT**: You don't get to say things like that. That's your choice, right?

**ME**: Please don't be mean.

**WYATT**: Not mean. Just honest. You could come with me, you know. You don't even want to teach.

**ME:** Of course, I want to teach.

**WYATT**: No, you don't. It's a means to an end. You come alive when you're in the lab, conducting research. You don't want to be teaching a bunch of asswipes about triglycerides.

It's annoying, how well he knows me. I guess every day he's been there with me in that classroom, he's seen past the surface to the truth beneath. Teaching has never been my passion. I do it solely because I need the backing of a university in order to publish.

**ME:** I wouldn't have the ability to conduct research without the teaching career. Or the credibility for my papers. The university gives me all of that.

**WYATT**: I think you've earned the credibility by now. You have a sterling reputation.

**ME:** Maybe. But I still need the lab.

**WYATT**: I feel like that's an easy problem to solve.

I decide to change the subject. This is getting us nowhere.

**ME**: So. What will you be doing with Noah while you're away? And what are we...? Are we just continuing as usual, pretending everything is fine until it isn't?

**WYATT**: IF I get an invite to spring training, my mother will carry on as usual, unless it turns into a long-term thing. Then we'll need to make other plans.

**ME**: Okay.

**WYATT:** And as for us. I'm not ready to end things, Harry.

**ME:** I'll see you tomorrow.

---

Later that afternoon, the phone buzzes again.

**WYATT**: I love you, Harry.

**ME**: I ...

I'm saved from replying when another text comes in, this one from my brother.

**OWEN**: Dinner at Landry's Pizza tonight?

**ME**: Nah. Tired today, think I'll grab a bowl of cereal and go to bed.

**OWEN**: What's up with Boy Wonder? Haven't seen him around lately.

**ME**: It's only been a few days. He's busy with practice.

**OWEN**: You need to stop moping and settle whatever's happening

**ME:** Francis, when I want your advice, I'll ask for it.

**OWEN**: We're eating pizza tonight. Be ready at six.

---

Landry's is packed when we pull into the half-asphalt, half-gravel parking lot. Owen finds a spot along the road, and we enter our local den of pizza, pasta, cheesesteaks, and wings to an enticing blend of aromas, red-checked vinyl, and the buzz of conversation.

I pull my scarf from around my neck, craning my neck to find a place to sit. "There," Owen says, pointing.

'There' is a large family booth in the back. My mother is standing beside it, waving madly. Closing my eyes, I groan inaudibly. "What have you done, Francis?"

He chuckles under his breath and shoves me forward with one hand, his other hand clutching Ava's. "Nothing at all, sis, nothing at all. I just mentioned that we might be here eating pizza tonight. At six."

"I will remember this. Momma!" I paste a bright smile on my face and hug her, then Dad. "Fancy meeting you guys here."

Owen and I slide into the side opposite our parents, while Ava sits between them like a princess surrounded by her subjects.

"She doesn't look down in the dumps, Owen." Momma surveys me with a critical gaze. "Are you depressed, Harry?"

"Oh, my God. No, I am not depressed!"

"You've been moping around for the past three days. Hasn't she, Ava?"

"Ammie Harry, are you sad?"

I glare at Owen. "No, baby, I'm not sad. Some people think you need to smile and dance all the time, and I don't do that."

"But why? Dancing is the funnest. I loves to dance."

Owen hides a smile behind his hand and turns to the waitress to order, leaving me to answer Ava. "Uh...I don't know, sweetie. I'm more serious, I guess."

"Ammie's a grumpy butt," Momma says, ruffling Ava's hair.

"I am not a grumpy butt. I am... Jes—eez. Can we just order some pizza, please?" I correct hastily as Momma narrows her eyes at me.

"Y'all leave the girl alone," Dad interjects. "She's not depressed; she's not grumpy. She's just hangry." He winks at me, and I flash him a grateful smile.

After his pronouncement, everyone leaves me alone until the pizza arrives. With his mouth full of cheesy goodness, though, Owen gets a second wind. "Mom. Dad. Did Harry tell you she was dating a younger man? A student, in fact."

"What is wrong with you today?" I punch his shoulder. "Momma, he is not a student. He is younger, yes, but he's also a father and very mature. I promise. Owen, if I were you, I'd lock your door tonight."

"Oh, my, a father? Tell us about him."

"I'm not even dating him. He's a baseball player and he's about to go pro, so there's really no point. It's all very casual."

"Casual? What does that even mean? How do you casually date someone?"

I groan while my brother's shoulders shake with laughter. "Not touching that one," he mutters.

"Moving on…" I fold my own slice in half and take a bite.

"We'll move on when I'm ready, dear. Do you feel like you're ready to begin dating again? So soon after Marcus, I mean."

"I know what you mean. And I'm fine. Like I said, it was casual."

"Was casual?" Dad is more interested than he appears to have caught my slip.

"I just mean that I'm not planning on anything serious with him. He's almost guaranteed to leave for a pro ball team, and I'm not interested in anything long distance."

"Mmpf." Dad returns to his pizza. Momma isn't as easily deterred.

"But it could be serious? If he wasn't going to play pro ball? And why is that a bad thing? It sounds exciting."

"Because he'd be gone all the time, just like Marcus was. I don't want that." I ignore her other question. I'm only just now beginning to understand how serious it could be, only now realizing the depth of my feelings. I'm not ready to share them with anyone.

Owen has no such reservations. "Yeah, it could be serious if he were going to stick around. Dude is whipped."

I turn a hot stare on him. "Okay, that's enough discussion of my love life. If y'all can't drop the subject, I'm calling an Uber."

Except for a grunt from Daddy and an "mmpf" from Momma, the table falls silent as everyone turns to their meals.

The pizza tastes like a cardboard lie, though. Everything I just said is wrong. Wyatt and I are anything but casual, and the potential—the probability—of his imminent departure is laying waste to the burgeoning growth of my soul.

Marcus... he was casual. He lit a match with his betrayal and flicked it with icy disregard for every finer feeling to the meadows of my heart. He set fire to my capacity for love and watched it burn and didn't care.

But Wyatt...he's been carefully nurturing every tender blade of new growth, coaxing fearful life from blackened ash.

He's my forty-two. My reason, my answer, my response to everything, and he's going to leave before I've even had the opportunity to accept that truth and watch it bloom.

Salt mixes with my next automatic bite and I realize I'm crying, noiseless tears tracking my cheeks as I bend my head over my plate. Everyone is silent, pretending not to see, until Ava's clear voice cuts through the pretense.

"Ammie—"

"Well, I think I need to make a trip to the little girl's room. Harry, come with?"

Momma doesn't give me a chance to decline but grasps my wrist with one hand and pulls me after her. I stumble, blind with tears, after her, dimly aware of Sugar on my heels.

In the restroom, I stand in the center of the tiled room while Momma wets a paper towel at the sink and wrings it out. "Now," she says, stepping close and wiping carefully at my face. "You want to tell me about what's got you in such a state?"

I bite my lip hard and meet her gaze. There's nothing there but love and concern and acceptance, and without letting myself think too much about it, I give voice to every fear I'm feeling. "He's going to leave, Momma. He's been putting me back together without even realizing what he's doing, and I'm terrified it's going to shatter me all over again."

When the words devolve into rough, gasping sobs, she says nothing, but instead gathers me to her and holds me like I'm small again, like every problem can find its solution and its solace in her scent and softness.

When I quiet, she strokes my hair back from my face and holds me out to look me in the eye. She speaks, her voice firm and brooking no argument or alternate possibility. "If that's the case...why then, we'll break out the super glue and the Mary Kay, and we'll put you back prettier than ever."

I stare, struck by the absurdity of her statement. And then I giggle, the sound echoing off the tiles and returning my mirth. "God, Momma..." I hug her hard, suddenly thankful for this woman. "I love you like crazy."

# Twenty-Nine

## Harry

Snow is falling, fat, lazy flakes sticking momentarily to the windshield before melting into slush. It's just starting to accumulate on the ground and pavement, and I know it won't take long to begin covering over everything with a pristine mantle of white.

I release a sigh as I watch out the window. "Pretty, isn't it?"

Owen steers with painstaking focus over the slippery mountain roads, driving considerably slower than his usual just-this-side-of-reckless speed. "Pretty annoying."

I laugh. He hates snow the way some people hate gray clouds and rain. I love it, though, and the sight of the plump flakes this morning put me in a cheerful mood.

Sugar loves the snow, also. In the back seat, she pants happily as she watches the scenery move by. I know there will be a warm bath in her future after I cut her loose to play later.

Owen spares me a sideways glance. "You're chipper today. Something happen?"

With Wyatt, he means. It sobers me. Wyatt should be finding out soon from his agent if the scout has an offer, either for a minor league team or spring training. If he does, Wyatt will leave immediately and be gone indefinitely. We continue to try, but the awareness has placed a damper on our burgeoning intimacy. It colors and imbues a different layer of meaning to everything from a careless word to a shared look.

"Nothing," I say. "Just kind of glad to be getting back to work."

"I hear ya. I've been doing some interesting stuff lately."

"Yeah?" I turn my attention from the snow to my brother.

"Yep. A client asked me to research the Lucy Falls mystery...to go deeper than the norm."

"The Lucy Falls mystery...that's the one with the missing girl, right? The one the town was named for?"

"Yes. I've managed to unearth some pretty wild stuff. So, you probably remember that Lucy Van Hollister was engaged to a wealthy financier, Landon Burke, out of Charlottesville?"

"Vaguely, yes."

"That was apparently purely a marriage of convenience. The Van Hollister family was land poor, so they needed Burke's influx of cash. Burke needed land to develop and was contracted half of the Van Hollisters' mountain property as dowry. But then Lucy up and disappeared."

"Which is where the mystery comes in. Where did she go? Was she murdered, and if so, why?"

"Exactly. I located old court documents, though, that explain some of the mystery. Burke eventually sued the Van Hollister family for the promised land, citing breach of contract. It had come out that Lucy was involved with a groomsman that worked for her family."

"Oh, my..."

"It doesn't look like Burke was vindictive about it. He had invested heavily on the outcome of his new property, and without it, he would have been ruined. Once he discovered that Lucy was involved with the groomer, it was a safe assumption that she had never had any intention of following through with the wedding. The court awarded him the land, which was the half of the mountain that our town ended up settling on. Burke called it Lucy Falls, I suppose still feeling some attachment for her."

"That's pretty wild stuff. What's next?"

"I want to figure out what happened to her. Chase down the groomer's family tree and find out what happened with him."

"How fascinating. I want to know when you find out more."

When I get to class, I'm mildly concerned to find Wyatt nowhere around. He's always here early, but maybe the snow held him up. I begin to set up for class, cursing under my breath as I realize I'll have to sync the projector and my computer myself.

It's a new computer. The old one is still with the Lucy Falls police department. I gave up on getting it back within any viable time frame after they'd had it for a week and discovered nothing except some embedded code and had asked the university to issue me a replacement.

With it being new, I have no idea how to do anything remotely technical with it. Though to be fair, I didn't know how to do anything remotely technical on the old model, either.

Students begin entering as I fiddle with it, clicking different things experimentally. Tongue between my teeth, I navigate to a separate menu. Maybe…

"Hey, Dr. Bee." I look up and offer a smile and wave to a young woman in the front row. "Are you going to let us leave early? It's snowing really hard out there. And glad you're back, by the way."

"Ah… thank you. And I'm not sure yet. Possibly. You wouldn't happen to know how—" The door opens again, and I break off hopefully as Wyatt enters. "Nevermind! Rescue has arrived."

Wyatt is not alone. As he moves down the risers to the semi-circle where my desk is located, I see a little black-haired mini-me behind him, a plush blanket in his arms and a small red backpack on his back. A feeling like awe makes my stomach flip. "Hi," he greets me breathlessly when he reaches me. "Sorry I'm late. The preschool was closed for weather and Mom had a thing with a friend… I hope you don't mind that I brought Noah?"

"Mind? I'm thrilled." I squat down so I'm on level with the boy and meet his eyes. "Hi, Noah. I'm Dr. Bee, but since you're my special guest, you can call me Harry. Are you excited about the snow?"

He grins at me, his smile all baby teeth and gums. "I'm gonna build a snowman. Wanna help me?"

"I sure will! I have to teach first, though. Would you like to help me teach?"

His eyes, the same clear amber shade as his father's, grow big. "How?" he breathes.

"Oh, I'm sure we can find things for you to do. Here, let's get your dad to fix my computer, and you can come over here and draw a snowman for the class on the board. How about that?"

He claps his hands and hops toward the board, then stops as he sees Sugar. "You got a doggo!"

"I do! This is Sugar and she's a very special doggie. She lets me know if I'm about to get sick. She's friendly, you can pat her. Gentle…like this…" My hand over his, I show him how to give Sugar pets, then pluck a dry erase marker from the desk and lead him over to the whiteboard. Wyatt watches, the corner of his lips kicked up, and then turns his attention to my computer.

Once Noah is settled, contentedly drawing pictures on the board, I survey the lecture room. Roughly a third of my students are present, likely because of the weather.

"Okay, let's go ahead and get started. I'm going to make this a quick discussion today because of the weather. I know you have other places you'd rather be, and frankly, so do I." I hitch my thumb at Noah. "We have a snowman to build." There's a general murmur of assent and I launch into a speed session where I provide highlights of the material and then make the slide show available online for further use. After giving a reading assignment, I dismiss the students who braved the weather to attend, deciding mentally to give them each extra credit points for the extra effort.

"Thanks," Wyatt says, beginning to pack the computer up. "Ah…were you serious about playing in the snow with him?"

I give him a sidelong glance. "Of course. I wouldn't have said it if I wasn't serious."

He nods. "I didn't think you would, but I wanted to make sure we weren't roping you into anything."

"You're not roping me into anything, Wyatt." I lick my lips. "I don't want this to be confusing, though. This doesn't change anything."

"So, what are we doing, exactly?"

My gaze drops to the floor. It's selfish, I know, but I can't make a clean cut. I miss him and he's not even gone, yet. "I just…I feel like I need to be with you. For as long as

I have." I falter through an explanation, but he seems to understand, gathering me into him in a hug that hurts. I bury my face in his shoulder and stay there, gripping the fabric of his shirt, praying he can feel exactly how much I need him. How much I long for things to be different.

After a long minute he sets me away from him and resumes packing our things. "My house or yours?"

I clear my throat. "It doesn't really matter. Sugar will want to romp around, too."

"That's not a problem. Let's go to my house so Noah has dry clothes to change into. He'll play for ten minutes and then want to go inside."

"Every kid, everywhere," I say, and wait as Wyatt lifts Noah to his hip. As we make our way to the parking lot, I send Owen a text, letting him know that I'm with Wyatt and will be home later.

Wyatt lives in a mid-modern ranch-style home. Its white-painted brick exterior blends into the snowy landscape of an expansive lawn bordered with a low stone wall and shrubbery. A deep red door boasts a wooden wreath shaped like the letter G and painted pale blue. "This is really pretty."

Wyatt shrugs and pulls the truck into the garage, pressing the button to close the door behind us. "It's home. Always has been. Mom keeps things nice."

"I like it."

"Thanks. All right, squirt. Let's go get a snowsuit on." He eyes me as we climb out of the truck and cross the garage to a door that leads inside the house. "Do you have enough clothes? I can give you something of mine…"

I look down at my jeans and boots. "I'll be okay. I'm not planning on rolling around in it. I'll leave that to Sugar."

The door from the garage opens into a mudroom with a tiled floor and shelving littered with shoes and jackets. Noah immediately kicks off his shoes and I start to follow suit. "No, you're fine." Wyatt stops me. "We'll go out through the back, so just leave them on."

"Okay. Is it okay if I go ahead and take Sugar out?"

"Yep…just through there. The yard is fenced so you can let her roam freely."

I wander through the wide hall he points to while he takes Noah in the opposite direction. The walls are lined with photos, and I pause to study them. School pictures of Wyatt, from the time he was a little boy missing teeth to a handsome young man in cap and gown, mixed in with casual black and white snapshots of other people—a petite woman with thick, straight dark hair grinning up from a workstation of some kind; Wyatt, looking exhausted and triumphant as he stared down at an infant; Noah in a diaper and a large pair of tennis shoes. It's the story of a life and I find myself a little blue as I continue through an airy kitchen to a door that opens into a spacious back yard and step outside. Sugar takes off immediately to dive into the snow, and I stand at the edge of a slate patio and watch her.

It's all I've ever wanted, if I'm honest with myself. A family. Children. A house full of love and life and laughter...messy surfaces and missing socks. A family dog and maybe even a mischief-making kitten. I've pushed the dream aside, invested my time and energy in other pursuits—those of academia, and Marcus, and research—because it was too depressing to dwell on the constant awareness that it wasn't coming true for me.

Maybe this whole thing with Marcus is just a way to move forward, rather than sitting still. Maybe I can have my dream...even if it's in other ways.

"Penny for your thoughts."

Wyatt's voice startles me, and I realize I've been standing there, staring at Sugar as she snuffles and rolls and wags her tail, for some time. Noah's out in the yard with her, tossing gleeful handfuls of snow in the air and at the dog. I'm chilled through, even with my coat, and hug my arms across my chest.

"Nothing exciting," I say. "They love it, don't they?"

Wyatt grunts. "We'd better get over there and build a damn snowman."

I watch for a second as he steps off the patio and makes his way to Noah, watch as he tosses a snowball lightly at his son and then teaches him how to pack his own. Then, as he turns and throws a snowball at me, I finally move to join them, to be part of them instead of an observer.

It's scary, how good it feels.

# Thirty

## Wyatt

Every time I think I can't possibly fall any harder for this woman, she proves me wrong. Seeing her with Noah today, carefree and happy...it made my heart clench. Somehow, I have to make her see that my career won't be an impediment. Not if we work at it.

It helps to know that she wants this. *Us*. I'm not alone in how I feel. It's so obvious to me that she wants to be with me, wants to say *yes*, and at the same time, *fuck off* to every fear and bad memory she has.

Maybe it's just too fast for her.

The thing is...she can deny what she feels all she wants, but her heart knows. Her heart won't let her forget, won't allow her to move on quite so easily.

After Mom returned from visiting her friend, Harry and I drove to her house and made tacos together. Now we're sprawled out on the sofa, her back to my front, watching *Frozen* of all things.

I think she picked it because it reminded her of this afternoon.

My phone buzzes in my pocket and shifting my arm from where it's wrapped around Harry, I dig it out and open my notifications. It's Brad, my agent.

**BRAD**: Dinner Wednesday with Phillies scout. Think we got something.

**ME**: 42.

I slide my phone back in my pocket and replace my arm around Harry, pulling her in against me even more snugly than before.

"What was that?" she asks, the question indifferent but her tone trembling with dread. I don't want to tell her. Don't want the peaceful day we've had to be over.

"My agent."

She tenses. "And?" The sound of "Let It Go" fills the room, but I can barely hear it past the rush of blood in my ears. We need more time. Just a little longer.

"Brad thinks he has something for me. I don't know for sure, yet."

She twists against me until I loosen my arms and she's facing me. Her eyes are sheened with tears she won't shed and swamped with pain, but she smiles at me. She fucking smiles. "I know for sure. You're going to get it." I start to shake my head, but she places a hand against my cheek. "No. Don't do that—don't undermine yourself.

You're one of the hardest working, most determined men I know. If anyone can do it, it's you, Wyatt Granger."

I swallow against the sudden lump in my throat. "It's everything I've always wanted," I say. "And I really, really need to know you'll be here when I get back." It's hollow, otherwise, a pyrrhic victory I'll never celebrate. I don't tell her that. I won't guilt her into compromising who she is.

"I know," she replies. "I know. But let's not talk about that right now."

Lifting her chin, she kisses me, her tongue slipping out to trace my lips and then lick into my mouth.

She tastes like tacos and tears. Angling my head, I deepen the kiss, shifting and pulling her over top of me as I do. She comes easily, eagerly, aligning her body to mine and settling against me with a comfortable familiarity. We've only made love once, but our bodies are synced as though we've been together for centuries. As though we know each other in ways hours and minutes can't convey.

It could be like this, all the time. We could make a mess of the kitchen, lay Noah down to sleep, and then make out while we pretend to watch a movie. Sugar could give us the side eye until we make her look away, and for a while, we could make the entire universe narrow to the space that lingers between our bodies.

The universe, contracted to millimeters.

But if it's up to Harry, that glimpse of a future I see will only ever be merely that—a glimpse. Because she's too damn afraid to take what I have to give.

I'll make her see what I see. Make her realize. I kiss her harder and she responds, our tongues dueling with something akin to desperation. Snaking together, sucking, licking...wanting and needing more. She answers my challenge, pushing upward into a sitting position and gripping the bottom of her shirt before pulling it over her head and letting it fall to the floor.

*God, so pretty.* The ripe curves of her tits, encased in pale lace the color of a blush, are a lure I can't resist. I have to touch, have to feel the heat of her skin and the weight of her curves in my grasp.

Of their own volition, my hands reach for her, and she takes them in hers, guiding them to cover her breasts. I want the contrast of skin and lace for a little longer and pull the cups down and beneath each plump tit, pushing them up in an erotic show with fingers that tremble just a little. "God damn," I murmur, the words a prayer and an invocation, before pulling her down to meet my mouth. A shaky exhalation sounds as I nip at the upper slope, and I meet her hooded gaze to gauge her reaction. Her eyes are wide, her bottom lip caught between her teeth.

"More," she whispers. It's a dichotomy—her murmured command—much like she is, herself. She knows what she wants, what she deserves, and yet life has made her hesitant to ask for it. I want to change that.

"Yes, ma'am." I comply, taking her nipple into my mouth and sucking hard, and my mouth waters at how delectable she tastes. Sweet, like vanilla, and salty. She groans, her fingers winding into my hair to hold my head in place. I love how responsive she is. How uninhibited. It's so different from how she is on the surface, and I can't help feeling as though I've been granted a rare glimpse of her private self. Her real self.

She rocks urgently against me, the heat from her core searing me even through our layers of clothes. A buzz shoots through my spine at the sensation, and releasing her nipple with a pop of sound, I grip her hips and pull her more solidly against my length. "How do you want it?"

"Hard," she answers, the word a whine. "And fast. I need—"

*Yes.* Releasing a hiss from between my teeth, I place my palm on her sternum and shove her swiftly to her back on the sofa, following her up and onto my knees. We've barely begun but there's no more foreplay needed. My body is primed and aches in readiness for her, and the flush of her skin shows she's every bit as eager for me.

Her eagerness...how overtly she wants me...it makes me feel like a god.

Hooking my fingers in the waistband of her sweatpants, I yank both those and her underwear off in one rough motion, then push my own down to my knees. She scoots toward me, her eyes locked on my dick, which is so hard it hurts, and wraps her thighs around my waist. With a moan she reaches for me.

"Greedy girl," I murmur, grabbing her ass with both hands. With my pinkies, I test her readiness and confirm she's soaking wet.

Eyes locked on hers, I shove forward and into her in one hard, swift thrust that makes her cry out. Just as she wanted. We hold motionless for a moment. She wants it hard and fast, but I want to savor every part of this—every sensation. The feel of her tightness clenched around me, the sheen of sweat on her skin beneath me, every sound she makes.

Even as the thought crosses my mind, Harry squirms beneath me, a silent demand to *move*.

As if to spur me on, with a faint thinning of her lips, she lifts her arms above her head, grabs hold of the arm of the sofa, and begins circling her hips.

"Tell me what you want, baby." I pull out and torment her with the head of my dick, sliding it over her folds and watching as she writhes beneath me. Her eyes darken, her pupils widening.

"Stop teasing me—"

"Talk to me."

Her gaze narrows on me, our eyes locking and holding. "Fuck me, damnit. Now—"

I stop teasing. Leaning over her, I link one hand with both of hers and with the other still gripping one hip, I slam back into her. She gasps, a breathy, high sound, and I do it again. And again.

There in the dim blue light of the television, Sugar snoring a few feet away, I thrust with a kind of sweet violence into her, over and over, our skin slapping together noisily, wetly, until she's sobbing out a prayer for release and sweat drips from my forehead to her lips. My heart thunders and my skin draws tight and hot sensation coils through my spine and gathers at its base at the sight and feel of her on my dick. Begging. Demanding.

There are no illusions as to what this is. We're in accord, intent on nothing more than fucking away the ache of what might-have-been, replacing it with a physical pain that doesn't hurt as much as it pleasures.

She comes with a keening wail I know I'll hear in my dreams for the rest of my life. With a few final hard pumps, I follow, letting the contractions of her cunt milk my cum with every rhythmic pulse.

Then I sag against her, resting my sweaty forehead against hers and breathing hard. Her hand comes up and her nails dig into the flesh of my pec, and she shudders beneath me in the aftermath.

It's only when I move to shift my weight that I realize her shudders are sobs and know this is a pain we can't fuck away.

# Thirty-One

## Harry

The pillow beside me is cold when I wake. Yawning, I sit up and look around, but I already know. Wyatt's gone.

I can't even be upset about it. I'm sure he left early in the morning so he could be home when Noah awoke.

I pull myself out of bed and let a tap-dancing Sugar out. Yesterday's snow lies nine inches deep, a mantle of ice crusting the top and shining brilliantly in the sun. Framed by the doorway, I squint against the glare, shielding my eyes and looking down.

Wyatt's footsteps track from the snow-dusted doormat and idly I follow their progression to where he parked last night. Sugar sniffs at something in the vicinity, and I look to find another set of footprints ringing the perimeter of the small stoop and then leading to the right around the side of the house before disappearing from view.

At first my blood chills. Why is there an extra set of prints, very clearly from someone walking around the house? My imagination runs riot, envisioning someone peeking in windows and testing their soundness. Almost as quickly I shoo the fright away. It had to have been Wyatt, checking something before he left.

Right?

From the doorway, I snap a quick photo with my phone. I'll check in with him in a bit.

Clucking at Sugar, I wait for her to finish up and return, and then head back inside and to my bathroom to get my day started. A notification stops me as I open the medicine cabinet. Classes are canceled pending the cleaning of the parking lot and sidewalks.

I text Wyatt to let him know and send the photo of the footprints.

**ME:** No class today. Are these yours?

While I wait for an answer, I fill a glass with water and grab my pill organizer from its shelf. Something…a wisp of a thought…niggles in the back of my mind, making me pause. It flees as soon as I attempt to grasp it, and I don't know if it had to do with Wyatt, or the footprints, or the dog…the pills? Rubbing my temple, I study my pill organizer carefully, then, feeling paranoid, I go through and count the pills in the different compartments. Everything is there, as far as I can tell, so that wasn't it.

Shrugging, I take my morning doses and return the pill organizer to its shelf. The phone buzzes with a text as I close the cabinet and begin to leave the bathroom.

**JACK**: Can you get to the station today? I have your computer ready.

**ME:** Yes. Hour or two okay?

**JACK**: I'll be here.

That's when the wisp of memory returns. It was my pill box. Rushing back to the cabinet, I open it and stare. The plastic box is on the second shelf, clasp turned out toward me, as always. I start to touch it and stop. It wasn't, though, when I first opened the cabinet. The back of the organizer was facing outward, instead.

"Just a fluke," I say. "You were distracted last night and put it in backwards. That's all."

Did I, though? I never do that. I'm particular about things. My books' spines are meticulously aligned and arranged in ABC order on their shelves, the cans and boxes in my cabinets always turned so I can see the labels when I open the door.

Marcus, on the other hand, would mess with the cans and such just to annoy me. He filled my pill box each month, and always put it in the cabinet backwards, so the hinges faced out, because he knew how deeply it irritated me.

A coincidence? A shiver races through me, and I pull the pill box from the shelf and open it so I can study the tablets more carefully picking each one up and looking at it. *One, two, three... square, white, round, cream...* everything looks normal. Shaking my head a little, I replace everything and leave the room. I'm being ridiculous. Wyatt and I had just had two rounds of delicious, raunchy sex before I took my meds. I must not have been paying attention when I put the box up, that's all.

As if my thoughts conjured him, a message flashes on my screen from Wyatt.

**WYATT**: Those are not mine. I saw them last night when we got home, figured your neighbor had been by to make sure all was well.

**ME**: Oh... okay, thank you.

**WYATT**: Ask him.

**ME**: I will... seeing him today at the station. He said he has my computer ready.

**WYATT**: Let me know what he says.

**ME**: I will. Dinner tonight with the scout, right?

**WYATT**: Yeah. Would you like to eat with us?

**ME**: No!

**WYATT**: What if I want your opinion?

**ME**: One, you know I'm useless with regards to baseball. Two, this is a decision you have to make without me. Take me one hundred percent out of the equation. Pretend I never was.

**WYATT**: Very funny, Harry.

**ME**: Not trying to be funny. It is what it is.

**WYATT:** I hate that saying. Harry?

**ME**: I have to go now, Wyatt.

**WYATT**: You can try to push me away, Harry. It's not going to work. I love you.

Ugh. This is so hard. And so necessary. After yesterday and last night…after meeting Noah and falling a little in love with him after just a couple of hours, I know more than ever that I'm doing the right thing. I'd never survive getting more deeply involved with Wyatt and then having to let him go for months out of the year. I'm already far deeper than I had ever intended.

Ironically, it's this awareness that tells me how completely *right* we are. By comparison, it was easy to say goodbye to Marcus and everything we had shared. It shouldn't be easy to let the other particles of your soul go. To know you'll always be connected, but separate.

That should be impossible. Agonizing. *Wrong*.

I press the heels of my hands hard against my eyes. *Acknowledge, move on.* I can do this. I *will* do this.

After a call to Owen, letting him know that classes are canceled and I don't need his chauffeuring for the day, I get dressed and schedule an Uber.

The police station is quiet when Sugar and I arrive, its eaves frozen with icy stalactites I eye warily as we enter. An officer directs me down the hall and I find Jack with the female officer from last time standing in front of a coffee pot. "Ah, here she is!" the woman says. "We were just talking about you."

I scratch Sugar behind the ears. "Good things, I hope."

"Nothing but," Jack murmurs, his eyes steady on me over the rim of his mug. "How are you this morning, Harry?"

"I'm good...well, actually, I have a weird question for you." Phone in hand, I shuffle to my photos and hold the one I took this morning up for him to see. "Are these your footprints?"

His gaze sharpens, a frown line appearing between his brows. "What am I looking at?"

"They're footprints, circling my house."

"No, they're not mine. You checked with Wyatt already, I take it?"

"Yes, not his, either." I swallow, trying unsuccessfully to quell my rising panic. "Jack—"

With a hand on my shoulder, he begins to steer me down the hall. "We're on it, Harry. Come on. Alex, can you bring her a cup of coffee? Cream and sugar, right, Harry?"

I nod. Thank the officer, whom I now remember is named Katy. *Alex Katy.* I like her name. Like how it works to convey strength in what is a predominantly man's world. Harriet has never said strong to me. It says gullible. Silly. Easily managed.

"Whatever you're thinking right now, stop," Jack says, opening the door to an office. "Have a seat."

"Is this yours?" I ask, gesturing at the room and easing into a leather chair in front of a dark wood desk. Sugar sniffs at the chair and then drops to lie down beside me.

"Yes."

"There are walls," I observe stupidly, looking around. "What happened to the other one?"

"I got a promotion," he says, sitting behind the desk and pointing to a brass name plate on its surface.

"Chief..."

"Nice, huh? The woman who was here last time you were was at retirement age, and just wanted out."

"I'm happy for you, Jack. Congratulations."

He waves a hand. "Thanks, but we're not here to talk about me. Tell me—"

A quick *rat-a-tat* on the door, followed by its opening, interrupts, and Officer Katy comes in with a mug of coffee. She sets it on the desk in front of me. "Anything else? I already got a team on the way to the house to take care of the prints."

"Perfect. Thanks, Alex. We're good." He shuffles some papers around, selecting one from a stack, and returns his attention to me as the door closes behind her. "So, your computer. As hack jobs go, it was fairly unsophisticated."

"Meaning what?"

"Meaning the perp did what any Joe Blow would or could do, and nothing more. Basically, someone that had access to your credentials logged into your cloud account at 3:52 A.M. on this date." He points to something on the paper and slides it over to me. There's a dizzying array of dates, numbers, times, and computer data listed. "There are timestamps that show corruption and/or tampering with a multitude of different files, logins...things like that. My tech guys said they can try reverting everything to an earlier date if you would like them to, but we recommend you change your passwords and anything else you think Marcus may have gained access to."

Somewhere outside the door, a phone rings. Someone laughs. Someone else curses.

I sit, my hands shaking with the depth of my fury. All my lessons, potentially lost. My research and notes, tampered with. I'll have to re-do everything. I can't trust that he left it alone. My banking and investment information... Swiftly, I pull out my phone and start looking to make sure he didn't take any funds from anywhere. "I...this is unreal, Jack."

"We will get this guy, Harry," Jack says from across the desk. He's all cop right now, his voice vibrating with conviction.

"He cleaned out my savings. Left the seven hundred and twenty-three dollars in my checking, thank goodness, but diverted every penny of the five thousand I had in savings." Jack picks up a pen and starts writing something down. Fingers shaking, I navigate to my investment portfolio. "And I'm locked out of the account that manages my trust. Damnit, Jack!" I fling the phone against the wall and grab two handfuls of my hair, pulling until all I feel is the pain in my scalp. "I can't deal with this! Why aren't you catching him?"

Dimly I hear Sugar jump to her feet and yelp in protest. She nudges her cold nose against my thigh but I can't respond just now. Everything has narrowed to a single realization: Marcus won't stop. He'll never stop. I don't even know what he wants, or why, so short of the police locating and arresting him, I have no way of stopping him.

"Hey…hey, now. Stop doing that—" I don't see him move, but Jack kneels in front of me all of a sudden, grabbing my hands and untangling them from my hair. He holds them between us, forcing me to meet his eyes.

"He's stealing my money, Jack! It's not enough that he committed bigamy and messed with my career…he's trying to take everything from me. What did I ever do to him? What did I—"

"Shh. It's gonna be okay, Harry. I promise you that." He gives me a little shake. "Now, we're going to call your investment company right now, and make sure they have a hold on that account until all this is resolved. It takes time to get money out of stocks, or bonds, or a trust… however you have it set up. That's going to work to your advantage. We'll also find out if Marcus linked an account to receive funds, and we'll put a trace on it. We *will* find him. Just breathe."

"Okay." I nod and breathe deeply through my nose, then let it out through my mouth. Repeat. "Okay. I'm fine." I tug my hands from his and he stands. "I'm sorry I lost it there for a minute."

"It's all right, Harry. I don't blame you. This would be a lot for anyone." He eyes me keenly before moving back around to the other side of the desk and sitting. "How have your seizures been lately?"

"Surprisingly good. I started a new medication after that last one and it seems to be working." I give him a wry smile. "One good thing, huh?"

"Hey, we'll take it," he returns. "And you and Wyatt?"

I tug on my earlobe, looking down. "Well, this suddenly took a turn for awkward."

"No...I get it, Harry. It's a little...different, I guess, with the age thing, but I can see that you guys just...you work." One shoulder lifts in a shrug. "He made a comment one day...answered forty-two to something I said, and that's when it hit me. You're like the same person. Just different."

Warmth spears through me and for the first time since I arrived at the station, I feel like smiling. "Yeah. He gets me, I guess."

Jack studies me soberly. "Well, I just want you to know that I'm here if you need me. Or, you know. There. Right across the backyard."

We both laugh a little.

"Thank you, Jack." I stop, gather my courage. I've never been good at feelings-kind of situations. Never been good at expressing stronger emotions. "I...uh. I'm really glad I found you again, after all these years. You're a special guy."

Jack clears his throat, shifts in his chair. "Well, tell me something I don't know. Now, why don't we call this investment firm?"

# Thirty-Two

## Wyatt

The restaurant Brad chose for dinner is a local steakhouse renowned for its prime cuts of beef, creative side dishes, and exceptional wine cellar. I cast a surreptitious look around as a hostess clad in classic black and white leads us to our table.

This is the kind of place I'd like to bring Harry to. White linen tablecloths, heavy red velvet curtains, and candlelight for ambience. I can see her here, dressed up in something pretty, sipping something dry and white that I'll taste on her lips later.

Although she's really not supposed to drink a lot of alcohol. I may need to amend my fantasy a little. She can have water. Or sweet tea.

Brad and the scout, a short, athletic-looking guy with close-cropped black hair, are already here and waiting at a table next to a gas log fireplace. They wave me over and the scout shakes my hand vigorously.

"Wyatt Granger, nice to meet you. I'm Hank Osborne, and I gotta tell you, I've had my eye on you for some time."

I feel my eyes widen at his enthusiasm. We're not even sitting, yet. "Thank you, sir. I appreciate you talking with us."

"Well, hopefully we'll be doing more than talking. Sit, sit." He seats himself and Brad and I do the same. "So, tell me a little about your goals, Wyatt. Where do you see yourself in the future?"

I shift a little in my chair, nerves fluttering in my gut. I'm afraid to make a wrong move or say the wrong thing. I guess I'll just have to be honest and hope it's good enough. "The dream has always been to play in the majors, of course. If I have to get there through the minors, I'll do it. I'm not afraid of proving myself."

"That's good to hear, and I can see it. I'll be honest with you…" He pauses as a waitress approaches, and for a few minutes the conversation is on hold as we order. "… I've been given leeway to offer you a minor league contract with an invitation to spring training." My heart speeds up, thumping rapidly in my chest, and I struggle to keep my expression impassive. "But we do have some concerns in looking back over your college career. Talk to me about your sophomore year. What happened there to have you red shirting? We couldn't find records of an injury…?"

Brad is uncharacteristically quiet, allowing me to answer the questions as they're thrown at me, and I realize...this is it. This is where my decision to take time off to devote myself to my child becomes a rubber meets road kind of circumstance. Inwardly, I send up a prayer that family and commitment to such means something to Hank Osborne. If it doesn't...well, maybe it just isn't meant to be.

Drawing in a deep breath, I meet his open, friendly gaze head on and explain. "Just before my sophomore year I screwed up and got a girl pregnant. She wasn't ready to be a mother but fortunately felt strongly that fathers have as many rights as mothers, and at least told me about the pregnancy. I had a choice to make. Continue as I had been and let her do as she wanted or make a commitment to becoming a father." I glance at Brad and he nods, encouraging me to continue.

"I chose to become a father. I got a job, worked my ass off to pay her medical bills, and made a plan for what I would do once the baby arrived. Baseball, though important to me, was the one thing I could put on hold at that time."

Osborne sits back in his chair and rests his hands on his flat stomach. "I see. That's quite commendable of you."

I lift my shoulder a fraction. "I didn't do it to be commended—"

"No, I understand that. And how about now? What is your situation?"

"Well, I'm a dad to an amazing three-year-old. My mother helps me manage parenting tasks, and we make it work."

He nods, chewing on the inside corner of his mouth. "If you did have a career in baseball, what would that look like for your family?"

"That's a fair question. I've spoken to my mother about it, because I know I can't do this on my own. She supports me fully. We would manage just like any other player with a child does."

"Okay. Oh, look—here comes our appetizer. Hope you're hungry."

Conversation turns to other things while we eat, and I attempt to restrain my impatience and nerves. It's not until dessert is being removed before he slides an envelope across the table to me. "So, here's what we're prepared to offer. Brad here has already looked it over, but I understand if you want to take some time and think it over. Basically, we'd like to offer you a minor league contract with, as I said, an invitation to spring training—which you'd need to leave for next week. After that, whatever happens is up to you. All the details are inside."

Exhilaration pumps through me but I—barely—manage to curb my excitement. "I appreciate the offer, Mr. Osborne."

"I think we're past that. Call me Hank."

"Will do. I'd like to take the night to look over everything, but..." I can't contain a grin. "...everything sounds really fucking great." I wince. "Shit, I'm sorry. I mean, *shoot*, I'm sorry—"

Osborne laughs. "No worries. Go home and read through that. Take your time. But not too much time!" He laughs, shakes my hand, and we say our farewells.

Still at the table once Hank and Brad are gone, I pull the sheaf of papers inside the envelope out just far enough to read a few lines of legalese.

We, the undersigned, hereby offer (Wyatt Katsuo Granger, hereby termed PLAYER) a one-year contract with the Lehigh Valley IronPigs, with a contingent invitation to Spring Training...

I don't bother checking out the salary. It won't be tremendous with a minor league team, but it doesn't matter. The invitation to spring training is huge. It'll give me a chance to show what I can do, and how I measure up to more seasoned players. It's the culmination of everything I've worked for, and more than I could have hoped for at this point in my career.

And I can't wait to tell Harry.

Gathering everything up, I leave the restaurant at a jog, hope riding high on the thought that maybe…just maybe it'll be what I need to convince Harry to take a chance on us.

Harry's house is dark when I arrive, the single light burning over the back door casting a mellow glow over the snow-dusted patio. From somewhere deep within the house, another light burns. Harry's bedroom, I think.

I knock, then enter the code and open the door, closing it behind me and resetting the alarm. Doing so reminds me of the footprints Harry saw. Did she find out who they belonged to?

"Harry?" I start walking down the hall. "It's me."

She's sitting upright in her bed, a book in her lap and her fingers in Sugar's fur. I pause and lean against the doorway, catching and holding her serious gaze as she looks up from beneath her brows. Her fingers still in their stroking. "You got it, didn't you?" Barely discernible, her chin trembles before she firms it.

"Right to it, hmm?"

Setting the book to the side, Harry folds her hands in her lap. "There's no point in delaying the inevitable, Wyatt."

I've been here less than a minute, but already this is not going the way I had hoped. I push my hands in my pockets and contemplate the floor. "The Phillies scout offered me a minor league contract with an invitation to spring training." For some reason, the words don't feel as good as they did in my head. They're dulled by her reaction, by the knowledge that arcs between us. "I leave Monday."

She nods. Silence pulses in the small bedroom and Sugar lifts her head, looking first at her mistress and then at me. Pushing the covers back, Harry swings bare legs over the side of the bed and comes to stand before me. She raises a hand and places it on the center of my chest. "I am happy for you, Wyatt. I truly am."

"Can you be happy for me in Philadelphia?"

She doesn't reply for an agonizing minute. When she does, the answer shines in the wet depths of her eyes first, her fingers twisting into the fabric of my shirt. "I'm sorry, Wyatt."

"You're not even going to try."

"I can't."

"You're a coward." I don't mean to say it, but the word slips out anyway, ugly between us. Harry curls her hand into a fist and thumps it once against my breastbone.

"No—"

"*Yes*," I hiss. "You're so fucking scared...of everything. You're scared of what I tempt you to be—the real you, not the manufactured you created for academia and society. You're scared of losing that control you hold on to so tightly. You're scared of taking a risk and getting hurt. Mostly, though—you're fucking terrified of the way I make you feel. Too much, too real, too honest...there's nowhere to hide and it's the single-most frightening thing you've ever faced." Pulling my hand from my pocket, I grab her fist and hold it between us. "But I'm here, Harry. I won't let you face it alone. You just gotta take a chance on me...on us."

She shakes her head, a frantic gesture, and tugs at her hand. "You don't understand what you're asking of me."

"Do you love me, Harry?"

Her mouth snaps shut, and she glares up at me, eyes narrowed. "It's not as simple as all that, Wyatt."

"It absolutely is. I love you. I knew the first time I saw you, standing on that bridge, that you were it for me. I felt it in my bones, Harry. You weren't new to me. It was like I had known you for centuries. My fucking soul recognized yours...it said, oh, hello. Finally." Harry closes her eyes tightly but a tear squeezes out from the corner. I continue pressing, relentless. "You know what it felt like? It felt like driving in the rain, and it's pounding on the roof, loud and invasive. You can't think. You can't hear the music on the radio. You can't hear each other talk. But then you pass beneath a bridge or an overpass, and for a moment there's this silence...this stillness. That's what happened when I saw you. Everything went still." Releasing her hand, I lift both of mine to cup her face. "You're my quiet place, Harry. I need you."

She opens her eyes and reaches up to cover my hands with hers. Leaning forward, she presses a hard kiss to my mouth, salty with tears, before she pulls away. Takes a step back.

"Goodbye, Wyatt."

Shock holds me speechless. It's not until she turns and walks to the bathroom and enters, closing the door behind her, that I'm spurred into action. I leave, walking on legs that feel like rubber down the hall and into the kitchen.

As I start to open the back door, a plastic bag on the table catches my attention. It holds the broken pieces of the vase Harry told me about, the one that belonged to her grandmother. On impulse, I grab it up and take it with me.

I'll do this one last thing for her, because I told her I would.

I'll fix these broken pieces, and return it, along with the broken pieces of my heart. She can carry the damn thing in her pockets, in her hands, wherever she chooses.

I don't need it anymore.

# Thirty-Three

## Owen

**ME**: FYI—Harry in hospital. Major seizure.
**JACK**: Status?
**WYATT**: On the way
**ME**: Status unknown. Unconscious upon arrival.

# Thirty-Four

## Harry

*Beep. Beep. Beep.*

From somewhere far away I hear the beacon. It sounds like it's pulsing through water, tinny and high-pitched. There's something about it... I don't like it. It makes me think of...

Hospitals. I'm in the hospital. My eyelids flicker, admitting painfully bright light and foggy shapes. Hushed voices murmur all around me. Is that my mother? Wyatt?

"Wha—" My voice is a croak and I struggle to clear my throat, half raising an arm that I quickly realize is bogged down with wires and tubes.

"Nurse...we need a nurse in here! She's waking up."

"Harry. Oh, Harry, baby girl—" Momma's face looms over me, clearing into focus as I squint against the light. Wyatt blocks it from the other side.

"What happened? Where am I?"

"You're in the hospital in Charlottesville, baby. You had a seizure. A big one." Momma's hand glides over my forehead and rests on my cheek. "How are you feeling?"

I try to think. Wyatt shouldn't be here. He was leaving.

"Fuzzy. Wyatt. What are you doing here? What day is it?"

"It's Friday, Harry. It's okay."

"You have to get ready to leave—"

"I'm okay. This is more important. You're more important."

A nurse comes in and steps to where Momma stands. "Excuse me a moment, ma'am. How are we doing, sweetie? Can you tell me your name and date of birth, please?"

I give her the requested information and we wait as she checks my vitals and data from the monitor beside the bed. "Okay, great. Everything looks really good. I'm going to get the doctor in here, though, and he's going to take a look."

"I don't understand," I mumble, pulling at a cord tickling my collarbone. "I want to go home."

"Give them some time, baby. You've been unconscious since yesterday when Owen brought you in."

"Where's Sugar?"

"She's at my house," Jack answers, surprising me as he enters the room. "Hanging out with Kota. She's doing fine. You, on the other hand...you gave us all a scare."

I look up at Wyatt, whose features are drawn and taut. "But I don't...I was doing so well. That medication was working, damnit. This doesn't make sense." Raising a hand to my temple, I try to think. There is something right at the edge of memory... a flash of a thought I had at another time. "My head hurts."

"Give it some time, Red," Wyatt echoes Momma's statement.

"No, I'm trying to tell you...the footprints..." I look from Wyatt to Jack. "Someone was at my house."

Momma's hand clenches on my fingers. "What are you saying, baby?"

"Someone was there—"

"Yes, but we don't know who, or to what extent," Jack says. "I'm not sure if they got inside, or just walked the perimeter yet. We may not ever know."

"Someone did this to me." Over my head, Jack and Wyatt exchange a look. "I'm not crazy. It was that same morning..." I stop to think, try to sort the thoughts pounding through my skull. "...yes. I remember thinking there was something off about my pill organizer, but I shrugged it off. It was in a different position from how I always put it on the shelf. Marcus knows how important my medication is. It would be nothing for him to swap something out—"

"Okay, calm down. I'll go get someone over there now, and we'll get it sent to the lab. I'll need a list of your medications for comparison."

"Owen has one. Where is Owen? And Daddy?"

Jack leaves, already tapping on his phone. Momma squeezes my hand again. "Owen's with Ava. He felt it best not to bring her yet. And your father just slipped out to take a nap. He was awake all night."

I close my eyes and sag into the pillow, suddenly fatigued. "Okay. I think I need to take a nap, too. I'm so—"

"Why don't we wait on that just a few minutes, hmm?"

My eyes fly open at Momma's sharp gasp. "Marcus!" Wyatt's hand fumbles at my side for the emergency call, but all I can do is stare, every muscle in my body inert with exhaustion and fear.

"Ah-ah-ah, young Granger. Step away from the bed, please."

Wyatt moves closer to me. "Yeah, I don't think so," he answers.

There's a gun in Marcus's hand, something black and deadly looking that sits far too comfortably in his grip. The barrel is long and wicked-looking with what I'm pretty sure is a silencer. Why does he have a silencer? Is he planning on shooting someone? Panic squeezes my throat shut as he closes the door behind him and comes stand at the foot of the bed.

"Always the hero," Marcus says, making a tsking sound. "Fine. If you end up shot, don't blame me." He turns his attention to my mother. "You, too, Momma Bee."

Instead of moving, Momma sniffs and clutches my hand more tightly. "Over my dead body. You should be ashamed, Marcus Lane. We took you in, gave you a family."

He sneers and begins to reply but I finally find my voice and cut him off. "What are you doing, Marcus?" Wyatt's hand, resting on my shoulder, tenses at my outburst. "What are you *thinking*? How on earth do you expect to get away with—"

"Don't you worry about that. Just do as I say, and you'll be fine. Probably."

"What do you want from me?" Frustrated anger rushes through me, covering over the fear, and I fist my hands in my lap. "Haven't you done enough? Taken enough?"

He laughs, a mirthless sound. "Not by a long shot. As for what I want—I want what's rightfully mine." He waves the gun at Momma, then back at me. "Not yours. Certainly not yours, or that useless brother of yours. Mine."

"What the hell are you talking about?" The question bursts from Wyatt. "You already cleaned out her accounts—"

"How did you know about that?" I gasp, looking at Wyatt.

He spares me a glance, his eyes flat and angry. "Jack told us. You should have told me."

"Save it," Marcus interrupts. "I was merely taking what was mine from the start."

"Yours? I earned that money!"

"Well, the savings was just a bonus. I was referring to the trust, but it appears you caught on to that and your cop friend placed a freeze on the account. So, here's what's going to happen. You're going to call the bank and remove the freeze, and then you're going to transfer every penny over to me."

I snort. "Not fucking likely."

"Or I can begin shooting." He swings the gun toward Momma, then to Wyatt. "Eeney, meeney, miney, moe."

Sweat trickles down my spine as I stare into Marcus' eyes. They possess that same blankness I've noticed on a few other occasions, that same intentness that tells me he won't be swayed.

I don't have any options here. Not if I want us to escape bullet-free.

With difficulty, I pull my hand free of Momma's and pat the top of it. "Get my phone, Momma."

Without moving my gaze from Marcus, I feel her start of surprise. "No, baby, don't give this..." Never one for cursing, she struggles to find a suitably terrible name. "...jerk... a dime. Not one red—"

*Pop.*

It's just a small sound, a puff of air making its presence known, but its impact screams as loudly as a siren. A bloom of red appears on Momma's shirt, high in the upper right quadrant, and begins spreading. She jerks and tumbles from her perch on the bed before I can catch her, the metal cart bearing the monitor breaking her descent as she drops with a thud and a whimper.

I scream and Wyatt's hand clamps over my mouth as Marcus swings the gun back at me. I don't stop, the sound interspersed with frantic cries for my mother, and struggle against Wyatt in a drive to climb out of the bed. "Let me go! Let me—"

Marcus returns the gun to bear on me. "Shut her up."

"Shh... shh—" Wyatt curves a hand around the back of my neck and pulls my face into his chest. With the other he holds me tightly against him, preventing me from moving. "It's okay. She's breathing. I see her breathing. Let's just get this done and get her some help, okay?"

"I see why you like him, Harriet. He's a bright young man." Something lands on my legs, and I look to see my phone. "Make the call."

Wyatt hands me the phone and I take it, working to stabilize my hitching breath as I open the phone app and scroll to the number I saved the other day. Putting the phone on speaker, I call and work through the automated options with shaking fingers until the system places me on hold.

"Oh, that's just grand," Marcus puffs out a peevish breath and looks at his watch. "Never anyone to take a fucking call."

I stifle a hysterical laugh. Momma doesn't have time for me to be on hold. I close my eyes, trying to conceal the desperate thoughts racing through me. *I could scream. I should scream, right? But he actually shot my mother, so no...no screaming. The call button...where's the call button?*

"While we're waiting," Wyatt says, his fingers tangling with mine and stroking them comfortingly. "Would you mind explaining this whole thing to me? How do you figure Harry and her mother owe you anything?"

"Because it was mine to begin with. That inheritance didn't belong to Tilda Bee. It belonged to me."

"I'm lost," Wyatt says.

Exhaustion pulls heavy at my limbs, but the urge to leap from the bed and sink my nails into this man's skin rides me hard. *Money.* Money is the reason Momma is lying on the floor, moaning into a growing pool of her blood.

"Hang in there, Momma," I murmur.

"Tilda Bee is a relative of my mother. Lucky bitch inherited my money when my family disowned me twenty-three years ago, when I was eighteen. I waited, patient as could be, year after year after fucking year for my parents to just fucking die...and when they were finally gone, your mother got my money."

I gape at him, my brain latching on to one thing he said. "We're related?" My stomach lurches.

"Relax. For Chrissake. We're so distant as to be strangers. So, you see, that's my inheritance your family has been playing with."

"But if you were disowned, then it's no longer yours." I speak without thinking, and Wyatt's hand on my neck tenses.

"That is *not* the way things work!" Marcus snaps.

But it *is* the way things work. He's insane. Greed has warped him, muted reason and common decency, and Momma's paying the price. I look at her again, Wyatt the only thing keeping me anchored to the bed. "Marcus, please let me get her some help. She didn't do anything—"

"She existed," he spits out. "You can get her help when I'm gone, so maybe hurry the fuck up."

"I can't do it any faster! No one's answering!"

The door opens silently behind Marcus and Gina steps in.

"Marcus, what is taking so... oh, my God! What have you done?" Catching sight of my mother, she blanches, her hands flying up to cover her mouth.

"She was being stupid," Marcus says. "And now we're on hold." He slaps the hand holding the gun to his forehead, making me flinch, then waves it in my direction. "Goddammit! None of this was supposed to happen! If you had just kept your fucking mouth shut...but noooo, you had to go and press fucking charges." He paces back and forth at the foot of the bed, visibly unraveling.

"This isn't what I wanted... it's not... Marcus, we have to go! Now!" Gina grabs his arm.

Through the tirade, Wyatt holds me together. "Stay calm, baby. Just stay calm—"

"This is all wrong—" Gina tries again, and Marcus shakes her off impatiently, pushing her backwards.

"Shut up and watch the door. You're in this as deep as I am."

"No, I never wanted all of this. All I ever wanted was to be with you."

"And I've been there, all this time. Even though it meant giving up fucking millions."

"You've only barely been there! You've been with her—" She points at me accusingly, and it's then I notice that she, too, has a gun. "—for the past seven years. I don't know what the hell I was thinking, agreeing to this stupid plan of yours." She takes a step right, then backtracks, the hand not holding the gun twitching in agitation.

"You were thinking we'd finally have what we deserved! And it would've worked! It would've worked just fine if they hadn't seen us at the goddamn mall."

"So now it's Santa's fault..." Gina puts her hands on her hips and views Marcus with exasperation. "What did you need seven fucking years for, anyway, Marcus? It was never supposed to take so long—"

"You stupid bitch. I didn't need seven years. I *took* seven years. Would've taken a lot more, too. It was fun, playing house with the hot professor, no whining kids underfoot—"

"You sonofabitch."

"You don't get it. If it wasn't for you, I would've had my money in the first place. But no—I chose you, Gina. And where did it get me? Four snot-nosed brats and a wife too tired to fuck."

"Marcus!" The exclamation flies from my lips and I struggle in Wyatt's arms.

Marcus pivots to sneer at me. "You weren't too tired, were you, babe? Always ready and willing—"

I can hardly fathom what comes next. As Marcus takes a breath to spew more venom, Gina raises her gun and shoots him in the back of the head.

There is no *pop* of sound this time. Her gun roars, unencumbered by a silencer, and she staggers back at the resulting kick. The bullet speeds in a blip of a second, before we can even process its utter finality, through hair and skin and muscle before halting deep within his cranium. It makes shrapnel of calcium and collagen casing, blood and brains spraying grotesquely across the white hospital blankets and my face, even as Wyatt reacts and curls protectively around me.

Marcus, reduced to a gruesome husk of skin and bones, falls to his knees and then forward, hitting against the bedframe before ending his descent in an ignominious lump on the floor.

Gina bends and with utmost gentleness, places the gun on the floor at her feet. She eyes the man she shot without expression, then places her hands behind her head and waits, lips trembling and eyes locked on mine, as the door behind her is flung open and Jack enters, gun drawn. A security guard follows him.

"Please..." I find my voice and begin to beg, shoving at Wyatt and working to climb from the bed. "Somebody help her! Help my momma—"

"I'm sorry," Gina whispers to the room, as Jack assesses the scene and begins shouting directives. "But it was the last time he was going to talk to us like that." Nurses and attendants flood in, one providing a brief check to Marcus while the rest swarm around Momma. Gina jerks as Jack pulls her arms behind her, cuffing her, but never looks away. "None of this was supposed to happen."

# Thirty-Five

## Harry

The waiting is always the worst. I twist my hands in my sweater, finding a loose string to twine around my finger, and stare vacantly at the blinds shuttering the window behind Jack's desk. They're closed, but flipped the wrong way, allowing a shaft of late-afternoon sunlight to peek through and blind me every time I turn my head the wrong way.

I start to stand, thinking to go fix the issue, but Daddy's hand grabs my wrist, halting me. "Just be patient."

I sit back down as the office door opens and Jack enters. "Afternoon, Mr. Bee. Harry. Owen." He nods at each of us and sits. "Apologies for the delay. I wanted to make absolutely certain I had everything I needed."

"No need to apologize," I say. My nerves are strung tight as piano wire. "We just want all of this to be over with."

"I understand. And I don't think you'll need to worry about things being over. Gina made a full confession and cleared up quite a few questions. I asked y'all to come in because honestly...it's a doozy of a story. I could tell you everything, but I think it'll make more sense coming straight from Gina's mouth." I nod, while beside me Daddy murmurs something inaudible.

He's been a wreck since Momma was shot. She's going to be okay, but her recovery won't be easy, and Daddy has been completely, brutally awakened to what life without his beloved Tilda would look like.

Owen, on the other hand, has been a rock, going between our parents' house, the hospital, and my house to make sure everyone has everything they need. He's bound to be exhausted by now, three days into the affair.

Without further introduction, Jack presses a button on a remote and a large screen on the far wall springs to life.

Gina waits in a small room, seated in an ordinary plastic chair at a table bare of anything except a telephone. The cameras show a face streaked with black mascara and smudged lipstick. She gnaws on the cuticles of one hand, her gaze skittering around like an animal freshly trapped.

When the door swings open and Jack, followed by Officer Katy, walks in, she jumps, half-rising and then dropping back into her seat.

"Mrs. Lane. We have some questions for you, as you might imagine." He slides another chair away from the table and sits, flipping to a fresh page in his ever-present legal pad, while Katy leans against the wall. Gina nods.

"I'll tell you anything you want to know. But first...is he dead?"

*Is he dead?* My jaw sags. Does she really believe there's the smallest chance Marcus could take a bullet to the brain and emerge unscathed?

Apparently, she does.

Her shoulders begin to shake when Jack tells her *why, yes, he is dead*. Finally, after seven tissues and a miniature bottle of water, she straightens in her chair and lifts her chin.

"What are your questions?"

Jack and Alex Katy exchange a look. "Why don't we start with what happened in that hospital room."

Gina grips her hands tightly together. "I killed Marcus. That's what happened. He had snapped. Gone completely mental. He had already shot Harriet's mother and he was going to kill Harry. So, I shot him."

"And why were the both of you there in the first place?"

After a sip of water, she speaks, her eyes distant. "Several days ago, Marcus learned of the freeze on Harriet's trust account. He was furious. He concocted this plan to force Harry to release what he considered to be his money to him, one way or another."

"Mm. What do you mean *his* money? And what were the details of this plan?" Jack makes a note on the paper before him and returns a cool gaze to Gina.

"He used to organize all of Harry's medication for her. Passed it off like it was an act of love, one that would remind her of how much he cared, even when he was 'out of town.'" The corner of her mouth crooks in an ironic grin. "Really, he was making sure she would always get her daily dose of birth control."

I can't contain my gasp, and almost instantaneously, my eyes well and spill over with tears. Jack pauses the video.

"Are you okay?"

I shake my head wordlessly.

*Birth control.*

All those years, making me feel like not being able to have children was my fault, my failure...it was nothing more than birth control.

Contrary emotions buffet me.

*Exhilaration*—I'm not broken, not at all. One day...maybe one day.

*Rage*—how dare he take that choice from me? Manipulate my feelings and my decisions and my freedoms in that way?

And then *relief*, a peculiar sense of respite that I hadn't had a child that would bind me irrevocably to this man. But...

"I don't understand. We went to a doctor...?"

Jack leans in, offering a grim semblance of a smile. "He probably paid someone to say what he needed him to say. We'll look into that."

Owen throws his arm around my shoulders and pulls me into his arm. "Keep going," he says. Jack presses Play once again, and Gina's voice fills the office.

"He figured he would tamper with her medication, replacing the newest one she was prescribed with tramadol. He'd done his research, knew that one could induce a seizure."

"But couldn't that—" Officer Katy bites her words off, but Gina has no problem picking up on her meaning.

"Kill her? Yeah. But see, that's the thing…before the mall, before she found out about us, Marcus *wanted* to kill her. That was the whole idea." She rocks forward in her chair and then backwards, laughing a little. "He had actually planned on killing her weeks ago…went to her house and everything. Decided to fuck with her, instead."

"That was the night he broke into her house?"

"Walked in, more like."

In the video, Jack rubs at his forehead with his thumb and index finger. "So, what you're telling me is that this man…your husband…he decided here's this random woman. I think I'm going to sweep her off her feet, marry her—while I'm already married, coincidentally—and then kill her? For what purpose? This makes no sense, Gina."

"Oh, she wasn't random."

"What?" Video Jack says.

I already know where this is headed, but it still hurts to have confirmation that everything, from the very beginning, was an utter lie. He played me false, played me for a fool, from the fender bender that brought us together to his to the little romantic things he did that tripped me up and made me fall.

"Jack knew exactly who she was. He picked her because of who her mother was." Gina jerks a hand at the room. "Mind if I move a little? I've got all this nervous energy."

"Go ahead."

Standing, Gina shakes her arms out and then begins to pace the room's tiny dimensions.

"You have to understand where we came from," she says. "What drove him."

"Okay, so, make me understand."

"Once upon a time—" Katy snorts, earning a glare from Gina. "—there were these two teenage kids who fell in love. One of them, the boy, was from a prominent, wealthy political family. The girl was trash. Definitely not in the boy's social strata." Jack looks as though he wants to interrupt, but he keeps his lips pressed firmly closed, allowing Gina to finish.

"The really unforgivable thing, though, was that they were cousins."

"Oh, my V.C. Andrews-loving heart," Officer Katy breathes.

Gina paints a dramatic picture of modern-day star-crossed lovers—born into the same family, doomed to love and to be punished for it. As first cousins, when their affection for each other was discovered, they were given two options. Cease immediately or be disowned.

Unfortunately for them, they were obsessed with each other. Marcus chose to lose his inheritance rather than lose Gina.

They left their homes in New York, went to Delaware, got fake documentation from someone Marcus was in contact with, and were married.

They hadn't counted on what it would be like to be poor. They had no real skills—hadn't gone to college and had never lifted a finger for anything in their lives. They traveled around, moving from state to state working odd jobs or running the occasional scam to get by.

As time went by, Marcus became more and more obsessed with the inheritance he'd given up. He kept an eye on news from their hometown, waiting for his parents to die so he could find out what was happening with the money.

Then they did die, and he learned that the estate had gone to a distant relative in Virginia. Our mother, Tilda Bee.

"Wow," Owen says.

Dad just shakes his head. "So, Tilda's windfall all those years ago…money we used to pay off the house. For college. Retirement...all of it was from Marcus Lane's family?"

"Apparently so. I take it that Mrs. Bee was not close to the relative who'd bequeathed the estate to her?"

"No. She had never met them." Daddy rubs at the corner of his eye while Jack makes a note on his pad. "I wish to God they'd never known about us."

"So, anyway," Gina continues, pulling our attention back to the screen. "He began investigating and trying to come up with a way of getting his money and he landed on Harriet. She was his way in. He persuaded me that he could 'marry' Harriet and eventually gain control of the money through her. I knew the marriage wouldn't be real, and I didn't see any other options to...settle...Marcus other than letting him pursue this crazy quest of his, so I went along with it. I didn't see it taking seven years." She spits the last sentence out.

"How on earth did he figure on something as asinine as that actually working?" asks Owen indignantly, as though Gina is right there to answer. "The money was our mom's, not Harry's. He'd have had to kill mom & dad, wait until Harry and I inherited, then kill her to get to her share."

"That's actually pretty much what he had planned," Jack says. "According to Gina, that plan was shot to hell when you guys ran into each other in the mall. He was no longer Harry's beneficiary, since they weren't legally married, and with the conflict surrounding them, he would immediately come under suspicion if anything happened to Harry."

He fast-forwards through a few frames, and then stops. "So then, he had to adjust his plan," Gina was saying. "He figured with the medication switch she'd end up in the hospital. As close as that family is, he counted on everyone showing up, and being able to leverage them against one another." Gina crossed her arms over her chest. "He was determined to get everything he felt he had coming to him." She shakes her head. "I didn't even care anymore. I just wanted to be done with all of it. Faking his death...killing that other man...his crazy hospital plan...everything had gone way too far."

Owen looks at Jack incredulously. "I guess killing her and the parents was okay, though? What. The. Fuck."

"Owen Francis." Dad's tone is sharp.

"It's all right," Jack says. "I get it. And I agree...it was just insane enough to work, though. Gina further explained that she was supposed to be his lookout and keep hospital personnel out while they worked on transferring the funds. When it was taking longer than expected, she went to check and realized how devolved Marcus had become." Jack leaned forward on the desk. "And that's when she shot him."

"God." We're all lost to our thoughts as we take in and try to process the utter depravity of the man I married. His insanity.

"But why did he fake his death?" I ask.

"Gina said he had completely flipped. He felt like everything was over and in order to get a fresh start, he was going to have to become someone completely different."

"Okay. That makes a kind of sense, I suppose. But who was the man he threw over the bridge? Did he kill some random bystander?"

Jack's look is sober. "He was pretty far gone with his plan to kill you guys. Had hired and paid someone off Craigslist, and then decided he was going to have to do something different to avoid having suspicion cast on him. Gina said the guy he hired—a complete amateur—was not happy and threatened him with exposure when he cancelled the contract, so Marcus killed him."

I don't say anything. There's nothing to say. The man I married was a con artist, a narcissist, and a murderer. That's pretty much a non sequitur, in my book.

A wave of exhaustion creeps over me, and I close and open my eyes in a slow blink. "Oh, but here's something interesting I turned up in our investigation. Marriage between first cousins is not permitted in Delaware, which is the state of record for Marcus and Gina's marriage. Which means—"

"That their marriage is void."

"And yours was legal."

I bury my face in my hands and shudder. "This is insane. And gross." A thought strikes and I lift my face to Jack. "What's going to happen to all those kids? Is there anyone that can care for them?"

"We're working on that. There are no living relatives except your family." His expression is flat. "I don't see the system being able to keep four siblings together, though. Sad."

It's more than sad. It's unacceptable. "We have to make sure they stay together. Can I...may I speak to Gina?"

Jack lifts his shoulder in a small shrug. "I don't see why not. Want to do it now?"

I nod. "Please." The revelations Jack passed along have gone a long way to resolving my questions, but I still need closure, and something is telling me Gina is the only one to provide it.

Pending her arraignment and removal to the regional prison, Gina is being held in a cell at county. Jack leads me to her and shows me a button on the wall. "I'll wait outside. Just press that when you're ready."

"Thank you, Jack."

Gina and I eye each other as Sugar sniffs at the bars. "What do you want?" She asks, her voice more tired than hostile.

"I wanted to say thank you," I reply. "You saved my life."

She lifts one shoulder and looks away, studying her fingernails. "Yeah, well, wasn't like I particularly wanted to. It just happened."

"All the more reason for me to thank you. Your action prevented Marcus from shooting either me or Wyatt and sped up the process of saving my mother's life. I—"

"My action." Her mouth twists bitterly. "Shooting Marcus. Killing him…the man I've been in love with since I was sixteen and he eighteen. Twenty-five years."

I don't reply.

"Anyway." She continues after a reflective sigh. "I guess it was the least I could do, what with all the other stuff. And honestly?" I raise my eyebrows. "He kind of pissed me off. Saying the stuff he did.

I tip my chin back in acknowledgement. "Yeah. That kind of pissed me off, too." We share a look.

"Bastard," she murmurs.

"Indeed. So. What happens next?" I ask, shoving my hands deep in the pockets of the jacket I'm wearing.

"All the court stuff, I think."

I feel immensely sorry for her, and don't know why. She was a willing, if misled, part of Marcus's scheming. She had the potential to end things so much earlier than she had. And yet… "Gina, what are you going to do with your children?"

Her face crumples for a split second before she presses her lips firmly together. "I do not know. I asked to see them. Just for a minute…but it wasn't allowed."

"I'm so sorry, Gina."

She presses the heels of her hands into her eye sockets. "Yeah. I'm sure."

I don't reply and for a while the only sound is the hum of the fluorescent light overhead. Then her breath hitches and I realize she's crying. "Gina—"

"My babies...my poor babies..."

My heart kicks and I lick my lips. There's a question on my tongue, but once spoken there's no reverse. No takebacks. "Jack told us there is no other family. That my mother is the closest relative, which is why she was chosen to receive Marcus's inheritance." *Here goes nothing,* I think, and *jump.* "Would you...how would you feel if we...I...fostered them?"

She says nothing but stares at me through the bars as if I have grown two heads and I rush to give her more information. "It would be a temporary thing. They're your children, and they always will be. I would never try to usurp that. And I will bring them to visit you if you want. I—"

"Stop." She holds up her palm to echo the word.

I stop.

"You want...you're offering to take on the care of my children? Marcus's children? After what we—" Her voice breaks and she bows her head. Her shoulders begin to shake, and for a moment, I can't tell if she's laughing or crying. A little of both, I think. She lifts her face, revealing wet, reddened eyes. "Is this a joke?"

"No! I mean it—"

"Why would you take care of the children of the people who made your life hell? Of the man who shot your mother, was going to kill you? I don't...I can't understand this." She bows her head and shakes it, raising fingers that shake to her temples.

Without thinking, I move closer to the bars and wrap my hands around them. "I don't understand, either, Gina, I promise you. If Marcus was here and I had a gun, I would shoot him, myself. But he's not, and I have to be happy with the fact that you did that for me. I would never, ever take my anger out on a child." Releasing the bars, I take a step away and begin to stride the length of the small area, Sugar following me back and forth until I drop the leash so she can sit and watch me pace, instead. "Those children...they're the reason I didn't file charges against the two of you immediately, you know. I couldn't stand the thought of both of you being in jail and the kids not having at least one parent to take care of them."

"Thank you, I guess," she replies, somewhat stiffly.

"I always thought I couldn't have children. It was a belief cultivated and perpetuated by Marcus. I don't even know what to do with myself now that children are a possibility. I don't know. I just have this feeling that I need to do this. Maybe part of me thinks taking care of someone else's kids...yours and Marcus's...will help make up for all those years I thought I was barren. And then there's my trust. That's not my money. It should be used to help—"

"Okay."

"Okay?" I stop pacing and turn my gaze on her.

Her expression is sober. "Yes. Okay. Find out what I need to do, and I'll do it. Sign custody over to you, whatever. You're a more than decent person, Harry."

"I'll ask Jack how to make it happen." Picking up Sugar's leash, I press the button on the wall and turn to leave. "Be well, Gina."

# Thirty-Six

## Harry

And that's how I find myself, in the space of just weeks, with temporary custody of four children of varying ages. Temporary, because there's a lengthy process I must undergo to make it permanent, beginning with a doctor's statement that my physical health is no barrier to providing care.

And it will be permanent. Although she has yet to undergo trial and receive sentencing, Jack has told me that it's pretty much a given: Gina will be in prison for at least twenty years for the murder of Marcus Lane without the possibility of parole, plus additional years tacked on here and there for other offenses.

My parents think I'm crazy, but Momma is secretly happy to be a pseudo-grandmother to a ready brood of children.

My department head thinks I've lost it, because I requested immediate leave of absence for the remainder of the year in order to get the children settled and thriving. I probably won't go back, but she doesn't know that yet.

Owen just shakes his head. My brother has always understood me better than most, and he knows my why. He knows my complicated feelings of guilt and concern coupled with the tiniest thrill of...happiness? Yeah. Happiness.

Wyatt...I don't know how Wyatt feels because he's gone.

I'm okay with all of this, because I feel, at last, like I'm doing what I'm supposed to be doing. Each morning the baby, Jolie, wakes me with babbled crib conversation with her sister, Ruth Anne. Ruth Anne is four going on sixteen and has so far expressed a sincere affection for bossing her brothers around and playing house with Ava. I think they're going to be fast friends.

The boys are eleven—Trevor—and seven—Barrett. Trevor is serious-eyed and quiet, while Barrett is a loud, spinning dervish of uncontainable energy.

All of them have adopted Sugar as their own with open arms and understand what to do if she goes on alert. Trevor and I have practiced making a phone call to emergency services if they're ever scared or worried when I have a seizure. I think he's secretly excited about the possibility.

They are, without a doubt, the best remedy for a broken heart I could possibly have received. There's no time to be sad, to sit and think about all the what-if's and might-have-beens. Not until the nighttime, anyway, when all the lights are off, and the quiet is broken only by the soft sounds of children sleeping.

That's when heartache lifts its head and reminds me of its presence. On nights like tonight, when I'm curled up in my bed with Sugar snoring softly beside me, I'm obsessed with questions. I want to know how he's doing. If he misses me. When he's coming back. What he would think of "my" children.

I want to hear his voice calling me Red, feel his fingers tangling in my hair.

I can't even see him on television, because it's not yet time for televised ball games, and who knows if he'll even play for a team that big, anyway. It feels like my oxygen supply has been cut off, and I keep grabbing for the mask and missing as it swings just above me, barely out of reach.

I miss him, and all I know is that nothing makes any kind of sense without him. I miss his hands that brought me back to life; I miss his lips that spoke truth and love to mine.

It's my own fault, I know. I did this to us. I killed us.

The weekend comes. Owen and Ava are here, helping me celebrate Barrett's eighth birthday, when the doorbell rings. I wade through the mountains of balloons and wrapping paper littering the floor until I reach the door and swing it open in time to see a delivery man climbing back into his truck. A package sits on the brick stoop, and I wave as I bend to pick it up. "Thank you!"

"What's that?" Owen asks as I return to the kitchen. He has the kids seated around the table, devouring cupcakes from Karla's and drinking red Kool-Aid.

"No clue," I say. "There's no return address."

"Maybe it's..." He doesn't finish his thought, but I give him a small nod. Maybe it's a gift for Barrett from his mother, although I wouldn't know how she could accomplish that. She hasn't allowed me to bring the kids to see her yet, not wanting them to see her in shackles or an orange jumpsuit. Trevor, in particular, is struggling with that. I plan on going to see her next visitor's day, see if I can't convince her to let the older children come.

I open the box and begin removing layers of crumpled brown paper. The object beneath the paper is wrapped in several layers of bubble wrap, and I carefully begin to unroll it. When I get to the last layer, faint white and blue shines through, and I know what I'm looking at. I drop it back into the box, snake bitten.

"Harry? What is it?"

I look up at him, my mouth working but the words refusing to come, and he pulls the object from the box and finishes unwrapping it.

Our grandmother's vase. It's been repaired, but it's not the same. Delicate threads of gold weave through the cracks where it had been shattered, binding each shard back together with an ineffable beauty and graceful strength. I take it from his grasp, turning it this way and that, studying the random tracks of gold. They weave a safety net in the middle of a battlefield.

"Watch them—" I mumble, my voice rough, and then stumble from the room with the vase in my hands. I don't make it all the way to my bedroom before the tears break through, streaming wetly down my face and accompanied by great, gasping sobs.

All I do these days is cry, it seems. I never used to cry, but now I'm a waterworks, tears erupting at the slightest thing.

Like a vase.

I set it on my dresser and sit across from it, on the edge of my bed, leaning forward with my elbows on my knees.

It's more than that, of course. It's that Wyatt fixed it for me, repaired every broken piece, even when I was breaking him. He knows what the vase signifies. Knows how I've avoided looking too hard at it, avoided trying to repair it, because it's *me*. I've become so used to feeling broken I don't even remember what it feels like to be whole. That kind of brokenness requires more than just glue, more than just being refitted into the correct spot.

Wyatt saw that and put it back together with gold dust, and patience, and care.

He's letting me know that he sees me, and he'll wait, until I consider myself as whole as this vase before me.

Love for Wyatt stole in slowly, carefully, one foot always poised and ready to run.

Actually, that's not entirely accurate. I think I may have fallen in love with him swiftly and inevitably as spring follows winter, but the realization of it followed slowly. It tiptoed in, not wanting to scare me. There was no blinking neon sign that flashed *I love Wyatt Granger!*…rather, awareness crept upon me like dusk stealing day.

Now that I know, there's no going back.

"Harry?" Owen stops in my doorway, his eyes flickering from where I sit on the end of the bed to the vase on my dresser. The tears have mostly stopped, but my face is tight with their drying remains.

"Wyatt did this," I say. "He fixed it for me."

"Ah." Owen comes to sit beside me. "It's beautiful."

"It is. I think it might be even more beautiful now, with its cracks."

"Broken can still be beautiful, you know."

I sniff. "Yeah. I'm starting to see that. Owen?"

"Yeah?"

"What are you doing tomorrow?" Tomorrow is Saturday. He doesn't need to work, but you never know. He could have plans.

"I don't know. Am I by any chance watching four extra rug rats?"

"Would you mind? I know they're a lot, but I think I need to go visit someone."

"Nah. It's good sibling currency." He cups his hand around the hair I've pulled into a knot on the top of my head and wobbles it back and forth. "Need any help finding a plane ticket?"

# Thirty-Seven

## Wyatt

"Granger?" Coach leans out of the room where he's holding a meeting with his batting coach. "The Man wants to see you in his office, stat."

*Shit.* We just came in from training and I am in nasty need of a shower. Guess it'll have to wait, because when Theo Booker, the manager, calls, you come running. Removing my ball cap, I run my hand through the sweat drying my hair into a stiff mess against my skull and leave the locker room to head up to the next level of the stadium, where the administrative offices are housed.

Booker's office is off of a plush, carpeted hallway with massive, floor-to-ceiling windows composing one wall and offices and conference rooms opening off the other. I find the right room and knock on the open door. Booker, sitting at his desk with his feet popped up on its surface, waves me in. He's on the phone and chewing a piece of gum, and as I enter, he points to a leather chair in front of the desk. "Uh-huh...yeah. No fucking way..."

I glance at the chair and then my grubby pants. I'm filthy. With a mental shrug, I sit. The Man said to sit.

"All right, well, I gotta go, Lloyd. I'll see you on Thursday night?" A pause. "Great. Bye, now." I wait while he hangs up and resettles himself more comfortably in his seat. "Wyatt Granger. Thank you for coming up so quickly. How've the past few weeks been treating you?"

"Very well, sir." *Is he fucking sending me home? Already? I* can't think of any major mistakes, but you never know what these guys are looking for. Maybe I'm just—

"Good, good; I'm glad to hear that. I have to tell you, Granger, I'm pleased with what I'm seeing and hearing from my coaches so far." *Oh, thank fuck.* I let out the breath I was unconsciously holding and relax a bit. "You're willing to work, have a good attitude, and a clean reputation, which I appreciate."

The praise makes me shift in my chair, uncomfortable. "Thank you, sir."

"I'm sure you've heard about Ross?"

"Just this afternoon." I scratch at the scruff that's begun growing into more of a beard, more because I don't have five minutes to shave than for any other reason. Hudson Ross is one of our lead pitchers, and as of today is officially out of commission for Tommy John surgery.

Booker nods, his eyes narrowed on me. "How would you feel about getting called up to the big leagues, son?"

I knew it was coming when he asked me about Ross, but my brain still stalls out for a moment. "Ah…I'd say tell me more."

Booker begins to do just that. As he talks, I nod and grin and make all of the appropriate responses. Another part of my brain is in Lucy Falls, though, with Noah and Harry and my mom. I can't do this without them. It doesn't mean they'd need to move to Philadelphia or anything. I just need the support. I need to know, when I'm on the road and playing a shitty game, that someone's watching and cheering me on.

I have this with Mom and Noah; no worries on that score.

But I need it from Harry. I need to know she'll be there when I get back home. Without it…without her…all of this is just killing time.

"Any questions about anything?" Booker asks.

I level him with a look, my elbows on my knees and hands clasped loosely before me. "Just one. I need to take the weekend…see my family…before I sign my life away. That okay?"

Booker chuckles. "Take your weekend. Get your ass back here on Monday and be ready to work."

"Thank you, sir." Standing, I clasp his hand in a firm handshake, and then make my way back to the locker room.

I need a shower before catching a flight back to Virginia.

***

The Philly airport is a sweeping expanse of wide-open spaces, interspersed by tall white columns and sheets of blue-green glass. My gaze skates idly over the tide of people hurrying back and forth or, like me, standing and waiting. The line is interminable, and I just want to get to the ticket counter and buy a ticket home.

It's probably stupid. Harry has been more than clear. I can't put it off, though, can't wait to see her and plead my case one final time.

I should have been ecstatic when Booker asked me to sub in for Hudson Ross. He's looking at a year-long recovery time, at least, with Tommy John surgery. As long as I perform, my place is set. It's the break I've been hoping for, the break most guys never get, and it's happening immediately.

I'm not ecstatic, though, and I know it's because everything is so unsettled with Harry. Unsettled as far as I'm concerned, anyway. Harry said she couldn't do the long-distance thing, but my brain refuses to compute the finality of that. I will find a way to convince her.

"Sir?" The counter attendant's question interrupts my musings. "Step forward, please."

I purchase a ticket for a flight landing in Richmond late this evening. It's later than I wanted, but I'll take whatever's available at this point.

"Are you checking any luggage?"

"No. I just have this carry-on." I gesture to the backpack slung over my shoulder and the attendant smiles.

"Okay, then, you're all set. Have a pleasant flight."

I make my way to the security checkpoint and, as the second way-too-long line creeps closer, begin to remove my belt and jacket and untie my shoes in preparation. I hate these fucking things. They take forever and there's something mildly skeevy about all these strangers getting half-undressed together. But I guess we do what we have to do to keep things safe.

A few minutes later, I'm able to start dumping my electronics and everything else in the plastic totes. I do so and wait, holding my ticket and license, to be checked through. As I wait, I look beyond the security checkpoint at the interior of the airport, where people are shuffling through in all directions. Hopefully, there's a fast-food place nearby. I'm about to starve.

That's when I see her. Harry, a small bag draped over her shoulder and Sugar close to her hip, walking with determined steps toward a sign that reads Exit.

I mutter a curse. What the hell is she doing here?

There are still two people in front of me. Frantic, I grab the shoulder of the closest. "Hey, man—can I cut in front of you? I just saw someone I have to catch up with."

The man waves me on politely. "Sure, sure. I'm in no hurry."

"Thank you—"

The other person is through. Hastily, I shove my license and ticket into the hand of the waiting officer and walk quickly through the metal detector. It beeps.

"Sonofa..." I spare a glance up. I can still see them. With panicked fingers I search for the random metal that I've forgotten, and finally remember my keys in my pocket. Tossing them with my bag, I walk through the detector again. Clear.

Grabbing the plastic tote as it comes through, I toss it to a waiting table and then sprint, sans shoes, after Harry and Sugar. "Harry!" She doesn't hear me, but Sugar does. Her ears prick and her gait pauses. "Sugar! Come here, Sugar!" She stops altogether, sitting down on the floor and looking back at me, then up at Harry. "Good girl," I breathe.

I watch as Harry tugs on the leash of an uncooperative dog and ease into a jog for the last several yards. "Harry!" I call again, and this time she hears. Her head jerks up and her eyes zero in on me. Her lips form my name, and then she's running herself, running toward me like something out of a movie. Something out of a dream.

I grab her up and hold her to me, so tight there's not a breath of space between us. Burying my face in her neck, I chant her name beneath my breath, over and over. "Harry, Harry, Harry..." Around us, humanity flows unchecked, as if we're simply a stone in the river the current sweeps through.

"What are you—"

I cut off her question with my lips. I kiss her mouth, hard and hungry, then sprinkle quick, hard kisses over her cheekbones, nose, and eyes, until I return to her mouth, speaking against her lips as the words pour out. "What are you doing here? God, I missed you. I missed you so fucking much."

"Me! What are you doing here?" Her fingers curl into my shirt, clinging for dear life.

"Sir." Something taps on my shoulder, and I turn my head to see a disgruntled-looking security officer. "I hate to break this up, but you can't just run off and leave all your things at the checkpoint. Please come with me."

I utter a breathless laugh and bend my forehead to Harry's. "Shit. Come on." Gripping her hand, we follow the officer back to the checkpoint, where he waits with tight-pressed lips for me to don my shoes and re-pack my bag.

"What are you doing, Wyatt? Where are you going? I can't believe I almost missed—"

"I was coming home, Harry." I lead her a few steps away, to a relatively empty row of chairs, and we sit.

"Home?" Her lower lip begins to quiver. "What have you done, Wyatt Granger?"

"I haven't done anything, yet. I just took leave for the weekend so I could see you. Talk to you. But what are you doing here? I can't even believe...I just looked up and there you were. Talk about luck." I push a curl that insists on falling over her eye behind her ear so I can look at her, really look at her. She's as beautiful as she always is, but there's something new in her eyes.

"Not luck...something more," she whispers, almost to herself. "It's serendipity. That's what this is. We were meant to meet like this. Charged particles...vibrating in unison..."

I have no idea what she's talking about, but it doesn't matter. Picking up her hand, I wrap mine around it. "Harry. I know I've said it a dozen times already, but I need to say it again. It came to me this morning, when the manager asked me to come up to the Phillies and fill out their roster, that it was all meaningless if I didn't have you to come back home to. I know you're scared. I know this is fast. I'm telling you right here, right now, if you can't do it any other way, I will quit. This minute. I'll come back to Lucy Falls and get a position somewhere...the university, maybe. And we'll be happy. I promise you, regardless of what either of us is doing, we'll be happy together. But I can't be happy without you."

She does that thing she always does when she's about to cry and doesn't want to—pinches the bridge of her nose and squinches her eyes closed.

"You're not going to fucking quit baseball," she says, and her voice is deep, thick with unshed tears. "That's your dream. You have to chase your dream, because it's not going to chase you, you know."

I shake my head. "I don't care about that—"

"Don't you dare. I'm here because I woke up, Wyatt. I'm finally awake. You...you fixed my grandmother's vase, and it made me see how foolish I was being. I'm finally whole! You loved me when I was nothing but heartbreak and war...now that's done and I'm good—more than good—but I've been doing my best to tear myself apart all over again." Bowing her head, she runs both hands wearily over her face. "I don't know what my problem was. Fear, maybe."

"What are you saying?"

Lifting her face to mine, she swallows visibly, then licks her bottom lip. "I'm saying I love you. That's why I'm here. I had to tell you, had to make sure you knew. I didn't want to. But you managed, somehow, to worm your way into the deepest parts of me, and I..." A line of confusion appears between her brows. "And I've decided I don't want to live this life without you. I want us to try, Wyatt. I want to try to be what you need, and I want you to try to be what I need, and if we fuck it up...well, at least we tried, right?"

I pull her over the arm of the chair and into my lap and hold her cheeks in my hands as I press my mouth to hers once again. "We're going to do more than try, Red. We're going to kick *try* in the ass. We're going to rock this love thing—"

"Forty-two," she says, laughing against my mouth, but then draws back and claps her hand over her own. "Oh, my God. I forgot to tell you something, and if it makes you change your mind, then so be it—"

"Nothing could make me change my mind."

"Four kids?" She smiles weakly. "Could four kids make you change your mind?"

I frown and can't help my gaze from dropping to her flat stomach. "What...are you pregnant with quads, or something?"

She snorts. "Or something. I'm fostering Gina and Marcus's brood. It seemed like the right thing to do, since she technically saved our lives." She keeps babbling as I stare. "I couldn't just let them be split up and sent to different homes. It wouldn't have been right! They're..."

"You're the most incredible woman I think I've ever known, Harry Bee."

She stops. Flushes. "Well, I don't know about all that, but—"

"I don't think I could love you more, or be prouder of you, than I am right now." I glance down at my ticket, wedged under my leg on the chair. "When are you supposed to fly back?"

"It's an open-ended ticket. I can get on any flight with room at any time."

"Let's go, then. I want to meet these kids."

"Now?" She stands when I do, gathering Sugar's leash closer.

"Right now. Let's check on this flight, see if there's room."

My arm around her shoulders, we make our way in the direction of the gate.

In the direction of forever.

# Epilogue

## Harry

*A Little While Later*

"Oh, my God, I am so sick of—"

The last word disappears into the toilet as I gag yet again and vomit. I've been puking non-stop, it seems, for the last week. I have to get this under control, because tomorrow Wyatt has a game in Philly he really, really wants me to attend.

His hands curl into my hair, lifting it away from my face and neck as I heave. He doesn't talk, simply stands, and waits until I finish, then helps me to my feet. "Here, babe. Drink up." He hands me a glass of water and I sip it, sending him a grateful smile before setting it down on the counter. "All right…back to bed."

"Let me brush my teeth."

When I finish, he's standing by the bed in the master bedroom of the furnished apartment we just decided to rent, after it became evident that he'd be pitching for the duration of the season. He won't be there a tremendous amount, but it makes things a hundred times easier when I come to watch a game and have the kids with me. I can hear them now, watching cartoons in the living room and having breakfast. Sugar is on the bed, chin on her paws, waiting for me.

I climb into the bed, and he pulls the covers up to my chin. "Better?"

I nod. "Just tired."

"Take a little nap. Your brother is in there with the kids, and he has everything under control."

Owen has become a lifesaver. Since he owns the tech company he works for, his time is flexible. He's become so intrigued by the mystery of what happened to Lucy Van Hollister that he decided he was going to take some time away from the company and write a book on his efforts to solve a centuries-old disappearance. We've taken to sharing childcare, both of us finding more kids easier to manage, since they keep each other occupied.

"I have to get to the ball field," Wyatt is saying, "but I called a doctor to come over and take a look at you."

"What? Wyatt, I'm fine. It's just the flu or something—"

"Well, it's been going on long enough. Get the doc to give you something." He bends and kisses my forehead.

"No arguments. You have to feel well enough to come to my game tomorrow."

I roll my eyes. "Fine. Forty-fucking-two, babe."

He grins, then kisses me again, this time on the lips, and regardless of the fact that I was just hurling my guts up, I can't help but respond. It's like this every time. He looks at me with eyes naked in their devotion, a gaze that devours me sweetly, and fire catches as soon as his lips touch mine.

He groans and presses a series of nipping kisses along my jawline. "Fuckkk. I have to go, Red."

"I love you."

"Love you more."

I ease back into the blankets as he leaves, intent on taking a nap. I'm still wide awake, though, when the doctor arrives, sleep eluding me. I raise up and sit against the pillows piled against the headboard.

"Hello, there, young lady," he booms genially. He looks to be in his sixties, tall and thin with a white Santa-like beard.

"Hi...thank you for coming. I really think I'm fine but Wyatt worries."

"It's my pleasure. Tell me what's going on with you."

"I've just been exhausted lately, and every time I turn around, I'm throwing up. It's some weird bug—"

"Or maybe some weird pregnancy?" He raises a bushy eyebrow at my O of surprise. "Hadn't occurred to you?"

"No! Oh, my..."

"Are you currently on birth control?"

I'm not. Until this very moment, it had not occurred to me to replace the ones Marcus had been slipping in with my other pills. I got every medication I take refilled while I was at the hospital and never thought twice about the fact that I was now missing one very critical pill.

If I didn't want children, that is.

"I...no. It's a complicated story, but I'm not." A thought strikes me, and I go cold. "What about the medications I'm currently on? If I'm pregnant, will they harm the baby?"

"Well, first things first. Let's give you a pregnancy test and if it's positive, we'll do an eval of those medications. Take this and give me some urine."

In a daze, I follow his instructions, emerging from the bathroom with a plastic cup of urine. He takes it into the bathroom, and I climb back into bed, then, too restless to sit, get back down and begin pacing the length of the small bedroom.

*Pregnant.* The possibility, always so far out of reach, never crossed my mind. It makes sense, though. We haven't been careful, haven't been thinking of the potential consequences. I utter a giddy, choked laugh. Between us, we already have five children. This...if I am pregnant...will be number six. "Fucking Brady Bunch, two-thousands edition," I mutter.

"Well, I have good news," the doctor says, emerging from the bathroom. "At least, I hope it's good news. You are definitely, absolutely, one hundred percent pregnant."

I start to cry. And laugh. And snot, all over the tee shirt I pull up to wipe my nose on. The doctor probably thinks I have lost my mind, but that's okay. I'm *pregnant*.

Awe steals over me and I cover my still-flat belly with my hands. There's a baby in there. "Oh, my God," I whisper. "Thank you."

"Well, ahem...excellent. Let's take a look at those medications, shall we? And then we'll get you set up with an obstetrician for future appointments."

"Yes, of course..." Nodding, I gather my medications from the bathroom and bring them in for the doctor to look through. He studies each carefully while I wait, notating information on a tablet and occasionally making a humming sound. Finally, he looks up at me. "First, I want to stress that everything is absolutely fine. That said, I do want to make a change to one of your medications, because it is not recommended for pregnant or nursing mothers."

"But you're sure it's okay right now?"

"Yes. There's no need to worry about any ill effects. I just want to make sure you're on the absolute best medication for your conditions."

The remainder of his visit flies by in a blur of instructions, prescriptions, and reassurances. When he leaves, Owen comes to stand in the doorway, expression neutral.

"Did I hear...?" I nod, not trusting myself to speak. I guess this explains why I've been so emotional lately. "Aww, sis..." He starts to walk toward me, then glances back into the living room, where we can hear an argument breaking out in high, childish voices. "Fucking hell," he laughs. "Someone has a sense of the absurd. Congratulations!"

"How am I going to tell Wyatt?" I wonder aloud. "This wasn't on either of our radars. He's going to be flattened."

Owen's mouth curls into a slow grin. "I have an idea."

---

The atmosphere at the next day's game is that of a party, with frenetic chatter and laughter and a sea of red, white, and blue. The scent of hot dogs and peanuts follows me as we hurry to section 121, Owen and I keeping a firm grip on the children's hands. The baby is back home with my mother, thank goodness. Noah, Trevor, Barret, Ruth Anne, and Ava are more than enough, and because no one can locate shoes when they need to be found, we're just about always late. Letting Owen go first, I usher the kids in after him and then take my place in the aisle seat, just as the first pitch is thrown out.

I've grown to love baseball, and especially coming to ball games. Win or lose, there's something magnetic about the diamond, the contrast of reddish-brown dirt, white bases, and the lush green of the outfield. There's something timeless about the men in their uniforms, the endless spitting of sunflower seeds, and the momentary blindness when a ball goes moonshot and all you see are lights.

I settle in, prepared to waltz on the razor's edge of enjoyment of the game and complete anxiety for Wyatt. My fingers dance lightly over my tummy. Maybe I should look into meditation…all that anxiety can't be good for growing a baby.

The game is a tense one. The teams trade off innings with no hits and others with bases-loaded home runs, until at the seventh inning the score is tied eight to eight. Wyatt has finished his pitching for the evening by the traditional seventh inning stretch and waits in the dugout with the rest of the team for the game to resume.

Or at least, that's what he usually does. Right now, he appears to be walking out on the field… "What's he doing?" I hiss down the row to Owen.

He shrugs. "He's your boyfriend." He chews a handful of popcorn, his posture relaxed. Too relaxed.

As my gaze narrows on him, the announcer begins to speak. "And now it's time for that seventh inning stretch! Stand up, walk around, but before you do…we have a little something extra from one of our players."

Almost immediately, Wyatt's voice fills the stadium and I look down to see him speaking into a microphone on the pitcher's mound. "There's a special lady here tonight. She's been a little under the weather lately, but she made sure to be here tonight because I told her it was important to me. I wanted to take a minute and let the world know what an amazing woman Dr. Harriet Bee is, but more than that, I wanted to let her know…in front of all these witnesses…exactly what she means to me. Harriet? Can you come down here, babe?"

"Oh, God." I send Owen a panicked glance.

"Get your ass down there, sis. I've got the rug rats."

Getting up, I begin to make my way down to the field. A park attendant is waiting at the bottom of the stairs and leads me to an entrance, where I walk through a short hall and emerge near the dugout.

I know my eyes are saucers as I pin them on Wyatt and walk forward. My legs are rubber, but somehow, they work, one foot in front of the other all the way to the mound where he waits, a smile that can only be described as enigmatic on his face.

"What are you doing?" I ask, dipping my head to hide my face as I approach. The stadium is a fishbowl and I'm dead center, the focus of thousands of pairs of eyes.

"Here she is, folks. Dr. Harriet Bee, scientist-extraordinaire, and the love of my life."

A ripple of response moves through the crowd, but I'm fixed on the man in front of me. "She's forty-two," he says, tugging at his jersey to indicate the number on his back, and I clap my hand over my mouth to hide the quiver of my chin. "She's the one. The question and the answer to absolutely everything."

A collective *aah* sounds just under the rush of time and space and blood in my ears. There was a time when I had a similar awakening and understood that Wyatt...this man in front of me who, even as I stand before him, mind racing, is lowering himself to a knee...was *my* forty-two. My...*ohmygod.*

My brain catches up with what's happening and a sound—part-sob, part-giggle, part-squeal—escapes my lips.

"Wyatt—"

He sets the microphone on the ground beside him and speaks solely to me. "I love you, Harry. I was drawn to you from the first time we met, pulled to you in ways I didn't fully understand. All I knew was that you were it for me. You would either destroy me or save me...I didn't know yet, and it didn't much matter. Now I know you saved me. Gave me purpose and reason and so much belief—I couldn't help but believe in myself.

"I want you to marry me, Harry. I want you to be mine, for now and forever." He gestures to the electrical sign behind him, at the opposite side of the field. Normally it displays flashing, ever-changing advertisements and motivational words. Now, the words MARRY ME HARRY scroll slowly by.

When I look back down, he's holding a ring.

My legs give out and I sink to my knees in front of him. "Stop…" he murmurs, wiping at my cheeks, and I realize I'm crying. "Please stop crying, Red. I love you, baby. If you don't want to marry me, it's okay! I promise. I shouldn't have—"

"No! Yes! God, I love you so much, Wyatt. I love you and I want to marry you!" I hold my hand out and tug his hand, the one holding the ring, to it. "Put it on."

Laughing, he slides the ring on my finger and then helps me to my feet, grabbing the microphone as he does. "Ladies and gentlemen…the future Mrs. Wyatt Granger."

Just then the announcer comes back on. "Congratulations to this lovely couple. But I do believe the future Mrs. Granger has a little something she would like to share, as well."

It's Wyatt's turn to stare at me in shocked surprise, a little smile playing around his lips. He tilts his head playfully and pokes me in the arm. "Been busy, hmm?"

I point to the sign behind him just as the crowd sighs. "I think we both have."

He turns to see a baby carriage trolling past on the electrical sign, and then turns back to me, mouth open and eyes dropping to my stomach. "Are you…?"

I nod. The announcer speaks in the background—something about it being a good thing Wyatt was finished pitching for the evening—but I barely hear him, all of my attention focused on Wyatt.

Wrapping his arms around my waist, he hefts me up and twirls me around, until all there is, is the sob of laughter, and the spin of stars, and the roar of applause, and...magic.

Everything's magic.

And as Wyatt carries me off the field, all I can think is that this is the kind of magic I'd sell my soul for. But I don't have to.

I don't have to, because Wyatt's the keeper of my soul, as much as I'm the keeper of his.

## AND THEY LIVED HAPPILY-EVER-AFTER.

Harry and Wyatt have their happy ending, but what about the other residents of Lucy Falls? Continue the journey with Shiloh in Speak No Lies.

# Acknowledgments

Alright, folks. It's acknowledgments time. I hate this part—not because I don't want to say thank you, but because I fear with all the passion of someone with a genuine phobia of A Thing *forgetting* someone. Because it's going to happen. I have ADD and I promise you...I will forget something.

So if I forget you...just know that one day a week from now, I will be sitting here watching a Yankees game, and suddenly I will remember. I will slap myself in the face—literally—and hope you haven't yet read these acknowledgments, and I will edit them as quickly as possible. And then I will repeat that, around seven times, for seven different people.

But here goes nothing.

I know a lot of us writers say "this book wouldn't be here if it weren't for" blah blah and blah...but I can assure you that it's not in the least an exaggeration for this girl. It takes a literal village to write and produce a book. It takes people to bounce ideas off of, people to read your initial trash, and tell you it's trash. It takes sensitivity readers when you write things that may potentially be... sensitive. It takes amazing cover designers, and editors, and so stinking many people to pull every little thing together. So without further ado, here is my incredible army of support:

**Vanessa Harradine Sheetz**. What would I do without you? Even while working on her own book, Vanessa takes time to read mine and give me encouragement and tough love. My favorite: "you're going to haaaate me, but I don't love it." Ha!

**Susan Clapp Hutchinson**. GODDESS. Susan pulls no punches, catches the tiniest of "oofs" and is always ready with some of the most brilliant of advice. So many times she pulled me back from the brink of scrapping this story with common sense motivation, and her baseball insight, in particular, was invaluable. (GO Yankees!! Haahahaha!)

**Becky Aksdal.** A late discovery and addition to my team, this woman began as an ARC reader and turned into an absolutely incredible, indispensable beta reader. I am blessed to have her!

My amazing beta/ARC readers: **Andi MacDowall, Jennifer Hahn, Sarah Beth, Chelley St. Clair, Jennifer Hartmann, Suzie Webster Franyo,** and **Jillian Cunningham**. Thank you all so incredibly much. It takes an army to find all those weird quote marks.

SO many people gave me incredible advice and research on epilepsy. **Lancy McCall** and **Tracey Moore Dawson**, in particular, were instrumental in providing key ideas for informing Harry and Sugar's characters and providing a thorough sensitivity and beta read. Others that assisted with epilepsy information and research were Kaitlin G., Rob Swanson, Paige Boggs, and Nora Phoenix.

Much appreciation to **Sarah Kil** and **Autumn Karn** for a sensitivity read involving Asian-American characters. Autumn also became an invaluable ARC reader, and I cannot wait to work with her on future projects.

Huge thank you to **Kim Wilson** of Kiwi Cover Design for the beautifully imagined cover design! Kim is a dream to work with!

Thank you to my PAs, **Paige Boggs** and **Ramie Kerschen**, for keeping me straight. It's a big job, but someone's gotta do it.

Finally…thank you to everyone who has believed in me, even when I was full of doubt and short on self-love. This has been the toughest year of my life. Cheers to better days. <3

# About E.R. Whyte

E(lle) R(ae) Whyte lives in south central Virginia with her youngest son. She's a textbook Capricorn with a tendency to overthink things and word vomit when she gets nervous. She loves good poetry, tacos, dirty jokes, and simple things like couch cuddles. An avid photographer, Elle can often be found wandering little-traveled highways or busy city streets in search of the perfect shot. E.R. writes contemporary reverse harem under her pseudonym Evie Rae.

## Also By the Author

### As **E.R. WHYTE**
*Contemporary*
LUCY FALLS

Play Me False
Speak No Secrets

STANDALONES

Remember Me

Entropy (with Jennifer Hartmann)

THE EAST COAST IRISH SERIES*
*coming SOON!

### As **EVIE RAE**
*Reverse Harem*

Bad Neighbors

Beastly Bullies

Printed in Great Britain
by Amazon